The Heartbreak Cowboy

INCLUDES THE COWBOY'S GOODNIGHT KISS: A PREQUEL

COLDIRON COWBOYS
BOOK ONE

MINA BECKETT

CURTISSLYNN
PUBLISHING

Experience the power of love, redemption, and second chances in the newly released edition of *The Heartbreak Cowboy* complete with the heartfelt prequel novella, *The Cowboy's Goodnight Kiss*. The story offers a poignant glimpse into the characters' pasts and the events that set their love story in motion. Fall in love with Eleanor and McCrea as they prove that true love can heal even the most shattered hearts.

The Cowboy's Goodnight Kiss

For as long as Eleanor Mackenna can remember, her heart has belonged to the irresistible McCrea Coldiron. A cowboy with rugged charm and a devil-may-care attitude, he has always been the embodiment of her deepest desires. But when he offers her a night she'll never forget, she's forced to choose between her love for the cowboy and the bitter truth behind his affections.

The Heartbreak Cowboy

Can an old flame reignite to become a fiery love?

Four years ago, McCrea Coldiron was thrust into a heart-wrenching ultimatum that shattered his tender and newly budding romance with Eleanor Mackenna. Settle down and find a wife or lose his inheritance.

Divorced and now proprietor of the Promise Point Horse Rescue Ranch, McCrea has no regrets about his decision to choose land over love as he watched

Eleanor storm out of his life — until he discovers they made more than love the night he proposed.

Eleanor knows all about choices and letting go. The single mom has come back to Santa Camino, Texas to sell her grandparent's ranch and sever all ties to her hometown. The only thing standing in her way is Mc-Crea Coldiron, the man she's loved since childhood.

Eleanor knows just how badly McCrea can burn a woman and how persuasive he can be when he wants something. When he asks for a second chance, she's forced to choose between trusting her heart again or running away from the man who has always owned it.

Reviews

"The Heartbreak Cowboy is a story about past hurts, family, forgiveness and love. So much love. This is a lovely story you need to have on your Kindle!" **USA Today Bestselling Author Naima Simone**

"An emotional and sexy novel. With a hero trying to do the right thing and a heroine struggling to set her heartbreak aside, this story is hard to put down. Great secondary characters and a cute four-year-old round out this compelling novel. Even better ... the heat level is in the sizzling range. Loved it!" **Kristy McCaffrey, author of the award-winning Wings of the West series**

"Are you looking for a book that you can't put down? Pick up The Heartbreak Cowboy... It is heartfelt and even had me laughing. I could see this book made into a movie on the Hallmark channel. I loved it so much." **Machiavellian Books**

"It was beautifully written and I look forward to reading more of her books. I'm a country girl at heart

living at the beach so reading this book made me feel at home." **Mommy Reads too Much Magazine**

"Caution! The Heartbreak Cowboy will break your heart but don't worry, it'll all be better by the last punctuation mark." **Clutter Your Kindle**

"Beckett writes her heart out in this hard-to-put-down book. She's made me a fan for life. I can't wait for the next book in the Coldiron Cowboys series." **Taking Time for Mommy.**

The Cowboy's Goodnight Kiss

A prequel to
The Heartbreak Cowboy

Originally, this prequel was written as the first ten chapters of *The Heartbreak Cowboy* but was cut after I submitted the manuscript to agents.

It was just too much backstory.

But I couldn't toss this bittersweet part of McCrea and Eleanor's story into a forgotten file. I wanted to share the emotion and angst of the night that changed everything for them.

Chapter One

Eleanor Mackenna made a quick exit across the side yard and over to the fence that separated her family land from the Coldirons'. She climbed to the top and slipped on her dime store shades to shield her eyes from the evening sun.

A cool breeze filtered through the hills and blew against her face. She closed her eyes and drew in a deep breath, savoring the sweet, earthy smell of hay and dirt.

Redemption, the Mackenna ranch, had been in her family for generations and had once been a top-notch breeding facility for horses. But without Granddad Charlie to oversee the day-to-day workings, it had become too much for Grandma Rose to handle.

Twenty years after his death, Rose was still holding on to the land and to Charlie's legacy. The last of the breeding horses had been sold years ago, leaving only a few workhorses for the ranch hands and Romeo, a silver roan quarter horse. However, Rose was still holding on to the land and Charlie's legacy twenty years after his death.

Eleanor's pride and joy.

Redemption's profitable days were over, and nowadays, they skimped by with raising and selling cattle. The meadows were overgrown, the stables and barns were empty, and the fences were rotting away with each passing year.

But after college, she planned on restoring the ranch to its former glory. New barns and paddocks, a new roof for the house… There were a hundred things that needed work and doing them rested solely on her shoulders.

With a deep sigh, she let her anxiety about the long road ahead of her drift away.

It was early August, and she had less than a month before the fall semester started. She would not worry about what needed to be done or how she was going to do it. She would figure that out when she came back home to rebuild the ranch after college. Right now, she wanted to enjoy the simple pleasures of country life before heading off to Austin.

She threw a leg over the top rail, twisted around, and jumped down to the other side. Then she sprinted across the pasture towards the barn, maneuvering past steaming piles of manure with precision. It was a skill she found useful the summer she came to live with Grandma Rose.

The last leap landed her near the fence, which separated the main house from the barn. She hooked a boot into the bottom of the four rails that were the perfect height for viewing, climbed to the top, and sat down.

In a dreamy state, she tilted her head up. There wasn't a cloud in the sky, and happiness enveloped her like a warm blanket. The feeling overtook her every time she set foot on the Coldiron Ranch.

Redemption was home and had its own feel, but sometimes it was a lonely place with only she and her grandma to fill the empty spaces.

For the past eleven years, Eleanor had called Santa Camino, Texas, home. The Coldiron siblings and cousin Dean felt like family to her, more so than her mother and half-sister..

She was a little jealous of her neighbors. Not for how wealthy they were or how much land they owned, but for the love they had for one another. The family bond they shared.

Family gave you a place in the world and made all the hardships of life easier. There was security in knowing someone loved you, cared for you, and wanted the best for you. Rose was nearing eighty, and a tiny ache nibbled at Eleanor's heart when she thought about losing her. When Rose was gone, she would have no one.

Louisa was her best friend, and Jess and Dean were like the brothers she was never fortunate enough to have.

A whinny brought her head down and her eyes to the woodline behind the barn. She recognized the distinct sound of McCrea's horse. She had a complicated relationship with McCrea, Louisa's older brother.

Somewhere along the way, her childish infatuation for him had grown into love, and her toe-tingling desire and falling-down attraction made it hard to be around him, so admiring him from afar seemed to be the best way to get her daily fix.

He was an untouchable dream she had loved and fantasized about since she was old enough to notice boys. It had taken years for her to give in to her feelings for him. Her mother's mistakes taught her never to let her heart go unguarded, so she fought the battle within. Loving him but fearing what might happen if she ever gave in to her feelings.

The sleek black coat of the gelding and the well-defined build of the rider kept her attention. Playing college football had changed McCrea's physical appearance. He was broader through the shoulders, and his biceps and thighs were more muscular than they had been when he was in high school.

The man was a spectacular sight. His wide brow and set jaw reminded her of an outlaw. That made her grin, but his hips moving in rhythm with the horse made her groan. "He is so fine," she sighed, watching him disappear inside the barn.

With her head towards heaven again, Eleanor basked in the last rays of the setting sun and her infatuation for the outlaw.

"Gotcha!"

She jumped and let out a scream as hands clamped around her waist, pulling her from the rail and into a set of powerful arms.

"God, Jess!" she yelled, recognizing the cowboy under the hat. "You scared the crap out of me!"

Louisa climbed the fence and took a spot on the top rail. "I told him not to do it."

Louisa was the youngest of the three children, with a slim build and a lovely face. Her parents and grandparents doted upon her, and her older brothers protected her. But their attention didn't make her spoiled or bratty. She was fiercely independent and headstrong, even if she didn't know what she wanted to do with her life. Louisa was confident, loyal, and the best friend anyone could have. Austin would be a lonely place without her.

"Sorry, El. I couldn't resist." Jess's blue eyes dazzled in a way that made most women stumble and swoon. His teasing, boyish charm and playfulness made him even more appealing. He was easygoing and loved to flirt in a harmless way.

He raised her back to the top of the fence without effort, stealing her shades as he did, and took a step up. He winced and brushed it off with a grinning wink when he knew she noticed.

Two years ago, a hard fall at the National Finals Rodeo ended his bronc riding career and his dreams of taking home the championship. A compound fracture of the femur left him with a slight limp and a thigh full of pins.

"What are you doing out here all by your lonesome?" he asked.

Her eyes followed McCrea from the barn to one of the ranch work trucks. "Admiring the scenery."

He slid the shades on and followed her eyes. "Are you lusting over him again?"

"Yes, I am," she said without an ounce of shame, and snatched the hat from his head.

The hat swallowed her head. "And a lot of good it does me. He doesn't know I'm alive." The obstacle threatened her bliss. She was a fool for the man, and he hadn't a clue.

"Sure, he does." Jess laid his arms over the rail and rested his chin on both hands. "He's just playing hard to get."

"Nope." The dingy brown hat he'd had since high school wobbled back and forth in a bobblehead motion, then fell over her eyes. "He thinks I'm a kid."

Would McCrea ever see her as something other than the girl next door? Or would she always be his little sister's annoying friend? She tilted her head back so she could see him. "You've got a fat head; you know that?"

Jess frowned, taking offense in her claim. "My head is just the right size, thank you, and any man with eyes can see you're not a kid anymore."

"Maybe I should wear a dress to the bachelor party." She lifted a jean-clad leg and twisted her foot from side to side. "I have decent legs."

With a finger, he eased the shades to the end of his nose and eyed her legs. "I didn't think you were working tonight."

"I'm not, but that doesn't mean I can't show up looking fabulous." Tomorrow night, McCrea would see her as a woman. She would be sexy and flirty, and everything would be different between them.

"Yeah, that's a great idea!" Louisa said with enthusiasm. "The little yellow dress you wore to the barbecue would be perfect."

"Did I leave it in your room?"

"It's hanging in the closet."

Jess gave the neckline of his t-shirt a tug. "That dress is indecent."

Louisa tapped his chest with the back of her hand. "It is not."

Eleanor measured a high spot on her thigh. "I could shorten the length to get his attention."

"Bad idea," Jess said from the corner of his mouth.

"Why is it a bad idea?" Louisa asked.

"McCrea won't be the only man at the bar tomorrow night, and if she walks in there with a skirt that high, there'll be another fight."

"I'm so country plain that McCrea will never notice

me." She pointed to her face. "There's no way I can compete with Vanessa Worley."

"There's nothing plain about you," Louisa assured her.

"And you have Vanessa beat in beauty, brains, and personality," Jess said as he pushed the shades back in place and craned his neck up to get a better view of the pasture in front of them. "Where is she, anyway? She's usually hot on his heels."

"Don't be surprised if we find her hiding in the bed of his truck." Louisa snickered.

"Tell me about it. With her around, I don't have a chance." Eleanor kicked the rail with the back of her boot, feeling frustrated with her inadequacy. "What I'd give for just a kiss."

"You should make him jealous." Jess made his eyebrows bounce up and down and flashed her a devilish grin. "Make him think he has competition."

"He's right," Louisa agreed. "Tell McCrea you have a date."

"But I don't."

"So, get one," Louisa said.

Jess sighed dramatically and bent his head to study the ground before throwing up both hands. "Okay, I'll do it."

"Do what?" they asked in unison.

"Be your date for tonight." He dusted off the shoulders of his dirty work shirt and rested his hands on his hips to mimic a James Dean stance. "I had plans, but…"

She closed her eyes with a grimace. "You're offering me a pity date? I'm pathetic."

"Be serious, Jess," Louisa ordered before leaning to

bump Eleanor with her shoulder. "I do not know what you see in McCrea."

Jess poked his head into the narrow space between them. "Me neither. You could do so much better."

Louisa put a finger to her brother's forehead and pushed him backward. "You're annoying. You know that?"

"Maybe." Without warning, he plucked Eleanor from the railing, tossed her over his shoulder, and spun her around, smacking her bottom. "But I am fun."

She shielded her backside with both hands, and his hat tumbled to the ground. "Stop that. Put me down."

He hauled her around so that she was in front of him, and grinned. "Come on, El. Let me be your date."

Struggling against his strong hold was futile. She was his prisoner until the game was over. "No," she said, laughing. "I'll ask Conner."

Like a rag doll, he lifted her off the ground, took her hand, and spun her around in a grand waltz. "Oh, that kid's not a threat to McCrea."

She laughed at the dance. "And you are?"

He let her slide to the ground and whirled her out. "Hell, yes. You know that I'm a ladies' man."

"Oh, good grief," she said, laughing again as he yanked her back into his arms. "Stop it."

"Nope. Not until," his fingers darted along her ribs, making her double over, "you agree."

"Stop." She tucked her elbows in to shield herself. "Please."

"I told you I was fun."

She jerked free while swatting at his hands. "Stop it!"

He made a leap forward, triggering her jump backward. "Nope. You're mine, lady."

She dodged his hand, snatched his hat from the ground, and set it on her head. "Don't make me hold it hostage."

His blue eyes squinted at her threat. "You wouldn't."

"Oh, but I would, so if you want to see it again, you'd better call a truce."

The thought of losing his hat made his hands fall. "That's dirty. Using a man's hat against him."

She grinned and prepared to run. Having been a victim to his bluffs more than once made her leery of him. "A girl has to do something."

In a flash, he bolted towards her.

She spun around, ready to run for home, and plowed face-first into McCrea's chest. The collision left her clutching his shirt for balance.

His leather-clad fingers grasped her forearm. "Whoa, there."

When she lifted her head, a teasing grin appeared on his lips.

The sun had scorched his face, leaving a thin layer of grime on his skin. A five o'clock shadow lined his jawline, giving him a rugged and sexy look. His light-blue Cambridge shirt was open in the front, exposing the ridges of his well-defined muscles that glistened with sweat. Her hand flattened against the toned surface of his chest.

An inexplicable sensation of intoxication overcame Eleanor as she drew in an uneven breath. Over the years, she had gotten a whiff of more than one sweaty cowboy. But there was something alluring and sexy about the way McCrea smelled.

"You running to or from, darlin'?"

Darlin'? The way he drawled out the word made her lower belly tighten.

She swallowed. "From."

He gave her a wink. "That's too bad."

"Can I have my hat back now?" Jess cut in with a begrudging frown.

McCrea removed the hat from her head and tossed it to him while keeping a hand at her waist. It was an odd gesture, seeing how he usually went out of his way not to touch her.

Jess tried reshaping the bent brim. "Where have you been?"

"Granddad's been looking for you," Louisa informed him.

McCrea's face hardened with furrowed lines across his forehead. "At the Point." Promise Point was his sanctuary from the world and a place he visited often when he and Wade disagreed.

Jess crossed his arms and leaned against the rail. "That bad, huh?"

"Could be. I'll know more after I talk to him."

"You are planning on being at the bachelor party tomorrow night, right?" Jess questioned.

McCrea's eyes could be soft and beautiful with gold specks when he laughed or teased. Other times, they could be black, void of color, and felt as though they were drilling into the depths of her. They were like that now. Boring into her soul in search of something. "I'll be there," he said, wiping dirt from her chin with his forefinger. "I need a distraction."

The tender action was innocent. Something he would do to a small child, but when the worn leather glove skimmed her skin, heat gathered between her thighs.

"A word of warning," Jess said. "He's still pissed about last week."

"Yeah," McCrea sighed and dropped his hand to peel away the gloves. "I know, but I didn't start the fight."

"We all know that, but Willard's granddaddy and ours go way back." Jess slapped his shoulder. "And that means you better walk the line if you want to get back into Granddad's good graces."

McCrea shoved his gloves into his back pocket and headed towards the house.

Eleanor watched him disappear through the door. "He looks worried."

Jess took his hat off and scratched his head. "He is."

"He finally told Granddad he didn't want to be a rancher," Louisa said.

"What?" Everyone always assumed McCrea would follow in his dad and granddad's footsteps. Ranching was in their blood.

But he was a different person now. Time away from home had changed him. He was more withdrawn and moodier. The carefree boy she had fallen in love with seemed lost, replaced by a man with drive and determination. A man who rarely smiled or laughed.

"That's the same as blasphemy to Granddad," Jess threw in.

"Yep." Louisa jumped down from the fence. "They've been knocking heads since he came home from college."

"I feel like this whole mess is my fault. Maybe I should explain what happened to Wade."

"It's not your fault," Louisa reassured her.

"Granddad has always been hard on McCrea," Jess said.

"Mom says it's because he and granddad are so much alike." Louisa hung an arm around her shoulder. "Are you staying for supper?"

"No. I promised Grandma I'd be back soon." She hugged Louisa. "I'll see you tomorrow."

Louisa cringed. "Probably not. I have a ton of things to do before I leave on Friday. Mom's helping me pack." She hugged her again. "But promise me you'll be careful at the party."

"Don't worry about me. I'm used to the bar scene. Besides, McCrea and Jess will be there if I need looking after."

"You know I won't let anything happen to our little El," Jess taunted and handed her shades back.

Louisa grabbed his ear and gave it a hard tug. "You'd better not."

He yanked away, nursing his lobe. "Damn, Lou. That hurt."

Eleanor climbed over the fence and jumped to the other side. "See you later."

"We'll have a girls' night out before we leave," Louisa yelled. "Just the two of us."

She waved as she headed towards home. "You bet."

Chapter Two

"You can't do this." Even as McCrea said it, he knew his granddad could do anything he wanted, including take away his inheritance. "That land is mine! You promised it to me!"

"Get a grip on that temper," Hardin directed his son from the leather sofa across the room.

McCrea did as he was told, ground his teeth, and rethought his strategy. He had laid awake all night dreading this conversation. "We've talked about this for years. Can you at least tell me why you've suddenly changed your mind?" This time, his voice wasn't as loud or as demanding. Respect would get him farther than anger. "Why now? Why, after all I've done to prove myself worthy?"

His Granddad Wade was in his usual spot. Hands clasped behind his back, facing the large picture window near his desk as he looked out over the ranch handed down to him by his father. The old man spent his life working the ranch, but in recent years had been forced to slow down. His heart wasn't as strong as it once was, and McCrea suspected the death of his grandmother had something to do with it. "You're not ready for it."

McCrea began pacing the room. He had earned a degree in ranch management just to appease his granddad, and he had been ranching since he was old enough to mount a horse. "I couldn't be any readier than I am now."

What would he do if Wade refused to give him the land? Be a rancher like the two of them? Hell, no. He didn't want to spend the rest of his life running cattle from one pasture to another, looking at the ass-end view of an animal he had grown to despise.

He could go north to Montana. He hadn't visited the Lucky Jack Ranch or talked with Colton since his discharge from the Marines last year. He knew Lauren wouldn't mind setting an extra plate at the table. And Colton would welcome a helping hand around the ranch until he could find a place of his own.

But that wasn't the life McCrea wanted, and by god, it wasn't the life he would settle for. He was a Texan and wanted his own spread in Hill Country to do with as he pleased. "Will you talk some sense into him?" he asked his father.

Hardin tossed his hat onto the couch and crossed an ankle over his knee. "It's his land to do with as he pleases."

Wade's arthritic fingers gathered the curtain and swung it open. "This view is something I never tire of. Rolling hills, fertile pastures. It used to regenerate me. Fourteen-hour days were nothing. Now, I'm lucky if I get in four without having to rest."

"You're recovering, Dad," Hardin reminded him. "You'll be back to your old self in no time."

They all knew that was a lie. The heart attack he had suffered in the spring had been a bad one, and McCrea would never forget the night it happened. Calving season produced nearly twice as many calves as expected, and Wade insisted on being present for as many births as possible. They were his herd and, in his eyes, his responsibility.

It was just 'McCrea and his granddad bringing the calf into the world. Witnessing the birth of an animal was a unique experience. Being the first to see it, hold it, and sometimes watch it take its last breath put everything into perspective.

At first, he thought it was the sight of that dead calf that brought Wade to his knees. Hand clutched tight to his chest, pale complexion, sweaty face... That night made McCrea realize his granddad wasn't indestructible and that it was just a matter of time before he left them.

McCrea sighed. Why couldn't he and his granddad find some common ground? "What did Doc Bowman say?"

Wade sat down in the chair behind his desk. His laugh lines deepened as a weary smile drew his lips upward. "That I could use a shot of youth."

"Couldn't we all?" Hardin chuckled. It was his dad's way of hiding what he feared. He, too, was afraid of losing Wade. They all were.

The old man let out a weighted sigh. "I don't fear death. It's as inevitable as the sunrise and comes to us all. I made my peace with it a long time ago but handing over a part of the family land to someone as reckless as you, McCrea, scares the hell out of me."

"Reckless?" he questioned.

Wade leaned forward in a commanding manner only he could accomplish and rested his arms on the desk. "Tell me again why you want the land?"

"We've talked about this. It's the perfect place —"

"For that damn game ranch," Wade finished.

His granddad had never been sold on the idea of cultivating wildlife for hunting, but McCrea knew it could be a profitable business. "There's a nice piece of land on the north side."

"No," he was quick to turn it down. "Give it to Jess or Lou or Dean. It's perfect for raising cattle." Jess and Lou wanted their own ranch. Dean had opened a law practice in Austin last year and they hadn't seen him in months. But he would come home to claim his portion of the ranch someday.

Wade's eyes fell on the desk. "I always thought you would be the one to take over after me and your dad were gone, but," he swiveled his chair around and faced the window, "I guess I was wrong."

"Damn it, Granddad." McCrea choked back a groan with the slumping of Wade's shoulders. "I have my own plans and ranching isn't one of them. Why can't you accept that?"

Wade's reply was interrupted by the familiar rattle of Rose Mackenna's old red Chevy rolling up the drive.

Hardin craned his head up to watch the truck roll to a stop. "We've got company."

McCrea knew it was Eleanor. Rose only drove the truck to church and to the market on Saturdays. "Jesus," he growled and scrubbed a hand over his eyes. "What's she doing here?"

"She's practically family," Hardin reminded him. "She doesn't need a reason to be here."

McCrea thought back over the years, and there wasn't a single activity, celebration, or holiday Eleanor hadn't been involved in. At first, she had been the shy little neighbor girl who blushed when he spoke to her.

She had a magnetic appeal which made her approachable and attractive in an indescribable way. She was kind, funny, and quirky, and McCrea felt his agitation start to soften. "I know," he sighed. "But there's never a moment's peace in this house, especially with Lou and Eleanor always running in and out."

"They're leaving for college soon, and this place will be as quiet as a tomb," Hardin said.

He would miss the two of them, but not the noise. Jesus, if he heard one more giggle…

Wade pushed himself away from the desk and panned his head towards the Mackenna home. "Rose and I go way back and have a lot in common. We've borne the same grief and loved the same people. Charlie was one of my closest friends."

McCrea knew the friendship between the Coldirons and Mackennas went back for generations. But his granddad didn't have a nostalgic bone in his body, so why was he talking about Charlie?

"I hear the taxes on Redemption are due again," Hardin said under his breath. "And we both know Rose is too proud for a handout. My guess is she'll be selling off more livestock and letting some of the hired help go."

McCrea walked to the window in time to watch Eleanor sprint up the sidewalk. His eyes were instantly drawn to the bounce of her breasts.

"Jimmy Ross told me he's thinking about leaving.

Says he can't make it on what Rose pays him.," Hardin said.

Wade sighed. "If he does, there'll be more work than that girl can handle."

"There's already more work than she can handle," McCrea said, knowing when Eleanor left for college in a few days, Redemption would lose its best workhand.

"There's a lot of prime land on that ranch." Wade's eyes glimmered covetously as they always did when he talked about money and land. "I've offered to buy her out several times, but…"

After Charlie's death, Rose held on to the ranch, but Redemption had been running in the red for years with little hope of ever making a profit. Eleanor knew that, but she, like Rose, held on to the hope that one day it would be more.

Eleanor worked tirelessly around the place and had since she came to live with Rose years ago. When she was old enough, she got a job at Lomer's Hardware, stocking shelves after school, and old Ed Tubs let her wait tables at his bar and clean up on the weekends.

She had spent her last year of high school saving for a second-hand car McCrea had nicknamed Old Blue. The Toyota Corolla came with a busted radiator and over a hundred thousand miles. It stayed in the shop more than it stayed on the road and was an eyesore with a duct tape bumper and missing hubcaps.

The money she earned wasn't spent on frivolous things like lipstick and new clothes. Her worn, faded denims were proof of that.

With the weight of last year's taxes bearing down on her, Eleanor was pinching the life out of every penny she made and was working her ass off to keep the ranch. To Wade, the ranch was just a way of expanding his cattle empire. But Redemption was Eleanor's future. It belonged to her, and Wade needed to be reminded of that. "The ranch is Eleanor's. She has her heart set on rebuilding it once she has her degree."

"I know," Wade said, affronted by the fact. "And when Rose dies, it will go to Eleanor and her husband."

"Husband?" he questioned, looking at his dad. "Do you two know something I don't?"

"Plenty," Hardin mumbled.

"She can't run the ranch by herself," Wade said.

"Yes, she can," he countered, knowing his granddad was raised in a different time. "Lots of women own and operate their own ranches. And if she needs help, there are plenty of cowhands looking for work."

"You know most of those cowhands." Hardin stretched an arm along the back of the couch. "How many of them would you recommend to her? Trust to work side by side with her? Sleep a hundred feet away in the bunkhouse?"

The cowhands McCrea knew were hardworking and dependable enough. But they were men who wandered from ranch to ranch. Most of them weren't looking to settle down or do right by a woman after a night of play.

His silence brought a smug smile to Hardin's lips. "That's what I thought."

Eleanor was too naïve to know the roaming tendencies of the opposite sex. But that would change when she started college.

"Can we get back to talking about my inheritance?" he asked, ignoring the jealousy pulling at his stomach.

Wade's gray eyes pinned him down. "Mildred said you started a fight over some floozy."

Mildred Satterfield was the leader of the Garden

Club, the Women's Book Club, and a board member of the town's historical society. She was also the head hen of the town's gossip committee. "Why do you listen to her? She doesn't know her ass from a —"

"It's not just Mildred," Wade interrupted. "The whole town's talking about how you beat the hell out of the Moore boy over some floozy."

He felt his temper rising. It wasn't the first-time Mildred had caused him trouble by spreading rumors, but this time it was different. This time, she had thrown Eleanor into her gossip.

"The woman wasn't a floozy," he said through gritted teeth.

"So you say."

He hated Wade's reproach. "Forgive me if my moral compass isn't what you want it to be. I'm sure you two were saints at my age."

"The hell we were." Hardin laughed.

"I remember what it was like to be a young man and what I'd give to be that age again. Riding through the backcountry, drinking and brawling with my buddies." Wade threw in his memories. "It was a hell of a life."

McCrea had heard those stories before. "And you turned out just fine."

"Thanks to your grandmother."

Wade always traveled around the mountain when telling a story, but eventually, he got to the point. Lately, that wasn't the case. "I'm not following you, Granddad."

"Life is a never-ending circle of birth and death, and in between are the memories you hold on to, the things that make it worth living."

He stared at his granddad. "I don't understand what any of this has to do with me getting the land."

"Your grandmother settled me down and taught me how to love. She was my anchor. You need an anchor, McCrea."

The conversation was going somewhere he didn't want to go. "By anchor, you mean a woman?"

"I mourn for your grandmother every day. The softness of her hands against my face, the gentleness in her voice as she sang our children to sleep, and the way she laughed. God, I miss her laughter." Wade paused to choke back his grief. "The love of a good woman is priceless, son, and I'd give everything I own to have one more day with her."

"The point is," Hardin cut in. "we grew up, son. We took wives and started families."

McCrea took a step back. "That's not going to happen anytime soon. I don't want either."

"That's what we're afraid of," Hardin said. "You have no direction. No drive. No plan for the future."

"I have a plan. Haven't you two been listening?" Lou didn't have a plan. She hadn't decided on a major or a career path, and Jess's had nearly cost him his life.

And while Lou was too young to be showing any real interest in finding the right man to settle down with, Jess had been a diehard connoisseur of rodeo buckle bunnies before his accident. But did his dad and granddad care? No! He was always the one under scrutiny.

"Finding a wife should be part of your plan," Wade informed him.

"The hell it should," he seethed.

"I thought going to college would straighten you out. Give you time to sow your oats, but it hasn't," Wade explained.

"The way I live my life shouldn't be an issue. We

made a deal. The land was mine when I finished college. I finished, and you're trying to back out because you think I need a wife. I'm not you, Granddad. I don't want to settle down."

"That shows me how little you know about this ranch," Wade shouted, unable to control his temper. "We are tied to the land. We've worked hard to be strong leaders and good-standing members of this community!"

"And I need a wife for that?" he questioned.

Three taps on the study door interrupted their heated conversation.

"It's open," Hardin answered.

When the driver of the Chevy eased her head in, McCrea stopped her at the door. "What do you want?"

The sharpness of his tone caused Eleanor to snap back. "Excuse me, grouch. I'm looking for Louisa. Have you seen her?"

"I'm not my sister's keeper," he grumbled, not knowing why he was directing his anger at her. "I have no idea where she is."

"Belle took her into town," Hardin answered with the same patient tone he used for Louisa.

She huffed out, "darn" before shoving her hands into her back pockets.

"Hang around," Hardin said, checking his watch. "They should be back soon."

Eleanor wasn't strikingly beautiful. Her creamy skin wasn't covered by layers of makeup, and her hair wasn't curled into the latest fashion. In fact, she was plain and seldom tried to make herself anything other than that. But damn if it didn't work for her.

Even as he tried to usher her out of the room, he couldn't help but notice how well her newly acquired curves filled every inch of her faded hip huggers.

"Could you hang around in the hall?" he asked, hoping he could move her along. "We're in the middle of something."

"Oh, sorry." A dusting of red colored her cheeks as she backed out the door. "I didn't mean to interrupt. Mr. C, do you care if I get something from Louisa's room? I left one of my dresses up there, and I have a date tonight."

"A date?" McCrea challenged, playfully. "Is it with the tuba player who took you to the prom?"

The blush on her cheeks darkened. "Conner didn't play the tuba. He played the saxophone, and no. He's not my date." She stuck her tongue out and crossed her arms over her chest like a pouting child.

McCrea wasn't a dumbass. He knew Eleanor had been chasing his spurs for years, but he had always ignored her because she had been a chatty, somewhat annoying little girl with braces and knobby knees, with the coordination of a newborn colt and the elegance of an ostrich.

But that wasn't the case anymore, and ignoring her was hard to do. She was a full-fledged, curvy blonde who turned heads and extracted whistles and cat-calls. In the past, he had been guilty of tempting her, but now the knobby-kneed girl he had left in the fall was the one tempting him.

"Get what you need," Hardin said, ignoring their bickering.

She began backing out of the door. "Thanks."

"How's Rose doing?" Wade asked, purposefully keeping her in the room.

Holy hell, McCrea swore silently. Would they ever get back to the land? With a heavy breath, he sat down in the chair across from the desk.

His impatience earned him a searing glance from Eleanor. She was adorable when she was mad. In an angry pup kind of way.

"She's sad that I'm leaving, but other than that, she's fine."

"That's understandable. You're a real comfort to her. Lou mentioned you earned a scholarship."

Her head bobbed up and down. "That's right. I worked my butt off for it."

"What are you studying?"

"Business."

"Can't go wrong there."

"Maybe you should help Lou decide on a major," Hardin suggested.

She lifted a shoulder. "Louisa is smart, Mr. C. She'll figure it out."

"Your plans for coming home after college haven't changed?" Wade continued his questions.

"Definitely." She took a few steps forwards, allowing McCrea another lengthy glance at her backside. "I'm going to rebuild Redemption."

He didn't have to see her eyes to know they shone with pride. He could hear it in her voice and see it in her stance. She was determined to make something out of the ranch.

"I'm glad to hear that." Wade seemed pleased by her plan.

"Those are awfully big dreams for a little girl like yourself," McCrea jeered.

"No bigger than finding gold in the ruins of an old church or landing that twelve-point buck you're always talking about."

He grinned at her comeback, remembering how excited she had been on her first visit to the Vera la Luz mission as a little girl. "Hey, the buck is real."

"So are my plans for rebuilding Redemption, and I'll start with Romeo."

Placing all her hopes for Redemption on a horse like Romeo was smart. Charging a premium price for his stud service would generate money for the breeding program she wanted to start and building a reputable name would ensure Redemption a future. The horse was an untapped goldmine.

Romeo was one of the best cutting horses he had ever worked with. The Quarter horse had a gentle disposition and a unique aura. An intangible, low current surge of strength and fluidity which allowed for a distinctive harmony between horse and rider. But more than that, he was smart. He had a special kind of cow sense all real cutting horses have. When the reins were loosened, he could isolate a calf and pull it from the herd like a gentle, guiding mother.

Because Romeo was only a couple of days old when his mother died, Eleanor bottle-fed him, nurtured him, babied him, and loved him as though he were a child, orphaned and alone. The colt had been a pitiful thing, and McCrea hadn't given him good odds at survival, much less growth. But she refused to give up on him, and in her care, the horse thrived. Eleanor never gave up on the things she loved.

"You should have named the beast Eleanor's Baby."

"He's not a beast and you're just mad because you can't have him."

"What's going to happen to your baby when you leave?" he asked, knowing she had already petitioned Jess to care for the horse. "I'll give you a hundred dollars for him right now."

His insulting offer was for the sole sake of instigation, and she knew it. That's what made their flirting quarrels so interesting. He teased her with a few light-hearted insults, and she retaliated with witty comebacks and pretended to be angry. It seemed to be the natural progression of their relationship since he came home from college. He didn't have a clue as to where that relationship might go, and for the moment, he didn't care. He was content living in whatever moment they had.

A convincing stare of anger narrowed her eyes. "Your brother has graciously agreed to take care of him, and it will be a cold day in hell before I sell Romeo to you."

McCrea smiled and fought the urge to kiss her, just as he had in the barnyard yesterday. "Colder weather is comin'."

He tried hard to keep his mind centered on the land, but he found himself wandering back to a conversation he had with her a couple of weeks ago.

She had been on the sidewalk outside of Sweet Sue's Bridal Boutique on Main Street when he drove by. Without knowing why, he parked and joined her at the large display window.

He looped both thumbs in the front pocket of his Wranglers as he gave the peach dress she was admiring a keen look of interest. "Do you think they have it in a thirty-six?"

She fought a grin. "Maybe, but I think the color is wrong for your eyes."

"Really?"

She bit her bottom lip. "Yeah, red is your color."

With a finger and thumb to his chin, he considered her suggestion, then heaved his size thirteen boot outward and twisted his leg in a feminine fashion. "I don't know. With that split, I'd have to get my legs waxed, and it hardly seems worth the effort."

A spew of giggles erupted from her. "Thank you for that mental picture of you in drag."

"You're welcome." Her laughter was like sunshine. He could never get enough of it, and right now, the only thing better than making her laugh at his own expense was seeing her in that sexy peach dress he knew she wanted. "Are you going to try it on?"

"No."

"Why not?"

"This is a dream dress, McCrea. Something I would have to save months for." She shrugged an arm. "Besides, spending that much money for something I'll only wear once seems like a waste."

"But it's the prom." He snatched her hand and, with a light tug, jerked her towards the boutique's double doors. "It's like your wedding dress. It's special."

Her boots didn't budge as she pulled her hand from his. "I'm late for work."

Her sudden withdrawal changed the air around them and the light in her eyes. "But what about the prom? The dress?"

"I have one. It's light blue with sequins running down the front. I bought it last month at the second-hand store down the block."

He knew the shop and anything she bought there could never compare to the gown in the window. "If it's the money, I'll pay —"

"It's not."

Her downcast eyes made him regret his offer. "I didn't mean to insult you."

"You didn't." She kicked the heel of her boot against the concrete. "The truth is, I have enough money in my savings account to buy the dress, but Romeo needs —"

"That horse is a burden you should rid yourself of. I'll give you ten for him."

Her retort was slow, deferred by temptation, he was sure. "Ten?"

"Yep. Say the word and I'll pull out my checkbook."

Her answer was plain and simple. "But he's more than a horse to me. He's the future of Redemption."

Damn the horse and Redemption. She needed the money. "We could make it a partnership."

She raised an eyebrow in question. "A partnership? With you?"

"I buy him, keep him while you're gone, and when you get back from college, we'll start breeding."

"And what do you want in return for your investment?"

A smart man would have spewed out a bullshit figure and let it go at that. Something to cure her curiosity, but he couldn't do that with Eleanor. She was too smart for bullshit. "Nothing."

She crammed her hands into the back pocket of her jeans and tilted her head to one side. "Then why would you do it?"

"For the same reason, I offered to buy you the dress." He felt something inside him give way. Something his pride couldn't hold back. "Because it would make you happy."

His words touched her. He could see it in the

changing color of her eyes, the nervous flex of her creamy throat, and the inward twist of her knees. She was the perfect mix of vulnerability and innocence, and an enticement that ignited a fire deep inside him. "Peach is your color," he lured.

"So is blue. No deal." She pointed to the boutique door. "But I think you should definitely try the red one on."

He watched her firm ass bounce from side to side as she retreated down the street. "I will. If you help me wax my legs!" His shout caused a passing group of teenage girls to giggle. Pride intact, he adjusted the waist of his Wranglers and pushed his chest out before entering the boutique.

Eleanor got her expensive peach dress, delivered anonymously to her mailbox the next day with a red bow that he tied himself. From a bush behind the fence, he watched for the Conner kid's arrival and reminded himself that acne and braces were safe, even if raging hormones were on the loose. Sure enough, at seven o'clock on the dot, the little green Volkswagen jolted to a stop outside Rose's house, backfired once, and produced a very nervous saxophone player. McCrea relaxed, knowing her virginity was safe.

"McCrea?" His granddad called his name, snapping him from the daydream.

"Sorry." He shifted in his seat and rubbed a hand over his eyes. "You were saying?"

"We were talking about Redemption," Eleanor said, glancing curiously at him before turning her attention back to Wade.

"Its heyday was before my time, but I've heard stories about how it was one hell of a horse ranch," Hardin said.

"Oh, it was." Wade laughed. "Your granddad was about the best bronc rider in the state and one hell of a horseman. You may have trouble finding someone as good as he was."

Charlie Mackenna had been the best in the state, and he dominated the sport in the 1960s until a broken back retired him. The old man was tough and a hundred percent cowboy.

"Jess offered to pitch in and help me with the horses when I get back," she told them.

He didn't want to think about Jess or any other man helping her with anything. Because every time he did, the jealousy returned to gnaw at his gut like a hungry bear.

But it was only natural she would enlist Jess's help. He, too, had been one hell of a bronc buster before his accident. After all the surgeries and months of rehab, his brother was still tough as nails.

"We'll help too, in any way we can — money, people, connections. Anything at all," Wade assured her. "And if your plans for rebuilding Redemption don't work out, you come and see me. I have just the job for you."

"You'd give me a job?"

"Sure, we would," Hardin answered for him. "We'd be crazy not to."

"Thank you."

"And don't worry about Rose. We'll take good care of her while you're gone."

"I would appreciate that. I worry about leaving her." She nervously glanced at McCrea. "Well, I better get going."

"Don't forget the dress," Hardin reminded her.

"I won't."

"Make sure you shut the door behind you," McCrea ordered.

She saluted him with a, "yes, sir," before shutting the door behind her.

Wade waited until he heard her run up the stairs before he spoke. "Eleanor's a sweet girl."

"And pretty too," Hardin threw in. "You should be nicer to her."

"She gives me a headache." McCrea scooted to the edge of his seat. "Back to the land."

"Hell, boy, you better not drag your feet with that one," Wade said. "If I were younger, I'd steal her right out from under you."

"What?"

"There's no use in trying to hide it," Hardin said. "We both saw the way you were gawkin' at her."

Damn. He pushed his Stetson higher on his forehead, a little embarrassed that he had been caught. "So, I was admiring her ass."

Chapter Four

W hen the front door slammed shut behind Eleanor, Wade leaned back in his chair. "You do know she's head over heels in love with you, don't you?"

"She's a kid with a crush. She'll get over it."

"But will you?" Hardin threw in.

"There's nothing to get over!"

"You sure about that?" Wade pushed. "Why did you punch Willard?"

"Because he slapped Eleanor on the ass and offered up a raw suggestion as to how she could deliver the next round of beers." He dragged his hat off and slung it to the desk, irritated they were talking him into a corner. "But you two already knew that, didn't you? What the hell is going on here?"

"You tell us," Wade said.

How could he justify kickin' Willard's ass without coming across as being jealous or protective of

Eleanor? The two of them would love that. "Willard has a big mouth, and he needed to know he was out of line."

"So, you broke his nose?" Hardin questioned with a smirk.

"He threw the first punch." He did feel a little guilty for breaking Willard's nose. He was a decent guy, just rowdy when he was drunk.

Wade raised his eyebrows. "Love provokes all sorts of emotions, and jealousy is one of the strongest."

Love? What the hell? "Whoa! I was just looking out for her," he said, raking a hand through his hair. "You would have done the same thing."

Wade's smile was wide. "Damn right, I would have. I once knocked out a guy's front teeth for asking your grandma to dance."

"This is crazy!" he shouted. "I can't believe we're having this conversation. I thought we were talking about my inheritance."

"We are," Hardin assured him.

Wade came to his feet. "I'll make you a deal."

"Oh, God." McCrea felt nauseous, and suddenly things were crystal clear. He needed an anchor. A wife. This entire conversation had been a setup, and he had walked straight into it. He dropped his head with the sentence of a man headed to an execution. "What kind of deal?"

"I'll give you the land if," Wade paused.

"I stop fighting and sleepin' around?" he asked, hoping he wasn't right.

"You get married."

Son of a bitch! Being right made him bring his hand to his face for a hard scrub. "Christ, Granddad. Have you lost your mind?"

"Maybe you should make it two years," Hardin's wit was dry. "We might get a grandson out of it."

Even without Wade's terms, he felt the weight of his family's expectations bearing down on him. The town was steeped in tradition, and family and ranching were two of its finest.

Twenty-four was too young to be tied down, but that's what they wanted. He was home and expected to make something of himself. And he wanted to. He had plans. Damn it, he had plans that didn't involve a wife.

"Find a wife and keep her for at least a year. And I'll hand over the deed." Wade held out his hand to seal the agreement. "What do you say? Do we have a deal?"

It was the heart attack. It had to be. His granddad wasn't thinking clearly. "I don't want to get married," he said and watched Wade's hand fall.

"Okay, have it your way. You can wait until I die to get the land. Maybe by then, you'll be responsible enough to inherit it."

Damn you, Wade. McCrea pinched the bridge of his nose and felt guilty for cursing a man he admired and loved. Waiting wasn't an option.

He had to have the land while Wade was alive. He needed to show his granddad he was responsible and that he could be a success at something other than ranching. He needed to see the approval in the old man's eyes. He needed Wade to know how hard he had tried to be the man he wanted him to be. And if he had to get hitched to do it, then by god, he would. "Okay," he sighed. "You got yourself a deal."

Wade grinned.

"I guess I'd better find a wife," he baited, knowing they had Eleanor in mind.

Hardin leaned forward and pointed outside. "Jesus, boy. The best woman just walked right by you."

Wade turned to the window. "Something about her reminds me of Sophia."

"Yeah, she is a lot like mom," Hardin agreed with a warm smile. "And she'd be perfect for you."

"She fiery." Wade smacked his palms together. "And just what you need right now!"

If he wasn't so pissed at being forced into marriage, he might have laughed at their pushy salesmanship. Look at the two of them, smiling their asses off. Damn, this is a mess.

At least he would get the satisfaction of picking his own wife. "No. Not in a million years."

Hardin's smile fell. "Why not? Eleanor is a good girl. She's hardworking and smart, and my grandkids would be beautiful."

"Stop talking about grandkids," he growled.

Wade pushed a finger into the desktop. "It's time you settled down and made something of yourself. The time for talking is over. Rose's days are numbered, just like mine are, and I intend on doing everything in my power to see that Eleanor is taken care of after she's gone. I owe it to Rose and Charlie."

"Are they the real reason you're trying to make me marry Eleanor?" he asked as the groggy hum of the old Chevy roared to life.

Wade blinked, a little disarmed by the blunt question but said nothing.

"We're not making you marry anyone," Hardin answered. His dad didn't have a clue about Wade's motives for his marriage. "But we all see how perfect you and Eleanor are for one another."

This ludicrous ultimatum was Wade's last chance to

own Redemption, and McCrea knew he could deliver. Sweet-talking and seducing Eleanor into marrying him would be easy. But could he live with himself afterward?

"Perfect or not, if I marry her, she loses Redemption," he said.

"That's ridiculous," Hardin answered, looking at Wade. "Feel free to jump in anytime and tell him he's wrong."

Wade rolled his jaw from side to side.

"Yeah, Granddad, tell me I'm wrong."

"Why do you care if she loses the ranch?" Wade asked. "You'll have Promise Point."

Anger and disappointment settled into McCrea's chest as his granddad's greedy agenda became clear. "I care," he answered, honestly because Eleanor deserved a real marriage with a man who loved her.

"Damn it, Dad," Hardin swore. "This was supposed to be about helping him settle down."

"It is," Wade assured him. "I was just making a point."

Maybe he was wrong. Maybe Wade wanted him to be happy and find love. Yeah, and maybe he would sprout wings and fly.

"Good, then I accept your deal, but," McCrea said, stepping closer to offer his hand to Wade. "I get to choose the woman."

Wade hesitated, knowing he had no choice but to accept.

He raised his hand and took McCrea's. "Choose wisely. Your future depends on it."

ELEANOR WAS sure the play in McCrea's eyes and the sharpness of his tongue was because he thought she had a date tonight. Jess was right. He needed competition, and she was going to give him some.

The flirty banter between them back at the Coldiron house left her flushed and excited. She rolled the window down, cranked up the radio, and bellowed out the upbeat tune with untalented enthusiasm.

At the end of the gravel drive, she felt the truck lurch and sputter. "Damn, what now?" Two days ago, Old Blue belched a gallon of water and gave up the ghost, leaving her stuck driving her grandma's rust bucket. She guided the dead truck off the road, pushed the brake until it stopped, and shoved it into park.

She pecked at the gas gauge and watched the orange hand fall to E.

"Great." She stuffed her dress into her purse and got out. It looked like she was walking home. She kicked a rock and sent it flying across the road. "Ouch!" Worn in all the right places, her favorite pair of Ariat boots did little to protect her feet, but she didn't care. At the risk of a broken toe, she aimed her frustration on a smaller rock and heard the unmistakable sound of the ranch diesel hauling ass down the road.

The work truck slowed to almost a stop, and the passenger side window came down.

"Need a ride?" McCrea asked.

Her quick stride never faltered. "After you practically bit my head off back there in front of Mr. C and Wade, and then tried to embarrass me with that snarky remark about Conner?" She shook her head. "No thank you. I'd rather walk."

"Don't be stubborn."

The temperature today was close to a hundred. She hadn't walked more than twenty feet, and she was already drenched in sweat. But she didn't want to seem zealous about accepting his offer. "Go away, McCrea."

"I wasn't trying to be hateful." He stopped the truck, and Eleanor knew that was as close as he was coming to an apology. "Now will you please get in? It's hotter than hell out here. Let me give you a ride home."

She held back a grin and gave in. "Can you take me to the mini mart instead? Grandma forgot to put gas in the truck yesterday." She climbed in and shut the door. "And I need the truck tonight."

"Old Blue out of commission again?"

"Yeah." With a wave of her hand, she dismissed the problem. "Something about a hose."

"Sure." He let off the brake and pushed the gas. In seconds, they were speeding along the road between his house and hers. "We wouldn't want to disappoint Conner."

"I told you; my date isn't with Conner." She turned the vent towards her face and leaned forward. The cool air hit her sweat-soaked skin, causing her to shiver. "God, that feels good." Aware of his eyes on her, she was nervous but determined not to let it show. The flick of her wrists sent the bottom of her thin t-shirt waving and him muttering a soft curse. "What's the matter?"

"Nothing." His hands tightened on the wheel. "I was just thinking how much things have changed since I've been gone."

She bit her bottom lip to keep from grinning and

twisted around to search the truck bed, giving him a better view of her breasts. "Do you have a gas can in the back?"

A quick glance at her cleavage told her he had noticed. "Yeah, I have one. I try to be prepared for anything."

"That's good to know." She slipped back into the seat and watched the fence posts pass as the song on the radio changed. "Oh, I love this song. The chorus reminds me of you." She listened for the beat and watched them pass her house.

He frowned. "Why does it remind you of me?"

"You drink too many beers on Friday nights. Don't deny it. And," she turned the volume up, pointed a finger at him, and bobbed her head side to side with the beat, "how many times have I heard you tell the boys at the bar you won't ever settle down?"

He let off the gas and merged onto the blacktop road leading into town. Murphy's Mini Mart was just a few minutes away, meaning she had to make the most of their time together. This was the first time she had been alone with him since he came home from college. She had to make it count by showing him she was all grown up.

McCrea was cocky and very confident in his ability to seduce a woman. If he wanted a woman, he got her, and he didn't play or chase. It made him dangerously irresistible. She purposefully lowered her voice to the sexy pitch she had practiced and said his name. "McCrea?"

"Yeah," he answered with a strained voice as he slowed for the sharp curve ahead.

She arched her back and closed her eyes. "Is it hard to seduce someone?"

The truck swerved off the road and down into the ditch.

"Watch it!" She gripped the dash, hoping he could gain control before they plummeted to their deaths. The cliffs jutted downward to the Sandusky Creek below. Locals were cautious of the curve and the potential hazard, but over the years, a few unfortunate souls had lost their lives.

He corrected the truck back onto the pavement and slammed the brake pedal to the floor. "What kind of question is that?"

She stared at him, not realizing the question would have such an impact. "I was just curious. Geez. Kill us, why don't ya." Composure regained, she fanned her face, fighting the adrenaline rush from her near-death experience.

He lowered the volume on the radio. "Are you thinking about seducing someone?" He seemed more disturbed by her question than by the threat of death.

Content with having his attention again, she drummed her fingers against her thigh in beat with the tune. "Maybe." She felt daring, and flirting with him was addictive. But after several intense seconds of him staring at her, she threw up her hands. "What? Why are you staring at me?"

Silently, he pulled back onto the road. "For someone like me, seduction isn't hard at all." He turned into the parking lot of the mini-mart and met her with a look that could melt steel. "But you've got a lot to learn, little Eleanor."

The "little" in that sentence pissed her off. When he opened the door and got out, she slid to the driver seat and glared at him as he dug in the back for the gas can. "I don't know if you noticed, but I've grown up."

"I've noticed." There was a meaning in his voice that sent a shiver up her spine. Had he really noticed?

After paying for the gas, he secured the can in the truck bed and came back to the door. "Are you trying to rope Conner into marriage?" His question seemed oddly out of place.

"God, no!" she protested. "Why would you ask such a question?"

"Scoot," he ordered her to the passenger side and climbed in. "You two have been dating a while, so I thought I'd be getting a wedding invitation soon." He slammed the door and started the truck. "You'll need someone to help you rebuild the ranch."

"Conner's not cut out for ranch life," she admitted.

"I figured as much."

"And I plan on rebuilding Redemption by myself," she clarified. "I don't need a husband for that."

"If Conner isn't the man you want to seduce, who is?" he asked, staring at the road.

"I'd rather not say."

"Then I'd rather not give you advice on how to seduce him," he answered with a glance in her direction.

"Fine," she huffed. "I'll figure it out on my own. I've read all about sex, and I don't think seduction will be hard for me to master."

His laughter filled the cab as they pulled out onto the road. "You and Lou still reading those smutty books?"

"They are not smut," she snapped. This was not going as planned. Maybe she should have gotten a real date for tonight. "They're romance."

"They're smut," he repeated. "Besides, you've read every cookbook my mother has," the daring look in his eyes excited her, "and you can't boil water."

"I can so." She scowled at him and felt part of her courage slip away. "You're an ass, McCrea."

There were those glittering gold specks dancing away in his eyes when he winked at her. "Oh, don't get mad at me. I'm just making a point."

She crossed her arms over her breasts. "And that is?"

"Sex isn't like cooking. There's no recipe to follow. No directions. You could read thousands of books and not know what the hell you're doing."

Score one for McCrea. "Forget I asked."

He shifted lower in the seat and lifted his hips as if he were uncomfortable. "How well do you know the guy you want to seduce?"

"Well enough."

"Seduction can be a dangerous game for someone like you, Eleanor."

Her back stiffened. "Why?"

"There's no delicate way to put it."

She twisted around in her seat to face him. "So, don't be delicate. Spill it."

When his eyes met hers, there wasn't one ounce of flirtatious fun in them. "You're a virgin, and if you try to seduce some of the young studs around here, there's a good chance you could get hurt."

Chapter Five

"A virgin," Eleanor repeated and felt the sting of truth penetrate her core. "That was blunt."

"You asked." McCrea looked forward as he explained. "Taking a woman's virginity is very arousing for a man, and dangerous for the woman if the man doesn't know how to control himself."

"I don't understand that at all. What's so special about taking a woman's virginity?"

He switched the AC on high and wiped his brow with the back of his hand. Was he sweating? "In the old days, it was a way for a man to claim his woman. Make her his. It's all through history."

She could see her truck as they rounded the curve. Damn. The quick trip was wasted.

"Well, chalk one up for the modern age. People have casual sex all the time and men don't," she made quotation marks with her fingers, "claim their women."

"Sure, we do." He guided the truck off the road and

braked a few feet away from hers. "And not all men believe sex should be casual. I don't."

A hard breath could have blown her over.

Her shocked reaction drew a smirk to his lips. "You don't believe me?"

Did she? "I–I–It's just," her words fell short of a sentence. "What about all the women you've slept with?"

"All the women I've slept with?" His question was made with a slight shake of his head. "There aren't that many, regardless of the rumors." The vein at his temple doubled in size when he paused to drape an arm over the steering wheel. His jaw tightened, then relaxed. "I don't screw everything with a vagina, and I am faithful when I'm in a relationship."

Could there be any truth to his claim? "But from what I've heard, you're with a different woman every night."

"Hell, Eleanor, this town doesn't have that many women in it. I'd have to drive all the way to Austin or Dallas to meet that quota." He did have a point. Santa Camino had a slim supply of women in it — eligible or not. "That's just small-town gossip. I used to think it was funny." He shoved the truck into park and stepped out, pausing at the door. "Now it just pisses me off."

The hard slam made her bolt from her seat and sent her racing to the back of the truck in pursuit of answers. "How many relationships have you had?"

After he loosened the bungee strap around the gas can, he lifted it and walked around her without answering the question. He unscrewed the cap, inserted the nozzle into the tank, and lifted the can until it made a guzzling sound. When the can was empty, he twisted the cap in place and closed the lid, then walked to the hood to find the release. The latch gave way with a pop and a chirr, allowing him to lean over the motor.

She raised on tiptoes and joined him for a look inside the foreign land of grease and oil. When her fingers touched the rusty, sunbaked body, she jerked. "Ouch! Why are we under the hood? I thought it was out of gas."

He stepped back to the work truck for an empty water bottle, took out his pocketknife, and unfolded the blade. A thumb to the side of the bottle kept the blade steady as he cut around the top. "Older trucks have to be primed."

It didn't matter to her. She was just grateful the hunk of junk was giving her more time with McCrea. "Oh."

All the men on the ranch carried a pocketknife, but none of them used it the way he did. She loved watching his hands. There was just something about them that intrigued her. Long, lean, and tanned. Callused, but soft. Strong, but gentle. Sweet lord, she wanted them to touch her. She wanted to experience all the pleasures his hands could give and know firsthand the love they were capable of. She was more than ready for that to happen. Years of wishing and dreaming about him wasn't getting her anywhere, and being this close to him was torture. A delectable, tangible ache that was getting worse.

Damn. Damn. Damn. Her hand fetish had her on the verge of squirming. Boots. Boots are safe. She forced her eyes to focus on his well-worn footwear. But boots are attached to calves, and calves to thighs. Firm thighs. With muscles and a dusting of dark hair. She cleared her throat and let her curiosity lead the way. Up. Up. Up to the rise beneath his zipper. Oh, yeah. This was a mistake.

"Get in and wait for me to tell you when to start it." The sound of his soft order brought her attention back to the truck.

She yanked the door open, climbed in, and watched him through the crack between the hood and the cab.

"Okay, try it now." She pumped the gas and twisted the ignition. After a few tries, it started.

He dropped the hood closed and rubbed his hands together, wiping away gas and oil. "They say a woman always remembers her first lover."

She squinted; one eye closed against the sunlight. "Are you making another point?"

"This guy's always going to be in your head." He cut a coy grin as he scrubbed his left thumb. "You might want to give that some thought before you go jumping into his bed."

Why was he trying to make having sex sound so vulgar? "Thanks for the advice."

"This guy." He rested an elbow on the side mirror. "He knows you're a virgin, right?"

"He knows, McCrea, and I don't need you to protect me. This guy's not like Willard or any of the other guys at Tubs." She stretched across the seat to roll the passenger window down, and a cool breeze rushed in, scattering her hair. She gathered it into a ponytail and twisted it into a crude knot at the base of her head. "I'm leaving for college in a few weeks, and I'm afraid if I wait for him to make the first move, I might not get the chance at all. The truth is, I think I'm falling in love with him."

His face drew into a deep scowl. "Does he know that?"

"No. He's clueless."

His quiet study made her uncomfortable. She had seen the same consideration a few times and knew his questions were brought on by a need to protect. McCrea was looking out for her. He wasn't worried about competition from her mystery date or losing her to another man. So much for giving him competition.

In need of a quick getaway, she pushed the brake down and pulled the truck into drive. "I trust him. Plus, he's older than me and more experienced."

His head lifted from its downward tilt with a deep breath. "That's what scares me."

"Don't look so worried. He's like you. He's always in control."

"Every man has his limits, darlin'." His eyes darkened with heavy lashes that lowered to her breast. "Even me."

"McCREA IS A BRAWLER AND A LOOSE CANNON." Rose pushed the limp brim of her straw hat up and held her arm out for assistance.

Eleanor took her grandma's thin arm and gently lifted. A brawler? Yes. A loose cannon? He could be. But she had, on many occasions, seen a deeper, gentler side of McCrea. The side that dried tears and soothed fears. That was the McCrea she had fallen in love with. The boy who had run to her rescue one rainy day when she was eight.

"And he has quite a reputation with the women."

Her talk with McCrea this afternoon left Eleanor questioning that so-called reputation.

With her help, the old woman rose from her kneeling position alongside the Zinnia bed. "I know he's a handsome man, but Mildred said she heard he started a fight over some floozy."

It was on the tip of her tongue to tell her grandma that she was the alleged floozy, and McCrea had chivalrously defended her, just like her granddad would have. Instead, she pointed to the ranch house across the road. "Mouthy Mildred Satterfield is a busybody."

She picked up the bucket of gardening tools and headed for the rusty green shed at the end of the driveway, careful not to dirty her dress. "I don't believe anything she has to say about McCrea, or anyone else for that matter. Was she there? No, she wasn't. But I was. I was working that night."

If her grandma only knew Willard Moore had instigated the brawl, which was now the talk of the town. "And it was just a fight. I don't see what the big deal is."

Rose studied the cracked sidewalk as she took slow, careful steps to the porch. "Okay, don't listen to me. God knows your mother never did."

Here we go again. Eleanor tried her best to tune out her grandma's voice. Agatha Rose Mackenna was the sweetest, most loving woman in the state of Texas, and she loved her dearly. But if she heard her explain, in detail, one more time how she had begged her mother not to get mixed up with the man she met at the bar, she might explode. Did her grandma realize she was the product of that mix-up?

By the time Eleanor came back to the porch, Rose had made her way back to McCrea. "Don't get me wrong. I like McCrea. He's always a nice, well-mannered young man when he drops by or when I see him in town. Wade wouldn't have it any other way but mark my words. He's a heartbreaker, and," Rose sighed when her rear contacted the porch, "not the marrying kind."

"God, Grandma," she groaned. "Marriage, again? You know I don't want to get hitched."

"I know." A corner of Rose's mouth turned down. "But I'm hoping that changes."

"It won't."

"Don't you dream of finding your one true love?" Her aged eyes sparkled with romance and hope. "Don't you want someone to share your life with? Give you children?"

"No." Her answer was like a chomp. "You know what I dream about."

Rose rolled her eyes towards heaven. "I do."

"My dream is to restore Redemption. I want new stables filled with broodmares and studs, and the only offspring I'm interested in are the four-legged kind."

That wasn't completely true. Eleanor wanted a man to share her life with, someone who loved her with the same fierceness of Charlie's love for Rose, and she wanted babies — lots of babies. But babies were made with love, and so far, McCrea was the only man to evoke that emotion from her guarded heart. And as sure as she was about being in love with him, she was just as sure he wasn't interested in bottles, babies, and settling down. At least, not yet.

Maybe after he got the game ranch he wanted up and running, he would want a family. McCrea and babies. The image of how those babies would be made flashed before her eyes. His masculine body pressed against hers in a passionate exchange of love and longing.

"Yes, well," Rose sighed. "I am hoping that changes. I want to see you walk down the aisle before I meet my Maker."

Eleanor made a snorting sound. "I doubt any of the men in Santa Camino would conform to my idea of raising a family without marriage, at least not the ones who are worth a damn."

"Eleanor!"

"And any man who is brave enough to bid for my heart will have to do so without sliding a ring on my finger."

"But — but marriage is a sacred partnership —"

"It's a trap. And hell will freeze solid before I vow myself into matrimonial bondage."

"You make marriage seem so wretched." Rose grimaced and raked silver wisps of hair from her damp face. "And it's not. Not at all."

"Our family is cursed when it comes to marriage," she said, watching Rose's mouth drop open.

"How can you say that?"

"Because it's true." Maybe she was stretching the truth for the sake of her argument, but she'd had the misfortune of witnessing her mother's failed one, so that was enough for her.

"Your granddad and I were married for fifty-five years!" Rose lay a hand over her heart. "And I would do it all over again in a heartbeat."

Oh, to love like Charlie and Aggie Rose. Her inner romance delighted in the thought, while her practical heart rebuked such nonsense. She had learned from an early age that love was volatile, and that marriage was a prison. "Some people aren't made for marriage."

"True enough, I suppose, but some are."

"Mom wasn't." Eleanor sat down next to Rose and let the bitterness of her early childhood claw its way to the surface. She had never known her real father. He had left before she was born, and her mother had married Rex Montgomery shortly after she left Santa Camino.

He was a bitter man with a bad temper and a serious gambling problem. He resented Eleanor and had refused to give her anything that wasn't a necessity, including his last name. Her mother never recovered from the heartbreak of losing Eleanor's dad. She often locked herself in her bedroom and cried for hours after Rex left for the casino. Those times were permanently embedded in Eleanor's memory. "What if I'm the same way? What if I marry the wrong man? What if I marry someone like Rex?"

"Oh, Eleanor, you won't." Rose patted her leg. "Just let your heart guide you. Don't live in the past or the future, but rather in the moment. That's what love is all about."

The uncertainty of Rose's logic ate at her. She wanted to argue that wasn't what love was about. It was about faithfulness and trust. It was about counting on someone to be there when you needed them. Giving and showing affection without coercion or manipulation. Love was about sacrifice and commitment. "Was that what mom did when she fell in love with my dad?"

The light in Rose's eyes dimmed. "Frances was… "

"Young?" she asked. "She wasn't much older than I am now when she had me."

"Confused," Rose answered.

Her mother was emotionally unstable at times but never confused about her feelings for the man she loved. "I asked Mom about him once," she said, suspecting Rose knew more about the man than she would ever admit.

"And what did she say?"

"That she loved him and always would." A bitter smile edged her lips. "He walked out on her and left her to raise his child on her own. He broke her heart, and she still loved him."

Rose looked down at her hands, unable to say anything.

"The heart is known for its faulty guidance, Grandma. Mom is proof of that, and as for living in the moment —" She pushed back her windblown hair. "We both can see where that got her. Pregnant and trapped in a loveless marriage."

Chapter Six

"You are not Frances," Rose said.

"No, I'm not." Pride made her agree even as her doubt took root and grew. She had convinced herself that McCrea was in no way a danger to her heart, but what if she was wrong?

Rose gathered Eleanor's hands in hers and held them tight. "If my Charlie were here, he would tell you marriage is a wonderful thing."

According to her grandma, the sun rose and set in her granddad, and Eleanor knew her argument would never be won. "Can't we just agree marriage is something we will never agree on?"

"McCrea is the spitting image of his granddad," Rose said, ignoring the truce. "Wade was wild like that, you know, hot-headed, unruly, and a real ladies' man."

No, she didn't know, and she was completely happy thinking of old man Wade as just that, an old man. She didn't want to hear about how wild he and her granddad used to be. Or how handsome they looked or a hundred other things that just creeped her out. Some things were better left untold.

"But then he met Sophia." Rose peered over her glasses, and her face softened with the glow of years passed. "Doe-eyed, soft-spoken Sophia had her work cut out for her, but she stuck with him. And she loved the wildness right out of Wade Coldiron."

That wasn't hard to imagine. The tiny, silver-haired woman they lost three years ago could have loved the wickedness out of the devil himself, and Eleanor missed her with a magnitude she couldn't express.

"Thank God your granddad wasn't like that. Charlie was a heartbreaker in his own way, but he wasn't a whore."

The word brought Eleanor back to focus. *Grandma Rose just said 'whore'.* She didn't know whether to laugh or gag, and Rose continued as if the word meant nothing at all. "God, I was so in love with that man. I'll never forget the day he brought me to Redemption and carried me over the threshold."

Not knowing her dad made her hunger for a father figure, and she knew Charlie Mackenna would have made a difference in her life. A larger-than-life character from a Louis L'Amour novel. That's the way she thought of him. Courageous and brave. True to his word, with a heart of gold. "I wish I had known granddad."

"Me too," Rose sighed with the thought. "He was handsome and strong, like your McCrea. Okay," she yielded. "I can handle having McCrea for a grandson-in-law."

"Don't start," Eleanor warned.

Rose's playfulness dwindled away. "Just be careful,

Eleanor. Marriage or not, all long-lasting relationships are built on trust, faithfulness, and commitment. Don't settle for a physical relationship or anything less than love."

A sharp, penetrating pain shot the length of her body. What if she was in love with a man who would never love her or be faithful to her? What if Mildred and the rest of Santa Camino's gossip mill were right about McCrea? What then?

"Now," Rose clapped her hands as her eyes beamed with friskiness. "Let me give you some advice on how to catch him."

Eleanor knew the story about the day her grandparents met. Their courtship and wedding. Rose told it often, and Eleanor was always eager to listen. It made her hopeful there were still men in the world like Charlie, and that maybe one day she would be loved with the same intensity. "The way you caught Granddad?"

"Don't look so skeptical. Remember, I was your age once." But Rose didn't launch into her usual story. "First things first, does McCrea know how you feel about him?"

Of course, not. She was no more than an orphan kitten that he gently pushed out of his path on the way to the barn. How could she tell Rose that hurtful truth when the old woman had such expectation in her eyes? She couldn't, so she answered as best she could without specifics. "I thought he might have figured it out by now."

Rose let out a laugh and winked. "Not likely. Men aren't that intuitive. If you're serious about that man, you need to help him along." Her grin turned wicked. "You know, show a little leg and cleavage."

"Grandma!" Eleanor gasped.

Rose let out an infectious giggle which tapered off into a deep-cleansing sigh. "Oh, it feels good to laugh."

She jumped to her feet before Rose could divulge more of her tips on how to catch a man and held out her hand. "Do you want me to help you inside before I go?"

"No. I don't." Rose pushed her hand away. "I'm going to rest for a spell and then get back at it."

She worked nonstop in the yard from early spring to late fall. The woman was obsessed with flowers, but her perennials and bulbs were the envy of the garden club. "Maybe you shouldn't do so much in this heat."

"It's therapy for the soul, honey." That's how Rose always explained gardening to her. "You should try pulling weeds and planting seeds."

Shoveling stables and helping Jimmy tend to what livestock they had left didn't give Eleanor much time for pulling weeds. "Maybe next summer."

"Maybe," Rose agreed.

"Do you need anything before I go?"

"If I do, I'll get it. I'm old, not helpless. Now, go! Get out of here!" Rose ordered playfully.

Eleanor walked to the truck but paused to look over her shoulder before getting in. Rose's blue-gloved hand waved back. Her grandma looked so thin and frail. Forgoing college was a temptation, but it was an essential part of her plan to rebuild Redemption.

Dreaming wasn't enough. She needed an education, to learn the ins and outs of running her own business. When she returned in four years, she would need money to rebuild, and a degree, along with a strong business plan, would help her get a loan from the bank.

One more look to satisfy her uneasiness found Rose knee deep in a bed of Blackfoot Daisies. She could always come back to Redemption. After all, this was her home. "I'll be late tonight. Don't wait up for me," she yelled and saw Rose nod.

MᴄCʀᴇᴀ ᴅᴏᴅɢᴇᴅ the fist aimed at his nose and counter-punched the man delivering the blow. The hard knock to the man's jaw sent him spinning around and into the bar. "Come on, Benny boy," he grinned. "Is that all you got?"

Ben blinked to focus, but before he could charge forward, an arm clamped around McCrea's neck and hauled him backward. "Shit!" he said, briefly seeing the faded Semper Fi tattoo of Old Ed Tubs as he watched his Stetson fly into the air.

"I've had enough of you two!" The bartender was strong for his age and mean when you pissed him off. And they had. He and Jess were always up for a healthy brawl, and when beers were involved, things could get ugly.

"Ed," McCrea croaked as Ed dragged him towards the door.

"Y'all are tearing my bar to hell!" Ed threw him to the floor.

"We were just having fun." He rubbed his throat and scooted against the wall to avoid being trampled by Jess and Scotty, who were brawling a few feet away.

Ed pointed a stubby finger at him. "This is the last time — Ooph!" his threat was interrupted when a hard right from Scotty sent Jess into Ed. The short and stocky frame of the ex-Navy Seal absorbed the blow and barely moved him.

When the creases in Ed's brow deepened, Jess said, "Oh shit."

Ed gritted his teeth, grabbed Jess by the collar, and delivered a hard, swift punch to his mouth.

Jess's head bobbed back. He blinked, dazed by the punch, and fell to the floor beside McCrea.

"Damn kids," Ed mumbled and stepped over them to break up another fight. Tubs Roadhouse was the only bar big enough or brave enough to handle tonight's much-anticipated bachelor party for the last unmarried Langford brother, Scotty.

Jess worked his jaw from left to right and scooted back to join him along the wall. "Old Ed's gonna kick us out for good this time."

Ed had been Old Ed for as long as McCrea could remember, but was, in fact, a year younger than his dad. The two had gone to high school together until Ed dropped out of his senior year to join the Marines. He came back years later and opened the bar. He had no family or close friends. He was a loner and seemed to like it that way. "How many times has he threatened to do that?"

"More than I can count," Jess said. "But two weekends in a row ain't good."

"He enjoys tearing up shit as much as we do." McCrea tried to savor the excitement he felt at this exact minute. Four years of college, with only intermittent times between semesters, left him missing high school and a time when life wasn't so complicated. The days when football and women were the only things that mattered. The days when he was free to do what he wanted.

He felt caged. He needed to punch something. He needed a release.

"Shit. I need a wife," he mumbled to himself, and with closed eyes, let his head fall back against the wall.

"Hello, boys."

The silky, honey-dipped voice opened his eyes to a pair of slim, tanned legs, and enticed them up to one of the sweetest asses he'd ever had the pleasure of being tempted by. He drew in a long breath while trying hard to clear his mind of the unchaste thoughts racing through his mind about his kid sister's best friend. None of which had ever been as strong as they were since his granddad suggest he make her his wife.

He had never tasted Eleanor, but damn if he didn't want to. Their ride into town this afternoon left him thinking about Wade's suggestion, and suddenly it wasn't so absurd. Maybe she was just what he needed.

She wasn't clingy. She was smart and funny. She was a woman with her own dreams and ambitions. Both of which revolved around Redemption, his conscience reminded him.

"Hot damn." A wide grin covered Jess's face. "This night just keeps getting better."

She ruffled the top of his shaggy mop. "I see Old Ed put you in your place again." She tucked a long strand of her blonde hair behind her ear and tilted her head to the side. "You boys 'bout done for the night?"

Her playfulness excited McCrea, and her tongue made him hard. He watched it dart along the edge of her full bottom lip and felt a cord of sexual tension tighten in his body. A man could stand only so much temptation before he dove in face first, and that's exactly what he wanted to do. Dive in.

"Hell, no," was his answer.

"Hell, yes," was Jess's before he jumped to his feet. "I'd like to spend tonight doing something other than getting my ass kicked. Where's my hat?"

McCrea pulled a pack of cigarettes from his shirt pocket and hit the top against his palm, producing a slightly bent cigarette.

He twisted the end of his new habit between his finger and thumb, hoping the nicotine would settle his nerves. He stuck it between his lips and stretched his legs out, preparing to enjoy. "Isn't it past your bedtime?" he teased and dug into the front pocket of his jeans for his lighter.

She took a step closer, twisted around on one hip, and folded her arms under her breasts. The action emphasized their roundness. "Like you said, McCrea. Things have changed since you left."

Damn right they had.

"I'm meeting my date here."

He lit the cigarette and took a long draw. "Oh, yeah," he mocked. "The guy you've fallen in love with."

Sneaking up behind her, Scotty looped an arm around her waist and twisted her around. "Hellooo, baby."

"Now, Scotty." She wedged her hands against his chest and pushed. "Don't make me tell Amy you've been misbehaving."

The threat didn't stop his drunken advances. "It could be our little secret." He slid a hand over her ass, only to have her smack it away.

"Damn it, Scotty, stop."

"Oh, come on," he jeered.

"Get your goddamn hands off her before you get your ass kicked," McCrea warned, knowing Scotty's rowdiness wasn't caused by alcohol. He was an asshole twenty-four seven, and his reputation went beyond that of a ladies' man.

Scotty flipped him the middle finger. "Screw you, Coldiron."

McCrea took another draw and exhaled before drawing a knee up to stand. "Fine by me."

"Don't, McCrea," Eleanor cut in. "I can handle this." But before she could react, Ben snagged Scotty by the shoulder and spun him around.

"You son of a bitch!" Ben rammed his head into his stomach. "My sister trusted you!" The knock drove Scotty back.

Eleanor tried stepping out of the way but was caught in the scuffle. She lost her footing and fell backward with a "Whoa!" into McCrea's lap, landing her ass hard against his crotch. He winced from the pain of having his hard dick hit but recovered quickly. A soft ass could work wonders.

The fight escalated out to the entryway and through the doors to the parking lot.

"Hoo! Wee!" Jess yelled and followed the fight outside.

McCrea grinned and took another draw from his cigarette. "Damn." He slid a hand up her calf and across her knee. "Things have changed."

He expected her to make a shy getaway, with blushing cheeks and downcast eyes, but she didn't. Instead, she placed both palms on the floor behind her and leaned backward across his lap as if she were lying on the beach.

That made him take another long draw.

"You say you're not the man everyone thinks you

are, but…" The arch of a single brow spoke of her doubt.

Shit. How could this sweet, young thing unravel him so easily? Behind the expulsion of smoke, he gave her curvy body a once over and noticed the outline of her breasts under the thin yellow dress. He had gotten a glimpse of the tantalizing pair when she had twisted around to look in the back for a gas can. They were round and firm. Not too big and not too small. They were just the right size for his palm. He swallowed. Was she wearing a bra? "Here we are with you in my lap and my hand on your leg."

"Yes," she agreed and removed his hand from her knee. "Here we are." The ease of her voice and the friskiness in her eyes were almost sinful.

She raised her lips, passing close to his as she slid from his lap and onto the balls of her feet. She tucked the edges of her short dress into the bend of her knees and drew a finger across his bottom lip before she slowly rose to her feet.

His throat constricted. "Aren't you the little flirt?"

She pressed a hand to her chest and offered an innocent look. "Me? Flirt?"

Sweet Jesus, there was an innocence about her despite her best efforts to look sophisticated and mature. She was ripe for the picking, and he would be damned if he let another man get the first taste.

Chapter Seven

To hell with her date. Eleanor would be his tonight, and if he played his cards right, his wife in a couple of weeks. His palms itched. He wanted the deed in his hand and Eleanor in his bed.

With his mind set on seduction, he crawled to his feet and walked back to the bar just in time to hear Jess yell, "Damn, what a fight," as he came back inside the bar.

By now, the ruckus had settled, and the men were nursing their black eyes, busted lips, and wounded pride. To avoid Ed's blistering stare, McCrea turned his back to the bar and braced his elbows against the edge.

One of the men handed Jess his hat. "Grab mine." McCrea pointed towards the floor next to his brother, and again, his eyes found Eleanor.

Jess tossed him his hat. "What's she doing here?"

He dusted a peanut hull from the brim. "Maybe she's working."

"She told me Old Ed wouldn't let her work tonight. Said things might get out of hand." Jess adjusted the position of his hat. "And those don't look like her usual work clothes."

"Nope." McCrea followed the length of her pale-yellow dress up to the elastic bodice. She had worn that same dress last week to his parents' anniversary barbecue, minus the jacket. The dress was strapless, and he knew it would be so easy to slide from her breasts.

"Don't do it."

McCrea stopped mentally undressing her long enough to ask, "Do what?"

"I know that look. Take my advice." Jess nodded towards a table in the back. "Let Vanessa scratch your itch and leave El alone."

He glanced towards the back of the bar to where the redhead from his high school days was flirting with a group of men. Vanessa had the face of a porn star and the personality of a blank sheet of paper. She was self-absorbed, money hungry, and wasn't adept at seeing anything past the end of a man's checkbook.

She was also very protective of the men she considered hers. McCrea was unfortunate enough to be one of those men. He had been since the night they'd both gotten drunk their senior year and ended up in bed together.

Vanessa was a convenience he hadn't indulged in a long time and he intended on keeping it that way. "Maybe I want more than a scratch."

"I doubt that, but if that's the case, take it slow. El is innocent and the kind of woman a man wants to settle down with."

McCrea knew Eleanor was a virgin even before their ride into town this afternoon, and he was willing to bet that her sexual experience had been limited to sloppy kisses and awkward handholding by teenage boys like the Conner kid. But he could remedy that. "Well," he said, grabbing his beer to down the last sup. "It just so happens that I'm looking for a wife."

"You? Married?" Jess laughed.

"You were right. The fight with Willard really pissed Granddad off, so he made a new demand." He doubted Jess knew Wade's true intentions, and he wanted to keep it that way. "If I find a wife and settle down, Promise Point is mine."

Jess studied him through narrow eyes. "And you picked Eleanor?"

"Granddad said she was fiery," he said without taking his eyes off Eleanor. "Said she was just what I needed."

Jess picked up an overturned stool and sat down next to him. "El's not the woman for you."

The barnyard chase from yesterday came to Mc-Crea's mind, causing jealousy to speak. "But she is for you? Jesus, that's rich. I saw the way you two were carrying on yesterday."

"I'd be lying if I said I hadn't indulged in a fantasy or two, or that I hadn't noticed how pretty she is, or that her dress offers just enough cleavage to keep a man looking." Jess grinned. "What man wouldn't?"

"Don't get any ideas about living those fantasies." If he laid a claim to Eleanor, Jess would never cross the line. "Eleanor is mine."

There was a touch of disbelief and humor in his brother's eyes. "Since when?"

"Since I decided granddad was right."

"That's your pecker talking," Jess said, dryly. "You're being ruled by a stronger power than common sense, and lust can make a man do some crazy things."

The whole notion of him taking a wife was crazy, but he didn't have a choice. If he wanted Promise Point, he had to marry Eleanor. "Crazy or not, I have to find a wife. Granddad won't wait forever."

"Are you going to blame him when you break her heart?" Jess asked flatly.

"That won't happen."

Jess took a couple of peanuts from the small bowl next to him and cracked one open. "And why won't it?"

He cared about Eleanor and had always felt protective of her since the day he found her, after she ran away from her stepfather. Cold, wet and bleeding, she had snuggled closer to him in search of warmth and protection. At thirteen, he had given it, wanting nothing more than to protect the small child who needed help.

He had thought then that the blood on her lip was just a scrape and a result of her trek through the underbrush and thickets. He learned later that wasn't the case. An old anger spread through McCrea's chest when he thought about Rex Montgomery.

He had vowed then and there that no man would ever hurt her again. And none had.

But he had never once considered that he might be the one to hurt her. But if he married her, if he slept with her, everything would change. Their relationship would change. They would be more than friends. She would be more than a tempting smile from across the room or a flirting partner when he felt cocky.

Eleanor would be his wife and lover. She would be a woman he would know intimately. A woman who might want more than he was willing to give.

He cleared his throat. "I'll explain everything up front, and she'll understand that it's just business."

Jess stopped chewing and raised an eyebrow. "By upfront, you mean before the marriage is consummated?"

McCrea ground his teeth together and looked away.

"That's what I thought," Jess said before washing the peanuts down with beer. "Don't you see? El is like a new colt, all jittery and nervous, and if you spook her, she'll run."

"No, she won't," he said, wishing he was as confident as he sounded. "She's done a lot of growing up. She's a woman now."

"A woman you don't know a damn thing about."

McCrea began making a mental checklist of all the things he knew about Eleanor. Blue eyes. blonde hair. Maybe those didn't count because they were obvious characteristics. He thought harder.

She loved Chinese food. Her favorite ice cream was strawberry. Her birthday was in January and…his mind drew a blank.

"How long are you going to think on the fourth one?" Jess asked, looking down at the three fingers McCrea didn't realize he was holding up.

He curled his fingers into a fist. "This is bullshit. I know all I need to know."

"You don't. Court her for a while and take things slow. When you get to know her, pop the question and then never let her go," Jess concluded with a big smile.

McCrea gave him a hard look. "The marriage is for a year."

"You've got to be kidding me. You're going into this with divorce in mind?"

"It's a business deal," he repeated.

"Christ, McCrea," Jess's curse was low. "Don't you dare sleep with her or — or let her think you care for her when you don't."

He looked over to where Eleanor was standing. The radiance on her face was as rare as pearls. The sweetness of her smile and the innocence of her body were his for the taking. He had within his grasp a precious opportunity, and suddenly seducing sweet Eleanor seemed wrong.

"Find someone else."

"There is no one else."

"Vanessa would be more than happy to be Mrs. McCrea Coldiron for a year."

"Hell, no," he said before turning back to the bar.

"Vanessa would be in it for the money. El wouldn't. She believes in love and romance. Marrying you for the sake of a piece of land won't be either."

"Granddad likes Eleanor."

"We all like her. Hell, mom and dad love her to death." Jess made a snorting sound. "And if you hurt her, Lou will murder you and leave your body for the buzzards."

He let out a shaky breath and ignored what might happen if Eleanor knew the truth behind his proposal. "I won't hurt her."

"The goddamn land will always be there. El won't. If you care for her, let the land go. You're going to get it sooner or later."

That's what everyone thought. But McCrea knew he would never inherit Promise Point without delivering Redemption to his granddad first. "I can't wait to inherit the land."

"El deserves a real marriage with a man who loves her, not some shitty marriage deal. If you do this, she will never trust another man enough to give him her heart or love. You'll ruin her."

Guilt washed over him. What if Jess was right? What if Eleanor was in love with her mystery date? What if he seduced her and the man found out? It might destroy her chances of having a meaningful relationship with a man who loved her.

"Did you know she has a date tonight?"

Jess rubbed his eyes. "She mentioned it."

"Did she mention that she's in love with him and plans on seducing him before she leaves for college?"

Jess let out a groan.

"You know who he is, don't you?"

"Jesus, McCrea. Forget the guy. Fix your screwed-up priorities before you entice El into bed and a marriage you can't commit to," Jess said before walking away.

A high-pitched laugh burst through the noise of the barroom crowd and pierced McCrea's patience. Out of aggravation, he threw a quick glance over his shoulder and made eye contact with the source. "Shit."

Vanessa scrunched her freckle-covered nose and gave him a wink to let him know she was on her way up to the bar. The last thing he wanted to do tonight was to catch her attention.

The quick tip-tap of her high heels crawled up his spine. Jesus. How could Jess suggest he make a deal with her?

Vanessa leaned closer to wipe the blood from the corner of his mouth. "You're bleeding."

He recoiled at her touch. "Don't."

Her red lips spread into a smile as she curled up against him and slid a hand down to the inside of his thigh. "But, baby, I thought we could go back to my place tonight."

"Not a chance in hell, Vanessa," he said coldly, and wished he had another beer.

She snuggled closer and palmed his dick without discretion. "I bet I can change your mind."

He shoved her hand away. "Damn it, Vanessa. Leave me alone."

She swiveled around with a giggle and headed towards the bathroom. "I'll be right back."

Hopefully, one of the other men would proposition her and spare him the job of pissing her off later. After all, she was there to work the crowd of drunken men. Every one of them knew what kind of woman she was. Cheap and easy to come by.

Someone dropped a few quarters into the old jukebox in the back and a slow country tune started playing.

Jess took Eleanor's hand and eased her into his arms. With one hand on her lower back, and the other around her waist, they moved around the dance floor, with perfectly synced steps.

Again, jealousy tightened in his stomach.

What the hell is he doing?

Jess spun her around and around. When the song ended, he gave her a quick kiss on the cheek. Eleanor laughed and stepped away to answer her cell phone.

She bent her head and pressed a finger against her ear to drown out the noise. The one troublesome strand of hair that always seemed to be in her way fell again. She tucked it behind her ear, skimmed the crowd, and smiled when their eyes met.

McCrea wanted a woman who reeked of innocence and virginity. A woman who was sweet and untouched.

The girl next door everyone loved, and every man dreamed of marrying. He wanted Eleanor.

"Here," Vanessa tossed his wallet onto the bar. "I found this on the floor. You must have lost it in the fight."

Vanessa with his wallet? Not good. He opened it, counted his money and credit cards, and was surprised it was all there. She clearly expected his gratitude, but he knew better than to offer it. So he shoved it into his pocket and went back to watching Eleanor.

After the call ended, she headed in his direction.

Christ. Here she comes.

She maneuvered her way through the men and over to the bar where he sat. The slinky motion of her hips as she crossed the room made the men teeter back in their seats to get a glance at her ass.

"Our waitress is here," Vanessa said loudly and tightened her hold on his arm. "Bring us a beer, Mackenna."

Eleanor tilted her head to the side and produced an unexpected sexy-as-hell smile. "McCrea, sugar," she practically purred out his name, "if I'd known you were this desperate for a date, I would have said 'yes' when you asked me."

"You little bitch!" Vanessa's voice trembled under the strain of competition. Her fiery red hair didn't match her temper, but she was always willing to put on a good show. Vanessa loved attention, even the kind that landed others in trouble.

"Shut up," he ordered, peeling her hands from his arm.

"She started it."

"I came here to have a good time. Not listen to you

whine." He passed a warning glance in her direction that made her glossy lips flatten. "Go home."

"But I thought —"

"You thought wrong."

"Fine," Vanessa grabbed her purse, flung it over her shoulder, and stomped towards the back.

"Now you've done it." Eleanor's grin widened, and a low, husky laugh worked its way up her slim throat. The sound seemed to vibrate down his body.

Does she know what that laugh does to me?

"Sugar?" he questioned.

She bit her bottom lip as she smiled. The sight of her white teeth raking across the soft flesh gave him another lustful jolt of pleasure, while the sexy grin that curved her lips made his dick twitch with the thought of pursuit. She hiked a hip onto the bar stool and twisted around in her seat to watch the door. "I thought it was a nice touch." Whether it was intentional or not, the movement thrust her breast and erect nipples outward.

Nope. No bra.

Whatever reservations he had about Eleanor went up in smoke. Jess was right, his pecker was in control, and walking away wasn't an option. He forgot every good intention he had. He didn't care about the guy she was in love with or what would happen after he seduced her.

"Did you come all the way out here just to piss off Vanessa?"

"No, but it was worth the drive." She glanced over her shoulder. "Like I said before, I'm meeting my date here."

"Do I know him?" he asked, trying not to let his jealousy show.

The faint smell of flowers hit his nose when she turned her head. "You do." Her blue eyes danced.

"But you're not going to tell me who he is, are you?"

"Nope."

"Why not? Afraid I won't approve?"

"I don't need or want your approval, McCrea." She propped an elbow on the bar and rested her chin on her palm. "But I will tell you he's about your height and weight. He has gorgeous brown eyes and lips," she took a deep breath and let it out, "that beg to be kissed."

McCrea did a glance over his shoulder at the men at the tables. It was hard to believe she was here for any of them. They were all way out of her league, and too drunk to care that she was a virgin. "That's too bad."

She raised her eyebrows in question. "You sound disappointed."

"Maybe I am."

"I doubt that." She nodded towards the back booth where Vanessa sat watching them. "Your date seems eager to please."

He felt the need to clarify. "She's not my date. She just showed up, as usual."

"That one's got her claws in deep."

"Not as deep as she thinks." He leaned closer so that only she could hear him. "About your date."

Her lips parted with hesitation before she asked, "What about him?"

"You could ditch him and come with me."

Her eyes darkened. "You're serious."

"Hell, yes," he said softly and with one finger, ordered her closer.

She hesitated, then slipped from the stool.

"Closer," he whispered and slid an arm around her

waist, pulling her between his legs. He stared into her eyes for a few seconds, purposefully arousing her curiosity. Then touched a finger to her bottom lip. "But just so you know," he returned her wink from earlier, "my dates don't end with goodnight kisses."

Without skipping a beat, she raised a slim eyebrow and gently grasped his hand, removing it from her lip. "McCrea, if that finger or those lips have been anywhere near Vanessa Worley tonight," her smile was superficial. "You can keep your goodnight kisses."

Her cleverness and spot-on response were arousing. "Trust me darlin'," he eased his hand to the base of her head and urged her closer, "when I get done with you, you won't care where they've been." He brushed his lips across hers and heard her draw in a sharp breath.

Piece of cake.

Chapter Eight

The sound of her pounding heart overpowered the noise of the drunken crowd, blocking out whistles and lewd cheers when their lips touched.

According to her research on sex, a kiss could cause an orgasm, and McCrea's had Eleanor seconds away from crying out in ecstasy. It was everything she dreamed it would be. Soft. Sweet. Sexy. And nothing like the boy kisses she'd had before. His skillful lips were magical and cast a spell that left her lightheaded and weak. Sweet lord, this was heaven.

Heaven that ended too soon when he pulled back. "We're drawing a crowd." The alcohol on his breath mingled with his rich cologne that left her holding onto his shirt for support.

"I don't care," she managed to say.

His low, coarse laughter penetrated every nerve in her body. "Normally, I wouldn't either, but…"

The unfinished sentence lifted her eyes to his. "But what?"

"I don't want people talking trash about my Eleanor."

His Eleanor?

"You know they'll talk about anything we do."

"After tonight, what they say about us won't matter, anyway." She wasn't sure what he meant by that. The hungry hounds of gossip weren't easily appeased, and the thought of tomorrow's chinwag headlines almost had her cringing. Mouthy Mildred's Hot Topic List would read: Local Playboy Seduces Innocent Neighbor Girl. She could see poor Rose as her face paled, and she tried to explain to Pastor Barns how it was all just gossip. Good luck, Grandma.

McCrea looped a loose strand of her hair around his finger and gently tugged. "What happened to the little girl in pigtails and braces who used to chase me around the barnyard?"

Oh, she's still chasing you. "She grew up," she whispered because it was too early to admit the truth.

His finger traced her jawline and ventured down her neck to her collarbone, which caused her body to shiver involuntarily. "She sure did." The depths of his eyes reflected a new fascination for the woman he saw in her.

The break of his lips and the slant of his head let her know another kiss was coming, and she didn't care who saw it. The touch of his lips fueled her hunger for something more, and the teasing war with his tongue drove her closer to the sweet release she craved. She was in the hands of a capable lover, one who could tease her all night. He was five years her senior and experienced in a way that made him a threat to any woman who wanted to risk her heart for more than one night in his bed.

What would that be like? Her imagination plunged deeper into a torrid scene of his body entwined with hers. She knew McCrea wasn't the teasing and leaving kind, and the scene in her head would happen if she didn't stop it. He wanted satisfaction just as much as she did, and his dates didn't end with goodnight kisses. Sweet Lord! What am I doing?

She broke the kiss. "McCrea."

The teasing specks of gold in his eyes were replaced by black pools of desire. His fingers gripped her hips and gently pushed her back so he could slide from the stool. "Give me my keys, Ed. We're leaving."

Ed eyed the two of them. "Like hell I will," he said and turned back to the men on the opposite side of the bar.

"Where are we going?"

"Someplace private," he whispered. "I want you all to myself."

Panic pushed a hand into his chest. "Wait."

"Why? Are you having second thoughts?"

"No. Yes," she stuttered.

"Which is it?"

"I don't know. I just thought…" She closed her eyes, unsure of what she should say.

"What did you think?" Something edgy was in his eyes. An emotion she hadn't seen before. Anger? Frustration? She couldn't tell.

"That things would move slower. I just wanted to get your attention."

"You got it." She loved the husky sound of his voice.

"I can't do this..." her voice broke into a deep breath.

"What can't you do?"

She hated herself for what she was about to say. With a flushed face and a racing heart, she stepped back. "I can't do more than goodnight kisses. I'm not Vanessa."

He caught her arm and gently eased her closer. "I don't want you to be. Trust me, Eleanor." His tender kiss soothed her second thoughts. "Tonight will be more than anything you could hope for."

More than anything she could hope for? "What does that mean?"

He thumped the bar with his fist. "Ed. Give me my keys. Now."

This time, Old Ed wasn't so easy about the order. He pointed a finger at McCrea. "Listen here, son. I'm not about to let you drive out of here drunk," he tossed the finger in Eleanor's direction, and she knew her boss's protective side was about to rear its ugly head. "And I'm sure as hell not letting you drive out of here with this little gal in the truck with you." Something about the way Old Ed said it made her think he wasn't happy about her leaving with McCrea, drinking or not.

McCrea's face changed into the hardness she had seen the night he punched Willard, but Old Ed didn't care. He showed his lack of concern by flipping the television to a different station.

"How the fuck am I supposed to get home?" Mc-Crea yelled back, and rather than see him make a fool of himself, she quickly jumped in with her offer.

"I'll take you home in my truck."

McCrea hammered another hard fist to the counter

to get Old Ed's attention. "I'm not leaving here without mine."

A sharp glance from her boss made her cut in before he could answer. "I'll drive him home, Ed."

The veteran bartender watched her carefully. "Are you sure you can handle this ugly cow chaser, honey?"

His gentle question caused her to smile. "I'm sure."

With a deep frown, he slid the keys across the bar to her and explained the policy she knew by heart. "I made all of 'em give me their keys before the first drink." He pointed to Jess, who was watching from the end of the bar. "I cut these two off a half an hour ago. Then," he pointed to McCrea with a scathing look, "this one started a fight."

She grabbed the keys before McCrea could take them. "Thanks, Ed. Don't worry about me. I'll be back later for the truck."

"It'll be here, honey. Just be careful." His finger took another aim at McCrea. "And son, you'd better mind your manners."

McCrea latched onto her elbow and practically pushed her towards the small entryway at the front of the bar. "Let's go."

His tone and grip made her wonder if the moment of desire between them could be rekindled. It could be on her part. Her body was still humming in all the naughty places. "Why are you in such a hurry?"

As they made the dark space of the entryway, McCrea hauled her into a corner, and the hard edges of his body pinned her against the wall, causing her to arch her body. His palm to the wall, throaty groan stirred her crux, and she knew his desire hadn't diminished either. "I'm in a hurry to have you all to myself."

Her hormones had been pin balling from high to

low since her close encounter with him in the barnyard, and his teasing foreplay was killing her.

The soft orange glow of the flashing "Open" sign in the window gave her a glimpse of his smile as he made a grab for the keys. She twisted her hand free and dangled them in front of his face. "Don't think you're going to sweet talk me out of these."

His arm fell, and he followed her to the door. "Keys are the last thing I want to talk you out of, darlin'."

Outside, she trotted backward with a grin. "Oh, really?"

She knew she was playing with fire, but she didn't care. She wanted to live in the moment and more than goodnight kisses from this cowboy.

"Get your ass in that driver's seat before I take another kiss and the keys," he said.

A light rain began to fall, cooling the hot August air and intensifying all the sounds and smells that made Santa Camino home. Fireflies twinkled under the trees, and the soft sound of crickets filled the air.

Once on the driver's side, she took a moment to fan her face, draw in a deep breath and collect herself. She didn't want him to see how shaky or nervous she was. She exhaled slowly, then hit the unlock button on the remote and climbed inside his truck. Unlike the ranch truck, the new leather in his smelled rich and felt wonderful beneath her legs.

Her hands caressed the steering wheel. "Boy, this is something," she said when he climbed in and slammed the door.

She watched him toss his hat onto the dash and rest an arm on the back of the seat. "Just be careful. It's got a lot of power."

"Oh, please. Why do men think women can't handle

a truck?" She heard him laugh as she turned on the ignition. She scooted the seat forward so she could reach the pedals and took off her jacket. "Buckle up," she said while fastening her own.

He leaned back in the seat, his fingers tapping impatiently against his leg. "Seat belts are too constricting. I don't like being tied down."

"Suit yourself."

She switched on the lights. "Where are the wipers?"

He reached across the seat to turn on the switch and brushed her breasts with his arm. "Right here."

Her nipples pearled. "Thanks," she breathed out.

He straightened and gently tapped her forehead with his finger. "What's going on in there?"

A knock-down, drag-out fight between this excruciating ache in my body and common sense. She managed a smile. "Nothing."

One corner of his mouth tilted up. "You're not a very good liar, are you, Eleanor?"

"I wish you'd stop calling me that."

To deepen her torment, he placed a hand on the seat between her thighs.

Ohmygod! What is he doing?

Her mind malfunctioned, blocking all rational thought, and her lungs ceased to work. She couldn't have taken a breath if her life had depended on it. It was like drowning in fire.

"Eleanor is a beautiful name," he said softly and laid his head against her thigh as his other hand searched for something under the seat. "For a beautiful lady."

She was sure she might die from the heat of his hand, which was only inches from her crotch. The stubble on his jaw slid against her bare skin, roughly stimulating her already heightened arousal.

When he had what he wanted, he raised to pause briefly at her lips. "Got it," he said, holding a bottle wrapped in a brown paper bag. The humor on his sexy face told her he was loving every minute of this.

Adjusting her seat belt gave her something to do and allowed her a second or two to find her voice. "I think it sounds old and boring. El sounds sexy and sophisticated."

"Jess tell you that?" His jaw ground together after the question.

"No, why would you say that?"

"He's the one who gave you the nickname, and it sounds like something he'd say." He ripped the bag open, smiled as if he were greeting an old friend he hadn't seen in years, and twisted the cap off a new bottle of Jim Beam. "Come to Papa."

She watched him take a long drink of the hard stuff. "Thirsty?"

"Maybe." He downed two more swallows that ended with a grimace. "Does it bother you?"

"A little," she answered honestly. "The last time I saw you chug JB was when you and Wade argued about college."

He let his head fall against the rest. "Same argument. Different demands."

"What?"

He raised the bottle for another chug. "Nothing. Drive and let me take care of my problems my way."

This wasn't part of his usual raillery. His tone warned her to stay clear of something he considered none of her business. Something she guessed stemmed from his conversation with Wade earlier today. But his harshness hurt her. "So much for trying to help."

A deep sigh turned his head towards her. "I was rude, wasn't I?"

"A little," she answered, knowing whiskey consoled silently, without questions or judgment. "I get it. I really do. You don't want to be a rancher or follow in Wade's footsteps."

He rested the bottle on his thigh. "My problems go beyond that argument."

"You have a great life and more money —"

"Don't be naïve," he cut in before taking another drink. Then he settled lower in the seat. "Just because I have money doesn't mean I don't have problems."

"I realize that, but you have a family who loves you. Wade loves you, and though you might not see it now, he has your best interests in mind."

He watched her for more seconds than she was comfortable with. "How long were you outside the study door?"

"Not long, why?"

"We were shouting after you left. Did you hear any of it?"

"No." Her lips twisted into a sheepish grin. "My mind was on my date."

A shake of his head made her feel childish. "Of course, it was."

"I'm listening now. Talk to me. Tell me about your problem," she urged him. "You have my full attention."

He wrestled a deep sigh. "You wouldn't understand."

"And the whiskey does?"

His eyes drifted down to the bottle in his hand. "Something like that."

"This must be a doozy of a problem. Are you going to be, okay?"

"Sure, why wouldn't I be?" The edge of his top lip turned up. "After all, I'm rich."

"That's not what I meant."

"I know what you meant, and I appreciate your willingness to listen." He recapped the bottle, sat it on the floorboard, and gave her a wink. "But I don't want to spend the night talking about my problems." He yanked the visor down and let a small box drop into his other hand. "I have something for you."

She was surprised. "For me?"

His mood lightened as he presented her gift. "For you."

"You bought me a present? Why?"

"I didn't buy it." He opened the green felt box. "It's not a big deal. I just saw it and thought of you."

The antique coin was tarnished and about the size of a quarter.

He lifted it from the box and looped the chain around his finger. The dingy coin swung back and forth. "I found it at the Mission yesterday."

"It's from Vera la Luz?"

"I dug it out of the ground myself."

She caught the coin to get a better look. To construct the necklace without damaging the gold coin, he had crudely wound a piece of thin wire around the circumference and twisted a loop at the top to hold the chain.

"I didn't have time to get it polished, but we can do that later."

She clasped it tightly. "No way. I like it just the way it is."

His hand brushed against her hip as he released the

buckle of her seatbelt and unclasped the chain. "Turn around."

She gathered her hair to one side and moved around in the seat with her back to him. "I thought the gold was just a story."

He moved closer to drape the chain over her head and fastened it in place. "There is always some truth to a legend. Remember the story Dad told us?" he whispered into her ear and ran his hands down her bare arms.

"I couldn't wait to see the Vera la Luz Mission. All the kids at school talked about how haunted it was. I was terrified, but so excited," much like she was right now. "That was my first camping trip, and Mr. C tried so hard to make me feel like I was part of the family."

"You are a part of my family." His voice was tender. "Haven't you realized that yet?"

"I always feel like I'm in the way. Like yesterday in the study."

"You're never in the way," he said. "I was just upset."

"About what?" She tried again to make him open up, but he was evasive.

"Nothing I can't fix."

She caressed the coin. "Do you think there's more gold up there?"

"Maybe the Wayfires Legend is real." With a raspy voice against her ear, he spoke of the ghost story from their childhood. "Maybe the gold is protected by the spirits of my Comanche ancestors."

She felt herself melting into his arms as his hands branded her with a fire only, he could extinguish.

Loud laughter erupted from a group of men exiting the bar. "Shit."

She scooted back into the driver's seat. "It's beautiful, McCrea."

"You like it?" He sounded pleased.

It wasn't beautiful or fancy, but to Eleanor, it was priceless. "I love it. Thank you."

"You're welcome."

"You'll be home for Thanksgiving in a few months. We can go back to dig for more and spend all weekend there if you like."

Her eyes moved to his lips. How many times had she dreamed about those sexy lips kissing every inch of her body? How many times had she dreamed of giving herself to a man she had loved and wanted for years? Would that night be tonight or the night after? Would it be in a bed with sheets or in a sleeping bag under the stars?

The particulars of when and where didn't matter. All that did matter was that they wanted each other. Tonight, was the start of something wonderful between them. "You really think there's more?"

"I suppose anything is possible, but if there is, I want to know how it got there." He reclaimed the bottle from the floorboard. "There are always more questions than answers whenever it comes to the Wayfires Gold."

That much she knew. McCrea and others had spent years digging and researching the legend without any answers to show for their work. "But now we have proof." She loved talking about the romantic legends of Santa Camino.

"I've found pottery shards and arrowheads. But this is the first coin I've found."

And he had given it to her. Why? Was it a token of love? Hope filled her heart.

"I've thought about calling one of the universities to

see if they'd be interested in doing a dig. There is so much we could learn about it." With a deep sigh, he laid his head against the rest and looked westwards towards Promise Point, where the mission lay in ruins. His passion for history was one of the things she loved about him. McCrea was an educated man, knowledgeable and worldly about so many things. He was also a conundrum. A puzzle as complex as the mystery he sought to solve.

"I wonder what it was like back then." Her gaze followed his to Promise Point, and she allowed herself to get lost in the romance of the past. "When the West was wild."

"Texas was a wild and dangerous place," he agreed.

"And romantic." She knew there was a dreamy look in her eyes, but she couldn't help it. Though her view on marriage was tainted by her mother's failed one, she was a hopeless romantic. Rose's influence, no doubt.

"Romantic?"

"Yeah, the Old West was romantic." She nudged his thigh and smiled before she put the truck in reverse to back out. "Don't you think so?"

He shot her a doubtful look. "No, I don't."

Out on the main highway, she held tight to the steering wheel and focused on the passing cars. The truck was twice the size of her grandma's. "Why not?"

"Indian attacks, harsh winters, blistering summers and," he paused, "men usually took what they wanted."

Her smile fell. "Thanks for bursting my bubble."

He laughed. "Sorry I spoiled the romance for you, darlin'."

"I'm sure not all men were like that. I can't imagine any of the Coldiron men taking what they wanted."

"What makes you say that?" he challenged. "Don't think we could ravish a few virgins?"

She rolled her eyes and took her turn at disagreeing. "No, I don't."

The bottle was on his lips when he hesitated. "You clearly underestimate us."

She knew he was joking. The Coldiron men had never treated her with anything but respect and kindness. And they made sure other men did the same. They were the perfect gentleman. "You would never mistreat a woman."

"No, I wouldn't. I don't take what isn't given freely." The deep pitch in his voice dropped another notch. "But I do know how to persuade a woman into giving me what I want."

"Oh, I bet you do," she said, and he laughed.

The drive to the ranch had her frustrated. In the bar, he was aroused and fervent for her. Now he looked as mellow as a house cat, relaxed against the seat and enjoying the ride. How did she get him back to being interested?

"By the way," she gave him a flirty glance. "I loved the way you were explaining virginity to me this afternoon. As if I know nothing at all about sex."

$$\textit{Chapter Nine}$$

"You know your books, Eleanor. Trashy fairy tales," he teased.

"They are not. And I'm nineteen." She gave him a "get real" glance. "I've had some experience."

"From the Conner kid or the guy that you're so in love with?"

"My experience didn't come from Conner."

He pointed towards the ranch road. "You're about to miss the turnoff."

She flipped on the signal and waited for a car to pass before turning. "Conner threw up in the parking lot, and I went in by myself. I told you spending all that money on a dress was a waste."

She knew he had bought the dress, and that he was watching from the fence when Conner picked her up.

"It made you happy, and that made it worth every penny." He indulged in another guzzle and recapped the bottle. "So, you're an experienced virgin?" Something about that seemed satisfying to him.

She shrugged. "Yeah, I guess so. Why?" The truth was, most of her knowledge of the art of making love did indeed come from the books he labeled as trashy.

"Drive out to the cabin."

She slowed the truck to a stop. He was referring to the cabin where they had first met years ago. She wondered if he remembered that day. "Why do you want me to drive out there?"

He shoved the whiskey bottle under the seat. "It's the perfect place for our date."

The cabin was vacant except for hunting season and was secluded. They would be all alone. Her heartbeat quickened. "I don't recall saying 'yes' to that date," she resisted with a hint of friskiness. "I volunteered to take you home."

"I don't recall you saying 'no' either."

She eased off the brake and let the truck roll closer to the cabin road. "True enough."

"Half the women in town would trade places with you in a heartbeat." He grinned at her open-mouthed expression. "After all, I'm rich, handsome, and irresistible."

"And arrogant," she added, and he winked. "Okay, if I accept this date," she paused, wondering if she should ask, "what can I expect?"

Against the dashboard lights, his expression changed from playful to serious. "I've already told you. My dates don't end with goodnight kisses. I'll teach you about seduction, but," the muscles in his jaw flexed before he continued, "not so you can seduce some other man."

As if. She almost laughed aloud.

"Sure, you may care for him, but it's just infatuation. Puppy love. Nothing more."

"How can you be sure?"

"Because you're considering taking me as a lover. Your first lover. If you really loved the guy, you would have told me to go to hell when I kissed you back at Tubs."

All that truth and he hadn't a clue. Now would be the logical time to tell him he was the man she wanted to seduce. The man she trusted. The man she was in love with. But if she did, would he dismiss her feelings as puppy love or infatuation? Would it change his mind about giving her a lesson in seduction? Her confession would have to wait.

She made the turn, drove to the cabin, and parked.

"Leave it running," he said, taking her hand as he twisted around to stretch one leg out in the seat. A quick but gentle yank positioned her between his thighs. "It will be pitch black in here without the dashboard lights.

"I'm okay with that."

He tilted her chin up, and the coolness of his dark eyes made her tremble with expectancy. "No hiding," he ordered with a tame kiss that soothed her. "Don't be nervous. Think of this as a dance with me leading the way."

"I have two left feet."

"No, you don't. I saw you dancing with Jess. You never missed a step."

"Jess isn't you."

His thumb slid across her bottom lip. "Meaning?"

"I don't get stupid when I'm around him, and," she hesitated before finishing, "he doesn't make me ache the way you do."

He sucked in a ragged breath. "Are you aching now?"

"Yes," she whispered.

"Good." He lifted her hand to his lips and grazed a kiss across her knuckles. "Seduction," he inserted his thumb into her closed hand, and pushed up, exposing her palm. "Requires intimacy and trust," he finished the sentence with a wet, tantalizing kiss to her palm.

"It's about," with his other hand, he unbuttoned the bottom button of his shirt, "skin," he freed two more buttons "against skin." Three more buttons and he slid her hand inside the shirt. "Touch me."

The need to do just that had her hands moving over the dark dusting of hair that tickled her palms. God, he felt good! His skin was warm and smooth, and she craved a taste. She lowered her lips to the rift between his pecs and kissed down to the muscles just above his navel.

"Seduction requires," his voice trembled, "control." He gently fisted her hair and lifted her lips to his for a deep kiss that screamed of wanton intrusion. As his tongue penetrated her mouth, she understood that his kiss in the bar had been a teaser.

His hands slid up her thighs, to her hips and waist, lifting the hem of her dress as she straddled him. The barrier of his jeans did little to hide his size, and the painful twinge building inside her made her arch into the hardness of his erection.

The rain, which had been a mist, now dashed against the truck, setting the tempo for the rhythm of a dance he knew well.

His fingers squeezed the soft flesh of her butt while his hips thrust upwards, coaxing her with his hardness. "Sweet Eleanor."

"McCrea." His name came out as a mew of sensual frustration.

"I know." One hand moved up her hip to her waist, then on to cup her breast. "You need more, don't you?"

"Yes," she breathed.

His fingers hooked on the elastic and moved her dress down to uncover her breasts. She didn't pull away or hide. She wanted him to see her as no other man had.

His thumb grazed her nipple, rousing a pleasure-induced moan from her lips. "So perfect and beautiful."

His thumb grazed her nipple, rousing a pleasure-induced moan from her lips. "So perfect and beautiful." His hand moved to the inside of her panties, and though he said not a word, the hypnotic gaze of his eyes convinced her it was okay to let go. It was okay to let him have what she so desperately wanted to give. "I won't do anything you don't want," he reminded her and claimed her breast with his mouth. The feel of his tongue on her nipple sucked the air from her lungs.

"More?" His question was hot against her skin.

A nod signaled her permission, and his fingers slipped into her yielding wetness. The shock of him touching her so intimately caused her to stiffen. "Relax and enjoy," he murmured.

She did. Over and over, his fingers teased her body, sensually, skillfully and patiently building her desire until her need was met with a hoarse cry of satisfaction. Her body clenched around his fingers. "That's it. Come for me."

After the peak of pleasure departed, Eleanor floated back to earth to rest as a crumpled mess against his chest. Her strength was gone, used up by the sweet ecstasy.

"I thought you were an experienced virgin," he teased.

"I've never experienced anything like you, McCrea."

He caressed her arms and kissed the top of her head. "Wasn't that better than goodnight kisses?"

She wiggled the dress over her breasts and raised to his naughty smile, which made her flushed cheeks hotter. Still straddling him, she was acutely aware of his own unmet need. A slow gyration of her hips against his erection closed his eyes and gave her a chance to mimic his naughty smile. "Shouldn't we do something about this?"

Tender fingers drew back her hair. "I intend to, but I'm not taking your virginity in a truck."

Her naughty smile broke into a frown. "Does that mean our date is over?"

"It's far from over, darlin'." He gently removed her from his lap, turned the truck off, and opened the door. "We're just moving it inside," he said, lifting her into his arms.

She let out a scream as the cold rain hit her skin and wrapped her arms around his neck. The short run to the porch had them soaked, but neither cared. The need to finish what had been started was driving them. He took the steps two at a time, stumbled through the front door, and headed for the bedroom. Tossing her on the bed, he peeled away his wet shirt and kicked off his boots.

The bare window didn't allow much light from the black night, but faint pulses of lightning delivered flashes of his face and chest.

She welcomed his deep kiss while working to unbuckle his belt. Once it was free, she unbuttoned his jeans and pushed them down. But the wet denim didn't make the simple task easy.

"Darlin', you're killin' me." At mid-thigh, he took over, stripping them off quickly. "Stay put," he said and disappeared into the other room.

She yanked her boots off as he returned with a camping lantern. He set it on the floor and tossed a condom on the bed next to her.

Birth control. She hadn't thought of that.

She rose to her knees, and let her eyes map out the places her hands wanted to go. She was fascinated by the hardness and beauty of his body, and the lantern gave off just enough light to make the exploration of her hands sinful. She yearned to look at him, naked in the light, touch him, hold him in her hands and feel him intimately.

He held her gaze, watching her discover his body as her palms glided over his rain-soaked chest, and lower to the black briefs which hugged his privates. Past the hard V-shaped muscles of his lower stomach, and downwards.

Oh! Wow!

His face contorted with pleasure when her fingers curled around him. His eyes closed with a moan. A clenched jaw and an inward breath enticed her to caress the length of him.

All the stories she had consumed hadn't prepared her for the physical experience of lovemaking. Sex isn't like cooking. There's no recipe to follow. No directions. You could read a hundred books and not know what the hell you're doing. His lecture on sex pierced her mind, invoking an impish grin and a laugh.

McCrea's lids peeked open. "What?"

She teased wet kisses along his jawline, to his chin, and down to his chest, hesitating long enough to add a flick of her tongue to the nipple. "Still think I can't cook?"

A lip-biting smile decked his face. "You're just beatin' the batter, darlin'."

Surprised, but not derailed, she quickened the movement of her hand into a long sensual stroke and met his lewd answer with a slow, lascivious lick from his navel to his sternum. "Do I get to lick the spoon?"

His fingers tangled in the hair at the back of her head. He tilted her head up. "Remember what I said about a man having limits?"

Smiling, she repeated the stroke which thrust his hips forward. "Uh-huh."

"You're about to push me to mine," he said, catching her hand to stop the next stroke.

She grinned. "Spoilsport."

He playfully shoved her onto the bed and climbed over her. "We'll see who's the spoilsport."

Giggling, she attempted an escape. "I was joking!" The delicious promise of a foreplay grapple coiled desire in the pit of her belly and slowed her retreat. She loved the game, and the consequences of losing were going to be excruciatingly sweet. His hand, twice the size of hers, snagged one wrist. She squirmed against him, fighting the capture of her other hand, but lost.

Above her, he waited with a corrupt smile.

She squirmed again. "I guess I'm at your mercy."

The smile dissolved and for the longest time, he simply stared at her.

Her arms, taut from the game, relaxed. "What's wrong?"

A slight lift to the corner of his mouth which could

have been remorse triggered panic to rise in her. The night was too perfect, and she had been too brazen. Now what? "Did I do something wrong?"

A brief frown grazed his forehead. "No. Why would you think that?"

"I thought maybe all that talk about licking spoons might have turned you off."

A tender smile darted across his lips. "No, darlin'. I love it when you talk about licking my spoon."

"Then why did you stop?"

He imprisoned both wrists with a single hand and lifted her arms above her head. With his free hand, he traced her cheek. "You're so beautiful. I had to stop and stare." His lips followed close behind, burning a sensual path of fire down her jawline.

Relieved he wasn't having second thoughts about making love to her, she basked in the way his lips made her feel. Attractive. Desired. Loved.

He tasted the shallow dip of her lower neck and the sensitive valley between her breasts. He shifted lower, without releasing her hands, to the dress she thought was a hindrance, but the thin, wet material clinging to the rise of her nipples like a second skin posed no problem for McCrea. The pointed sensation of his teeth raking over her peak through the garment arched her back, and he made sure he gave each breast the same expert attention. His was nothing like her amateur foreplay. "McCrea." The guttural cry gained her an intermission by way of a long, hard kiss that left her panting for more.

Catching the thin material of the dress between his teeth, he unveiled her from breast to belly inch by inch. Eleanor knew she was completely at his mercy, and playing the captive amplified the intensity of his every move. She was his to do with as he pleased, and the thought made her body writhe beneath him.

His knees at her waist shifted wider and allowed his hand to glide down towards the apex of her thighs. The earlier demonstration of his dexterous fingers vaulted her pelvis upward in expectancy and urged a moan from her throat. Under her panties, his fingers advanced into her folds to graze her already sensitive nub. Persistently but softly, he manipulated and filled her until the threat of a climactic spiral edged closer. "Don't make me —" Her voice broke with the plea.

"Come," he finished with another plunge, which curved her body again.

In the truck, he had played her body with the skill of a master violinist, hitting all the right notes at just the right time. Even now, he had her body humming with a sensual song. But she wanted more. Craved more. "Please…"

He released her hands and slipped the dress past her hips, thighs, and ankles. Her wispy panties came next, followed by his briefs. He tore open the foil packet, removed the condom, and rolled it down his shaft. Its size had grown and caused her eyes to widen with a silent question.

He bent to kiss her lower belly, and his tongue traced a ring around her navel. With his knee, he divided her legs and pressed his erection against her. "Your body was made for mine."

The erotic encounter of hard and soft brought a moan to her lips. Her nails raked down his chest, to his waist and around to latch onto the hard muscles of his buttocks as her hips reached to his with an instinctual urge to become one.

He shifted his weight to a hand beside her head, and

the other found the space between the small of her back and the mattress. The texture of his slightly callused palm lifting her upward opened her legs in an unspoken invitation.

"That's it," he exhaled against her ear. "Open up for me." With that sensual command, he entered her, tore past the threshold of her virginity, and claimed her.

A searing pain, far worse than she expected, briefly overpowered her desire, but she endured, knowing it was part of her body merging with his.

She buried her face in his chest and held her breath, fighting past the discomfort and openness that came from giving herself to McCrea. Her first lover. The man who would always be in her mind.

"It won't last long," he promised.

The penetrating sting lessened, and the sweet desire she had felt before slowly crept back in. Its fire torqued in the pit of her stomach and burned down to where their bodies joined. The delectable ache controlled her once again.

She twisted her hips with a call of his name. "McCrea."

"Are you ready?"

She knew now the control he spoke of and that he was exercising it at a great cost. His whole body vibrated with a restraint she couldn't comprehend. When she answered with a nod, he dropped to an elbow to kiss her forehead and drew his hips back. The friction lifted her head up with a gratifying moan.

He shuddered and pushed into her again. "So tight," he whispered against another thrust. "And so damn sweet."

Hoarse cries of an unfamiliar voice escaped her lips, and she transformed in his arms. He took down the fortress around her heart and freed her. The cold, lonely world she knew before disappeared. With McCrea's love, everything was possible. All things were new, and she was his, and though he hadn't said it, she knew he loved her. How could he not? Everything he was doing said he did. His touch. His words. His kiss. His eyes all spoke of it.

The poignant moment brought her to tears, and she was moved to honesty. "You're the one, McCrea."

"The one?" His voice was rough with the question.

Her lips trembled under the weight of her words as she gazed up at him through misty eyes. "The one I love."

He froze.

She held his face with both hands because she wanted to savor the memory of this moment. He kissed her palms. First one and then the other. She waited for him to say something — anything. But his words never came.

As he made love to her, a twinge of hurt mingled with their unbridled passion. She reminded herself that McCrea wasn't a man who expressed love easily, and his intimate and ardent love making was enough. He would voice his love in his own time.

When he couldn't hold back, he unleashed what restraint he had left. He drew her higher and closer to the sun than she had ever been before. The thrust of his hips was tempestuous, and his body tight like a whipcord.

Her legs clenched tight around his hips. "Please."

A final heave finished him with a groan and washed her in ecstasy. He fell, spent, to her breasts, and with hearts pounding, neither said a word.

Chapter Ten

McCrea shifted his weight to the bed and rested his head on her shoulder. She kissed his forehead and caressed his back with a brush of her fingertips. Never had she felt more attractive, desired, and loved than she did right now. He couldn't deny the love between them or the magic of what they had just shared.

He was so still; she thought he had fallen asleep. "McCrea?"

"Yeah," he answered in a hollow voice.

"I love you."

He rolled onto his back and closed his eyes. "Darlin'," he said with a sigh as he sat up on the edge of the bed to grab his jeans from the floor. "Never let sex make you say things you don't mean."

Wounded by his coldness, she sat up to explain. "Sex didn't make me say it. I wanted to tell you earlier, but…"

He heaved one leg into his jeans and then the other, jumped to his feet, and headed into the living room.

"Where are you going?"

"To the truck. I need a cigarette."

She heard the front door open, the truck door slam, and his footsteps on the porch. He didn't return to the bedroom, and the longer she waited, the more nervous she became. Why was he suddenly distant? Had she done something wrong?

She slipped his shirt on and took the lantern into the living room. He was at the door, staring out across the porch and into the rain with his back to her.

Smoke from his cigarette billowed around him as he exhaled.

She set the lantern on an old table near the fireplace and circled her arms around his waist to lay her cheek against his rain-soaked back. "What's wrong? Was it me? Was it because it was my first time?"

His hand covered hers and lifted it to his lips for a kiss. "No, Eleanor. Your gift to me was priceless."

Her gift? He considered her virginity a gift. A priceless gift. God, she loved this man. Her arms tightened around him. "Then what is it?"

A long draw filled the air with more smoke, and his silence persisted.

"Please talk to me. Let me help you."

A quick flick sent the cigarette out into the rain, and his hands gripped the frame around the door. With his head down, he stared into the dark night as if he were on the edge of a great abyss. "You really want to help me?"

"I do."

"Then marry me."

A blast of hot needles pricked her body. Numbly, her hands fell, and she took a step back. "What?"

Her retreat brought him around to explain. "I told you tonight would be more."

She swallowed back the nausea. "I didn't think you had marriage in mind."

He shoved his hands into his pockets, and the weight shifted his jeans lower to the tan line around his hips, exposing more of the V-shaped muscles she had felt against her thighs minutes ago. "I thought you'd be happier."

Happy about being trapped? "You thought wrong."

"But you just said you loved me."

"All the more reason not to marry you."

He frowned. "I don't understand."

Marriage? The very notion terrified her. "Love and marriage are two different things, and I want no part of the latter."

"Why not?"

She glared at him, hoping he would accept her refusal without an explanation.

He didn't. "I'm waiting." His face was hard and drawn, nothing like a man seeking a loving marriage. If he was this dismal before, how would he be in six months, or a year? In a lifetime?

Like, Rex.

He'll be just like Rex.

Bitter. Heartless. Cruel. Malicious.

And I'll be as miserable as my mother.

When she couldn't summon a truthful answer without diving into her life before coming to Santa Camino, she went to the obvious faults of his proposal. One she knew he couldn't deny. "You're a roamer. You like your freedom and having your choice of women."

He took her hands in his. "I told you the truth this afternoon. I don't sleep around. I'd take my vows seriously, and I'd expect you to do the same."

"Don't lie." She jerked away. "I know your type!"

"My type?" he asked, tautly. "You know what everyone says about me."

"I know what I see, McCrea. Vanessa Worley is one of your whores!"

His face twisted. "Vanessa is a whore, but she's not mine!"

"You've never slept with her?"

He looked away. "That was a long time ago."

"But you did sleep with her!"

"It was high school," he yelled. "Everyone had a turn at Vanessa. It's a mistake I've had to pay for over and over!"

Mistakes. She was guilty of a few herself. The biggest being opening her heart to the man standing in front of her. "This is crazy."

"Why is it crazy?"

"I'm not the marrying kind either."

"Why? Do you have trouble with fidelity?" he snarled. "Can't give up the other guy? The one you're so in love with."

"God!" She threw up her hands. "Are you really that blind?"

"I guess I am," he seethed.

"I wasn't meeting anyone at Tubs."

He blinked.

"I was there because I knew you'd be there."

"But this afternoon you said you wanted to seduce —"

"You, McCrea! You're the one," she repeated.

Another blink. Then another.

"I wanted to seduce you. Don't you see? It's always been you, but you've never noticed me. Until I practically threw myself at you!"

His face softened with a smile that made her heart flutter. "I've always noticed you, darlin'. I've just been waiting for you to grow up."

Tiny moments of his affection over the last couple of years flashed through her mind. The moments when no one was watching. The moments when they connected without a word. Quick kisses on the forehead. Tender hugs. Loving glances. Teasing smiles. All things they had shared that could be interpreted as notice, but nothing which would have brought about a marriage proposal. "You were?"

"Yes. I was." The chalice of his hands on her face and his gentle kiss made his answer nearly convincing, but his words lacked sincerity.

She drank in the taste of his lips, the feel of his tender hands, and the magic of her love for him. She wanted time to stop. She wanted to keep McCrea this close, this real, and this devoted. But something inside her told her there was more to his proposal. She drew back and lifted her eyes to meet his. "I know you, McCrea. You don't want to get married."

His hands fell from her face.

"So just cut through the crap and tell me what's going on."

A shift of his lower jaw signaled annoyance. Her directness had caught him off guard. "I have to find a wife."

"Why?"

"Wade promised me a piece of land when I finished college."

"Land?" Why was he talking about land?

He propped a shoulder against the door. "My inheritance is over three-thousand acres. It includes Promise Point, the old homestead, and most of the original land that started the ranch. It's been in our family for generations, but now," he scrubbed a hand over his eyes. "The fight with Willard has made Wade reconsider mine."

The well-worn wood of the floorboards creaked beneath her feet as she began backtracking across the room. Marriage? Land? Her mind rattled with questions. The whiskey. Solving his problems his way. Piece by piece, the night came together.

"He doesn't think I'm responsible enough to inherit it. He thinks I need a wife."

That was it. His motive behind all the kissing and cuddling. He needed her. His tender lovemaking was nothing more than a scam to lure her into accepting his proposal.

She sat down on the stone hearth because her legs were weak. "That's what the three of you were talking about this afternoon in the study?"

Both hands raked up the back of his head. "Yes, and Dad kept talking about how much he wanted a grandkid. Hell, I don't want kids. Ever."

He doesn't want children. Her fingers rubbed the edge of an overhanging hearth rock. No babies. No kids. Ever.

"Diapers and droolin', that's not me."

The level of disdain in his voice triggered something inside her. An anguish which caused her to rip the loose rock from its mortar. The razor-sharp edge sliced into her finger. She let out a yelp and clutched her hand.

"Careful." Two quick strides brought him kneeling in front of her. "Some of those are sharp."

She winced and bent forward, holding her bloody ring finger. "God, it hurts." Everything hurt. Her finger. Her heart...

"Let me see," he said, leaning over to draw the lantern closer. "I don't think it needs stitches." He rose and went to a cabinet along the wall. After searching through it, he came back with a first-aid kit. He used an antiseptic pad to wipe it clean and dressed it with a band-aid. Tenderness and concern laced his face, drawing her back to his proposal.

Not only was McCrea asking her to marry him, but he wanted her to do so for the sake of his inheritance. Not because he loved her or wanted to spend the rest of his life with her.

He finished with a kiss on the tip of her finger. "I may have to buy you two rings. One for the wedding and one for after the swelling goes down."

She withdrew her hand from his. "Don't bother." Her eyes closed as the awful truth of his intentions tore through her. Grandma Rose was right. McCrea was a heartbreaker. No truer words had ever been spoken. How could she have been so blind? "I'm not marrying you."

"I have plans for the land. A game ranch with trophy bucks and elk..." The scald of his eyes pinned her down. "This is a chance for me to have something of my own."

What about love and commitment? Children? Home? Family? They meant nothing to him. She meant nothing to him. "I'm leaving for college in a few weeks." She whispered her last argument and pushed him away, hoping he would land on his ass.

He staggered backward without falling, and oddly enough, his face brightened. "I'll pay your tuition."

Wasn't he listening earlier? "You're a real sweet talker, McCrea, but I have a scholarship. Remember?"

"Then use the money for Redemption."

She didn't want him to have any part in rebuilding the ranch. "No, I'm not the type of woman who can be bought."

"I'm not trying to buy you, only compensate you for your time." His knuckles grazed the side of her breast. "Look at it like a business agreement with benefits."

"God. Stop." She shrank back, revolted by his touch. "How could you suggest such a thing?"

"What can I offer you?" Desperation replaced enticement. "What do you want?"

Did she dare answer that? Did she tell him her heart's desire? Or did she walk away? "If I marry you, what happens after you get the land?" She hurried back to the bedroom and snatched her panties and jacket from the floor. "What then?"

He followed her. "After a year, I pay you and," he shrugged, "we go our separate ways."

A year? That's all he was offering her? She shivered out of his shirt and found her dress to whisk over her head. "The marriage is over," she snapped her fingers, "just like that? I say, 'I do' and a year later you hand me a check along with divorce papers?"

"Yeah. It doesn't have to be complicated." To him, it was simple. To her, it was a stab in the heart.

"What if I don't want a divorce? What if I want a white picket fence and — and growing old together?" The kind of love Charlie and Rose had. "What if I want children?"

A quake of dark emotion ripped through his eyes. "I'm not the type of man who takes to the bridle or babies."

Her heart made one last bid. "What if what I'm feeling isn't puppy love? What if it's the real thing? What then, McCrea?"

His smirk not only insulted her, it crushed her. "Fairy tales and happily ever after only exist in your books."

"They do exist," her defense was weak. "In people like Wade and Sophia. Charlie and Rose. Your mom and dad."

His face hardened. "The marriage is a twelve-month business agreement."

A year. That's all he was willing to give her. God, this was a nightmare! There was a part of her that wanted to agree to this stupid business agreement just to keep him, but she wasn't desperate enough to be trapped in a loveless marriage. And though his tenderness during the night suggested he cared about her, his cold business agreement shined a light into the dark recesses of the truth.

She sat down on the bed and shoved her bare feet into her wet boots. "I see, and if I don't marry you?"

"I'll find someone else." She never suspected he could ever be this heartless.

"So this," she waved a frantic hand between them. "All your gentle persuasion, and — and lovemaking was for —"

"No," he cut her off.

She felt like melting through the floorboards. "I trusted you. I thought you cared for me."

"I do!" he belted. "I want to take things one day at a time, but if I don't get married, I don't get the land. I have to find a wife. Now!" He gave the air in a frustrated punch. "Damn, it! I asked you first. Doesn't that count for something?"

"I suppose I should feel flattered, since half the women in Santa Camino would trade places with me in a heartbeat." Sarcasm wasn't her style, but it helped to hide her pain.

"They would want more than the cost of tuition," he returned with the same amount of cynicism.

"That's why you asked me, wasn't it?" Pain tore through her heart again. "You thought I would jump at the money. You —" her voice broke. "You thought you could buy me like that damn dress or Romeo."

"No. I don't even want that goddamn horse!" His voice cut through the oak rafters, scattering her nerves so much that she flinched. Her reaction softened his demeanor. "I didn't mean to shout. Let's just calm down and talk."

"There is nothing to talk about. You planned this."

"You're the one who came looking for me, remember?"

She recoiled at the sobering truth. "You're right. I did. I was stupid enough to think you might love me." A mocking laugh emerged from her tight throat. "I guess all the guys down at Tubs had a good laugh watching me bounce out of there on your arm."

He stood firmly planted in his cause without any emotion. "Fuck the guys."

"I made myself a prime target, didn't I?" She wiped away her tears and attempted a smile. There was no way in hell she would let him see her pain. "Lesson learned." When her face threatened to crumble into uncontrollable tears, she started to the door. "Don't worry about giving me a ride home. I'll walk."

He was too fast for her quick getaway. She hadn't gotten one foot out the door before he caught her by the arm and whipped her around. "You don't understand. Wade likes you."

"Wade?" she repeated and understood why he had chosen her. "Wade likes me?"

"He thinks you'd be good for me, and that you'll settle me down. You remind him of Grandma."

Any other time, the comparison to Sophia Coldiron would have been a welcome compliment. She had been the heart of their family. A true lady who would have been appalled by her grandson's proposal and behavior.

A frosty bite of animosity ran over her. "You asked me to marry you to pacify Wade?"

"No."

"It all makes sense now. The three of you were in a deep discussion about Wade's new terms when I walked in today, weren't you?" She had seen the imprint of something serious on their faces, even though they had tried to hide it. Wade's interest in her plans for the future. His offer to help in any way he could... She felt sick.

"Would tonight have happened if Wade hadn't given you those terms? Would you have kissed me?" She hesitated with another wave of nausea. "Made love to me?"

He stepped closer to caress her arms. "Let me take you home, and we'll talk about it after you've had time to —"

The smack across his cheek was hardly enough to cause damage, especially to a man as tough as McCrea, but it did rouse his temper. She could see it in his eyes. He blinked and gritted his teeth. "Calm down."

She drew back for another blow, but his fingers closed around her wrist. "Stop smacking the piss out of me!"

"Tell me tonight wasn't about the land." Please tell me you love me, her heart cried.

He gave her a gentle shake. "Don't you see? This way, we can both have what we want."

With a quick jerk, she freed herself. "I'll never have what I want."

Her heart was broken. Shattered into a million pieces by the one man she thought she could trust. How could she have been so blind? How could she have thrown caution to the wind and fallen in love?

An indescribable sadness entered her as she walked the long distance back to her house. The path was one she had taken years ago, the day McCrea found her. The day she fell in love with the boy next door.

All her hopes and dreams for what they might one day have together died, and she couldn't help the tears that rolled down her cheeks as the flame of her love was extinguished.

The Heartbreak Cowboy

BOOK 1 IN THE COLDIRON COWBOYS
SERIES

Chapter One

As co-founder and chairman of the board for the Promise Point Foundation, McCrea Cold-iron had been eager to volunteer for this year's annual bachelor auction.

But the crowd of women clustered around the large window of Sweet Sue's Bridal Boutique hoping for a glimpse of bachelor number three being fitted for his tux made him uneasy about strutin' his stuff down a runway, even if it was to raise money for a worthy cause.

He wedged his index finger into his collar and tugged. "How long is this going to take?"

Sue raised from her crouching position at the hemline of his right pant leg and removed the straight pin from between her lips. "Forever, if you don't hold still."

He wanted to remind her that it was her fault they had drawn an audience. A month before the auction, Sue's marketing committee had run a two-page ad in the local paper featuring biographies along with fitting dates and times of each of the participating bachelors. She said it was like giving the ladies a sneak peek at what was to come and added fuel to the fire. And it had.

He knew each of the twelve bachelors, and all but one was taking bets on who would draw the biggest crowd. That money, too, would be donated to the foundation. Judging from the number of women in front of the window, he had a good chance of winning that bet.

He should have been pleased with himself, but he wasn't. He was antsy as hell because the woman peering through the window had marriage in mind. In Santa Camino, getting hitched was as much of a tradition as ranching and the rodeo.

Brook Tidwell, the local dry-cleaning heiress and two-time Miss Gilmore County, elbowed her way to the front of the crowd and gave McCrea a sultry once-over that made his skin crawl.

He wasn't ready for love or any of the other things he knew a real marriage brought with it. And once he was up there on that catwalk, he was fair game.

Suddenly, the fitting platform he had been standing on for the past hour felt eerily close to the gallows. And the constricting bowtie of his tux, a noose. "I don't know if I'm ready for a polite dinner conversation." He gave his collar another tug. "Or to be auctioned off like some prize bull."

"Well." Sue snorted. "You can't spend the rest of your life being a surly hermit."

Sue had known him since birth and was his mother's dearest friend, so she knew more than most folks did about the hell Vanessa had put him through.

For twelve long months, McCrea had endured his

wife's compulsory need to spend his money and had turned a deaf ear to the rumors about her infidelity until he had caught her in bed with Tony Chaves. A sleazy pothunter who had slithered into town after a local news station did a story about the excavation of the Vera la Luz Mission located at the top of Promise Point.

The marriage had been hard on McCrea's pride, and he had dealt with it by throwing himself into the horse rescue ranch and foundation.

Three years after his divorce and he was still putting business before pleasure, before his pathetic love life, and before his need for female companionship.

But he was neither rude nor a recluse.

And he wasn't going to admit he was tired of cold showers and eating alone. That would put a big ole' bullseye on his forehead for his mother and Sue to aim at.

He replied to her comment with a low growl.

"Oh, stop," she said with a frown that made her perfectly drawn eyebrows almost touch. "It's about time people saw you in something other than crap kickers and dirty Wranglers."

He liked his old jeans. And he liked being single. Bachelorhood was comfortable and without constraints. With the impatience of a two-year-old, he scratched his unshaven jaw and shifted his weight from one foot to another.

"Stand up straight and hold still," Sue ordered, brushing her hands over his lapel.

"I haven't worn a tux since Colton's wedding."

She smiled up at him, her brown eyes softening at the mention of her son's name. "You two were so handsome that day."

"Colton was so nervous," he said, smiling at the

memory. "I was still nursing a hangover from the night before." He let out a weighted sigh, feeling decades older than his twenty-eight years. "All that seems like a lifetime ago. I can't believe Little Jack will be seven in a couple of months."

Sue's eyes became teary as she glanced across the room to the small office where her grandson was. Jack sat behind the desk playing a game on the iPad Lauren said he was too young to have. "Time has a way of flyin' by. It seems just yesterday Colton was his age."

McCrea remembered those carefree days. The days when he and Colton dreamed of starting their own game ranch. The days of riding and roping and before Post Traumatic Stress Disorder started kicking Colton's ass. "It sure does."

The bell over the door jingled, alerting them to Sue's next appointment.

"Would you look at that?" Ed Tubs usual frown deepened with distaste as he ducked inside. He scowled at the gaggle of women who now had their eyes on him. "What self-respecting woman ogles a man like that?"

Sue's smile was saucy as she gave the bartender a thorough inspection from the soles of his well-worn Justins to the top of his thin, gray hair. "I do, and I can't wait to see you up there on that runway." She fanned her face, trying to cool her suddenly red cheeks, and headed into the back room. "I'll be right back with your tux."

Grinning, McCrea stepped from the fitting pedestal and slapped Ed on the back. "That woman has the hots for you."

Ed's scowl flatlined. "Don't you have horses to mend or shit to shovel?"

"There's always shit to shovel," he said, taking a

seat on one of the plush sofas near the counter. "But I'm partial to your company, and I like the smell of the wax warmers."

Ed picked up a red lace garter from the counter and held it between a finger and thumb as if it harbored a flesh-eating disease. "We aren't going to talk about our feelings, are we?"

McCrea's life was on autopilot, and he tried not to think too much about how he felt. He just sat back and let his system maneuver him through what had to be done. "No," he sighed. "I'm fresh out."

Ed tossed the garter to the counter and dusted his hands. "How about give-a-damns? Do you have any of those left?"

Despite his cranky demeanor, the veteran bartender had the patience of a priest when it came to hearing confessions. But he usually did so while refilling a glass, not on social visits to Sweet Sue's Bridal Boutique.

"Sorry, all out of those too," he answered. "Promise Point might be the only reason I get out of bed in the morning."

Ed let his eyebrows rise and fall quickly. "That's a shame. A man needs more than a job to roll over to in the morning."

The rescue ranch was more than a job to him, and Ed knew that. It was more than a business and about more than making money.

Promise Point had given McCrea a purpose in life and an opportunity for him to serve someone other than himself.

"You don't want to end up like me, McCrea."

Ed was a good guy and a respectable member of the community. He never failed to lend a helping hand to those in need. Tubs Roadhouse was a place the working class went to have a good time on the weekends. It was a place where guys like McCrea could drown their troubles in a couple of shots of whiskey.

Not that he was that guy anymore. He had learned the hard way that whiskey wasn't the answer. "What's so wrong with you, Ed?"

"The Roadhouse is my life. I have no wife, no children." A shadow passed over his face. "I'm alone." The ex-Marine had never married, and the only family he talked about were the men in the framed Camp Pendleton platoon photo he proudly displayed behind the bar.

The loneliness in Ed's eyes gave McCrea's conscience a hard kick in the ass. In all the years he'd known the man, he had never once invited him to a holiday dinner or family get together. But Ed wouldn't take kindly to pity, so McCrea opted for a wide grin. "Hell, Ed. You have me."

"We're both doing our own laundry."

"I like doing my own laundry," he defended, lying about the chore he hated most. "And if you weren't such a stubborn old son of a gun, you'd have Sue to cuddle with."

Ed mumbled a curse under his breath.

"You've been dancing around something since you walked in. What is it?"

"She's selling the ranch."

"Who's selling what ranch?"

"Eleanor is selling Redemption."

As it always did with the mention of her name, a deep sense of culpability and warmth churned inside McCrea. "What?"

"It went on the market this morning," Ed said, looking grim.

"Didn't you see the For-Sale sign on the way into town this morning?" Sue asked, walking back into the room.

"I've been out of town visiting a donor this week," he said, giving his eyes a hard rub. "I haven't been home yet."

He and Eleanor had been neighbors growing up. Her grandparents' ranch bordered his parents'. But they had shared much more than a fence line four years ago.

Sue made a clicking sound with her tongue. "It's a shame. She hasn't been home since Rose died, and now she's selling the ranch."

Nausea hit McCrea's stomach. "Her plan was to rebuild the ranch after she came home from college. Why would she sell it?"

Sue's eyes softened. "I have no idea, dear. Why don't you ask her?"

How was he supposed to do that? A week after they had made love, Eleanor had knocked the dust of Santa Camino from her boots and never looked back.

There wasn't a chance in hell his sister would tell him anything. He was sure that if given half a chance, Louisa would douse him in gasoline and shove a lit match up his ass. But that was to be expected when you slept with your baby sister's best friend. Lou blamed him for Eleanor's detachment from their family. She seldom spoke to him and when she did, it wasn't pretty.

He dropped his gaze to the floor, unwilling to let anyone see the regret he knew was plastered across his face. "I — uh — we kind of lost touch after she went to Austin."

Sue hung Ed's tux on a rack and straightened the sleeves. "I heard she's hiring the Davis twins to do all the packing and that she's meeting Sage Parsons at the ranch at noon."

McCrea removed his jacket, handed it to Sue, and checked his watch. It was eleven-thirty.

The boutique phone rang, and Little Jack picked it up. "Hi, Mom. Yeah, she's here. Grandma! Mom is on the phone!"

"Poor Rose," Sue sighed, walking towards the office. "She probably rolled over in her grave when that For Sale sign went in the ground."

Ed clamped a hand over McCrea's shoulder. "Don't make the same mistake you made four years ago."

McCrea walked to the dressing room and slid the curtain shut. "That was a record year for me, Ed. You're going to have to be more specific," he said, wanting nothing more than to drop the conversation.

"Wade is dead."

He missed his granddad but was relieved the old man wasn't here to remind him of how miserably he had failed him.

He yanked the hem of the dress shirt free from the pants and began unbuttoning it. "So?"

"Don't let her leave town without telling her the truth."

When Eleanor wouldn't answer his phone calls and refused to see him, McCrea had done what he always did when life threw a punch. He had gotten rip-roarin' drunk. But when the whiskey didn't ease the guilt of what he had done, he had cleared his conscience to Ed about his Granddad Wade's plans for Redemption and about why he had to let Eleanor go.

He had expected his confession to be plastered on the front page of the newspaper the next morning, but Ed was as good at keeping secrets as he was at listening.

But confession never solved anything. It sure hadn't eased McCrea's remorse one bit. "It's too late for the truth."

"Not if you love her."

"I don't," he snapped.

"That's not what I heard," Ed chuckled.

He jerked the curtain back. "I was three sheets to the wind that night."

Ed smiled smugly. "Just drunk enough to let that damn pride of yours go. But keep telling yourself you don't. A lie is easier to face than the truth."

Eleanor swerved to the right and braked as the truck in front of her came to an abrupt stop.

Santa Camino hadn't changed much since she had left home. Longhorn and Angus cattle were still grazing unhurriedly in the pastures, and Mr. Crawford's John Deere was still holding up traffic.

When he turned off, she rolled her window down and drank in the picturesque landscape of the backcountry. It was late September in Hill Country and the afternoon sun shone brightly through the thin scattering of clouds drifting across the blue sky.

She fought with the wisps of hair escaping her

ponytail and drew in a deep breath, filling her lungs with the sweet smell of fresh country air.

As she rounded the curve, the white two-story ranch house she had grown up in came into view. She slowed the car, flipped on the signal light, and turned into the long drive.

She stayed left when it split midway of the fenced-in yard and parked in the circle near the walk leading up to the wrap- around porch.

She shut the engine off and sighed.

With a heavy heart, she opened the car door and planted both feet on the ground. Coming back to Redemption was a mixture of sweetness and pain for Eleanor. The last time she had been at the ranch was for Grandma Rose's funeral. It lasted only a couple of hours, followed by a long procession up the hill to the Mackenna family cemetery behind the house. There, next to her beloved Charlie, Rose had been laid to rest.

And after not seeing her mother or half-sister in over a decade, Eleanor felt as though she had buried the last of her family that day. In some ways, it had been too long and in others, not nearly long enough.

Kicking at a patch of dry dirt with the heel of her boot, she crouched down and scooped up a handful. Knowing McCrea wanted nothing to do with her or Sophie in the months after she left Santa Camino made Eleanor blame herself for loving him. And the guilt of knowing she had taken the same path as her mother nearly drove her insane. The path of falling in love with the wrong man. The path of finding herself pregnant and alone.

Her hand tightened into a fist, and the dirt crumbled like her dreams of rebuilding the ranch had. She opened her fingers and let the dirt fall away. When there was nothing left, she raised and dusted her hands.

A gust of wind kicked up a wave of dust and leaves. The rattling of the brittle foliage dancing across the porch beckoned Eleanor back to the task at hand.

She grabbed a stack of moving boxes from the back seat. She made her way up to the porch and to the door. She let the boxes fall to the porch and dug into her purse for her keys. One by one, she fumbled through them...house key, car key, bar key, storage rental key. The last brass-colored key caused her chest to tighten.

Was she really doing this? Was she selling Redemption, her family ranch and childhood home? A place filled with wonderful memories and love?

Yes, she was. She had exhausted all other resources. Selling Redemption was the only way she could afford the partnership she had been offered in the Rebel Road.

The sound of a car engine brought her eyes to the drive. The mid-sized sedan with a Parsons Realty logo on the door parked behind her. She waved to her friend Sage.

With a large leather bag slung over her shoulder and a portfolio in her hand, Sage hurried over to where Eleanor stood. "Oh, El," she said, hugging her tight. "It's so good to see you."

"Hi, Sage."

Sage drew back with a smile. "Look at you. You're even prettier than you were in high school."

"I don't know about prettier, but I am wiser."

"Yeah, me too," Sage returned under her breath. "I'm grateful for the commission from this place, but I'm sorry you're selling it."

Eleanor crammed her hands into her back pockets and sighed. "It was a tough decision, but it's time. Now that Jimmy's gone to live with his sister in Tucson, there's no one to keep an eye on the place."

Jimmy Ross had worked for Granddad Charlie for years and had tried hard to keep Redemption running with meager pay after Charlie died. A sacrifice he made from loyalty to her grandparents. He had even organized the sale of livestock after Rose's death to pay the past due taxes, which allowed her to keep Redemption.

Sage opened her bag and pulled out a small camera. "Can I go inside and take pictures?"

"Oh, sure." Eleanor handed her the keys. "Make yourself at home. I've got more boxes in the car. I'll get them and be right in."

She set her purse on the small table beside the door and hurried down the steps to her car, hoping to wrap things up quickly. She opened the door and reached into the back seat for the boxes, ignoring the vehicle driving by. There had been numerous ranch trucks rolling down the road since she arrived, and it was most likely a work hand coming back from town. Unlike Redemption, the Coldiron Ranch was flourishing.

There were a few things she wanted to take back with her, like Grandma Margaret's bible, Granddad Sutton's pocket watch, and her grandparents' wedding photo that hung over the fire —

"You're home."

The two words knifed into her neck and cut a trail of hatred down her spine. She stilled, hoping the voice was a figment of her long crawl down memory lane on the way into town.

"And you're selling Redemption?"

Nope. That's McCrea. Damn it.

Chapter Two

Eleanor's skin prickled as the air around her became charged with sexual tension. Even after all McCrea had done, or rather not done, her body was still hypersensitive to him. She supposed fire had the same effect on burn victims and though she didn't consider herself a victim, he had burned her.

Bad.

"That's what for sale means," she said as her second thoughts about selling Redemption evaporated like a gin and tonic in the hot Texas sun.

With a knee in the middle of the seat, she re-stacked the empty, overturned boxes and prayed marriage had made him bald and fifty pounds heavier.

She backed out of the car, a little self-conscious about her butt being up in the air for him to gawk at, raised and swung around to face him.

No such luck.

McCrea stood muscular and tall, just the way he had

four years ago. A well-oiled heartbreaking machine with a confident demeanor. He was wide through the shoulders and narrow through the hips, with a penetrating stare that made her legs weak. He was more virile and handsome than ever.

Damn. The man didn't have the decency to show a little wear and tear!

"You're selling the house?" he asked, clarifying with a hard rub to his forehead that pushed his cream-colored Stetson higher.

Bastard. Not even a receding hairline.

His scruffy beard and worse-for-wear appearance offered her a bit of consolation. But not much. His body, hard and callused like his heart, emanated sex appeal and coercion that made her mouth dry. A hint of gray at his temples suggested wisdom and experience.

Of the latter, she had no doubt. The gray, wrinkled t-shirt clung to the well-defined muscles in his chest, and the dark blue jeans hugged his long, powerful thighs.

"And the land," she said as Sophie's face flashed in front of her eyes, causing a red-hot hatred to bubble to the surface. The you-son-of-a-bitch speech she'd practiced a thousand times rolled to the tip of her tongue.

McCREA'S FEELINGS for Eleanor had always been so deep and complex, and he had never been able to make sense of them. Over the years, they had gone from wanting to protect the frightened little girl he had found one rainy day to teasing the teenage girl that had a crush on him to covet and seducing the woman.

She had always triggered intense sensations inside of him. Standing less than three feet away from him now, with a death glare in her eyes, she was setting off urges, twitches, and desires. Sizzling sparks that ignited deep inside his chest and rocketed outward. It was better than any adrenalin rush he had ever had, which explained why he was suddenly dizzy and was having trouble breathing.

Eleanor took a step forward, and when he didn't move, she shoved a box into his chest. "Get out of my way."

Startled, he blinked a couple of times and stepped aside to let her pass.

He knew this day would come, and he knew that he would be on the receiving end of her anger before he was in her good graces again. Judging from the rage in her eyes, he might never be.

"Are you interested in buying it?" she asked, hurrying up the walk. "Oh, wait. It's land. Of course, you're interested."

He ignored the snide comment because the last thing he wanted to do was resurrect the argument they had had the night he proposed. "I'm more interested in why you're selling it."

"Because I can."

"That's not a reason."

"Grandma left the ranch to me, and it's mine to do with as I see fit."

"I don't think she had selling it in mind."

She stopped abruptly and swung around to gaze up at him with wide, wondering eyes. "Wow. Thinking. That's something new for you, isn't it?"

The late summer sun darkened the scant dusting of freckles across her nose and brought out the natural blonde highlights in her hair. He sure had missed those freckles and the untidy ponytail at the base of her head. He wanted to give it a playful tug, the way he had when they were kids.

But he also wanted to keep his hand. "Don't be a smartass."

Hell couldn't hold a candle to the fury in her blue-diamond eyes. She turned and ran up the porch steps to where Sage stood just inside the door.

"I think I have everything I need from in here. But we should go over some paperwork." Sensing the tension, Sage's eyes darted to him and back to Eleanor. "Do you want to do that later?"

"Yes." Eleanor swept past her to toss the boxes inside. "I need to get out of here."

"That's fine. I'll call you to set up a time." Sage handed her the keys and a Post-It note with numbers on it. "Here are the young ladies I told you about. I can vouch for both Tiffany and Kara. They're hard workers and you won't have to worry about your grandma's things being stolen."

"I'm so relieved about having someone reliable to do the packing and," she shot an evil eye his way, "even more relieved that I won't have to spend days here doing it myself."

"Tiffany babysits for me, and Kara helped out in the store when Esmeralda and Matilda went on vacation. Oh here," she said, pulling a small box from her bag. "I almost forgot. It's a sample of their new blend."

The fragrant aroma of herbs and spices floated from the purple tea package and down the steps to him. He wasn't a tea drinker, but the smell was enticing.

His mother and Sue were regulars at The Teaspoon Magic Apiotherapy Shop and swore their unusual blends helped cure everything from heartburn to heartache.

Eleanor drew it to her nose and sniffed. "It smells heavenly. What's in it?"

"I haven't a clue. My aunts never tell me, only that the secret's in the stir." Sage slipped the portfolio into her bag and descended the steps. "Hello, McCrea."

He gave her a curt nod. "Sage."

Sage gave his wrinkled shirt a questioning look. "Laundry day?"

He shifted his shoulders uncomfortably and gave the front a quick tug. "Uh…yeah."

As Sage headed back to her car, Eleanor stepped inside and came back with her purse.

He knew her intentions were to run right past him, hop in Old Blue, and leave him standing high and dry the way she had the night they made love.

But he wouldn't let that happen again.

Tell her you love her. Ed's words began bouncing around in his head like a pool ball meant for the corner pocket.

But he wasn't here because he loved Eleanor. He was here to apologize for seducing her and then breaking her heart with a shitty marriage proposal.

That's why he was here. Being a red-blooded man overcome by lust didn't mean he was in love.

He had been five years older than Eleanor and a hell of a lot more experienced. Four years ago, she had been naïve and thought love was a prerequisite for sex.

But the woman standing on the porch wasn't the shy little waitress with a bashful smile and love-filled eyes that he teased when he came to the Roadhouse for a drink. She was a mature woman who knew by now that what had happened between them was based on lust, not love.

McCrea indulged in a long look at her figure. Her hips were rounder and the low-rise jeans she wore hugged the feminine curve of her hips. Hips, he remembered, as smooth.

After locking the door, she turned and started towards the steps.

His eyes jumped from button to button, up her trim waist to the swell of her breasts. Breasts that had fit perfectly in the palm of his hand.

Damn, she was gorgeous.

Snap out of it. Here she comes.

He rubbed his sweaty palms over his jeans and stepped in her path, risking bodily harm to clear his conscious.

She moved left, then to the right, each time he countered her move and blocked her path.

"Just give me a minute," he said, holding up a hand. "It's the least you can do after leaving town without so much as a 'Goodbye,' 'See you later,' or 'Go to hell.'"

OH, she had told him to go to hell, many, many times. Through tears, she had cursed and screamed until her throat ached. But McCrea hadn't witnessed that pain or any that followed.

"Fine," her smile was plastic. "Goodbye, see you later and," the smile disappeared, "go to hell."

The corner of his mouth edged up, spreading a warm rush of desire through her lower belly. *Ugh. Stop,* she ordered her sex-starved body. *You're not that desperate.*

"You can't sell this place," he argued.

She blew a stray strand of hair from her eyes, venting her frustration. "The house needs repairs, the fields are overgrown, the barns are falling in, and Old Blue needs fixing – again."

He glanced in the direction of her car. "I can't believe you still have this piece of sh —"

"Neither can I. It spews water like a geyser and is running on four bald tires, but I can't afford a new one. I'm scrimping to pay my bills and the taxes on this place."

"But you love Redemption," he argued.

"We can't always hold on to things because we love them," she bit out. "Can we, McCrea?"

His head dipped with guilt. "Eleanor..."

Sophie had the same expression when she didn't put her toys away and knowing her daughter carried the traits of a father that didn't want her pissed her off. Plain and simple. The wishy-washy maybes and what ifs were gone.

"Save it," she said, shoving him out of her way so she could hurry down the walk. She hated that her fingers burned from touching him, hated the way he looked at her, and more than anything, she hated that she'd been foolish enough to think he could ever love her. "Whatever you have to say to me is four years too late. If you're interested in buying the ranch, you can talk to Sage."

"Redemption is your home."

There had been safety at Redemption and before

Rose died, love. But without her grandma, the ranch was a place full of memories and reminders of how alone she and Sophie really were. "Redemption isn't my home anymore. My home, job, and friends are in Austin."

She was almost to Old Blue when he latched hold of her arm and spun her around to face him. "Stop running from me."

She yanked her arm free. "Don't flatter yourself. I'm in a hurry."

"Your dream was to rebuild Redemption," he reminded her.

"Dreams?" She laughed to keep from bursting into tears because her only dream was for McCrea to want his daughter. "Is that why you're here? To talk about my dreams?"

"Yes."

Could it be? Was he here because of Sophie? "I'm listening."

"I—I just wanted to..." He scrubbed a hand over the back of his neck. "Redemption has been in your family for generations. You can't sell it."

She forced herself to take a deep breath as his words saturated her with a familiar hurt. The irony of just how consumed he was with family mocked her. "I have new dreams, McCrea. Ones that don't involve broken-down ranches or – or hard-hearted cow chasers!"

And those dreams didn't include wearing her heart on her sleeve or yearning for the affection of a man who would never love her. She had shoved all of that into a mental file marked Over and Done With.

"Ranches can be fixed and hearts can be softened by the right person," he said.

She had always feared that like her mother, she, too,

was cursed when it came to love and marriage. A fear that had manifested itself early on in her life and was proven four years ago when she gave her heart to the selfish bastard standing in front of her.

But she was stronger and wiser than her mother. She had spent the last four years raising her daughter alone and building a life for them.

She was her own person and a strong and level-headed woman who wouldn't be swayed by love again. "I'm not that person," she answered. "Besides, neither are worth the effort."

"They are if your hearts in it," he said, swallowing hard.

She threw her purse on the hood and began rummaging through it for keys. "Mine isn't, not anymore."

"Eleanor, please, don't do this."

"Do what, McCrea? Sell the ranch that's been in my family for generations? Give up on my dreams?"

"Walk away."

His voice sounded so tender, so concerned, so genuine. But Eleanor knew better. She knew what kind of man McCrea Coldiron really was.

Her throat was so tight with hurt and anger that she could hardly speak. "I walked away a long time ago."

He took a step closer and looped his finger through the chain, dislodging the coin from the crevice of her breasts. "You still wear my gift."

Four years of worry and regret had worn the tarnish from the antique coin, allowing gold to shine through in spots. The reality that it would soon sparkle like a new penny weighed heavy on her heart. It would never be the way it was the night he gave it to her.

Nothing would be.

She had thought that the coin was an invitation for

her to be a part of something he loved doing. Searching for answers about the Wayfires Gold, a ghost story from Santa Camino's past.

But she knew now that the coin had been but a prelude to heartbreak. The setup, seduction, and proposal had been orchestrated to fulfill his Granddad Wade's ultimatum. A yearlong marriage for his inheritance of Promise Point.

If I marry you, what happens after you get the land?

I pay you and we go our separate ways. McCrea's answer had been clear and to the point.

What if I want a white picket fence and growing old together? She had believed in love then. *What if I want kids?*

I'm not the type of man who takes to the bridle or kids. It's a business agreement.

Apparently, he was that type of man. Shortly after Eleanor had left town, he had made Vanessa Worley his wife. But to her knowledge, the marriage hadn't produced children. She doubted either one of them wanted the responsibility. Vanessa was a shallow, self-absorbed woman with two things on her mind. Sex and money.

They made the perfect couple and knowing they had what they deserved — each other — helped to brighten Eleanor's spirits.

But Sophie was growing up without a father, and every time she thought about that, she wanted to boil McCrea in oil. Thick, black, overused motor oil.

The selfish bastard.

And no matter how much she wanted to, she couldn't make McCrea be something he wasn't. She couldn't make him love their daughter. And she couldn't make him be a part of Sophie's life any more than her mother could her own father. She wondered if she and Sophie were caught in some sort of fatherless cycle.

McCrea had made his choice, and it wasn't her or their daughter. Hell, choosing Sophie would have earned him some respect, but he hadn't. He hadn't done a damn thing.

She snatched the chain from his fingers. "I wear it to remind myself that falling in love isn't worth the heartbreak," she said, not misconstruing the look in his eyes as hurt.

"There are ways to deal with what needs fixing," he said, going back to Redemption. "Lease the land, rent the house."

"No," she said firmly and remembered she had put the keys in her pocket. "At some point, you have to face the facts, know when it's time to cut your losses, and walk away while you can."

The words spoke to her heart because finally, after all these years, she was doing just that. She was walking away from shattered dreams and salvaging what remained of her heart.

"And when Redemption is gone, I'll be gone too." She swung the door open, hitting him in the midsection. "This time, for good."

"Just like that?" he questioned, his voice gruff.

She flung her purse into the passenger seat and slid in, slamming the door. "Just like that. Now get out of my way before I run you over."

Chapter Three

E leanor parked behind Hank's black GTO and wiped tears from her eyes once more before climbing out of Old Blue. Resigned to the fact that today had been a total waste of time, money, and emotions, she slammed the door and let out a low scream.

McCrea was still an asshat, and she was still broke, in more ways than one.

"Car trouble?" The deep baritone voice belonged to Nix Rebel, a man who had come to her rescue nine months after she had moved to Austin.

His unshaven jaw, a product of his days off, and rippling biceps decorated in ink made him look more like the leader of a motorcycle gang than a cop for the city of Austin.

Nix was a regular at the Lucky Lizard Tattoo Shop down on South Congress Avenue and had an assortment of Gabe Vega's beautiful artwork across his upper body.

She suspected more of Gabe's work was present on the lower half, but that was past the limits of their friendship.

She suppressed another scream and stomped up the driveway. "No."

Nix continued wiping grease from his hands as she walked by him. "Want to talk about it?"

Even if she wanted to spill her guts to Nix, she was too angry for words. Why did McCrea care if she was selling the ranch? If he wanted Redemption, he could have just called Sage and skipped dealing with her completely. Instead, he had shown up at Redemption and tried to talk her into keeping it. "No."

"Yeah, you do."

She stopped and took a deep breath before saying, "Men are assholes."

One side of his lip lifted with a grin. "Feel better?"

"A little," she admitted, spinning around on her heel.

"Glad I could help," she heard him say.

She opened the door to the Rebel house without knocking. She was met by Hank and Tracey's son, Harley, who, upon seeing her, wrapped both arms around her thigh and asked, "Can I go?"

"Please, Mommy!" Sophie pleaded and hugged the other thigh. A tendril of dark hair escaped the ponytail at the back of her head. Its color may have been Mc-Crea's, but its fine texture was her own.

Harley, who was older than Sophie by three months, tilted up his cookie-covered face. "Pwease, El."

Eleanor bent to wipe away the crumbs. "Go where?"

"To see the horses," Sophie answered for him.

Flecks of gold sparkled in her eyes as she patted her little palms together.

"What horses?" she questioned.

"They overheard us talking about the ranch," Tracey explained, walking into the foyer with a hand on her hip. "And no, you can't go, Harley. We talked about this. Remember?"

His little shoulders slumped, but Eleanor knew she could use his sweet tooth to soothe his disappointment. "How about I take you and Sophie to the park? We'll stop for ice cream."

His smile returned and that was the last of it.

"Thanks for watching Sophie."

Tracey caught Harley before he could escape. "No problem."

"Put me down!" Harley complained and wiggled against Tracey's hold. The kid was almost half the length of his mother's petite frame.

"This one escaped when he heard the word bath." Tracey waved her in and kicked a fire engine out of their way as they walked into the kitchen. "Come on in, if you can get through the mess."

"That boy's going to be bigger than you in a few years," Nix said, entering the kitchen through the laundry room.

"Tell me about it. He's going to be tall like his daddy." Tracey grunted as she lifted Harley onto the counter.

"You bet he is." Hank crunched his face and growled. "He's going to be a raw dawg, just like me." He pumped his biceps and made a fist. "Ain't that right?"

Harley mimicked his daddy's face, pumped his non-existent muscle, and growled as best he could.

"Nice." Tracey rolled her eyes. "Now he's going to be telling everyone he's a raw dawg."

The microwave beeped, and Hank opened the door to retrieve his bag of popcorn. "Ouch!" he blew his fingers. "Damn that's —"

"Darn, Hank. Darn," Tracey amended, and Eleanor smothered a snicker.

"Oh, yeah. Darn, that's hot." His face crinkled into a distasteful frown. "It doesn't sound right, Tracey." He popped a handful of popcorn into his mouth and chewed. "It's like the P word."

Eleanor set Sophie on the counter, wiping cookie from her mouth. "The P word?"

Tracey rolled her eyes again. "Poop. Hank hates the word, poop!"

"I'm right there with you," Nix said, grimacing before he opened the refrigerator to pull out a box with leftover pizza.

"See, Tracey, someone else agrees with me," Hank defended.

Tracey waved a hand in Nix's direction. "He doesn't count. He's just as bad as you are."

"There's something wrong with a grown man saying," Nix's face scrunched, "poop."

A giggle bubbled up in Eleanor's throat and Hank shuddered. "I'd rather hear the word shi — "

"Hank!" Tracey clamped a hand over his mouth. "Not in front of the kids!"

He patiently pried it away and smiled. "Yes, dear. I'll try harder."

"See that you do." Tracey's face softened as she laid a protective hand on her lower belly. "I don't want the baby picking up your bad habits, too."

Hank's big hand covered hers. "Especially, if it's a girl."

"You're pregnant?" Eleanor gasped.

Tracey nodded with a bright smile.

Eleanor wrapped her arms around her. "Oh, Tracey! I'm so happy for you."

"That's great news." Nix took his brother's hand. "Congratulations, bro."

Hank's smile was wide and prideful. "Thanks, man."

"The doctor confirmed it a few weeks ago, but because of the miscarriage we had after Harley, we wanted to wait before telling anyone," Tracey explained.

"So, Daddy," Nix bit into the cold pizza and spoke between chews, "are you planning on getting' your hands dirty today? Or am I doing all the work?"

"Yeah, yeah," Hank said, following Nix into the laundry room. "I'm comin'."

Tracey let Harley escape to the floor, and Eleanor set Sophie down so she could follow him into the playroom. She swatted her bottom. "Help Harley pick up the toys."

Hank and Tracey tempted Eleanor to consider love again. There had to be more Hanks in the world. Men who were destined to be loving husbands and fathers. Men who wore their penchants of love and loyalty proudly, as if it were a mantle. Men who held their family close and protected it.

But marriage required trust and loyalty, perseverance and commitment, and knowing she had been such a poor judge of character by trusting McCrea made guarding her heart a priority. "You two make marriage look so easy."

"There are hard times, but I wouldn't trade it for anything."

She had witnessed some of those hard times. The miscarriage they had after Harley and all the emotions that had followed, raising a family, and building a business together... But their love had brought them through it.

"And the sex is great," Tracey threw in.

She shook her head. "You are awful, Tracey Rebel."

"Blame it on Hank," Tracey told her with a virtuous smile. "I was a good little Presbyterian girl until he came along."

"You?" she questioned. "A good little girl? I doubt it."

Tracey's smile turned wicked. "You know you could have a wild tumble with that brother-in-law of mine if you'd just give in."

Give in to what? she wanted to ask. She and Nix were friends. They went to ball games together, drank beer together, and spent the holidays here at Hank and Tracy's house. And she had never considered him with a lover's eye.

Eleanor glanced out the window to where Nix was standing beside the hotrod.

He was handsome and there was no doubt that the man was built. His rough and tough physique turned heads, and dark-set eyes, along with self-confidence, gave him a presence and commanded attention, especially from women. And though his muscles weren't formed from lifting bales of hay, wrangling cattle, or working on a ranch, they were impressive.

Damn impressive. Flat abs, tight chest... Yeah, sharing the sheets with Nix shouldn't be a problem for her, but it was.

Aside from their relationship not having the heart-stopping chemistry that made her head spin and her heart flutter, there was a tortured side to Nix. A darkness that loomed just behind the whiskey color of his eyes. A darkness Eleanor suspected had something to do with a scar at the back of his head and a woman named Sabrina. And though she was curious about both, she never asked.

No, she and Nix would never be anything but friends. She checked the time on her make-believe wristwatch. "It took you a whole fifteen minutes to work Nix and sex into our conversation. Not your best time."

"You haven't had a date in months, and I'm pretty sure you haven't been laid in —"

"That is none of your business," Eleanor snapped.

Tracey gave her a rueful smirk. "Come on, admit it. It's been a while since you've had sex."

A while? More like forever. Eleanor pulled out a dinette chair and sat down, giving up on an escape. "Sex isn't a necessity."

"I knew it!" Tracey snickered, sitting in the chair beside her. "How long has it been? Weeks? Months?" Eleanor raised an eyebrow and Tracey's eyes widened. "Years?"

Eleanor held up four fingers.

"You haven't had sex in four years?" Tracey's voice exploded.

"Shhh! Lower your voice," she ordered.

"Sorry," Tracey apologized. "You must go through a lot of batteries."

"Really, Tracey?"

From the laundry room door, she heard Nix ask, "What's going on in here?"

Heat rushed to Eleanor's cheeks. God, how long had he been there?

"Girl talk," Tracey was quick to explain.

He took a bottle of beer from the fridge and twisted the cap off. "Girl talk, huh?"

"Yes, girl talk," Eleanor agreed, praying he'd just walked in.

"We're in the middle of something, Nix. Do you mind?" Tracey was in a hurry to get back to the details of her sainted sex life.

His lips inched higher. "I heard sex and batteries. What kind of girl talk are you two having?"

Eleanor cringed, but Tracey, who was a hell of a lot braver than she would ever be, didn't miss a beat. "Product review."

"Tracey!" Eleanor gasped.

Nix's eyes changed from amused to predacious as they drilled into Eleanor. "Any chance you could give me a demo?"

"Oh my god," Eleanor groaned and covered her face with both hands.

"Get out of here!" Tracey ordered.

Laughing, Nix did as he was told, and Eleanor jumped to her feet. "Hank is a bad influence on you," she whispered harshly.

"Just have sex with him," Tracey shot back in the same whisper.

"Sophie!" she yelled. "Let's go!'"

"You two are perfect for one another," Tracey urged.

"Goodbye, Tracey," she said, taking Sophie's hand before walking out the front door.

MCCREA UNBUTTONED HIS SHIRT, tossed it onto the railing, and grabbed a wheelbarrow from the work shed.

There wasn't an art to shoveling shit. That's what he liked about it. He could walk into the stables, grab a shovel, and clear a stall without caring about the process.

Hard work was good for the body, mind, and soul because being ankle deep in horse manure brought a man's life into perspective. According to his dad, shoveling shit kept him humble and honest.

But McCrea had learned early on that his dad's philosophy was wrong. His granddad had shoveled plenty in his younger days, and it hadn't done a damn thing to help his integrity.

Wade had been a man of prestige and high morals who left behind a legacy of generosity and kindness with the townspeople. But he ran his family and business with an iron fist of high expectations, unwavering obedience, and little forgiveness when things didn't go his way.

McCrea let out a long sigh, feeling the weight of those days settle into his soul. There had been only one way to please Wade, only one thing the man valued more than money. And when McCrea had failed to get it for him, he had paid the price.

But he didn't regret making that choice. Redemption belonged to Eleanor and seeing her yesterday was like catching a glimpse of sunlight through barred windows. She was a beautiful promise just beyond his reach. It had awakened old desires and stirred his discontent about where his life was headed.

McCrea was a Coldiron. In Texas, it was a name synonymous with cattle ranching and prosperity, admiration, and dignity. His parents and grandparents had been respected members of the community. His dad was a successful businessman and cattle broker who had taught McCrea how to invest his money wisely. His mother had a law degree and served on the town council. His dad and granddad had married women who loved them. With their wives by their sides, they had built homes, had children, raised families, and made a living by working the ranch.

Louisa had graduated summa cum laude and was applying for veterinary school. Eventually, she would find the right man, settle down, and have those grandkids his folks wanted.

Grandkids neither he nor his brother Jess stood a snowball's chance in hell of having.

Jess had never been much for steady relationships. Riding the rodeo circuit and recovering from a fall that ruined his career had left his love life in worse shape than his own.

McCrea had done more than fall. He had gone down face first and skidded to a dead stop. He had broken the heart of the sweetest, most adoring woman he had ever known and married a woman he hated for the sake of a piece of land he valued more than love.

Hell, he deserved a medal or a plaque of some sort for the fiasco he called a personal life. Right in the middle of town square next to the newly erected City Hall, or better yet, a billboard flashing updates on his bad decisions.

He tossed the shovel into the wheelbarrow and

wiped his sweaty brow before pushing it out the door. He dumped the manure on the compost pile out back and returned the wheelbarrow to the work shed. He peeled off his leather gloves and headed up the hill to the cabin.

Built in the early 1800s by his Granddad Jedidiah, the cabin was a piece of his family's history. He had wanted to preserve it after he purchased Promise Point, so he had called on the craftsmanship of a contractor with a reputable reputation for restoring historic homes. The cabin was now a fully restored, two-bedroom modern home with a fantastic view overlooking the lake and plenty of solitude.

It was also the place he and Eleanor had made love. He told himself more than once that the comfort he felt there had nothing to do with her, and at times, he almost believed it.

Whatever the reason, the cabin was his home and had been since he and Vanessa were married.

He showered and was zipping up a pair of clean jeans when he heard a knock on the front door.

He hadn't expected to see Sage Parsons standing on the opposite side.

Smiling politely, she raised her brows. "Did I catch you at a bad time?"

"No, I-uh." He snatched the wrinkled t-shirt he had worn yesterday from the back of the couch and whisked it over his head. He shoved his arms in and nodded towards the McDermott Construction truck parked down the hill next to the ranch office. "I thought you were Carter."

Sage was always polite and friendly, but she didn't make a habit of paying him a visit. So, McCrea was more than a little curious to know why she was here.

"Everything looks terrific," she said, glancing over her shoulder to the new porch railing before she stepped inside. "I hear the man is a miracle worker."

"Carter does great work," he agreed. "I'm pleased with how everything turned out." He closed the door and walked the short distance to the kitchen. "Can I offer you some coffee? I just made a fresh pot."

"No, thanks. I stopped by Pixies on the way over," she said, holding up a cup with the local coffee shop's logo. "I followed a white caravan of KCR vans up the road. How's the dig going?"

As co-chair of Santa Camino's historical committee, his mother had employed KCR to evaluate the mission's historical significance.

"Slower than Sunday service," he complained. "My mother should have never suggested bringing in a cultural research group to the historical society."

Sage chuckled softly. "I'm sure your mother means well, and the town will profit from it."

Ten years ago, the small town born of cattle ranchers, outlaws, and pioneers hoping for a new life out west had threatened to pass peacefully into Texas history. But thanks to his mother and others like her, Santa Camino was growing by investing money in the heritage tourism movement. Businesses were moving in, and the local economy was bouncing back.

"Maybe so, but those archies," his nickname for archaeologists, "are still in the way."

"Word around town is the historical society has hired Tony Chaves as their new dig liaison," she said, lifting a skeptical eyebrow as she sipped her coffee. "Mildred told me they want to make sure everything coming out of the ground is accounted for."

"And they think he'll do that?" he asked, suspecting

Tony had talked his way into the position to smuggle artifacts from the dig site.

"Apparently so," Sage said.

"Have a seat," he said, picking up empty water bottles and cups from the leather chair.

"I'm fine," she said.

"Sorry the place is such a mess," he said, kicking a pair of dirty jeans into the bedroom and shutting the door. He had grown accustomed to living, sleeping, and dining alone. He had learned that guzzling milk from the jug, throwing his clothes on the floor, and eating out of fast-food containers were the joys of bachelorhood. "Have a seat."

"I'm fine, really," she said, holding up a hand. "I have to get to the office. I just dropped by to tell you that I have an interested buyer for Redemption."

He gave his jaw a stroke and tried to hide his disappointment. He was holding onto the chance that the ranch wouldn't sell so soon. "That's good news."

"Is it?" Sage questioned, incredulously.

"Sure," he said, rubbing the back of his neck. "But I'm not sure why you thought I needed to know."

"I thought you'd be interested in buying the ranch because the western side borders Promise Point."

That was true, and buying the ranch was a smart business move. He could double the exercise trails and add barns and paddocks. There were a hundred things he could do with Redemption. But the bottom line was that without Eleanor, he wasn't interested in the land.

"I talked to the guy yesterday," she continued. "He wants the ranch to be a surprise for the woman he's head-over-heels in love with."

He couldn't imagine loving any woman enough to buy her a ranch, but to each his own. "Is this guy an out-of-towner?" he asked, knowing new people were moving into Santa Camino because of Sage's salesmanship.

"No, he's a local." He didn't know Sage well enough to read the smile on her face, but he was sure it could be considered crafty. "They both are, though she's been living in Austin for the last four years. She'll make a beautiful bride if the guy ever gets his head out of his ass long enough to tell her how he feels."

Heat crept up McCrea's neck and spread to his cheeks. "I'm not looking for a ranch or a bride."

Sage pulled a business card from her purse and held it out to him. "I hope the extraction won't take you long."

Hesitantly, he accepted the card. "If the real-estate market goes under, you have a promising career as a matchmaker."

Her lips blossomed into a grin. "I'll be expecting your call soon."

He held the door open for her.

She pointed to his wrinkled shirt before stepping out onto the porch. "Seriously though, you might want to try the dry cleaners on Main. Tell Brook I sent you."

He shut the door and looked at the business card in his hand. Okay, maybe his head was up his ass in a metaphorical way, but he wasn't in love with Eleanor.

His cell phone vibrated against the coffee table. He snatched it up and answered it with a, "Yeah."

"Did you get my message?" Jess asked.

"No." He grabbed his boots from beside the door and sat down on the edge of the sofa. "I haven't checked my messages."

"We're meeting Jasper and Bill Baxter for beers."

The Baxter brothers were businessmen from

Chicago in their late fifties, and two of the foundation's biggest donors. They usually arrived a day or two before the charity event and treated McCrea and Jess to a beer and dinner. "But the auction is two weeks away."

"Be that as it may, they are expecting us," Jess said. "We're meeting them at the Rebel Road Bar in Austin at six. I'll text you the address."

"I'll be there," he said, catching sight of the dingy duffel bag sitting beside the door. But first, he had laundry to do.

He shoved the phone into his pocket and picked up the bag once bearing the colors of his college alma mater.

He didn't want Brook Tidwell anywhere near his underwear.

Chapter Four

McCrea unbuttoned his shirt, tossed it onto the railing, and grabbed a wheelbarrow from the work shed.

There wasn't an art to shoveling shit. That's what he liked about it. He could walk into the stables, grab a shovel, and clear a stall without caring about the process.

Hard work was good for the body, mind, and soul because being ankle deep in horse manure brought a man's life into perspective. According to his dad, shoveling shit kept him humble and honest.

But McCrea had learned early on that his dad's philosophy was wrong. His granddad had shoveled plenty in his younger days, and it hadn't done a damn thing to help his integrity.

Wade had been a man of prestige and high morals who left behind a legacy of generosity and kindness with the townspeople. But he ran his family and business with an iron fist of high expectations, unwavering obedience, and little forgiveness when things didn't go his way.

McCrea let out a long sigh, feeling the weight of those days settle into his soul. There had been only one way to please Wade, only one thing the man valued more than money. And when McCrea had failed to get it for him, he had paid the price.

But he didn't regret making that choice. Redemption belonged to Eleanor, and seeing her yesterday was like catching a glimpse of sunlight through barred windows. She was a beautiful promise just beyond his reach. It had awakened old desires and stirred his discontent about where his life was headed.

McCrea was a Coldiron. In Texas, it was a name synonymous with cattle ranching and prosperity, admiration, and dignity. His parents and grandparents had been respected members of the community. His dad was a successful businessman and cattle broker who had taught McCrea how to invest his money wisely. His mother had a law degree and served on the town council. His dad and granddad had married women who loved them. With their wives by their sides, they had built homes, had children, raised families, and made a living by working the ranch.

Louisa had graduated summa cum laude and was applying for veterinary school. Eventually, she would find the right man, settle down, and have those grandkids his folks wanted.

Grandkids neither he nor his brother Jess stood a snowball's chance in hell of having.

Jess had never been much for steady relationships. Riding the rodeo circuit and recovering from a fall that ruined his career had left his love life in worse shape than his own.

McCrea had done more than fall. He had gone down face first and skidded to a dead stop. He had broken the heart of the sweetest, most adoring woman he had ever known and married a woman he hated for the sake of a piece of land he valued more than love.

Hell, he deserved a medal or a plaque of some sort for the fiasco he called a personal life. Right in the middle of town square next to the newly erected City Hall, or better yet, a billboard flashing updates on his bad decisions.

He tossed the shovel into the wheelbarrow and wiped his sweaty brow before pushing it out the door. He dumped the manure on the compost pile out back and returned the wheelbarrow to the work shed. He peeled off his leather gloves and headed up the hill to the cabin.

Built in the early 1800s by his Granddad Jedidiah, the cabin was a piece of his family's history. He had wanted to preserve it after he purchased Promise Point, so he had called on the craftsmanship of a contractor with a reputable reputation for restoring historic homes. The cabin was now a fully restored, two-bedroom modern home with a fantastic view overlooking the lake and plenty of solitude.

It was also the place he and Eleanor had made love. He told himself more than once that the comfort he felt there had nothing to do with her, and at times, he almost believed it.

Whatever the reason, the cabin was his home and had been since he and Vanessa were married.

He showered and was zipping up a pair of clean jeans when he heard a knock on the front door.

He hadn't expected to see Sage Parsons standing on the opposite side.

Smiling politely, she raised her brows. "Did I catch you at a bad time?"

"No, I-uh." He snatched the wrinkled t-shirt he had worn yesterday from the back of the couch and whisked it over his head. He shoved his arms in and nodded towards the McDermott Construction truck parked down the hill next to the ranch office. "I thought you were Carter."

Sage was always polite and friendly, but she didn't make a habit of paying him a visit. So McCrea was more than curious to know why she was here.

"Everything looks terrific," she said, glancing over her shoulder at the new porch railing before she stepped inside. "I hear the man is a miracle worker."

"Carter does great work," he agreed. "I'm pleased with how everything turned out." He closed the door and walked the short distance to the kitchen. "Can I offer you some coffee? I just made a fresh pot."

"No, thanks. I stopped by Pixies on the way over," she said, holding up a cup with the local coffee shop's logo. "I followed a white caravan of KCR vans up the road. How's the dig going?"

As co-chair of Santa Camino's historical committee, his mother had employed KCR to evaluate the mission's historical significance.

"Slower than Sunday service," he complained. "My mother should have never suggested bringing in a cultural research group to the historical society."

Sage chuckled softly. "I'm sure your mother means well, and the town will profit from it."

Ten years ago, the small town born of cattle ranchers, outlaws, and pioneers hoping for a new life out west had threatened to pass peacefully into Texas history. But thanks to his mother and others like her, Santa Camino was growing by investing money in the heritage tourism movement. Businesses were moving in and the local economy was bouncing back.

"Maybe so, but those archies," his nickname for archaeologists, "are still in the way."

"Word around town is the historical society has hired Tony Chaves as their new dig liaison," she said, lifting a skeptical eyebrow as she sipped her coffee. "Mildred told me they want to make sure everything coming out of the ground is accounted for."

"And they think he'll do that?" he asked, suspecting Tony had talked his way into the position to smuggle artifacts from the dig site.

"Apparently so," Sage said.

"Have a seat," he said, picking up empty water bottles and cups from the leather chair.

"I'm fine," she said.

"Sorry, the place is such a mess," he said, kicking a pair of dirty jeans into the bedroom and shutting the door. He had grown accustomed to living, sleeping, and dining alone. He had learned that guzzling milk from the jug, throwing his clothes on the floor, and eating out of fast food containers were the joys of bachelorhood. "Have a seat."

"I'm fine, really," she said, holding up a hand. "I have to get to the office. I just dropped by to tell you that I have an interested buyer for Redemption."

He gave his jaw a stroke and tried to hide his disappointment. He was holding onto the chance that the ranch wouldn't sell so soon. "That's good news."

"Is it?" Sage questioned, incredulously.

"Sure," he said, rubbing the back of his neck. "But I'm not sure why you thought I needed to know."

"I thought you'd be interested in buying the ranch because the western side borders Promise Point."

That was true, and buying the ranch was a smart business move. He could double the exercise trails and add barns and paddocks. There were a hundred things he could do with Redemption. But the bottom line was that without Eleanor, he wasn't interested in the land.

"I talked to the guy yesterday," she continued. "He wants the ranch to be a surprise for the woman he's head-over-heels in love with."

He couldn't imagine loving any woman enough to buy her a ranch, but to each his own. "Is this guy an out-of-towner?" he asked, knowing new people were moving into Santa Camino because of Sage's salesmanship.

"No, he's a local." He didn't know Sage well enough to read the smile on her face, but he was sure it could be considered crafty. "They both are, though she's been living in Austin for the last four years. She'll make a beautiful bride if the guy ever gets his head out of his ass long enough to tell her how he feels."

Heat crept up McCrea's neck and spread to his cheeks. "I'm not looking for a ranch or a bride."

Sage pulled a business card from her purse and held it out to him. "I hope the extraction won't take you long."

Hesitantly, he accepted the card. "If the real-estate market goes under, you have a promising career as a matchmaker."

Her lips blossomed into a grin. "I'll be expecting your call soon."

He held the door open for her.

When the door opened, McCrea glanced up from his lukewarm bottle of beer and did a double take as a blonde in thigh high stiletto boots glided through the door of the Rebel Road Bar. Her hips moved in a sleek, cat-like rhythm to Eric Church's "Broke Record" that pounded through the jukebox speakers.

Lips and hips.

Moves and grooves.

Lust and thrusts.

An appropriate song for her walk. The sway of her hips and the bounce of her breasts swelled his dick to an uncomfortable size while the mystery of her eyes, shaded by a pair of stylish sunglasses, drew him to the edge of his seat.

To McCrea, the man with her could only be described as a biker dude. Because of his black leather jacket, worn blue jeans, and black leather boots, he fit in well with the other patrons of the bar. Most were in similar outfits, minus the black leather jacket and huge biceps. This guy wasn't an average bald, thick-bearded biker. Nope. Bubba was all muscle with neatly trimmed hair and beard.

Bubba placed his hand on the blonde's back as he led her to the bar and waited for her to take a seat. She removed the purse from her shoulder, laid her sunglasses on the bar, and peeled off her leather jacket and draped it over the bar.

"Hell, yes. Take it off, baby," McCrea said under his breath when he saw the woman's bare midriff. The black leather number she had strapped across her ample breasts made him want to lick his lips.

The troop of beer chugging frat boys in the adjoining billiard room stopped in mid-strike and let out loud whistles and lewd comments about how she could chalk the end of their sticks.

She ignored them, but Bubba didn't. His big form unfolded into a stance, quieting the gawkers with just a look. Heads ducked, and the men returned to their game.

She hoisted her perfectly round ass onto a stool and brushed back a wave of hair with a slender hand.

Bubba shrugged out of his jacket, threw it over the bar, and took the stool next to her. The cute brunette bartender set a beer in front of him, and he gulped down half. The blonde tilted her head to the side and rested her chin on her palm.

The dim light of the bar and his view from the back made it hard for McCrea to see the details of her face. But that didn't matter. He was already filling in the void with a different blonde. One filled with passion and dreams. One who came to him willingly.

McCrea leaned back in his seat and closed his eyes, unable to keep his mind off Eleanor. He could feel her body wrap around him as he took her, hear her soft whimper, and feel her nails rake down his back. "Shit," he groaned.

He sat up and attempted to rearrange himself discreetly. Seeing her again had awakened old desires. Desires he hadn't indulged in for a long time.

But she was selling the one thing that connected her to Santa Camino. "When Redemption is gone, I'll be gone too. This time for good," McCrea repeated her words and felt them seed deep in his soul.

The blonde slid off the stool and disappeared around the corner to the restrooms. McCrea tried to get his mind off her and back on business. He had been hesitant about entertaining two of his best clients in a bar located on Austin's Dirty Sixth. But after navigating through the website, he found the Rebel Road had a long list of positive reviews, which helped ease his mind.

The bar had a tasteful interior. The rich walnut panels covering the walls and floors helped to keep the atmosphere dark and intimate. Mirrors in the back and across the bar gave it space and helped with lighting. The showpiece was a black vintage Panhead Harley which sat overtop the bar with the bold red Rebel Road sign above it.

A couple walked through the door and behind them was Jess. McCrea held up his hand to get his brother's attention, and Jess raised his chin with a nod, to signal he had seen him.

With a familiar limp, Jess made his way through the crowd and over to the table to where McCrea was sitting. "Have you heard from the Baxters?"

McCrea's question was in hopes they had canceled. He didn't want to spend the night entertaining a couple of divorced, balding, out of shape, Baby Boomers who were probably the mirror image of him and Jess in thirty years.

Jess pulled out a chair and sat down. "No, not yet."

He picked up a menu holstered between the steak sauce and ketchup, noticing a mouthwatering assortment of appetizers and entrees. "It's after six."

"They'll be here," Jess said.

When the blonde walked back to her stool at the bar, McCrea tossed the menu down. He knew exactly what he wanted, and it wasn't on the menu.

Good God Almighty, he swore silently when she hooked a boot heel in the ring around her stool and pushed up, extending her reach down the bar to a bowl of peanuts. The black leather pants hugged her ass like a glove.

"It's a hell of a place, ain't it?" Jess asked, unaware of the blonde behind him. "A long way from Tub's, that's for sure,"

"I like Tub's and bikes are more your thing. I'd rather ride a horse."

"Are you sure you don't want to reconsider?" Jess asked, doing a double-take when a pretty redhead walked by. "Steel horses are a real turn on for women."

"Oh okay, sign me up," McCrea said, dryly.

"Humor." Jess's face contorted with suspicion. "Are you really my brother or a clone, sent down by aliens to take his place?"

"Aliens?" he chuckled. "You've been talking to Lilly Winters again."

"I'm always open to new theories about the Way-fires lights," Jess said, grinning.

McCrea had his own theory about the mysterious lights associated with the legend, and none involved aliens.

During the time of slavery, Vera la Luz had served as a station for runaway slaves and the lights, which were rumored to burn red and blue, could be explained as nothing more than signals indicating when the way was safe.

He seriously doubted Lilly had any logical insight since her enlightenment came by way of herbal teas and meditation. "Was her theory part of this morning's pillow talk?"

"Hardly." There was a scoff to Jess's rebuke. "Lilly's a looker, but she's lost her vertical hold on reality. I saw her and her sister at Pixies this morning."

McCrea didn't bother mentioning that he had also seen Sage this morning.

"It was either jump into a polite conversation or skip the latte, and you know me. Nothing gets in the way of my Salted Carmel Mocha Latte."

The image of his brother strolling through the doors of the local coffee hangout in search of his second favorite addiction caused McCrea to shake his head. "You're a cowboy. Have some dignity. Drink it black."

"Dignity be damned." Jess snorted. "I'd parade my bare ass through town in a pink tutu if it would get me a Salted Carmel Mocha Latte."

"Since most of the town has seen your bare ass, I don't see how that would be a sacrifice," McCrea said.

Grinning, Jess slid around in his seat to survey the women at the bar. "Wait, a minute. Is that who I think it is?"

He pretended to be interested in the menu again. "One of your old conquests?" he asked, fighting a sharp stab of jealousy.

Jess slapped the table with his palm. "Hot damn! It is her."

He took a mental step back. Jess knew the blonde. Okay, so what? It wasn't like he had a claim on her.

"I think I'll go say hi. Do you want another beer?" Jess asked, walking towards the bar.

"No." He didn't want another beer, and he didn't want to watch his brother flirt his way into the blonde's tight leather pants. But the alternative was to leave without having dinner with two of the foundation's best donors.

So McCrea sucked up his pride, downed what was left of his warm beer, and watched as his brother slipped up behind her.

Jess bent over and whispered something in her ear. She spun around, threw both arms around his neck and shrieked, "Jess!"

Her voice poured over McCrea like a shot of well-aged bourbon. It was rich, smooth, and familiar in a way that made his body burn. The blonde in skintight leather was Eleanor.

McCrea tossed the menu down and started for the bar.

Laughing, Jess spun her around. "How about it? You, me, and a night on the town?"

Eleanor snatched Jess's Stetson from his head and tousled his hair, much like she would a small child. "Oh, you're a big flirt. Put me down."

"Nope," he answered her with a mischievous wink. "I think I'll take you home with me."

She let his hat drop to his head. "You haven't changed a bit. You're still a rascal."

Jess let her slide to her feet with an impish grin. "Did you want me to change?"

"Absolutely not." She laughed.

Jess's grin turned coy when he saw McCrea. "Recognize her now?"

Growing up, Eleanor's smooth and creamy complexion had rarely seen a hint of makeup. And apart from her prom, McCrea had never seen her hair shaped into anything other than a ponytail. A stark contrast to the woman in front of him.

Her long hair was fashioned in an I-just-climbed-off-a-Harley style that suggested wildness. The dark brown eyeshadow and black eyeliner added sophistication to her flawless beauty.

Though he was enthralled with the temptation, the overall look provided, he wasn't comfortable thinking his sweet and innocent Eleanor had become an untamed woman sporting stilettos and black leather.

THE COLDIRON BROTHERS had a distinctive build. They were athletic, lean, and tan. Their Stetsons always rode low on their brow, swaying first impressions towards modern-day outlaws.

They were rugged, handsome and could be debonair when they needed to be. But Eleanor was past the phase of being beguiled by the angle of a hat, especially when the cowboy was McCrea.

McCrea had money, yet he rarely looked like anything other than a hardworking rancher. But damn, the man did clean up nicely. He looked completely at ease in his camel-colored corduroy sports coat, jeans, and boots.

She crossed her arms over her chest — wishing she was dressed in jeans and boots instead of the ridiculous leather costume — and faced McCrea. "Are you stalking me?"

The chocolate centers of his eyes darkened with mischief, and the shallow grooves anchored at the corners of his mouth deepened with a hint of a smile. "Maybe."

"We're meeting donors," Jess rushed to explain.

"Donors for what?" she questioned.

Jess reached into his jacket pocket. "The Promise Point Foundation," he explained, handing her a folded piece of paper.

She unfolded it and read the elegant red-lettering:

The Promise Point Foundation
presents the 3rd
Annual Bachelor Auction
Friday, September 25th at 7:00 p.m.
At the Tall Oaks Winery

Promise Point was McCrea's coveted inheritance, and the reason he had proposed to her. It was the three thousand acres he needed for his beloved game ranch. So what was the Promise Point Foundation? And what cause, other than himself, was so important to McCrea?

"I'm one of the bachelors," McCrea announced.

Well, la dee da. McCrea was a bachelor again. "Congratulations. I'm thrilled for you."

"You should come," McCrea suggested.

"Yeah, you should." Jess grinned. "There'll be plenty of eligible bachelors to choose from."

"It looks like quite the shindig," she said, handing Jess the flyer. "But I'm sure I have something to do that night."

McCrea summed her up like the last steak in a butcher's window. "So what brings you to a bar in this getup?"

"I'm working."

His lips twisted slowly into a sexy grin. "Just what line of work are you in?"

"Watch it, Cowboy," Hank warned. "I don't like what you're implying."

"I don't give a damn what you don't like, Bubba," McCrea said, evenly.

Hank stiffened and rolled his jaw from side to side.

"El, introduce us to your friends," Tracey said, trying to alleviate the tension.

"We're more than friends," Jess informed her. "We're family. Right, El?"

His dark blonde hair and country boy grin made him the embodiment of cowboy eye candy to a large percentage of the female population. He was an affectionate guy who was the first to laugh and the last to lose his temper. Eleanor envied the woman who lassoed his heart.

She grasped his chin with an affectionate shake. "This handsome fellow is Jess Coldiron. He was like my big bro when we were kids." She finished the introduction with a loud kiss on his cheek and pointed to Hank. "This is Hank, the owner."

Jess offered his hand to Hank and he accepted. "You've got a hell of a place here."

The compliment eased Hank's defenses a fraction. "Thanks. We're proud of it."

She pointed to Tracey. "And this is his wife, Tracey."

Jess gave her a polite doff of his hat. "Ma'am. Good to meet you both."

Eleanor fell silent when it was McCrea's turn to be introduced and gave Jess her full attention. With her thumb, she smeared her red lipstick from his cheek. "How are your mom and dad?"

"They're fine," he answered. "I guess Rose's funeral was the last time I saw you."

"Yeah, I guess it was." The morning of the funeral, she left Sophie in Tracey's care and headed for Santa Camino with a knot the size of Texas in her stomach.

Thankfully, McCrea hadn't attended, and she'd been able to brush Jess and Louisa's invitation to dinner off with working the next day. They knew she was lying but said nothing and let her go with hugs and a promise of a future get-together that never came.

"I'm sorry I didn't make it to Wade's funeral," she said, feeling guilty she hadn't attended the memorial of a man who had felt like her granddad.

"We understood."

The ever-churning electric charge coming from Mc-Crea made Eleanor nervous and edgy, and she knew he wasn't a man who would be ignored. When he shot her a cocky side grin, she knew she'd made a mistake by not giving him a proper introduction.

But honestly, what could she say? This is my best friend's older brother? The guy I was stupid enough to sleep with? The guy I thought loved me? Or how about, this is Sophie's dad, the deadbeat?

"Do you always wear leather to work?" he asked, taking a step back to inspect her outfit. "Or is it a clientele fetish?"

"Cowboy," Hank cautioned through thin lips. "You're walking a fine line."

Fine line or not, McCrea wasn't done. His smile widened as he reached into his back pocket for his wallet. He opened it, pulled out a crisp one-hundred-dollar bill, and held it out to Eleanor. "What will this buy me?"

Playful banter and lighthearted jabs had once been a part of their rapport. But the days of flirting quarrels and humorous comebacks were over. She was past witty retaliation and sassy remarks. And she wouldn't stand by while he threw teasing innuendos at her, joking or not.

So, with a feline sway to her walk, she stepped closer and met his playful insinuation with a sexy face she only used for the camera.

A bite to her lower lip and a lusty glance at his zipper parted his lips with expectation.

Hook.

"Oh, McCrea," she said, snatching the money from his fingers.

Line.

She ran a finger over his bottom lip, gave him a sensual smile, and crammed the bill into the front pocket of his jeans.

Smile.

Her touch made him draw in a breath that amplified the challenge in his eyes.

And sinker.

She tilted her chin up for a kiss but didn't deliver because she was only willing to take this game so far. "You of all people should know that I can't be bought."

He pushed the brim of his Stetson up with one finger and, in true McCrea fashion, stuck his thumbs through his belt loops before leaning closer to whisper in her ear. "Money didn't get you into my bed the first time, darlin'."

Mortification enveloped her, causing her cheeks to burn. No, not money, not land, but love, and for that, she was the biggest fool of all.

Chapter Five

"**P**rick."

"Tease," McCrea drawled out with an extra helpin' of Texas.

Eleanor stepped back to the bar. "Whiskey Sour. Now," she ordered Tracey, who delivered the drink quickly and with wide eyes.

"So, El," Jess cut in. "What's with the sexy getup? Did you become a model?"

"Hardly," she choked out as the whiskey left a trail of fire down her throat. "I'm all about the business. Dressing up like Biker Barbie isn't my style. You know that. It's helping promote the bar."

"Thanks to El, we have more customers than we can handle," Hank said, eying her reaction to the alcohol she never consumed. "She's got a real nose for business."

Jess wiggled his brows. "Brains and beauty. All in one sexy leather-covered package."

"That's me," she agreed, giving in to his playful antics, if for nothing more than a distraction.

But the diversion ended when he excused himself to answer a call. "Sorry, I have to get this."

With a brash smile and a languid saunter, McCrea approached the bar and made himself at home in a vacant seat.

Typical. The smug son of a —.

"That was one hell of a show, darlin'. You had me bursting at the seams."

His voice was too close and the pain from their past was too real. Another sip of her drink and she prayed the whiskey would take hold. But her nerves were shot in a way alcohol couldn't allay.

She propped an arm on the bar and stared him dead in the eye. "You aren't allowed to call me darlin'. We aren't friends, lovers, or anything that would give you that right. I'm not the stupid, love-struck girl I was then, and your cocky cowboy act isn't working."

"Cocky cowboy act?" He questioned with a fake scoff. "I thought I was being irresistibly charming."

She downed the last of her Sour. "You're neither irresistible nor charming, so don't think you can come sashaying in here, laying down the same bullshit lines that conned me out of my virginity."

"The Baxters canceled," Jess said, returning to the bar.

McCrea's eyes focused on her. "Looks like I'm free for dinner."

"Hell, yeah," Jess agreed. "That's a great idea. How about we take you to dinner and catch up on old times?"

"Sorry, man. She's mine tonight," Hank said, helping her with her jacket as she stood.

Eleanor offered Jess an apologetic smile. "Hank's right. I'm working. Some other time?"

Jess gave her a wink. "You bet."

Hank handed her the sunglasses. "Don't forget the shades."

Before she could take a step, McCrea caught her elbow and snatched the sunglasses from her hand. "I'd like a word with Eleanor before she goes to work." He nudged her towards the hallway and tossed the sunglasses to Hank. "Hold these. Will you, Bubba?"

Hank juggled the glasses, finally catching them before they fell to the floor.

She tried yanking free. "Stop. Let go of me." Walking in the five-inch heels wasn't a problem but running in them was.

"That's it." Hank hit his fist against his palm and shoved a stool out of his way. "I'm going to kick your ass."

McCrea scooped her up, threw her over his shoulder, and headed down the hall to the storage room. "Yeah, yeah, later, Bubba."

"No, Hank," she yelled, seeing him storming down the hall after them. "Fighting isn't good for business."

When they reached the storeroom, McCrea slammed the door and turned the lock.

"Put me down," she ordered.

He wrapped an arm around her hips and tipped her back to let her to the floor. Despite the situation and the anger churning inside her, Eleanor felt her nipples draw into pert points against the thin leather top. She chalked it up to the friction of his corduroy jacket, not attraction. Because being manhandled was not arousing and neither was being trapped in a small room with a man she despised.

Hank's big fist pounded on the door. "Goddamn it! Open up!"

"What are you doing? Do you have a death wish?"

Hank drilled another round of beats into the door. "Tracey, where are the extra set of keys?"

"Come on, McCrea. This isn't funny. Hank's going to have a coronary." She reached for the doorknob.

"Don't, please," he pleaded, wrapping a hand around hers. "A few minutes of civil conversation is all I'm asking for."

"You want civility after what you just did?"

"Please?" He gently squeezed her hand and let it go before stepping away from the door, allowing her to leave if she wanted to.

Eleanor wrestled with the urge to knee him in the balls and be done with all of his bullshit. This whole uproar was probably about Redemption. She should march right out the door and let Hank kick the crap out of him.

But if she did, she might never know why he had hauled her back here. And as insane as it sounded, she was holding on to the slim chance it might be about Sophie. "If this is about Redemption —"

"It's not." One side of his mouth hitched upward. "Do you really think I'd haul you back here, kicking and screaming, if it was about the ranch?"

"I wasn't screaming, and you have until Hank gets the keys." She shrugged one shoulder. "Or breaks the door down."

"Thank you," he said, smiling. His large hand rubbed thoughtfully over his jaw as if he were searching for common ground to start a conversation.

She tapped her foot and waited. *When is he going to ask about Sophie? When is he going to make an excuse for turning his back on his daughter? Any second now. He's just trying to work up the nerve. Yep, the dumbass-look on his face is just his way of stalling.*

When a couple of minutes passed, she huffed *Jesus,* inwardly, and gave up. Two complete strangers with a minimal vocabulary could have managed a single sentence about the weather or politics or a thousand other topics, but for them, simple, polite conversation had been lost to the four years they'd been apart.

It was sad.

Whatever acquaintanceship they shared before their brief interlude of passion had diluted, and they were strangers. And for her, the watered-down familiarity was overpowered by the resentment and downright bone-deep animosity she had simmering inside her.

"Let's start with the bar?" he suggested.

Whatever. "Fine."

Her acceptance eased the stiffness of his shoulders and allowed his eyes a more tasteful admiration at her outfit. "So, you've been posing in front of the cameras for the last four years?"

McCrea was not the simple, thumbs through the belt, country boy he appeared to be. He was an intelligent and educated man who could direct a conversation and people as easily as he could rope a steer. And the sly way he maneuvered the conversation from the bar to her was reminiscent of the days before they'd become lovers. The days before she knew how selfish and manipulative he really was.

"No, I started out waiting tables and moved up to manager." She dug into one of the boxes along the wall, pulled out a calendar, and handed it to him. "We're doing a shoot for next year's calendar. We have props set up in the space next door and a photographer who will be here later. That's why I'm in this monkey suit and five-inch boots."

Guys flirted with her, that came with working in a bar, and she didn't take a lot of stock in the compliments she received from boozed-up roughnecks and college boys. But it was hard to believe she was the woman in those photos — sexy, confident, glamorous.

A part of her wanted McCrea to see that woman. The woman he had let walk away. But the other part of her wanted him to see all she had accomplished since leaving Santa Camino. She was a successful business-woman, a savvy marketer, and a single mother raising their daughter without him. "I came up with the idea and wanted to hire professionals, but Tracey suggested we do it."

He flipped the calendar open, then backtracked to what she knew was the July page and raised both brows. "Damn, darlin'," he said. "You're good."

The red leather bikini, which was Tracey's idea, revealed more of her Star-Spangled Banner than she was comfortable with. Nevertheless, she took one for the team and straddled Hank's bike with the ease of a person born on the back. Butt up, breasts out, lips wet with her best sultry look.

He flipped to August. "I'm impressed, but not surprised. You always were a smart lady."

Not too smart. I did sleep with you.

"Hank and Tracey have offered me a partnership," she said, paying close attention to his reaction. "Which is why I'm selling Redemption."

She expected him to shoot out a curse word, or at least a scowl. But he didn't. Instead, he closed the calendar and laid it on a box, giving her his full attention. "You're selling the ranch for a bar?"

"Unlike Redemption, the Rebel Road is already a profitable business that I don't have to pour thousands of dollars into before I see a profit." She piled up a stack of medium-sized t-shirts and continued talking as though she were giving a lecture on bowel movements. "Thanks to Ed Tubs, I know a lot about operating a bar, so I thought, what the hell? I'll give it a go. I already do the marketing, the website, and promotions."

His eyes softened. "That's my Eleanor. I guess that business degree paid off."

The warm fuzzy feeling of accomplishment and praise he lathered on earlier hit the wall and slid to the floor with a hefty *thwap*. "I am not yours and I didn't get the degree."

That truth was painful in a way a man like McCrea would never understand. College, land, and money were all things he had a birthright to. Something he never had to struggle for.

She held out the shirt and covered the tremble in her hand with a slight wave. "Extra-large, right?"

His brow knotted. "What happened to your scholarship?"

The wrinkled black shirt dangled from her fingers while the urge to question his intelligence clawed at her tongue like a caged dog. "I lost the scholarship because my head was buried in a toilet."

His frown deepened. "You were sick?"

With her mouth agape, the caged dog was released. "Are you really that stupid?"

His frown gave way to surprise, and both brows lifted. "I must be."

"That's what happens when you're pre — "

"El." Hank pounded on the door for signs of life. "You okay?"

"I'm fine," she yelled back, irritated by Hank's obsessive need to protect. "Give it a rest." She ran a hand through her hair. "Anyway, without the scholarship, there was no way I could afford tuition."

She held the shirt up by the shoulders and wondered why she was offering him a shirt, let alone a backstory, when he hadn't offered her a damn thing but a ridiculous, freakin' proposal. "Do you want the shirt or not?"

"Of course, I want it," he said, taking the shirt.

Keys rattled outside the door. "Damn it, Tracey. These don't work."

She heard Hank's booted feet stomp back down the hall to the bar in search of the right keys. "It doesn't matter. None of it matters now. We've both moved on. Now, get out of here before he gets back. Hank can be a real badass when he gets mad."

"I'll take my chances."

McCrea could afford to take chances. He could walk away from responsibilities whenever he wanted to and act on impulses. She could not. "Don't when they involve me."

He moved closer and gently took hold of her upper arms, drawing her closer.

"McCrea, let me go," she warned, watching his head lower.

"I let you go once, and I've regretted it ever since."

She pulled back. "Don't you dare."

He took her mouth, much like he had her heart. Hard, fast, and without warning.

While Eleanor could cut out her own tongue for letting his slip past her lips, she felt herself give in. Her hands flattened against the hard contours of his chest, and her body leaned in, lax against his.

One of his arms circled her waist, drawing her up

and into the kiss, while the other slipped into the opening of her jacket. The tips of his fingers skimmed along the waist of the low-cut pants, and she moaned as the heat from his fingers sent a rush of desire through her pelvis. She felt the rise of desire building.

But even as her body gave in, her mind kept fighting. This wasn't happening. This couldn't happen. He was a bastard. A bastard that could kiss. A bastard that could take her from ice cold to sizzling hot in seconds. She was powerless to stop him because when McCrea Coldiron kissed her, she had no sense, no control, and not one ounce of willpower.

"El!" The clinking of keys resumed along with Hank's threats. "Cowboy, when I find the right key..."

He nibbled on her bottom lip, deliciously breaking the kiss. "Damn. Bubba doesn't give up easy, does he?"

Even now, amidst the desire, it was so tempting to open the door and let Hank dish out the beating McCrea deserved. She wanted him as broken and as hurt as she was, but Hank couldn't do that. Only the woman he loved could break him the way he had broken her, and she wasn't sure that woman existed. Or ever would.

Her fingers tightened into fists. "He's going to kick your ass," she repeated the threat.

"I'm not afraid of Bubba." He laughed and kissed her forehead.

His thumb rubbing across her bottom lip made her heart ache. It was tender, loving, and seductive all at the same time.

"And a second chance with you is worth getting my ass kicked."

The sound of screeching brakes skidded through the shower of her raging endorphins, bringing Eleanor to her senses.

"Second chance?" Her push to McCrea's chest was so hard he grunted. "Just who the hell do you think you are?" Her finger followed the push. "You came barging into the bar like you own the world. You insulted me in front of my friends and customers."

She gave her mouth a hard swipe because the taste of him made her sick. "You hold me prisoner, act like a dog in heat, and then have the balls to think a kiss is going to get you somewhere?"

He raked his hat off and busied himself by picking invisible lint from the brim, nodding slightly. "You're right. I've been an ass."

Is he nervous?

"It's just..." His Adam's apple bobbed up and down with a hard swallow. "I was shocked to see you yesterday. And tonight, all the old feelings came rushing in."

Feelings? What feelings?

He set his hat back on his head, crammed his hands into his front pockets, and shifted his feet. "I should have thought before I acted. I'll apologize to Hank and Tracey if you want me too."

"Apologize to Hank and Tracey?" she questioned as her temper spiked.

The self-centered bastard was akin to a dingleberry for not wanting anything to do with his own flesh and blood. And over the last four years, Eleanor had found great solace in the misery of his regret. Who was she kidding? She had partied in it, drank it in and danced the night away in the celebration of knowing one day he would tell her he was sorry for deserting her. But instead, he was offering to apologize to two complete strangers.

"They don't give a damn about you or your apology,

and neither do I. You hurt me!" The pitch of her voice drowned out the hum of the fan above them. "And then left me high and dry when I needed you!"

His frown was deep. "What are you talking about? You took out of Santa Camino like a cat with its ass on fire and never looked back. You shut Lou and Jess out of your life."

"You think shutting them out was easy?" She had turned down countless invitations and even missed Louisa's graduation to avoid running into McCrea.

She went back to the boxes and started stuffing shirts in to keep her hands from shaking. "It wasn't, but they're your family. What was I supposed to do? Make them take sides?"

"There was hardly a side to take, Eleanor. It was one night of sex." His voice was low and condescending as he repositioned his Stetson.

She threw one leg over the stack of boxes and met him in the middle of the floor, ready to draw blood. Her eyelids burned from the Scots-Irish anger gene she inherited from Grandma Rose.

With a flick of her hand, his Stetson went flying off his head. "Is that how you think of her? As one night of sex you can just forget about?"

His Tony Lamas did a two-step backward, the edge of one catching on a case of Scotch which nearly landed him flat on his ass. He staggered but found his footing. "Forget about who?"

Tight fists stiffened her arms. "Your daughter!"

"McCrea," Jess yelled through the door, wiggling the knob. "You should really get out of there! Hank's gone to find a crowbar. Oh, hell," he groaned. "He found it."

A loud "whack" broke the knob. "Hank, you hot-headed — oooh!" Eleanor yelled out as she rushed to the door. To do what, she didn't know. Hank Rebel was a powerhouse and stopping him would be like going head-to-head with a charging rhino. "This is going to get ugly. Let me do all the talking. I can calm him down."

McCrea stood glued to the floor like a department store mannequin. What was he doing? Didn't he realize what was about to happen?

Hank swung the door open, threw the crowbar onto a stack of boxes, smacked his square fist against his palm, and smiled in a way that made Eleanor's teeth ache. "I warned you, Cowboy."

She wedged her palms against his chest, the bottom of her stilettos sliding against the concrete floor. "Hank, don't you dare. Jess, help me!"

Jess leaned his shoulder against the door, somewhat amused by the show. "What do you want me to do?"

Hank couldn't be stopped, and she knew there was about to be one hellacious fight. "Hank, don't."

Hank gently moved her to the side and drew back a fist as he went. Without warning, McCrea came to life and planted a hard punch to Hank's jaw. The blow knocked him backward and down. "Not now, Bubba."

"Are you insane?" she yelled.

He stepped over Hank as if he were a fallen tree. "I have a daughter?"

The air that escaped her lungs was a hollow laugh. "Is that a question or a declaration after years of pretending she didn't exist?"

His eyes widened as he took a step back with a hand clutched to his chest. "You were pregnant when you left Santa Camino?"

"Right," she agreed, mockingly. "Like you didn't know."

His mouth closed and opened. "How could I have known?"

His true-to-heart shocked expression almost threw a wrench into her anger, but she refused to believe he didn't know. "I left you messages."

"Messages?" he questioned. "You were going to tell me you were pregnant with a message? Jesus, Eleanor! How cold-hearted are you?"

"Cold-hearted?" she asked, stunned by his words. "You were the one who abandoned her."

"How could I have abandoned a child I didn't know about?" The muscle in his jaw flexed as it always did when he was furious. "You should have come home."

He had no right to be angry with her. This was his fault, not hers. "I did!"

"When?"

A wave of rejection and hurt caused tears to spill down her cheek. "I drove out to the ranch before she was born because I thought you might want to be there for the birth. I thought that if you saw her, you would want her. But Vanessa stopped me at the door."

"What?"

"She said you didn't want anything to do with our baby."

His dark eyes became rheumy with an unexpected mix of pain and disbelief. "And you believed her?"

"She only confirmed what you told me the night we made love. You didn't want kids."

Chapter Six

An oncoming car blew its horn, rushing McCrea's exodus across the street outside the Rebel Road.

"I thought that punch you threw would keep him down," Jess said, crossing behind him with less speed.

He hit the unlock button on his key chain and opened his truck door. "Yeah, well, you were wrong." He climbed in and tilted the rear-view mirror down. The puffy rise under his eye was already turning blue. "Damn, Bubba packs a punch."

"What did you expect him to do?" Jess asked, catching up to him. "Tell you it was okay to toss El over your shoulder and pack her off like a caveman?"

In retrospect, that hadn't been one of his better decisions.

Jess propped his hand against the door, keeping it open. "The way El was crying, you're lucky he didn't kill you."

He crammed his keys into the ignition. "Shit, Jess," he swore softly, letting his forehead fall to the wheel. "I have a daughter."

"I heard. Did you propose to her before or after you seduced her?" Jess asked, with an undertone of disappointment.

When he didn't answer, Jess swore under his breath. "How could you do that to El?"

"Don't act like such a saint," he sneered, raising his head. "We both know you wanted her for yourself."

"Screw you, McCrea. I've always treated El with kid gloves and like a sister. I'm not low enough to seduce the woman who was in love with my brother."

He knew that, but he wanted a fight. He wanted to hit something.

"Believe me, there were times when I could have manipulated and wooed her into sleeping with me, but I'm not you," Jess continued, not caring how close he was to getting his teeth knocked out. "And if I had been lucky enough to have her love, I sure as hell wouldn't have traded it for a piece of land."

That fact didn't help the overwhelming regret and anger swarming inside McCrea. It made it worse.

"And," Jess continued his rant. "The only thing I've ever been guilty of is playing matchmaker between the two of you. But after tonight, Lou can find someone else to be in cahoots with. I've learned my lesson."

He might have known this was his sister's brainchild; his death by way of a big ass biker dude.

"Hell, I don't know why I try. You've always been like a goddamn Brahma Bull when it comes to El, slinging your horns, pawing the ground, snorting..."

He couldn't argue with the comparison, not after his behavior tonight. He had been a jackass on a monumental scale. But that was him. Go big or go home, and he saw no reason to stop now.

He gave Jess an arrogant grin as he came out of the truck, slammed the door and planted his feet, ready to fight. He wanted to hit something, hoping it would help purge some of the self-loathing that consumed him. "I knew what you were doing that night at Tubs. Say wasn't the woman for me, while you were planning your own itch scratching party—"

Jess's fist caught him just under the eye and sent him backward into the side of the truck. "Don't make this about me." He rubbed his knuckles. "You're the one who seduced El for the land, and now you're paying the price." He took two steps back and held up his fists. "Now, get up and let's finish this."

He grabbed hold of the truck bed and pulled himself up, feeling his bruised eye as he did. "You had to hit the one Bubba pounded on, didn't you?" The question came with a punch to Jess's stomach.

Jess coughed up an "oph!" and staggered backward, then retaliated with an equal punch to McCrea's stomach, knocking him into a parked car. The movement sounded the car's security system and caused a chain reaction of beeping alarms through the parking lot.

He recovered quickly and lunged for Jess, locking both arms around his midsection as he drove him to the ground.

From that point on, they fought like two armadillos. Through blinking headlights and ear-piercing alarms, they punched, dodged, and rolled until a blue light flashed.

McCrea swung, missed, and swiveled around so that he was face to face with the bright headlights of a police cruiser pulling into the parking lot. Its siren joined in with the alarms and drew more attention from patrons gathering outside the bars.

A cop with huge biceps, bearing an uncanny resemblance to Bubba, opened the door and stepped out. "Let me guess. It's over a woman."

"Something like that." McCrea rested his palms on his thighs and tried to catch his breath. "You wouldn't happen to have a brother, would you?"

The cop shined a flashlight into his bruised eye. "I see you've met Hank."

The crowd of onlookers laughed and pointed, and McCrea stood upright, trying to salvage some of his dignity. "Briefly. Shit," he said, breathlessly. "I'm getting too old for brawlin'."

Jess rolled onto his side and crawled to his feet. "Yeah, me too."

"Okay, against the hood and let's see some ID," the cop instructed.

Jess took out his wallet and removed his license.

"Have you gentlemen been drinking?" the cop asked.

"We're well under the limit," Jess assured him.

McCrea felt his back pocket for his wallet. "Mine's gone."

"It probably came out when I threw you against the car." Jess pointed behind him. "Look over there."

He saw something lying on the covered pavement, bent over and picked it up. "I found my license, but my wallet is gone." He handed them to the officer for him to examine under the flashlight.

"Can this night get any worse?" he mumbled. With a deep sigh, McCrea waited for his fine, but instead of whipping out a ticket, the cop whipped out a shiny pair of handcuffs.

"It just did," Jess groaned.

"What's the charge?"

A quick slap secured one wrist as he shoved Mc-Crea belly-first into the cruiser. "Disorderly conduct. Terroristic threatening. Kidnapping."

"Kidnapping? Aw, come on!"

He locked the other wrist behind his back. "Being an asshole. Making my lady cry. I'm sure they'll be more after I have a chance to talk to her."

"Your lady?" McCrea asked, connecting the dots.

Jess placed his hands behind his back and turned around, knowing his ass was going to jail, too. "Damn it, McCrea. I can't take you anywhere."

After handcuffing Jess, he placed him in the back of the cruiser and McCrea followed on his own accord. "I got it."

The cop shut the door and walked towards their vehicles.

After Eleanor stormed out of his life, McCrea made torturing himself with the image of her being in the arms of another man a habit. Most of the time, his mind gave him leniency with that man being some college kid with her level of experience, looking to get off. Not the cop walking towards the cruiser. A man with a predatory vibe.

McCrea's cuffed hands closed into tight fists. "You could have waited until we got back to the ranch to throw a punch."

Jess laid his head against the back of the seat and closed his eyes. "You deserve more than a black eye. You knew she loved you, and you used it to get what you wanted."

"It wasn't like that," he confessed, remembering their night together. "I cared for her."

Jess raised his head and frowned. "The woman bore your child, and that's all you can say? You cared for her? Holy shit, McCrea, you're a grade A, number one, major fuck up."

The cop returned, his voice cutting into the monotone voice of the female dispatcher. "All right boys. Let's take a ride," he said, buckling his seat belt before pulling the cruiser into drive.

As they passed the bar, he saw Eleanor make her way through the crowd and onto the curb. She looked so alone and lost.

"Vanessa knew and didn't tell me," McCrea said. "All this time she knew."

Jess laughed half-heartedly. "I would have loved to have seen her face when El showed up at the door pregnant with your baby."

He didn't share the humor. Vanessa had taken something from him. Something he valued more than money, land, or life itself.

He closed his eyes. In the blackness, a light emerged, and in the middle was Eleanor. Her hands reached for him, drawing him closer with a loving smile. A flash of his hand caressing her expectant belly caused a lump of emotion to rise in his throat. The thought of her carrying his child sent a warm wave over him. He was a father. A daddy. Emotions of happiness, love, hurt, and anger mingled inside him.

He opened his eyes in time to see Hank shelter Eleanor with an arm and nudge her back inside the bar as they drove by. That let the air out of McCrea.

He should have been the one protecting her. The one loving her. But instead, he'd had his head so far up his ass that he hadn't seen what was right in front of him.

McCrea felt the hell he had made for himself grow exponentially to snare the innocent. And seeing the consequences of his selfishness in the eyes of the woman who had loved him made him physically sick. "I've been a selfish bastard, Jess."

"No shit," Jess snorted. "There is no way I'm calling Mom or Dad for bail money, and Lou would never let us live this down."

"Call Dean," he said, not caring about his destination. Jess was right. He deserved a lot more than a black eye and jail. "We'll need a lawyer."

THE NEXT MORNING, McCrea pushed open the door of the Austin City Jail and took a deep breath of morning air.

He hated the city — any city. He hated the noise of passing cars and honking horns. He hated the concrete terrain, the iron buildings, and the reflective windows. And he hated the smell. But after a couple of hours in a holding cell, he was damn happy to fill his lungs with something other than the smell of body odor and urine.

"When are you two going to grow up?" At the bottom of the steps, Dean shoved a hand into the pocket of his black slacks and waited.

McCrea massaged the tense muscles at the base of his neck. "I told you he would answer."

"He didn't," Jess said out of the side of his mouth.

"Then why is he here?"

"One minute I'm in bed with a beautiful redhead,

and the next minute, El's beating down my damn door." Dean's pragmatic voice was fueled by anger.

"There's your answer," Jess said before stiffly making his way down the steps to slap his cousin's shoulder. "Couldn't keep it up with all that noise, huh?" He stuck out his forefinger and let it fall.

"Fuck off," Dean ordered, expanding Jess's grin. "Kidnapping? Terroristic threatening? Drunk and disorderly?"

"We weren't drunk," Jess clarified.

"Which means you can't blame alcohol for the shit you did," Dean noted.

Dean was one of the best criminal defense lawyers in the state of Texas. He was a hardass in the courtroom and didn't like losing, which was why he was always upfront with his clients. Do what I say, when I say it, or get another lawyer. He could be intimidating and vicious, but McCrea didn't give a damn. "Spare me the goddamn lecture, Dean," he said. "I don't need you to tell me I screwed up."

Dean let out a long sigh before looking away. "You two are damn lucky El called the arresting officer to explain that it was all a misunderstanding."

The arresting officer, Eleanor's tattooed lover. Jealousy fired through him, twisting his stomach into a knot.

She was a beautiful and desirable woman with needs. Why shouldn't she have a lover? What did he expect her to do, stay celibate? Hell, yes. He wanted to be her one and only lover. But he had blown his chances of that four years ago when he let her walk away.

This was his fault. He was the one who had broken

her heart. He was the one who had pushed her away. And as Jess said, he was paying the price.

He had wrestled with that fact all night. He needed to see her. He needed to make things right. He needed her to believe that he hadn't known about the child and that he hadn't abandoned her.

Whatever had happened between him and Eleanor might never be resolved, and he would have to live with the consequences of that. But he needed to be a father to his little girl. And he wasn't going to waste any more time.

He stuffed his shirt into the waistband of his jeans as he walked down the steps to where Dean stood. "Are our trucks at the impound?"

"Yeah," Dean answered.

"Where's your car?" McCrea asked.

"In the parking garage."

He quickened his steps and headed that way.

"Hey," Jess yelled. "Where's the fire?"

His walk turned into a jog. "I'm not leaving Austin until I talk to her."

Jess kicked his bad leg into high gear, trying to keep up with him. "How? You don't have her number or know where she lives."

"Dean does."

"No, I don't," Dean said, walking at a brisk pace behind them. "I haven't seen or heard from El in years."

McCrea stopped to pull his cell phone out of his pocket. "I'll ask Lou."

"Or I could just kick you in the balls," Jess chuckled. "Which is what she'll do when she finds out what you did to Eleanor."

McCrea shoved the phone back into his pocket. "Then I'll wait at the bar until Eleanor shows up."

"Like hell, you will," Dean all but barked.

"If Hank doesn't kill you, you'll be able to add stalker to criminal resume," Jess said, rubbing his thigh. "Besides, what are you going to say to her? I'm sorry. I didn't know about the baby?"

Dean's eyes narrowed. "What baby?"

"I didn't, damn it," McCrea said between clenched teeth.

Jess held up his hand. "I believe you, but put yourself in her shoes."

He couldn't empathize with being alone and pregnant. He had never been in love. He had never given himself to someone and watched them walk away. He had never suffered heartbreak. He had never loved anyone like Eleanor had loved him, selflessly, unconditionally.

"What baby?" Dean repeated.

"McCrea's a daddy," Jess said, giving Dean a side-glance.

"A daddy?" The lines on Dean's forehead deepened. "How the hell did that happen?"

Jess's lips distorted into a mocking grin. "Do we need to have a talk about how babies are made?"

Dean gritted his teeth. "Again, fuck off."

McCrea rubbed his temples, knowing nothing he did would budge the full-blown, four-alarm headache he had. Would he ever be able to convince Eleanor that he hadn't abandoned her or their daughter?

Jess clamped a hand over his shoulder. "Go home. Get drunk. Nurse your hangover and give El time to calm down."

"You know I don't drink anymore."

"Make an exception," Dean said.

"She won't calm down and the longer I wait to talk to her, the worse it will be when I do."

Jess grimaced and rubbed his thigh. "Don't go off half-cocked and do something stupid."

"I'll make some phone calls. It shouldn't be hard to find her home address," Dean said, pointing a finger at McCrea. "But you have to swear you won't go to her house or back to the bar. Women love flowers. You can start with that."

Chapter Seven

Stepping over crayons and coloring pencils, Eleanor maneuvered her way across the living room to where Sophie colored contentedly next to the couch. She took a seat in the recliner and laid her head against the back, yawning widely.

After a night of tossing and turning, she had rolled out of bed at dawn and left a message on Tracey's voice mail that she was taking a sick day. She made breakfast and had spent the rest of the morning cleaning the house.

Little by little, she had made the two-bedroom Victorian house next door to Hank and Tracey's into a cozy home for her and Sophie. The enclosed backyard had been used as a parking spot by the previous renters. But Eleanor had sown grass to cover bald spots, added a stone path leading to the garage, strung lights around the pergola and bought miss-matched lawn furniture at yard sales and thrift shops. Her elderly landlord, Mrs.

Bruce, was a sweet woman who welcomed the improvements she had made.

From the patio door, Eleanor could see the Austonian and the Frost Bank Tower, two of Austin's tallest buildings. Though she had grown used to the imposing structures of the city's skyline, she longed for the sloping hills of Redemption. The morning sun would rise over the pecan and oak trees and shine brightly over the ranch.

She closed her eyes and drew in a deep breath, trying to remember the rich aroma of hayfields and livestock that permeated the air around the ranch. But the imaginary scent of cattle was overpowered by the sweet, fragrant perfume of peach roses, white cushion spray chrysanthemums, alstroemeria, and statice sitting on the counter. The classic and elegant arrangement had been delivered this morning with the words, "To forgiveness, family, and redemption" written on the card in McCrea's sprawling penmanship.

Seeing him had not only ripped open the hurts and heartaches from the night she had gotten pregnant, but it had also awakened demons from her childhood. The ones she thought she had conquered.

Her father's identity had always been a secret. He had left before she was born and was never spoken of by her mother or grandmother. Eleanor had taken her mother's maiden name and an unhealthy dose of resentment from her stepfather before coming to live with her Grandma Rose.

The positive influence of the Coldiron men had taught Eleanor real men were protective, loving, and gentle. But not knowing who her biological father hadn't cared enough to stay around after she was born hurt Eleanor more than her step-father's slaps on the face. The abandonment. The lingering question of, "Why am I not good enough?" The emptiness she couldn't shake. These were things she didn't want Sophie to suffer.

"Do you want boots or sneakers today, Mommy?"

Sophie's little fingers moved selectively over the box of well-worn crayons. She chose a light color to make three circles and outline bodies on the blank page of the drawing pad. Bright yellow locks of long hair adorned the middle circle. She picked a mahogany brown color for the hair on the smaller circle.

Eleanor eased to the floor beside her. "I think sneakers," she said, going along with the drawing game they played often.

"What color?"

"You choose."

After embellishing the two figures with clothes, Sophie meticulously added details to their faces.

Eleanor pointed to the much taller third figure. "Who is this?"

"My daddy," Sophie declared.

"Oh," was all Eleanor could manage. Apparently, the ranch wasn't the only thing Hank and Tracey had discussed.

Sophie hesitated at selecting the next color. "What color is his hair?"

She combed her fingers through Sophie's hair, remembering the way McCrea's shined when the light hit it. "He has dark hair."

Her face brightened. "Like mine?"

"Yeah, baby. Like yours," she said.

Sophie pointed to her eyes. "Eyes like mine too?"

"Exactly like yours."

Enthusiasm moved Sophie's little fingers as Eleanor

gave her specifics about McCrea's features. It wasn't a surprise to see she had captured him perfectly. Straight nose, dark eyes, long legs, and a Stetson.

"He's a cowboy," Sophie decided. "Does he have a horse?"

"Yes, several of them."

Expectation beaconed in Sophie's eyes. "Do you think he would let me ride one?"

Even if she were game for showing up unannounced on McCrea's doorstep, she didn't know where his doorstep was. Granted, it wouldn't be hard to find out where he lived in a town as small as Santa Camino. But how could she be sure he wanted to see Sophie? "We'll talk about it later."

Sophie's bottom lip protruded. "Promise?"

"I promise."

With her mother's promise given, Sophie scrambled to her feet. "Can I give Daddy my drawing?"

Eleanor had given up on trying to figure out how McCrea hadn't gotten the messages or why Vanessa hadn't told him about her visit to the ranch. The woman was manipulative and that was reason enough for her to keep McCrea and Sophie apart.

But if he truly hadn't known, then Sophie was no longer the daughter he didn't want. She was the daughter he never knew existed. And that shifted everything in a different direction, into Eleanor's lap.

"Mommy," Sophie frowned impatiently and repeated her question. "Can I give Daddy my drawing?"

Eleanor swallowed the lump in her throat, realizing she had the opportunity to give Sophie something she never had, a chance to know her father. "I think he would love that, baby."

The zeal in Sophie's eyes was heartbreaking.

"Yay!!!" Clutching the picture to her chest, she hurried into her bedroom.

Eleanor raked the crayons into a pile and dumped them into the plastic box. She rose to her feet and began pacing. Sophie had her heart set on giving McCrea her drawing, riding one of his horses... Dear lord, what had she done?

She could call McCrea. And say what? Do you want to see your daughter? He might say yes. But there was a good chance he would say no. He had been crystal clear about not wanting children. No, she was not calling him.

She picked up the card and stared at the last word. Maybe Redemption was the answer. Maybe the ranch could be neutral ground. She could take Sophie back to the ranch and use her vacation time to do the packing herself. Two weeks in the country. Sophie would love it, and if McCrea didn't want her, then there wouldn't be a brutal rejection. She and Sophie would just walk away when the packing was done.

But was going back to Redemption the right thing to do? Eleanor had learned the hard way that McCrea wasn't the man she thought he was. Would he fall in love with their daughter the minute he saw her? Would he hold her, cherish her, and always be there for Sophie? How could she be certain he would be the father Sophie needed and not walk away one day?

She couldn't. The only thing she could do was take a chance that McCrea wanted Sophie. He had to want her. The message on the card all but said he did.

But what if McCrea did want to be a part of Sophie's life? What then? Though Eleanor had dreamed about him wanting Sophie, she hadn't thought about what that might mean. And she didn't want to start now. If she did, she might back out.

An hour later, she had their bags packed and was dialing Tracey's number when she saw a familiar black Chevy truck pull into the drive.

Nix killed the engine and climbed out. With a bottle of red wine and a bag of egg rolls she knew was from Uncle Kim's Chinese restaurant, he jogged up the walk.

"Perfect," she groaned. Nix thought she needed comforting, or he was just fishing for information so he and Hank could plot McCrea's disappearance.

She opened the door before he could knock and glanced at the bottle. "It's a little early for wine, isn't it?"

"It's lunchtime and I'm hungry. Are you in or what?"

"It's greasy food and alcohol," she said, grinning as she snatched the wine from his hand. "Of course, I'm in."

He stepped inside and glanced at their bags by the door. "I guess I should have called."

She searched the drawer for an opener. "It's fine."

"Want to talk about it?" he asked, eyeing the flowers.

She handed him the opener. "There's nothing to talk about."

"You haven't called in sick in three years," he said, sliding the card around so he could read it. "And you've been crying."

"So I am an emotional mess." She shrugged, trying to downplay the flowers and card. "Chalk it up to PMS."

"PMS or Cowboy?" he asked, inserting the corkscrew.

She grimaced at Hank's nickname for McCrea. "I know what you're doing, Nix Rebel."

With a few twists, he removed the cork and poured wine into the glasses she set in front of him. He leaned closer, taking great interest in her face. "What am I doing?"

For all his toughness and brawn, Nix was a sensitive and affectionate man. His presence calmed her, and at times, persuaded her to divulge more than she wanted to.

She tapped her short nails against the Formica countertop. "You're baiting me with greasy egg rolls and red wine, hoping I'll spill my guts. You know alcohol makes me stupid."

"I won't argue with you there." He laughed before reaching into the bag for an egg roll. "But if it were PMS, I'd be dodging the wine instead of consuming it."

"I'm not a suspect, so don't start with the questioning," she said. "Comprende?"

"Si, senorita," he said, devouring half of the greasy wrap in one bite. "Don't bother with the plates. Bring the bag."

"Nix!" Sophie ran into the living room, waving her drawing in the air. "My daddy's a cowboy!"

Oh God, Sophie! Really?

"Is that right?"

Her little head bounced up and down. "Mommy told me all about him. He has dark hair like mine and eyes too!"

He crouched down beside her to inspect the drawing. "You did a great job, Sophie."

Sophie pointed to the newly added horse beside McCrea. "He has horses and Mommy said I could ride one!"

His smile never faltered. "That sounds like fun."

"We're going to see him soon." Holding the drawing as if it were her most prized possession, she went skipping back into her room.

Eleanor took a spot on the end of the couch, licking the grease from her fingers. "These things are addictive."

He sat down next to her and popped the other half of the egg roll into his mouth. It was somewhere between his third and fourth one that an awkward tension meandered into the room and made itself at home between them. "You're going back to the ranch?"

Deciding she liked the awkward tension much better, she tossed her uneaten egg roll back into the bag. "There are a lot of things I need to sort through."

"Things like teacups and lace dollies, or memories and old lovers?" he asked, digging into the bag for a napkin.

"We all have a past," she defended.

"True, but Cowboy gets under your skin."

"No, he doesn't," she lied.

"The Whiskey Sour says he does."

"Don't make this into something it isn't." She purged her frustration by crunching the empty bag into a tight ball. "Oh, and by the way, I love the way you and Hank swung in to save me like Tarzan," she said, throwing the bag at him. "But it just made the situation worse."

He dodged it, gathered the empty glasses, and headed into the kitchen behind her. Setting them on the sink, he crossed his arms over his chest and leaned his butt against the counter. "If it wasn't something, then there wouldn't be a situation, Jane."

Eleanor busied herself with washing the glasses.

"There is no situation, only a little girl who wants to meet her daddy."

"And a woman who is still in love with the little girl's daddy."

She no longer had a just cause for wanting to slow roast McCrea over an open pit. And if she were being fair, she had to shoulder part of the blame for what went wrong four years ago. McCrea hadn't seduced her. In fact, she had gone to the Roadhouse that night with her mind set on seducing him. Sure, he had been older and more experienced.

But Eleanor hadn't been blind to his intentions, nor naïve about how the night would end. She had gone to his bed willingly and without any expectations of marriage or commitment. Only love.

But McCrea hadn't loved her. And she had decided a long time ago that she was done with wasting time wishing he did. "McCrea was my first crush, my first real kiss, my first lover." She paused, remembering each of those times. "He's the father of my child. But the love I had for him died when he let me walk away four years ago."

"I know a thing or two about being in love, and real love, true love, can't be killed or forgotten, no matter how much you want it to be."

Her grip on the glass loosened, and it slipped to the bottom of the sink.

"Careful," he said, leaning over to pick the glass up. He dipped it under the running water and set it in the drainer. "Letting things slip through your fingers can hurt you."

She knew what he was implying. And for the longest time, Eleanor had blamed herself for what had happened. She knew about McCrea's reputation with women.

And the guilt of knowing she had taken the same path as her mother nearly drove her insane. The path of falling in love with the wrong man. The path of finding herself pregnant and alone.

But when the nurse laid Sophie in her arms, Eleanor knew her love for McCrea hadn't been corrupt. It hadn't been in vain or wasted. She had loved a man with all her heart and given herself to him without suspicion. Because of that, she had been blessed with the perfect gift.

A beautiful baby girl.

Sophie was her world, her proudest accomplishment, and the only thing she didn't regret about her one night with McCrea.

But she hadn't let him slip through her fingers. She had taken what was left of her heart and walked away. And he had let her.

"How do you know so much about being in love?" she questioned. "You haven't had a steady relationship in the four years I've known you."

Ignoring her, he smiled smugly. "Cowboy is the reason you're selling the ranch. You're running away — again."

Damn it, she wasn't a runner. She didn't quit or pull up stakes when things got hard. And if Sabrina had hurt him the way McCrea had hurt her, then he wouldn't be acting like a jackass. He would be compassionate and understanding. Not accusing her of running away. "Like you're running from Sabrina?"

His posture stiffened, and a pale wash came over his face. "Don't. This isn't the same."

"I think it is. What if the tables were turned? What if Sabrina walked back into your life?"

His eyes lost their luster at the question. "She won't."

She turned and gripped the edge of the sink with both hands. "I thought the same thing about McCrea, but he did." And that was the problem. McCrea Cold-iron had walked back into her life, bigger than the devil himself, and a hell of a lot scarier.

Minutes passed without any response from Nix, and with the silence came uneasiness on her part. With an apology on the tip of her tongue, she turned to find the front door open and Nix gone.

Chapter Eight

As the sun slipped lower in the sky, beams of gold splintered through the trees to bathe Vera la Luz in the sunlight. McCrea dismounted when Romeo cleared the tree line. He led the horse along the edge of the fence and walked up the trail to the highest hill.

The solitude of Promise Point had always brought McCrea comfort and renewed him, which was why he had decided to take a ride up to the top. But as he looked out over the land, he'd never felt more confused. His eyes focused on the green valleys and blue rolling hills below. From here he could see the office, cabins, equine clinic, barns, paddock, and covered arena of the rescue.

The facility had been birthed from necessity, not planning. Metal buildings had been hastily built to care and accommodate some of their first patients. But now it was time to give the place a facelift.

The veterinarian and surgical center had been fitted with all the most up-to-date and modern equipment. But the outside had been built with the same rustic tongue-and-groove design as the cabin.

After his Granddad Wade disowned him, McCrea had been desperate to start over in a place where his family name didn't precede him. A place where he could do what he wanted without the approval of his granddad. A place where he could drown his regrets in a bottle of whiskey.

He had packed his bags and headed north, ready to start over in Montana at the Lucky Jack Ranch. Little did he know that his life and Colton's would take drastic turns.

A week later, he returned to Texas, and the Promise Point Horse Rescue Ranch was born. He had rolled up his sleeves, started building, and never looked back. He had immersed himself in work and in building a business that served a cause greater than making money.

He had worked long days and nights with his own two hands to build something he could be proud of. He had done that. He was well pleased with the rescue ranch and the foundation.

McCrea found a profound satisfaction and fulfillment in serving people. But something was missing from his life. Something success couldn't give him. Something he hadn't known was missing until last night.

Love.

For so long, his dreams had revolved around building the rescue and raising money for the foundation. He realized that now his dreams were about rebuilding what he and Eleanor had before he had fucked everything up with a proposal.

A low rumble brought his attention to the western sky. A storm was blowing in and the evening sunlight fought futilely to penetrate the thick canopy of bulging gray clouds that dominated the horizon.

He mounted Romeo and took the trail back to the ranch, arriving before the rain, and pulled the horse to a stop in front of the stables. He dismounted as a mixture of warm and cold air swirled around him, blowing dust and twigs into the air.

He removed the gloves from his hands, shoved them into his back pocket, and set about removing the saddle and supplies.

After making sure Romeo was fed and inside his stall, he made his rounds to see that the horses in the field were secured in the barn and made one last stop to check on Hope. She was the pregnant mare he and Curt Porter had rescued late last night from the Twisted J, an abandoned ranch located on the far side of the county. It hadn't housed animals for years. But in the last six weeks, McCrea and his staff had rescued four horses from there.

The other horses had been in such poor condition that euthanizing them had been the only humane thing to do. Rescuing an emaciated animal that might have to be put down was just what he needed to make this week a perfect damn disaster.

Various staff and volunteers had worked around the clock to get her stable. If she lived, she would need rehabilitation and love before she recovered from her obvious long-term neglect.

McCrea opened the stall door, slipped inside, and knelt beside her. Her rib and hip bones were prominent, with her bay-colored skin draping over them. Her head was disproportionately large in comparison to her thin body. When he reached out to pet her, she didn't recoil or pull away. She was too exhausted, but he knew she wanted to. Her eyes reflected her anxiety, fear, and mistrust, causing both pain and anger to settle into his chest.

He moved closer so he could cautiously run a hand down her neck. Her ears flickered once, then stilled. "It's okay, girl. No one is going to hurt you."

A labored sigh flew from her nose and her eyes closed. At least she was resting well. After a couple more strokes, he rose and slipped out of the stall. From there, he walked down the hall to where the offices were.

Doc Tolbert was standing at the reception desk, bifocals low on his nose as he looked over the paperwork in his hand.

"Give me good news."

Doc laid the papers on the counter before removing the glasses to massage the bridge of his nose. "She's alive and she hasn't aborted the foal."

"And?"

"There is no and," he said. "You know how this goes."

He knew. But he needed to hear something different this time. He needed to hear that they would both make it. He needed to feel good about something.

Doc repositioned his glasses. "We've given her electrolytes and probiotics. And we will slowly introduce food —"

"Will the foal make it?"

Doc frowned. "You're as concerned as a new papa."

He *was* a new papa, he wanted to say, but didn't. The foal, his daughter... His daughter. Tears sprung to his eyes. Damn, all this baby business was making him soft in the head and the heart. He felt like he had been turned on his head, shaken from side to side, and rolled around under the hooves of two dozen wild horses. "How long until she delivers?"

"It could be any day."

He walked towards the double doors leading outside. "Let me know if anything changes."

He followed the flagstone walk up to the cabin and opened the door. Inside, he plopped down on the sofa and was hit by an overpowering loneliness. He had never been lonely before, never thought the cabin too quiet or too empty. But as he stared out into the dimness of the room, he was left with a troubling truth. The cabin was a representation of his life: lonely, dim, and cold.

He rubbed a hand over his chest, feeling it tighten the way it had when he found out he was a father. He and Eleanor hadn't just had sex. They had made love, and the evidence of their love was their daughter. He would always have a connection with her — a love and life to share. And he would always be a father.

He couldn't quite wrap his head around that. He was a father. The man who said he would never take to the bridle or kids was a daddy.

He dragged himself up, dumped the left-over coffee from this morning into the sink, and made a fresh pot. As he waited for it to brew, he walked onto the porch to watch the approaching storm clouds. In the distance, lightning flashed erratically through a curtain of seething rain, and thunder clamored with an offbeat rhythm.

Storms brought with them an electricity. A vibe that could be felt in the restoring rain they delivered. But

McCrea knew the weather wasn't a cause for the restlessness he was feeling.

The prospect of spending the rest of his life without ever laying eyes on his daughter made him want to jump into his truck and head to Austin. He had wasted enough time. It was time for him to meet his little girl.

He dug into his pocket for his phone and found Sage's business card where he had left it on the kitchen counter. After he dialed her number, he hit the speaker icon and filled his travel mug for the drive to Austin.

She answered on the third ring. "Parsons Realty."

"Sage," he said, riffling through his dresser drawer for a clean shirt.

"Hi, McCrea," her voice was pleasant. "I hope the extraction wasn't too painful."

"It's an ongoing process," he replied dryly.

"Well, that's a start," she chuckled. "Have you called to make an offer on Redemption?"

He found a shirt. "No, I'm calling to get Eleanor's number."

"Your timing is perfect. She called earlier today to say she was coming to Santa Camino this afternoon."

"She's home?" he asked.

"Yes, I dropped by earlier to return the key she left me. I think she's planning on staying a couple of days. She's made an appointment to finish up the paperwork. And," Sage paused. "Her little girl looks just like her daddy."

He tried clearing the lump from his throat. "She does?"

"Very much. Maybe they'll be here long enough for you to visit them. I'll text you her number."

After she hung up, McCrea buttoned his shirt, found his hat, and slid his jacket on. The storms were bringing unseasonably cool weather to the region, and he knew the rain that was now coming down in sheets would be cold.

He opened the door as a loud clamor of thunder vibrated the windows. He flipped the collar of his jacket up and grabbed his coffee before making a dash for the truck. By the time he was in, he was drenched.

He set the cup in the console holder and flung the water from his hands. When his phone beeped with Sage's message, he hit the number and waited for Eleanor to answer.

"This is El. Leave a message."

He ended the call and tried again. But she didn't answer.

Lightning sparked and rippled across the western sky, and seconds later, another clamor of thunder sounded.

Rain in Hill Country could be brutal at times, causing flash floods and mudslides that could demolish roads, houses, barns, and wipe out entire herds of livestock. Tonight could be one of those times.

He started the truck, pulled it in drive, and headed towards Redemption. He turned off the gravel road and on to Clearview Road. It was covered by runoff, and if the rain didn't stop soon, it would be impassable.

He drove slowly, knowing the truck could hydroplane if he drove too fast. He turned into Redemption and followed the circle around. Old Blue was nowhere to be found. Maybe she had changed her mind. Maybe they were both safe and sound in Austin. He dialed her number again and heard her voicemail pick up.

Another clash of thunder vibrated the ground and his uneasiness worsened. What if Old Blue had broken down again? They could be stranded, or worse. What if they had wrecked? He fought against thinking about those scenarios and continued down Clearview.

The rain had tapered into a mist as the storm moved on and left the night sky clear. The only light was the headlights from passing cars and an occasional streak of lightning across the sky in the distant storm clouds.

As he rounded the curve before the bridge, he saw Old Blue sitting on the side of the road. He cursed when he saw Eleanor straighten from her crouching position near the deflated back tire.

He eased the truck to the side of the road, switched on his flashers, and parked, then grabbed a flashlight from the glove box before getting out. When he stepped into the beam of the truck lights, she backtracked a couple of steps.

"It's just a flat tire," her voice faltered anxiously as she held the tire iron with a white-knuckle grip. "Nothing I can't handle."

With the flashlight, he pointed to the jack under the car. "I don't doubt that, but," he shined the light into the trunk, catching the back of a child's car seat as he did, "you wouldn't want to injure my pride by changing the tire while I watched, would you?" he asked, feeling all the excitement of a new daddy racing through him. His daughter was within reaching distance.

Holding distance.

Eleanor's lips lifted at the corners, generating an unsure half smile, which she traded for a thought-filled bite to her lower lip. "I guess not."

McCrea hauled the tire out and rolled it over to where she was standing. As much as he loved seeing her teeth sink into that luscious lip, he didn't like seeing her close to tears, and she was. God help him, she was.

Eleanor Mackenna wasn't a frail, feminine mess of

emotions who teared up when the wind changed directions. And she wasn't the type of woman who fell apart over a flat tire.

This was more raging hostility mingled with a desperate attempt to keep a deadbeat dad at bay. A title he had claimed unknowingly. But, nonetheless, one she thought he deserved. So he kept the conversation easy and bolstered his grin. "I appreciate that."

McCrea entertained the possibility that she might refuse to let him see his daughter or use the tire iron on his thick skull before this was over. After all, she thought he had left her to raise their child alone. "How long have you been out here?" he asked, seeing her shiver.

She sniffed and wiped away the rain from her blanched face before holding out her left hand, bound by a bloody rag. "A while. I had it licked until my hand slipped."

He tucked the flashlight under his armpit and carefully unwrapped the blue bandanna she had used as a makeshift bandage. A cut on her lower thumb. "God, honey. This might need stitches. Let me take you to the ER."

She withdrew to re-wrap her hand, wincing slightly. "It's not that deep."

The hell it wasn't. The challenge came to the tip of his tongue, but he held it back. Arguing wouldn't help ease her anxiety or the situation.

And things were different now. There was a child involved, and he had to remember that when he wanted to throw out whatever came to his mind.

He handed her the flashlight and took the tire iron. He leaned the spare against the back fender and bent to loosen the lug nuts. "I tried calling you."

"My phone went dead," she explained.

When the last lug nut was off, he traded the flat tire for the spare and screwed the lug nuts back on. After they were tight, he lowered the jack, and the spare flattened as the tire before it had.

"Are you kidding me?" she groaned.

He tossed the flat tire into the trunk. "You're lucky I came along."

"Can I use your phone to call a tow truck?" she asked with wide eyes.

"There's no one to call," he lied, knowing he could call one of the ranch hands to tow Old Blue back to Redemption. Something she would have thought of if she hadn't been so upset. "The only tow truck service we had around here went out of business last year after the owner died."

The tire iron and jack followed the flat tire into the trunk. He slammed it shut before making his way back to where she was standing. He gathered the front of her thin jacket together, expecting a protest, but none came. She was cold and tired and in need of long overdue comfort.

Large blue eyes made her face seem smaller, and her hair, void of its usual bounce and fullness, left her resembling a street urchin from a Mark Twain novel.

McCrea gathered her cold hands in his to ward off the chill in them, taking careful consideration of the left one. She welcomed the warmth he offered by easing closer to the shelter of his arms. She felt good there, damn good.

In this very instant, she didn't look much older than the day they met all those years ago. The frail expression of an eight-year-old and a gaze of untrusting vulnerability, cloaking something much deeper. Then it had been fear, but now it was mistrust.

All those emotions were vividly clear to him now. He hadn't seen them before because he'd never allowed himself to look at her through the eyes of a man who loved her.

Holy shit.

He was in love with this woman. The epiphany hit him with the force of a fist to the chest. There was no doubt about it. Eleanor owned his heart, whether she wanted it or not.

Their bodies were touching now, connecting with a different type of intimacy. She wasn't just a woman who fomented his body to an ache, and she wasn't simply Eleanor Mackenna. The woman he had fallen in love with years ago.

She was the mother of his child, the nurturer and protector of the love they had made. Damn, that kindled something primal deep within him. Something exigent that went beyond physical pleasure.

The urgency moved his hand lower to her abdomen, to the place she had carried their daughter. A small gasp escaped her throat and their eyes met. "How could you think I didn't want our baby?"

Her chin trembled with the weight of his question, and her eyes welled up with tears. "What was I supposed to think? You didn't return my calls. After I left town, it was like I didn't exist. And then when I came to see you..." Her voice fell away, and she burst into tears.

It was hard for McCrea to swallow back his own tears. "I didn't know, honey. I swear, I didn't," he said, enveloping her in his arms. "I'm sorry, so damn sorry."

His apology unraveled her. It opened the infected

wound of their past and let everything spill out in a release of shuttering sobs which rocked her small body.

McCrea's lungs grew heavy. He couldn't blame it on the passing storm, but rather the one churning inside the woman he was holding.

When her sobbing ceased, he didn't let her go. He loved the feel of her soft body against his, and at this moment, everything was right.

He lifted her chin to lovingly kiss her lips. "What's my daughter's name?"

She looked up at him with red-rimmed eyes. "Sophia Rose."

"Sophia Rose," he repeated and felt the coldness of night being chased away by the warmth of her words. "After our grandmas."

She held tight to the front of his coat. "Yes."

"Can I see her?"

The tension in her face eased. "She's your daughter." She sniffed and wiped away the remnants of her tears with the cuff of her jacket. "Of course you can see her."

He followed her around the car to the back passenger door. "Wait," he said, holding a hand against it. "Does she talk?"

Eleanor's brows lifted. "She's four, McCrea. Of course, she talks."

"Yeah, yeah, that was a stupid question," he said, remembering what a talker Little Jack had been when he and Lauren moved in with Sue. "But she doesn't know who I am. How are you going to explain me?"

"Trust me," she said. "Introductions won't be necessary."

"Are you sure? I mean…" He rubbed his forehead, trying unsuccessfully to express his uneasiness. "I don't want to confuse her or do something she'll have to see a psychiatrist for later."

"Sophia Rose Mackenna is the most levelheaded and intelligent four-year-old on the planet. Meeting her daddy isn't going to cause a mental meltdown."

He was grateful their daughter had her mother's intelligence and levelheadedness, but he was still nervous as hell. "What do I say?"

Her face softened with a warm smile. "Hello?"

He took a deep breath and dropped his hand, allowing Eleanor to open the door. He stepped up to it, slowly bending his knees to squat.

He compared the descent to losing his grip on a horse. A man knew he was going down, knew he was hitting the ground hard but was effortless to stop the landing.

But instead of landing hard, McCrea felt like he was floating as eyes that were the color of his own stared back at him. "Hello, sweetheart."

Her pink bow-shaped lips parted, then lifted into an angelic smile. "Hello, Daddy."

His throat constricted. "Daddy? You know who I am?"

She dug into the small bag beside her seat and withdrew a folded piece of paper which, she held out to him.

He took care when he unfolded it. The three figures clearly defined each of them. Eleanor with long blonde hair, Sophie with dark hair, and him, complete with a Stetson and boots.

She pointed to the tallest figure. "Mommy told me about you." Her voice was delicate, like the webs formed on dew-covered leaves, and her face was the purest form of childhood innocence. She was breathtaking.

"She did?" his voice cracked.

Her little head bobbed up and down, spilling a lock of dark hair across her forehead. "She said my hair was like yours." Her point moved to the horse. "And that you would let me ride one of your horses."

"I said we would talk about it," Eleanor corrected from behind him.

Seeing disappointment bend her brow, McCrea leaned in to whisper. "I'll see what I can do. Okay?"

"Okay," she agreed with a giggle.

He tucked the picture into his shirt pocket for safe-keeping, unbuckled the belt, and lifted Sophie out, loving the feather-light weight of his daughter in his arms.

Chapter Nine

The love in McCrea's eyes and in his voice emanated with the beauty and strength of the sun. Never in her wildest dreams could Eleanor have imagined his love could be so strong and transparent.

"I have a daughter. A beautiful and perfect little girl."

"It's a wonderful feeling, isn't it?" she asked, elated by his reaction.

He didn't feverishly try to wipe away the tears that gleamed in his eyes. Instead, he palmed the back of Sophie's head and tenderly kissed her forehead. "It's indescribable."

McCrea was never emotional, never expressive about his feelings. She had never seen him shed a tear or utter an apology. But he had done both.

Eleanor felt something inside of her melt. Something that was once cold and icy, run hot. Something she said she wouldn't be foolish enough to feel again.

He held Sophie with one arm while he reached into the back for her car seat. "Go ahead and get in the truck. I'll take care of her."

Sophie laid her head against McCrea's chest with her face snuggled to his neck. Eleanor remembered what it was like to be wrapped in his arms and completely content in the love she thought he had for her. Thankfully, Sophie wouldn't have to worry about having his love. His hold on the child was precious and true.

Eleanor grabbed her purse from the front because there wasn't an ounce of protest left in her. She had cried it all out. Right there on Clearview Road in the arms of a man she thought hadn't given a damn about her. Yet he was there, holding her and trying to rid her of more than a rainy night chill.

The storm had abated into low rumbles and quiet flashes that moved slowly into the horizon, exposing an indigo sky above them. But the storm hadn't passed without leaving its mark. It had dumped several inches of rain and scattered branches and debris along the road. In places, water glided across the asphalt like sheets of glass.

But Eleanor had been touched by a different storm. A storm of forgiveness and new beginnings. A downpour of promise and expectations for Sophie's future with McCrea.

She took a deep breath and let it out. For the first time since her daughter was born, she felt like she could breathe.

McCrea wanted Sophie. Her daughter had the family she needed, and no matter what happened, someone would always be there to take care of her, love her, and shelter her. Sophie had a father who loved her.

Eleanor shivered as a deep yawn opened her mouth.

He pointed to the insulated cup sitting in the console. "It's hot and fresh."

"Thanks." She yawned again, unable to muster a worry about how bad she must look and reached for the camouflage coffee mug.

His ride was nothing like Old Blue. There wasn't a single animal cracker, toy, or milk stain anywhere. The tan leather seats and woodgrain dash gave it a new truck smell.

"I didn't get much sleep last night."

"Me neither."

She winced when the hot liquid hit her lips. Coffee sloshed over the edge, hitting the seat. "Shit."

"That's a bad word, Mommy."

She fished a damp Kleenex from her pocket to wipe up the spill. "You're right. Mommy's sorry."

Amusement tweaked his lips. "I don't know what else you've learned since you've been working at the Rebel Road, but your swearing's gotten better."

She took another quick sip of coffee and handed the cup back to him before putting the jacket on. She settled back into the seat.

Here they were. In the evening hours of a new day, indulging in a friendly conversation like two normal adults. It was strange how in the span of a few days she had gone from hating McCrea's guts to sharing a cup of coffee with him.

The ring of his cell phone caused him to reach inside his jacket pocket. He answered with a, "Hello." The pinch to his brow was followed by a low curse.

"Are you sure? I mean, it might have been a couple of kids — Yeah, yeah, I'm on my way."

"What's wrong?"

Eleanor watched his face harden into a scowl. "There's been a break-in at my house at Sunset Terrace Estates. That was Wayne Brewster. He lives next door."

The ritzy community was on the north side of town and adjacent to the country club. "You have a house at Sunset Terrace?"

He kept his eyes fixed on the road. "I bought it for Vanessa when we were first married."

He had offered to get an apartment in Austin, so she could attend classes and come home on the weekends. But she doubted her apartment would have been this nice. "Oh."

"It's not what you think," he said, giving her a hard glance before he made the turn into the posh community. "It was part of the deal I offered her."

"That's none of my business," she said, stiffly. "But I never thought you would live in a house at Sunset Terrace."

"I don't. After we were married, I moved into the cabin at Promise Point, and she moved into this place. I considered the house and property an investment I could make a quick return on after we were divorced." He slowed the truck and rolled up to the gate. After punching in the code on the keypad, he waited until the gate opened and drove through. "But the cabin needed work, so I stored my stuff here while the restoration was being done."

He stopped the truck next to the curb a few feet away from where the sheriff's car was and shoved it into park. "Stay here until I know it's safe." He hurried up the sidewalk to shake hands with Wayne and then disappeared inside.

Wayne, who was dressed in a pair of blue striped pajamas and a black bathrobe, stared suspiciously at the truck before walking back to his house.

A short while later, McCrea returned to the door and motioned Eleanor in. She unbuckled Sophie and walked through the double wooden doors to where he was waiting.

The elegant, yet rustic interior of the sprawling ranch house was a tasteful mix of both Tuscan and Texas design. Textured walls — painted pale yellow — created an airy feel and enhanced the natural light of the wide windows.

Native American rugs woven in earth colors anchored the open floor space and gave it a cozy atmosphere. A two-toned sectional couch of rich brown and buttercream leather faced the floor-to-ceiling stone fireplace, which displayed a giclée of a lone cowboy. Off to the side, love seats had been added to form intimate clusters of seating arrangements.

She stared up at the vaulted ceiling and exaggerated, "I could fit my entire house into this one room."

A faint smile tugged at the corner of McCrea's mouth but didn't extend to his eyes. "Buying this place is number four on my list of regrets, while the marriage holds strong at three."

She sat Sophie down and cocked her head back, studying the huge chandelier hanging from the hand-hewn cross beam in the middle of the room. The bronze finish and soft radiance of the iridescent, amber-covered glass were sophisticated, luxurious, and probably cost more than her entire wardrobe. "This place is a pricey regret."

He dragged his hat off and knelt beside Sophie, aiming a finger at his cheek. "How about a kiss from my favorite girl?"

Sophie gave him a quick smooch and then jumped onto the couch, belly-first.

He raised slowly, looking down at Sophie with remorse. "It's nothing compared to what number one and two cost me."

Undoubtedly, the time he had lost with Sophie was his number one regret. Did that place her at number two or did one-night stands even make the list?

"So, what happened?"

"The door was jimmied, but the alarm wasn't triggered. A security officer saw the door open and called it in," McCrea said, scrubbing a hand over his face.

"What did the sheriff say?"

"That he should get the hell out of here and let us do our job." Ted Bailey had been sheriff of Gilmore County for years. He was pudgy in the middle, weak through the shoulders, and thin on top. But the man strolling towards them with a trim middle, stout shoulders and a thick crop of dark blonde hair was not Ted Bailey.

It was Finn Durant, a roughneck bad boy from high school who had broken more rules than he had followed.

Holy crap.

"Who'd you bribe to get that badge, Durant?" she teased.

"Hold up, little lady," Finn ordered with eyes that zoomed in on her. "That's how gossip gets started, and I don't need that kind of negative publicity." He directed his thumb towards Wayne's house. "Brewster would love to see me drawn and quartered on the courthouse square."

"Oh, yeah," she said, remembering that Wayne had caught Finn in the backseat with his daughter on prom night. "How is Tess?"

Finn's authoritarian face broke into a grin. "Happily married with three kids, the last I heard."

"This was Chaves," McCrea said, running a hand through his hair. "The Vera la Luz coins are the only thing missing. That has to say something."

Finn shifted his weight from one hip to the other and hung a thumb through his duty belt. "I agree with your theory about what's going on at the Twisted J, but this is a little farfetched, don't you think?"

The Twisted J. Where did she know that name from? She thought for a moment and remembered. It was the old Johnson ranch. "What's going on at the Twisted J?"

"Nothing good," Finn answered and turned his attention back to McCrea. "But Chaves wasn't the only pothunter that story drug into town. This could have been one of them or a dozen other lowlifes."

"Hey, guys, I've been gone for a little while," she cut in. "Fill me in. What story?"

"The town council is pushing tourism, so a few months ago, they hired a cultural research group to evaluate Vera la Luz."

As kids, McCrea's dad took them on camping trips up to Promise Point and let them look for clues among the ruins of the old Spanish Mission.

Maybe the Wayfires were real. Maybe the gold was protected by the spirits of my Comanche ancestors. McCrea's voice as he told the story could be seductive and alluring, drawing her into his tale of legends and gold.

"There's an archeological dig going on at the Mission?" she asked, excited by the news and by what they might find.

"As we speak," McCrea answered without enthusiasm.

"There was a big write-up in the local paper about the Legend of the Wayfires Gold," Finn explained. "Social media got ahold of it, and a news channel in Dallas picked it up."

"Eventually, the story made it to the national news and Santa Camino was bombarded with reporters and sleazy pothunters like Tony Chaves," McCrea said, taking a seat on the arm of the couch. "I had the Mission and surrounding dig sight safeguarded with a high-security fence and hired around the clock guards. No one can enter without the proper credentials."

"The historical society thought it would be a great way to draw in tourists," Finn said. "But it's been a nightmare."

"Now they've hired Chaves as their dig liaison," McCrea added.

"People seriously think there's gold up there?" She laughed.

Finn shrugged. "People like Chaves aren't after gold."

"They're in it for the artifacts," McCrea cut in. "The same artifacts we found at the Twisted J when we rescued the first horse. The historical society should know their dig liaison is an antiquities thief. And that he's been stealing and auctioning off horses for slaughter."

"God, no," she gasped. "Slaughtering horses?"

"It's a very profitable business," McCrea said.

Finn scrubbed his forehead. "You don't have anything to back up the claim that Chaves is involved in any of this or what's going on at the Twisted J. Just because you caught Chaves in bed with your wife doesn't mean he's a thief."

"Ex-wife," McCrea was quick to correct him.

Eleanor wasn't sure if the ruddy tint to McCrea's cheekbones was from anger or embarrassment. A few days ago, her inner bitch would have pushed the knife in deeper by asking him if the land had been worth the humiliation.

But she was past being bitter and past wanting him to pay for what had happened four years ago. She wanted a fresh start for the three of them. One where she and McCrea could eventually be friends. Because she knew better than most that a child needed both parents.

"Look, I know Chaves is a piece of garbage," Finn said with more patience than before. "Unfortunately, that's not a crime. The house hasn't been lived in since Vanessa moved out, right?"

"No," McCrea sighed.

"We'll try lifting prints and run whatever we find through AFIS. But since he and Vanessa were lovers..."

"He can justify his prints being here," McCrea finished.

Finn nodded. "I don't have the manpower or the resources to keep the Twisted J under twenty-four-hour surveillance. But I'll question Chaves and follow any leads we get. Now, how many coins were there?"

"Five."

"I'll need a description."

She reached for the coin around her neck. "Were they all like mine?"

"Yes," McCrea answered softly. "I went back to Vera la Laz the winter you left."

That was the camping trip they were supposed to take together when she returned home for Christmas break.

"May I?" Finn asked, pointing to the necklace.

"Yeah, sure," she said, handing Sophie to McCrea. She quickly unclasped the latch and gave it to him.

Finn's smile was polite and official. "Thanks."

Sophie yawned and nestled her head against McCrea's chest.

"What's your name, beautiful?" Finn asked.

"Sophia Rose Mackenna," she answered.

"That's a pretty name." It was nice to see Finn's charm extended to all the ladies, not just the ones of a datable age. "I have a niece about your age. We're planning a big birthday party next week with balloons, pony rides, and lots of cake and ice cream. Would you like to come?"

Sophie nodded bashfully.

"Thanks, Finn," Eleanor answered. "But we won't be staying that long."

Finn's frown was one of confusion as he moved a finger between her and McCrea. "But I thought you two were..."

"No, I'm just here to tie up some loose ends," she was quick to say, then hurried to explain. "I'm selling the ranch. We'll be here just long enough to get everything packed and ready for the movers."

"Oh well," Finn smiled. "That's a shame. I thought you might give Brook Tidwell some competition at the bachelor auction."

McCrea cleared his throat, catching Finn's attention so he could dish out a deadly stare. Finn dropped his eyes and went back to inspecting the coin.

So, McCrea was fraternizing with Brook Tidwell.

Typical. The man had always been attracted to a pretty package. Eleanor shoved her hands into her pockets and backed out of the conversation, feeling like she did in high school. The plain Jane girl from next door, only noticeable to McCrea when in the way. She was most definitely in the way now.

She turned and walked to the French doors leading to the veranda. A variety of plants and shrubs lined the edge of the house. Ornate terracotta pots and planters with seasonal flowers decorated the large rock patio and steps leading down to the infinity pool.

The outdoor kitchen and fire pit were perfect for entertaining numerous guests. Guests that Vanessa would have gladly entertained to up her ranks with the town's elite. She had always had a thing for men with money and power, which was why she'd sunk her claws into McCrea years ago.

Eleanor's eyes followed the horizon. The hilltop had a scenic view overlooking the rolling hills ,and off to the right, the country club. Its lush golf course and high dollar clubhouse were cut out of what used to be ranch land.

The view, like the house, was perfect. There wasn't a single throw pillow or rug out of place. The lawn, the furniture, flowers, and view were immaculate. Yet the marriage between McCrea and Vanessa had been a union littered with adultery, malice, and distrust. Money could buy anything but love, and she was starting to see that McCrea had paid dearly for Promise Point.

She rubbed her palms over her thighs, trying to expel the icky feeling she had bubbling inside her. She didn't like being here. It felt wrong. She walked back to where McCrea and Finn were standing by the door.

Finn let the coin dangle from his finger as he handed it back to her.

"I think I'll wait in the truck. Do you want me to take Sophie?"

"No, I'm right behind you," McCrea said, placing a hand on her lower back to guide her toward the front door.

"It was nice seeing you again, Finn."

"You too," he returned. "If you change your mind about the party, Griff's house is in the new development over on the east side."

"The east side was bluebonnets and pastures when I left." She laughed.

"I guess it was," Finn agreed. "I'm picking up Debbie and Wendel Norman's little girl. I can swing by and get Sophie, too."

"Do you also carpool and bake brownies, Sheriff Durant?" Eleanor asked.

A rosy tint covered Finn's cheeks. "Only until my brother hires a nanny."

Chapter Ten

Eleanor had told Finn she was here to tie up loose ends. That's how she had justified being with him tonight. As if he meant nothing at all to her. He was just an unfinished chapter in her life she was here to write him out of.

We can't always hold on to things just because we love them. McCrea didn't believe that. Eleanor never gave up on the things she loved, and she might not love him, but she loved Redemption. And he couldn't let her sell it.

"In a town as small as Santa Camino, not much can be hidden," Eleanor said as she looked out the window. "Especially when it concerns a family as prominent as yours."

He knew she was making a point and that this was more than just chitchat. "That's small-town life."

"Catching Chaves isn't personal for you, is it?"

"In a way it is," he said, glancing over at her.

"I get it. Finding out he was sleeping with Vanessa had to be hard on your pride."

"I don't have much pride left these days, that's for sure." He laughed. He hadn't felt anything but relief when he found them in bed together, and he was past giving a damn about what people thought about him. "But that's not why I'm after Chaves. Stealing artifacts is one thing, but what he's doing to those horses is…"

"Atrocious."

"Yes, and I may be the only thing standing in the way of those horses and the slaughterhouse. So, yeah, catching him is personal."

Nothing more was said, and the cab filled with silence as they drove across town. Runoff from the storm-flooded ditches made travel slow, but McCrea didn't mind. And from the relaxed state of her body, neither did she. There were things they needed to talk about, sort out, and discuss. But there was peace in the silence. A peace he hadn't felt in ages.

Eleanor sighed heavily as they passed Old Blue. "Poor guy."

"That damn thing has got to go," he said.

"Buying a new one is first on my list after I sell the ranch."

"That might take months." But he knew Redemption was already sold to a man who had finally gotten his head out of his ass. "You need a dependable vehicle now."

"I'm not in the financial position to go whipping out my checkbook for a new ride."

"I am," he said without flinching because a new car wouldn't dent his bank account, and neither would him buying Redemption.

Her lips thinned. "I'm not taking a handout."

Those were the exact words Rose used when his Granddad Wade volunteered to lend her money or help pay the taxes. Maybe Rose knew what his granddad was up to, or maybe she was just like Eleanor, too damn proud for her own good. "It's not a handout. If you figure up all the child support I haven't paid, I owe you a lot more than a new car."

She chewed her bottom lip, thinking of an argument. "You have a point, but I'm not comfortable with you giving me money."

"Sophie is my daughter, and I am going to support her. You need a car and I need peace of mind."

Her bottom jaw rolled from one side to the other. "Fine, but nothing extravagant or fancy."

"Right." He laughed and gave her knee a squeeze.

He turned into Redemption's drive and parked in the circle near the walk. He shut the engine off and turned to her. "We have a lot to talk about."

She unlocked her seatbelt and tucked a leg under her as she swiveled around to face him. "Let's start with how you didn't get my messages. I left more than a dozen, McCrea. How could you have not gotten them?"

"How did you get pregnant when I used a condom?"

The question made her shoulders lift timidly as she reached into her purse. She held out his wallet. "Maybe the condom was defective or old. The one in your wallet is expired."

"You found it?"

"It was by the curb. Your license is gone, but your credit cards and cash are there. I thought about tossing it into Lady Bird Lake, but my conscience won the fight."

He chuckled. "Aren't I lucky?"

He unfolded the wallet, took out the condom, and held it up. Before his marriage and a long bout of celibacy, he hadn't had a promiscuous sex life, despite what people thought.

But his condoms never had a chance to expire. Because he did make practicing safe sex a habit. And the odds of it being defective were slim. Eliminating expiration and defectiveness left only sabotage.

Vanessa had been a woman desperate enough to use an innocent child as a money-making scheme. A thousand how's and a million replays couldn't have explained how Eleanor had gotten pregnant any better. "Remember Scotty Langford?"

"Sure, why?"

"A few months after his little boy was born, he found out Amy set him up by sabotaging the condom."

Her eyes widened. "You don't think I—"

"No," he was quick to say. "But I think Vanessa did. She and Amy were friends, and she had access to my phone, which explains why I didn't get the messages you left."

Her mouth dropped open. "I saw her with your wallet that night at the Roadhouse."

"I lost it in a fight, just like I did in the parking lot. It's the perfect setup," he continued, knowing what Vanessa's intentions had been all along. "The guy figures he's doing the right thing by using protection, but the girl ends up pregnant, anyway. Bingo. It's an instant catch for the girl. Amy divorced him a year after they were married and sued him for child support. There was a huge scandal."

"The Langford name was dragged through the mud. Scotty's dad resigned from his position at the bank, and his mom was close to a nervous breakdown."

"That's horrible."

"Yeah, and the poor kid only gets to see his dad every other week." He shoved the condom back into his wallet so he could discard it later. "And if I had slept with Vanessa instead of you..."

She drew in a deep breath and released it. "Now we know."

"Yeah, now we know. But it doesn't matter to me how you got pregnant, darlin'. Only that you did."

She gave him a smile that made his heart drop to his boots. "When I realized that you were telling the truth, I knew I couldn't be selfish by allowing what happened between us to stand in the way of Sophie meeting you."

Eleanor had never been selfish a day in her life. She was the most caring and considerate person he had ever known. He, on the other hand, hadn't given a damn about anyone but himself.

He looked over the seat at Sophie. She was perfect, from the crown of her dark head to the tips of her dainty toes, and he couldn't imagine his life without her now. "I've missed so much."

Eleanor placed a hand on his arm, offering him the comfort he didn't deserve. "Knowing she has a father who loves her is going to make a big difference in her life."

He covered her hand with his. "I won't disappoint her." He wouldn't disappoint either of them ever again.

She opened her door, pausing to look at him. "Please don't. You're either in this for the long haul or you walk away now."

"I'm not going anywhere." He was in this for the long haul. Marriage, babies, diapers, and droolin'.

But he would save that revelation for later.

He opened his door and went around the truck for Sophie. "There's something else."

She waited.

"What Finn said about Brook —"

"Who you sleep with is your business," she interrupted.

"I am not sleeping with Brook," he said as his body did an involuntary shiver. "The woman gives me the willies."

The cards were already stacked against him. And if there was the slimmest chance he might win Eleanor back, she didn't need to think she had any competition, especially from a woman like Brook.

"Whatever you say." When cocked high on her forehead, that one damn eyebrow spoke volumes.

"Don't do that?"

"Do what?" she asked, reaching inside the cab for her purse.

"Give me that look," he said, opening the back door. He released the buckle and pulled Sophie into his arms. She rested snug against his chest and drifted back to sleep.

Eleanor stopped at the bottom of the steps, eyebrow lowered, eyes without humor. "You don't owe me an explanation, McCrea. I'm not your wife or girlfriend. I'm Sophie's mom. The women in your life aren't any of my business, just like the men in my life aren't any of yours."

She had moved on, but he hadn't. He wanted to tell her that she was the last woman in his bed, that he hadn't dated or thought about sleeping with a woman because of her and that she was the one woman he wanted to be accountable to.

But it was too soon into their developing relationship for that sort of detail. Plus, maybe he had more pride than he thought.

But there was a part of this that didn't sit right with him because of Sophie. Her feelings, wellbeing and safety came first, and he knew Eleanor felt the same way. "I'm not sure I agree with that. Think about what you just said from a parental point of view."

She stopped halfway up the walk and turned back to him. "Meaning?"

"As parents, we have a right to know about the people in Sophie's life."

Her eyes narrowed as she considered his words. "I think we should trust each other to make the right decisions for Sophie when considering a husband, wife, or lover."

Husband. Lover. He cringed inwardly.

"And I think the four of us should at least be on speaking terms."

"The four of us?" he questioned.

"You, me, and our significant others," she explained.

Hell, no. He drew in a steady breath. "Do I need to remind you about the conversation officer Rebel, and I had in the parking lot the other night?"

Her smile was one of confusion and amusement. "His name is Nix, and he's an easygoing guy, in and out of uniform. You just rubbed him the wrong way by holding me hostage and treating me like a hooker."

"I didn't," he contested, because he felt like an ass for what had happened at the bar.

She pointed a finger at him and laughed. "You did."

"It was all a misunderstanding," he said.

"So you say," she jeered, but her smile dimmed. "You do have a valid point about Sophie. But…"

There was always a damn 'but' with this woman.

"That doesn't give either of us the right to pry into the other's personal life. Who we sleep with is not up for debate or discussion. Agreed?"

He tried not to scowl. "Agreed."

"Maybe the four of us could have dinner together or have drinks—"

"I get it," he cut in, rubbing a palm over his eyes. "You want me to play nice for Sophie's sake?"

Her face was deadpan. "And mine."

Their eyes locked, and McCrea knew this was the standoff. Eleanor was drawing a keep-your-distance line in the dirt, and if he crossed it…

He shrugged indifferently. "Whatever makes you happy, darlin'."

Having said her piece, she climbed the steps and unlocked the door.

He watched her enter the house and flip on the light in the living room. Seeing her here in Redemption's window wasn't something he was used to. There had been a few times when he came with Wade or dropped something off his grandma had baked for Rose. He saw her then, but Eleanor usually met him at the door with a blushing smile.

But that was usually the extent of his visits. He hadn't made coming to see her a habit. She had been the one who made the effort. She had been the one who walked across the pasture or up the road to see him. He hadn't made much effort at all where Eleanor was concerned.

That had to change.

He hurried up the steps and once inside, kicked off

his boots by the door. He hung his hat on a hook and did a double take at the stacks of boxes covering the living room floor. "You've been busy."

"I haven't made a dent yet," she said with a grimace. "Grandma was a hoarder and she kept everything. Can you believe I found a store receipt from 1962?"

"Maybe you'll find a stack of bearer bonds."

"I'm more likely to find a set of false teeth," she said, climbing the stairs. He followed behind her, enjoying the sweet sway of her behind. She pointed to the first door and hurried around him to open it. "In here."

She switched on a lamp beside the bed, pulled back the bedspread, and went to get an extra blanket from the closet to ward off the chill. He lay Sophie down and felt her little arms tighten around his neck. She held on to him as if he might disappear into thin air. "Don't go, Daddy."

The words squeezed his heart. "I'll be back in the morning, sweetheart."

"Daddy can have breakfast with you. I'll make pancakes," Eleanor said.

"No," she whined. "I don't want you to go."

In just a brief time, his daughter had become attached to him. Sophie wanted him close and needed him. "Okay, I'll stay," he agreed, giving Eleanor a wink that made his intentions clear. He would stay until Sophie fell asleep.

He shrugged his jacket off and tossed it onto the chair next to the door. "But you have to go back to sleep."

Sophie smiled with a drowsy nod as Eleanor removed her shoes and socks, tucked a doll in beside her, and pulled the quilt up to her chin. McCrea snuggled in and wrapped an arm around her before Eleanor closed the door as she left the room.

The small lamp gave off just enough light to let McCrea look around. He had never set foot in Eleanor's room when they were growing up, and as they grew older, Rose would have used Charlie's double-barrel shotgun on him if he'd even glanced in its direction. But he knew from the numerous books, cheerleading pompoms, country music posters, and academic trophies that it was hers.

As Sophie's breathing leveled off into a peaceful slumber, McCrea gave her a kiss on the forehead and eased from the bed.

He heard the shower faucet creak on, and water rumble up the pipes. And his mind dove into a place it didn't need to be. To the way Eleanor's body had felt under him four years ago, soft, supple, and yielding.

He rubbed his eyes, trying to block the images of her standing naked in the bathtub. In a few minutes, she would be out of the shower, and he would be on his way. Surely, he could keep it together that long.

As the water warmed, Eleanor lifted a strand of plastered hair from her forehead and winced at her smeared mascara and ghostly reflection in the bathroom mirror.

She peeled away the bandana and inspected the wound. It wasn't deep enough to require stitches, but it did need cleaning. After searching through the medicine cabinet, she found a bottle of outdated peroxide and washed the wound. She stepped into the claw-foot tub to let the hot water relax her tired and now aching muscles.

She hadn't been prepared for changing a tire in a deluge or for what had happened when McCrea pulled up behind them. It had all happened so fast. One minute he was changing the tire and the next, he was holding her. McCrea had comforted her, warmed her, and revitalized her just by wrapping his arms around her.

She thought she knew him, but the man he had been tonight was a stranger. A man she hadn't seen before, but a man she wanted to know. This McCrea was also much more attractive than the old McCrea and tempting to more than her eyes. This new, paternal man awakened something in her, something deep and untouched. Something desirable and scary.

The sexual tension between them hadn't faded over time. If anything, it had gotten stronger. It was an attraction that sparked and sizzled every time he touched her. A spark that might burn them both to ashes if she didn't keep him at a safe distance.

She let out a long sigh. Sexual tension and awkwardness. Not the best way to rebuild a friendship. A friendship that now had to be centered on Sophie, not on their attraction or her feelings for him. That was a whole other problem and something she didn't want to think about.

Sophie was completely enamored with him and saying goodbye to her daddy was going to be hard. She and McCrea had to sit down and lay out a practical plan for shared custody. Scheduled visitation, birthdays, holidays, and summers.

She crinkled her nose at the thought. Navigating the

dark waters of the ocean of history they shared wouldn't be easy.

After she shut the water off, she stepped out of the tub and squeezed the water out of her hair, remembering she hadn't brought her hair dryer or clothes with her from the bedroom.

That meant she had to traipse back in there wearing nothing but a damp towel or crawl back into her muddy jeans and t-shirt. Not an option.

"Friggin' fantastic, Eleanor," she applauded herself.

Okay, so what was the worst that could happen? McCrea would see her in a towel? Big deal. *He's seen you in a lot less,* she reminded herself. But that was four years ago. A lot had changed since then. Her body was far from perfect before she had Sophie. But now she had stretch marks...

You're being childish, and your cowardly indecision might be the reason you freeze to death.

She wadded her dirty clothes into a ball and clutched them to her chest before opening the bathroom door. The door to the bedroom was just as she had left it. Maybe he was asleep. That was a very likely scenario.

She tiptoed down the hall. He did look tired and ruggedly sexy. His mussed hair and square-cut jaw. The memory of how it felt grazing the inside of her thigh popped into her head. Desire coiled tight in the bottom of her stomach. The fantasy flushed her skin and left her a little breathless. "Stop it," she said, fanning her face.

She'd had dates, several thanks to Tracey, but none of them ever made it past her front door. And that was the way she wanted it. A nice dinner with aimless chitchat and friendly smiles helped her to feel normal and placated Tracey's concern.

But McCrea wasn't a date. Nor was he an average Joe off the street. He was her first and only lover. He was the father of her child, and the man who had broken her heart. He was off limits.

But so much of what had happened tonight — seeing his love for Sophie, feeling the concern in his examination of her hand, knowing he wanted her — endangered her tenacity.

Eleanor took a deep breath and held it as she turned the knob. It clicked loudly with the turn, causing her to wince. If McCrea had fallen asleep, he probably wasn't now. She pushed it open and there he was with his jacket draped over an arm.

So much for slipping in. She clutched the towel tighter. "I forgot my clothes."

"She's asleep," the husky sound of his voice sent a shiver up her.

The question of what sex between them would be like had been answered four years ago. Hot. Passionate. Consuming. Her nipples perked underneath the cotton covering and chill bumps drew her skintight. "I didn't expect her to be so attached to you so soon," she said, slipping past him to her bags. "Leaving you is going to be hard for her."

"It's going to be hard on me too," he admitted. "I don't want Sophie to feel like she has to choose between us. And I don't want chopped up Christmas visits and scheduled visitations."

"Neither do I," she returned, nervously. "Sage brought me a sample of her aunt's new blend when she dropped off the extra key. I was going to make myself a cup because I'm too wound up to sleep. Would you like a cup before you go?" *Tea? Now?* "It would give us a chance to talk about how we're going to handle saying goodbye."

His brows knitted. "I…uh..."

She felt the flush on her face deepen. "You probably don't drink tea and it's late. We can talk later."

"No, ah, I'd love a cup." The words tumbled from his mouth and even that was sexy. Anything coming from those lips was sexy.

"Okay, then," she said, managing a polite smile.

McCrea didn't take the cue to leave. Instead, he stood there fixed to the floor, much like he had been in the storeroom right before Hank barged in.

"I'll be down in a minute. Make yourself at home," she said when his heavy-lidded gaze lowered to her breasts.

He blinked and nodded before leaving the room.

When the door shut, Eleanor let out the breath she'd been holding and hurried to her bags. She slipped into a pair of yoga pants and a faded t-shirt and ran a comb through her hair.

She quietly gathered her bags and turned back to the bed to give Sophie a kiss before slipping out the door. In the guest bedroom across the hall, she plugged her phone into the charger and turned to walk out as the floodlight beside the barn flickered on and off. It hadn't worked right in years. But it was drawing her eyes to the broken fence separating the Mackenna land from the Coldirons.

Its weak posts and broken rails mirrored the boundary between her and McCrea. It had once been strong and resolute, like the animosity she had for him over abandoning Sophie. It had divided them, but a part of that barrier had been torn down tonight. So where did they go from here? Back to being friends? Or a step closer to being lovers?

The light flickered again and then faded to black.

"What the hell are you doing?" she asked herself, knowing that playing with fire was going to get her burned all over again.

Chapter Eleven

There wasn't a chance McCrea could forget what had just happened.

Eleanor's creamy skin, damp from the shower. Her beautiful face flushed from the hot water. Her legs, smooth. Her pink-tipped toes, wiggling as one sexy little foot crossed the other. Her nipples, cresting beneath the thin towel covering her breasts.

He growled and scrubbed both hands over his face. And now he was staying for tea.

"I forgot how cool the house could be this time of year." She interrupted his thoughts, rubbing away the chill from her upper arms as she joined him in the kitchen. "I guess I should light the furnace."

She had changed from the towel into a pair of yoga pants and a t-shirt. And they failed miserably at detouring the ache in his crotch. Hell, she could be wearing one of those muumuu dresses and the damn thing would still be pitching a tent.

She opened the top cabinet adjacent to the stove and raised to her tiptoes. He should have been a gentleman and offered to help her with the cups. But he was no gentleman. And seeing her stretch to reach the top shelf had him remembering just how she tasted. Sweet. Warm. Innocent.

The muscles in her thighs extended, accentuating the smooth lines of her body. With her arms up, her t-shirt lifted to unveil the smooth skin of her lower back.

Shit.

"I could build a fire," he volunteered, because he needed something to do other than watch her. And it would be romantic.

Hold on, Casanova. Where're you going with this? Nowhere. We're having tea.

And nothing sexual could possibly happen where tea was involved. Tea was as incorruptible as lace curtains and fluffy white rabbits.

Yes, tea was safe. Lace curtains and fluffy white rabbits, he reminded himself, trying to adhere to non-sexual objects.

Concentrate.

Lace.

White, see-through material. Material that allowed the hint of nipples and curves. Eleanor in white lace. White lace panties and bra. Or better yet, Eleanor in one of those sexy little lingerie numbers that hugged her breasts without panties.

Damnit.

Fluffy, white rabbits. Long ears. Furry tails. Fishnet stockings. High heels. Fuck!

She turned with the tea kettle in hand, her lips parted and her eyes soft and compliant. "That would be nice."

Nice? *Oh, baby, if you only knew what I was thinking!*

He scrubbed his jaw, returned her smile, and headed for his boots near the front door. He was so damn far from nice right now. Because all he wanted to do was strip those sexy little yoga pants off her round ass and go balls deep into her soft, wet body until the ache in his dick was gone. Instead, he was building a goddamn fire.

He snatched his boots as he went outside and didn't bother with his jacket. The night air was cool, but it did nothing for the burn he was feeling. He shouldn't be staying for tea. But he was. He was staying for any damn thing she offered.

On the porch, he yanked on one boot and then the other and then jogged down the steps and across the backyard on his way to the lean-to where Rose had kept the firewood. He rummaged through the unused pile, stacking one arm with split logs and grabbing a handful of kindling before turning back into the house.

He took deep breaths, trying to clear his thoughts, and concentrated on the path in front of him. More so, the path this night was headed.

He wanted her, but there was the history between them.

She had opened her heart to him, trusted him, and given herself to him out of love. He had misused that trust and let his dick talk him into making love to her before he proposed, and before he told her about his granddad's demands. A part of him wasn't sorry about that. If he had proposed first, they would have never made love, and they wouldn't have Sophie.

He relished that night, held on to it as if it were the only lifeline in a turbulent ocean. Her virginity was his.

He was her first, no matter how many lovers she took to her bed.

But she had moved on, and he was just a mistake in her past. She wasn't interested in rebuilding Redemption. She was a successful businesswoman with a lover.

He shook his head as if he could shake away the thoughts of her in bed with the tattooed cop. He couldn't. "Shit."

McCrea pushed the door open and kicked his boots off as the teakettle whistled.

"After Grandma had the furnace installed, we hardly used the fireplace," she said from the kitchen. "There hasn't been a fire in it in years. I'm not sure it still works."

He stacked the logs on the wood rack. "It's probably full of bats and bird shit," he mumbled under his breath. "You could have just lit the furnace. But no, a fire is more romantic. A fire with a cozy cup of tea." He laughed, but despite his humor, the whole domestic thing felt good. The three of them under one roof. Sophie asleep upstairs. Eleanor in the kitchen and him building a fire. "You'll be wading through the flower beds come spring."

God, he hoped so.

Eleanor popped her head into the living room. "Did you say something?"

"Nope." He crouched on his knees, looking up to find the damper. He tried pulling the handle open, but it wouldn't budge. So, he rolled onto his back and used both hands. "The damn thing is —" His words were lost in a thick blanket of soot. He sat up, spitting and blinking, and Eleanor burst into laughter. "Oh, you think this is funny, do you?"

She held up a finger while trying to catch her

breath. "I'm — sorry! It's just — " She took a deep breath, tears edging her blue eyes.

It was good to see them filled with happiness and laughter instead of hurt and sadness. And it was good to know that he was the cause of it, even if he looked like a total jackass right now.

She cleared her throat, but the smile stayed. "I'll get the paper towels." She hurried into the kitchen and returned, rolling off a handful. With her bottom lip held in place by her teeth, she looked him up and down as she held them out. "Maybe I should just take you out back and use the water hose."

McCrea playfully snatched the roll from her, forgoing the ones in her hand. "And freeze my balls off? No, thanks." He rolled off a plentiful amount, wiped his face, and unbuttoned his shirt. "Any chance you could throw this in the washer?"

Her smile wavered slightly. "Sure."

He handed her the shirt, catching her eyes on his chest. It was the sexiest, most bashful gaze he had seen in a while. And hardly the reaction of a woman with a lover like officer Rebel.

He swatted his thighs, purposefully drawing her eyes downward to a very evident hard on. "It looks as though my jeans escaped damage."

A quick glance at his crotch dusted her cheeks crimson. "Uh — that's good. There are towels and shampoo in the bathroom." She backed away and retreated into the laundry room adjacent to the kitchen.

Did experienced women blush? None that he knew did.

Interesting, very damn interesting.

McCrea took the steps two at a time and tried not to leave a trail into the bathroom. He stripped off his jeans and winced at his pale pink underwear. A red shirt had made it into the whites yesterday and now all his under-wear — he wiggled his toes — and socks were pink. He made a mental note to buy new ones and hid them under his jeans before climbing into the shower.

The water in the pipes quickly ran hot. McCrea ducked his head under the spray and began rinsing off a layer of soot. Black water swirled around his feet as he looked for the shampoo she had mentioned.

It hung from the shower caddy along with the soap and a mesh sponge. He picked up the sponge and cra-dled it in his palm. In his mind's eye, he saw the sudsy sponge sliding over Eleanor's nipples, down to the soft-ness of her belly and lower, to the dark blonde curls at the apex of her thighs.

"Shit," he hissed, cramming the sponge back in the caddy. He flipped open the shampoo lid and sniffed the flowery scent that was uniquely Eleanor, and quickly snapped it shut. The shit was an aphrodisiac. It also went back into the caddy.

He whisked the shower curtain back and grabbed a bar of soap from the sink to wash his hair with.

After the soot was gone, he braced his arms against the wall to let the hot water pour over his head as the memories of his one night with Eleanor returned.

The feel of her silky skin sliding across his had gen-erated a low throaty groan from her lips. The arch of her back and the rhythm of her hips rocking against his aroused him while the soft purr of her satisfied cry as he took her tormented him. He hissed and flipped the water to cold.

He made himself endure the frigid water to cool his body. But even then, there was no guarantee his hard-on wouldn't come back. He hadn't had sex in four years, and the last time he had, it was with her.

His body had one hell of a memory.

McCrea dried and redressed, save his socks, and headed back downstairs. He was unexcited by the promise of tea, but was thrilled to be spending time with her. As he hit the top step, Eleanor walked back into the living room, holding two cups.

She glanced up, smiling. "Your shirt will be ready for the dryer soon."

"Thanks. I think I got most of it," he said and crammed his pink socks into his boots by the door. "But you may have to trash the shower curtain."

"I'm sorry my fireplace threw up on you." She winced and set both cups on the coffee table. "Maybe I should light the furnace instead."

McCrea gave her a wounded look. "Are you trying to take away my man card?"

"No. Never." She chuckled. "Have at it."

He set about the task, and when the fire caught, he warmed his hands. "Success."

"Your man card has been saved," she declared and handed him his tea.

Swallow and smile. Remember that, no matter what it tastes like.

"Have you had herbal tea before?" she questioned, the edge of her lips lifting with the hint of a grin.

"No. This," he held his cup up to toast his induction, "is my first."

"Are you worried about your man card?"

He was about to partake in tea while wearing pink underwear. Hell, yes, he was worried. "Extremely."

"It will be our little secret," she assured him.

There was something dark and naughty about them doing something that needed to be kept a secret.

Damn naughty.

"Sophie will be pleased to learn her daddy is a tea drinker," she said, blowing softly across the hot surface of the tea. "We have regular tea parties."

"I can't wait," he said, ruefully.

"Don't worry," she said. "You're not the first guy who's attended. That was Harley, Hank, and Tracey's son. They're best friends. She even talked Nix into it."

A bitter taste coated McCrea's mouth. "Officer Rebel doesn't look like the kind of guy who's into tea parties."

The humor in her eyes dimmed. "Nix is a good man and a very dear friend."

Friend?

"Oh, I have something for you," she announced, before darting into the dining room. She came back to the couch with a small trunk. "I found it under Grandma's bed."

He set his tea on the table and took a seat next to her. "What's in it?"

She laid it in his lap and sat down next to him. "See for yourself."

His fingers moved over the worn leather. "It looks old."

"Are you one of those sick and twisted people who won't tear the wrapping paper off their gifts?" she asked, her eyes bright with excitement. "Open it!"

"Okay." He laughed and did as she instructed. Dozens of folded letters, some still in the envelope, were stacked neatly inside.

Her smile widened. "They're addressed to a woman

named Callie Coldiron. I'm assuming she's one of your relatives."

"Callie was my great-grandma," he said, pulling a letter out.

"I thumbed through a couple of them. I hope you don't mind," she was quick to say.

"I don't mind."

She leaned closer to examine the letter with him. "Her penmanship is so beautiful."

The only beauty McCrea saw was Eleanor's. The thin arch of her brows, the delicate line of her cheek-bones, and the soft, supple redness of her lips. "Have I ever told you about her?"

"No." She tucked her feet under her and leaned in closer, ready to listen the way she did around the campfire when they were kids.

"My granddad was orphaned as a little boy and taken in by Callie's father, a wealthy businessman from Virginia. When my granddad came to Texas searching for answers about his family, he was arrested and thrown in jail for murder. Callie made the trip to Texas to find the killer and free him."

Eleanor's eyes held a familiar dreamy glaze. "Did she?"

"She must have." He laughed. "I'm here."

She gently punched him on the shoulder. "Now who's being the smartass?"

His laughter dwindled off, but his smile remained. "This never gets old."

"What?"

"Sharing my family history with you. You're always so attentive to what I have to say about it. Why is that?"

Her lips lifted to one side as she thought. "I guess

it's because I don't know much about my own family history. I'll probably never know who my real father is, and the only things I know about the Mackenna's are what little Grandma told me as a girl."

"Your great-granddad was the sheriff who arrested my great-granddad for murder," he informed her.

Her eyes grew wide, and her jaw dropped open. "Are you serious?"

"I am. I learned that last year while digging through the county archives. It turns out my great-granddad was helping yours infiltrate a ruthless band of outlaws."

"Wow," she whispered in awe. "We share a lot of history."

"We certainly do, more than either of us ever suspected," he agreed, thinking more about their future than their past. "My great-grandparents were married for over fifty years and had six children together. I'm named after one of them."

"I didn't know that." She looked intrigued. "So, there's another McCrea Coldiron in the family tree?"

"Tucker McCrea Coldiron made a name for himself in the oil fields. And from the stories I've read, he was quite a hell-raiser."

"He was a Coldiron," she said, grinning. "That goes without saying."

That sexy grin had the potential to be devastating, and like a moth to a flame, it drew him closer. A few more inches and he could claim those lips and savor the sweetness of her mouth.

But she pulled back to reach for her cup on the table.

"I've been looking for these since I was a kid," he said, slipping the letter back inside the trunk. "Thank you."

"You're welcome," she said and handed him his cup.

She sipped her tea, carefully as not to burn herself, and he followed the path it took, watching her throat contract. The heat of the liquid deepened her lips to a dusky red. Her tongue appeared, waxing her bottom lip glossy.

Risking pneumonia in the cold shower had been in vain. And an icy plunge into the Antarctic Ocean wouldn't stave the erection he had right now.

Front and center, long and mean.

"Delicious," he said, setting his cup on the coffee table.

Her brows pinched slightly. "You haven't tasted it yet."

"No, but I've tasted you." He lowered his head to salvage the remnants of the tea from her lips. It wasn't meant to be an intrusive kiss. But rather a sample of the herbal elixir which threatened his manhood, a remedy and an indulgent reminder of how hot they were together.

As always, Eleanor's lips capitulated to his. It was an exciting power he couldn't get enough of. Would it always be like this with her? Would his heart always thrash around in his chest when she was near? Would she always excite him with a mere brush of her lips, a touch, or a whisper?

She broke the kiss and placed her cup beside of his. "You," she inhaled a ragged breath as she stood, "can't keep doing that."

He reclaimed his cup and tasted the tea without her sweetness. "The tea is good," he said calmly, as if the kiss hadn't happened at all.

He picked up her cup and held it out to her. "Aren't you going to finish yours?"

McCrea's cool composure needled Eleanor.

Damn him!

How could he prance around in nothing but a pair of jeans, looking like a cowboy god straight out of rodeo heaven, kiss her and then have the audacity to act like it was nothing?

Why weren't his hands shaking? Why wasn't he at a loss for words? *Because he's McCrea and this is a game to him.*

A game that, if she was willing to play, would allow them to pick up where they left off the night Sophie was conceived.

The fact he was still able to take her from ice-cold to red-hot with just a kiss made her want to throw the tea in his face.

She didn't accept the cup or attempt to be amicable. "Are you trying to seduce me?"

He coughed and wiped his mouth. "That was frank."

"Yeah, well," she massaged her temple. "I've never been good at games, McCrea, which is why I lost the last one we played."

He set the cups down. "That night wasn't a game, and neither is this."

"Then what is it?"

He stood and scrubbed the back of his head, looking down as if answers were going to sprout from the floorboards.

"I'm not a girl who thinks the sun rises and sets in

McCrea Coldiron. I know now that you're a man who values land and business over love."

The desire in his eyes turned cold, but he said nothing.

"I'm thrilled you want to be a part of Sophie's life," she said. "And I asked you to stay and have a cup of tea, so we could talk about custody and visitation. Not so we could have sex. You hurt me. You slept with me, then made it clear the only way we could be together was if I accepted that damn business agreement. An agreement that would have made me a divorcee by the time I was twenty."

The muscle in his jaw flexed. "I said I was —"

"Sorry. I know. You've made your apologies, but that doesn't make everything magically disappear. I don't trust you, McCrea, and being with you isn't easy for me. I have a lot of scars where you're concerned. Scars that are only now starting to heal. Know that before you try charming your way into my panties again."

She stood there, stripped of her pride with her heart open and raw, waiting for him to say something.

But he didn't. He just stood there too, making a quiet summation of what she had said. When she couldn't stand his silence any longer, she started for the stairs. "I'm going to bed. Lock the door when you leave."

Chapter Twelve

Eleanor woke to the inexplicable aroma of coffee and the sound of giggles. She rolled onto her back and stared up at the ceiling.

Though she knew right away, the giggles belonged to Sophie, her mind couldn't explain the coffee until she heard a rumble of deep male laughter.

"McCrea," she groaned and covered her head with the pillow. But the blaring ringtone of her cell phone made Eleanor fling the pillow into the air. She raised on an elbow, squinted to make out the name, and hit answer. "What was in that tea, Sage?"

"Good morning to you too," Sage chuckled. "They never tell me what's in their brews, only that the secret —"

"Is in the stir." Eleanor plopped back onto the bed, thinking there could have been some serious stirring last night if she hadn't walked away. "Tell me you have a buyer for Redemption.

"I have a buyer for Redemption," Sage announced.

"Don't toy with me. I haven't had my coffee yet," she grumbled, knowing she would have to face McCrea to get it.

"I'm serious, and so is the buyer."

She bolted upright.

"I got a call early this morning from a lawyer with an offer from a client who wished to remain anonymous."

"That's strange."

"Not really," Sage reassured her. "It happens all the time. Is it a problem?"

"No, I mean, I don't think so. Money is money, right?"

"My thoughts exactly."

She glanced around at all the furniture, linens, and pictures that were in this one room. There was still so much to do. "But I didn't expect it to sell this quickly."

"The lawyer says his client wants it to be a wedding present for a woman he's head over heels in love with."

Eleanor was moved to tears. "Oh, that's so sweet."

"And romantic," Sage agreed with a long sigh. "I can see him carrying her over the threshold. They'll have a baby or two and buy a dog."

Sage painted the picture of the perfect life. A life Eleanor wanted to believe was possible. But love was a volatile emotion. It was faulty and unpredictable. It burned and left scars. It scattered families, left children fatherless, and it hurt. Yes, love and marriage were as incompatible as oil and water. "What time should I come to your office?"

"Give me a few days to get everything ready," Sage said.

"A few days?" she questioned.

"The storm uprooted one of the old trees next to my building. I have busted glass all over my office, and most of my files are waterlogged."

She winced. "I'm sorry."

"I feel pretty lucky, considering some folks lost barns and cattle," Sage said. "So I'm not going to complain, but I'll be in touch. I just wanted you to know."

"Thanks, Sage." She tossed the phone onto the bed and fell back. It was done. Redemption had a buyer. In a few days, the home she grew up in and the ranch her grandparents had worked so hard to keep would be owned by strangers. A pang of sadness enveloped her. Was she really doing this? Was she selling Redemption, her family ranch and childhood home? A place filled with wonderful memories and love?

The sound of McCrea's deep voice floated up the stairs. Each time he laughed, it reverberated through her body, hitting all the right notes. A familiar ache swirled and tightened her lower belly, making her body hum with a sensual melody. One he had written four years ago.

More than once, Eleanor had dreamed about moving back home and teaching Sophie how to ride.

She could find Romeo and bring him home, or buy a new horse and a dog, a Labrador or a Shepherd. And maybe she could love again, with a man who wanted babies and would be supportive. A man unlike the heartbreak cowboy downstairs.

It was nice to think about finding a guy to settle down with, but doing so would require more than woolgathering. It would require her to date, mingle, and get to know the eligible bachelors in town.

But how would she support herself? By going back to work for Ed? She wasn't above waiting tables, but a ranch the size of Redemption would need a crew to operate efficiently. And repairs would have to be made before that happened. She would never make enough money to do that by working at the Roadhouse.

Staring at a crack in the ceiling, Eleanor reminded herself that there was no use in deviating from her plan or in daydreaming about things she couldn't have. Selling Redemption was the only choice she had.

Another round of Sophie's infectious giggles floated up the stairs, replacing her sadness with love. Yesterday had been wonderful. McCrea was ecstatic about Sophie. And today was a new day with giggles and laughter between father and daughter. A day of new possibilities and beginnings. And she was going to enjoy it.

She showered, brushed her teeth, and whipped her hair into a ponytail. She rummaged through her bag for a comfortable pair of jeans and a top, ready to busy herself with packing away family heirlooms and memories.

Downstairs, she tiptoed quietly across the living room to watch Sophie and McCrea.

He leaned against the sink with her grandmas Don't Cook Bacon Naked apron stretched across his chest. It had been a gag gift from the ladies at the garden club.

But there wasn't anything funny about the way it fit over the width of his broad chest, hiding just enough of his torso to make a woman wonder what was behind it. Not that she had to wonder. Eleanor knew, in detail, what was under that apron and those low-riding jeans.

McCrea cradled a mixing bowl in the crook of his arm. The smooth lines of his forearms, covered by a sparse dusting of dark hair, flexed with each flip of the whisk. His long fingers curled around the handle, making it appear miniature in size.

She loved the way his hands held things, small

things no one else thought mattered. Broken things that needed mending. The way they fought, the way they loved, and the way they held their daughter.

Sophie, who was sitting on the counter next to him, swung her feet in wide circles. "Do you think Mommy is pretty?"

McCrea added an unmeasured helping of pancake mixture to the bowl and sloshed the watery mix with the whisk. "Your momma is a beautiful lady, and you look just like her."

Sophie's feet stopped in mid-swing, a sure sign she was thinking. "Are you and Mommy going to sleep in the same bed? Harwley's mommy and daddy sleep in the same bed."

Oh, no. Eleanor's stomach flipped at Sophie's unexpected question.

"Er — uh—," he stammered and sat the bowl next to her. "Do you want to mix while I look for the griddle?"

Sophie held the whisk up and watched batter drip from the end." He said they make funny sounds, too. Why do they make funny sounds, Daddy?"

Eleanor clamped a hand over her mouth to quiet her laugh and hurried into the kitchen to rescue McCrea. "Good morning."

"Mommy!" Sophie yelled.

His shoulders relaxed. "Thank God, you're here."

"We're making pancakes!" Sophie said and held up the whisk as proof.

Eleanor held her hand under the loaded utensil, catching a glop of batter before it hit the floor. "Yummy."

He moved Sophie to the dinette chair. "How's your hand?" he asked, wiping the batter from her fingers with a dishrag.

"It's fine." The antiseptic ointment she slathered on it last night had taken the redness out, and it wasn't as painful as before. "I thought you went home."

"I fell asleep while waiting for my shirt to dry. Sophie woke me this morning." When the batter was gone, he took both of her hands in his. "I owe you an apology for the way I acted last night. I was completely out of line. I'm sorry."

Because of Sophie, she would always be tethered to him. There would always be disagreements and problems to work through. They needed to be able to find solutions and function as a parenting team. They couldn't do that if they weren't able to move past their mistakes. "Apology accepted."

He lifted her hands to his lips for a quick and polite kiss. "Thank you."

The softness of his lips grazing her knuckles heated her core, and her second thoughts about selling Redemption evaporated like a gin and tonic in the hot Texas sun. "Are you going to explain why Harley's mommy and daddy make funny sounds?"

"No," he chuckled and switched on the gas burner. "Where is the griddle?"

"Down here," she said, reaching into the cabinet beside him for her grandma's cast iron griddle. "Sage called."

"And?"

"She has a buyer."

He glanced at her, lifting both brows. "So soon?"

"Yeah, I know," she said, sighing as she surveyed the kitchen. "Maybe I should have hired Kara and Tiffany to help me pack."

He pointed the spatula at her. "I'll make a deal with you. You come to the auction next Saturday night and bid on me with the money you would have used to pay them. In return, I'll help you pack."

The scent of a set-up mingled with the sweet smell of the pancake batter. "Why would I do that when I can just hire the girls?" she asked.

"The money from the auction is going to the foundation. Plus, you'd be saving me from Brook Tidwell."

She had to grin because maybe he was telling the truth about Brook. "Why would I want to do that? I've heard revenge is sweet."

A wince hit his face before he turned back to the stove. "I guess you enjoyed watching Bubba throw that punch."

"I'm not really a vengeful person. If I were, I would have told Hank the truth about what happened in the storeroom, and you would have more than a black eye."

"That would have been your mistake, darlin'. I wasn't in the mood for an ass-kicking." He scratched the sexy stubble on his jaw. "And it would have been one hell of a fight."

Eleanor knew that which is why she didn't divulge details about their kiss to Hank or Nix. "Well, contrary to what you believe, I don't enjoy watching you get beat up."

"I'm not sure I believe you," he teased with one eye skeptically narrow.

"Okay, so, if I agreed to help you —"

"When you agree. I am confident in my powers of persuasion."

So was she, and that was disconcerting to her because she had fallen under the power of McCrea's persuasion more than once. And the last time had left her with one hell of a hangover. Maybe there was an antidote for the magical spell. "Brook has more money than I do. What if she outbids me?"

"She won't. I'll make sure of it."

She remained doubtful about McCrea's motives. First, that he would want to be saved from the clutches of Ms. Gilmore County. Ha. That was laughable, and second, that he was willing to help her pack when he had been so fervently against her selling the place. "Hmmm… I don't know. It sounds hinky."

"There's nothing hinky about it. You're the one doing all the bidding," he shrugged a shoulder. "I'm just writing the check."

"I've attended a bachelor auction before, and they were less than tasteful."

His face lost all humor. "People around here take the Promise Point Foundation very seriously. It'll be tasteful. The guys don't strip, and the ladies don't grope."

She leaned a hip against the counter, intrigued by the sudden change in McCrea's demeanor. "What exactly does the foundation do?"

"It provides financial and emotional support for returning veterans and their families," he explained.

She was surprised by his answer. But she wasn't surprised about the support the small town had for its veterans. The courthouse lawn had several monuments dedicated to war heroes from all eras, and many businesses, like Ed's, showed their patriotism by erecting hero walls which proudly displayed the photos of service men and women, past and present. "Okay," she sighed. "What happens if I win?"

He pointed the spatula at himself. "You win a date with me."

Maybe McCrea wasn't sleeping with Brook. Maybe

she cared. Maybe she didn't. Maybe this was his way of tricking her into sleeping with him.

"A date with you? No, thanks." She dug into her pocket for the Post-It note only to have him snatch it from her fingers. "Hey! Give that back." She made a grab for it.

He held it up out of her reach. "No, I'm desperate and you need help packing," he stated ,then winked at Sophie, who was watching everything. "Besides, I want to spend all the time I can with Sophie before you leave."

Sophie's face lit up with joy. Damn. He had her. "Okay, fine," she groaned. "I guess it would be nice having someone around who could do all the heavy lifting. But there's a lot to do. I haven't even started in the attic."

"I'm your man." He grinned. "We can start this afternoon. But right now, we're making pancakes."

Sophie pushed a chair to the counter and climbed up for a better view.

Eleanor watched from a safe distance. "Are you sure you know what you're doing?"

Sophie crossed her little arms and adopted a frown. "Yeah, Daddy. Are you sure you know what you're doing?"

McCrea's lips twitched as he spooned small mounds of batter onto the griddle. "Watch and learn, ladies."

Eleanor was watching and learning, but nothing about pancakes. What she was learning was more dangerous than a failed flip. She was learning that waking up to giggles and coffee was something she could get used to.

She leaned a hip against the counter. "I'll be impressed when it doesn't land on the floor."

He glanced at Sophie. "Ready?"

Sophie shook her head up and down.

"How about you?" he asked, Eleanor.

She gave him a saucy look. "Impress me, Cowboy."

His sexy smile roasted her socks. He leaned closer so that only she could hear him. "I love it when you call me Cowboy. It makes me want to wear my spurs to bed."

"Sounds kinky," she dared, because flirting with him was addictive.

"Darlin', you have no idea." He eased the spatula under the edge of the pancake and started counting. "One, two —"

"Three!" Sophie yelled, and McCrea sent the pancake into the air.

It landed perfectly.

Sophie clapped. "You did it, Daddy!"

Eleanor was too busy picturing McCrea wearing nothing but boots and spurs to notice the flip. But she clapped anyway. "I'm sorry I ever doubted you."

"Do you have paper plates or are we dirtying the fine china?"

"Grandma didn't have fine china," she said wryly. "And if she had, she would have sold them to pay taxes or meet payroll. I brought paper plates, plastic cups, and utensils with me. Sophie, can you run into the living room and get them? They're in the grocery bag by the door."

Sophie scooted from the chair and took off running towards the living room.

Eleanor took the opportunity to watch McCrea flip more pancakes. With his back to her, she could admire his body without being noticed. And her fingers itched to trace the apron strings that hung low around his sexy backside.

God, she was insane for accepting his apology. Insane for asking him to stay for tea and a complete lunatic for checking out his ass. She shouldn't smile, laugh, or flirt with the man. McCrea was the enemy. Okay, maybe not the enemy, but he wasn't exactly a comrade either.

In less than twenty-four hours, he had gone from plaguing her dreams to standing half-naked in her grandma's kitchen, flipping pancakes. At this pace, they'd be having sex before the griddle had time to cool.

He was too comfortable and too assuming of his place in her life and in her house. And now he was going to be here every day until the packing was done.

She needed to lay out boundaries. "As Sophie's mom and dad, we have to learn how to get along and work as a team."

"I agree."

"It's obvious that we're attracted to each other. But we can't have a repeat of last night. So I think you should know where your boundaries are."

He turned with a surprised mien to his face. "My boundaries?"

"No more kissing," she whispered. "Period. You can't spend the night again. And no more walking around half naked."

"I get it," he said, giving her a sexy wink. "This," he waved a hand over his apron-covered chest, "is too much of a temptation for you?"

Damn right it was.

She crossed her arms. "I'm serious. I don't want Sophie to get confused about our relationship."

"Sophie or you?"

"Sophie," she snapped. "I am not the least bit con-fused about you, me, or us."

"Sophia Rose Mackenna is the most level-headed and intelligent four-year-old on the face of the planet, remember? So don't use her as an excuse for your ridiculous boundaries."

"They are not ridiculous."

"Just admit that what happened last night scares the hell out of you."

"I found them!" Sophie shrieked as she ran back into the kitchen holding the bag.

"Thank you, sweetheart." McCrea accepted the plates ,and the subject was dropped.

She was sure he was building a case for a future talk about his boundaries. But for now, they both would play nice for Sophie's sake.

He stacked three pancakes on a plate and handed them to her. She set it in front of Sophie, added syrup, and used a fork to cut it into small bites.

"I want milk, Mommy," Sophie said.

Eleanor opened the refrigerator and groaned at its contents. A can of Diet Pepsi, a pint of milk, and six eggs. The cupboards and pantry were the same. And her only option for filling them—other than limping Old Blue into town on three wheels—was to ask the cook for a ride.

She took out the milk and poured Sophie a glass. "I hate to ask, but I need a ride to the grocery store."

"Don't think twice about asking me for anything," he said as a sharp tap on the front door was accompa-nied by a, "Hello!"

Eleanor cringed, and McCrea swore.

"That's a bad word, Daddy," Sophie informed him and stuffed more pancakes into her mouth.

"Sorry, sweetheart," he apologized with a pained expression. "You better open the door before Mouthy Mildred beats the thing off its hinges."

Hank couldn't hold a candle to the power in the old woman's knock. Wishing she had at least one cup of coffee in her, Eleanor hurried to unlock the deadbolt and open the door. "Hi, Mrs. Satterfield."

The woman She caught Eleanor's face with both hands. "I didn't know you were in town!"

She withdrew, fighting the iciness in Mildred's bony digits. "It's nice to see you, too."

Mildred stretched her neck to see above Eleanor's shoulders. "I thought I heard voices. Are you alone, or did your husband come with you?"

Most of the town worked hard to appease Mildred because of her money and influence. Rose had tolerated her to keep peace and because of her association in the garden society. An almost sacred organization in her grandma's eyes.

"No, my husband didn't come with me — "

"You are married!" Mildred clapped her hands together. "Rose was so afraid you were never going to get married. Or that you would marry McCrea."

McCrea had been the subject of Mildred's gossip since he had been old enough to mutton bust. So, it didn't surprise Eleanor when he yanked the door open with a chafed smile. "Morning, Mildred."

Mildred jumped, startled by his sudden appearance, and decorated her wrinkled face with a sour smile. "So, the rumors about you two are true."

"Most of the rumors in this town start with you, Mildred. So, I doubt they are," he said without politeness. "Is that why you're here? To poke your meddlesome old nose in where it doesn't belong because you saw my truck parked in the driveway?"

"Well..."

"Let me satisfy your curiosity."

With the movement of a boa constrictor, he eased behind Eleanor and wrapped his arms around her waist. "I spent the night, and we had sex in her old room. It was teddy bears and pompoms all night, just the way daddy likes it."

Eleanor bit her lip to keep from laughing as Sophie bounced from the kitchen and up to the door. She smiled up at McCrea and licked the back of her syrup covered fork. "I want more pancakes, Daddy."

"You can have mine, sweetheart," he said.

Smiling, Sophie skipped back to the kitchen to devour his portion of pancakes.

Mildred's gray eyes grew wide, and Eleanor knew everyone in town would know about Sophie before lunch.

He moved to the doorway. "Are the rumors true about the historical society hiring Tony Chaves as their dig liaison?"

Mildred's posture straightened, and a droll expression donned her face. "Tony is a capable young man with a background in archeology."

"He's a thief," he said flatly. "I've told the guards to turn him away at the gate. He's not allowed back on my land or around any of the artifacts. And I don't give a damn who it pisses off."

Mildred's gasp was audible. "You're completely incorrigible and uncouth, and nothing like your granddad!"

"No, I'm not," he agreed before slamming the door

in her face. He raked both hands through his hair and took a deep breath before letting it out slowly.

It was obvious that Mildred's snippy remark about Wade being disappointed in him had cut him deep. McCrea had practically worshiped his granddad and always worked hard to live up to his expectations. That was not an easy task.

He whipped the apron over his head. "I have to go," he said, snatching his shirt from the back of the couch. "Mildred has Mom on speed dial, and I don't want her to find out she's a grandma by way of that old busybody. I'll be back soon."

Chapter Thirteen

The door to the mudroom opened and a wet and muddy Jess dragged in, winding McCrea's chipper whistle to an end.

With circles under his eyes, Jess hung his hat on the row of hooks beside the door and squinted at the clock above the sink. "Why are you whistling at eight o'clock in the morning? Hell," he swore, his hand gripping the place on his thigh where the pins were. "Why are you whistling at all?"

McCrea filled the reservoir with water and added coffee to the filter before he answered his sleep-deprived brother. "I had breakfast with two beautiful ladies."

Jess shrugged off his wet coat, hung it beside his hat, and sat down on the bench to remove his boots. "If one of those beautiful ladies was wearing stiletto boots and tight leather pants at the Rebel Road the other night, I want details."

He knew this was Jess's humorous attempt at distracting the pain in his thigh because they didn't share the details of their love life with anyone. "She was wearing a smile when I left, and that's all the details you're getting."

"Such a gentleman," Jess said, with a half grin. "At least one of us had a good night."

His good night consisted of sitting in a dusty laundry room listening to the dryer while reflecting on what an ass he had been. But the pancakes had been excellent. And so was the company.

He watched Jess wince as he raised his leg to remove his boot. "Where have you been?"

"The storm hit the Gates Ranch—hard. Logan called me after it was over to help round up what was left of the bulls."

"You should have called me."

"I did."

He pulled out his cell phone and sure enough, there were several missed calls from Jess. "Sorry. I guess I left it in my jacket pocket."

"Don't worry about it," Jess said.

"How bad was the damage?"

"They lost the lower barn and some good bulls. But no one was hurt."

He didn't have to see the grim look on Jess's face to know the Gates Ranch wasn't in a financial position to lose bulls or barns. Since their father's death, the brothers had been struggling to keep the family ranch afloat. Violet's coffee business helped, but they were a long way from being profitable.

"Logan has a good head on his shoulders, and with help from us and the community, they'll bounce back."

"Jesus," McCrea groaned, hearing the unmistakable

sound of Lou bouncing down the stairs. "I forgot she was home."

By the time she was done taking her pound of flesh, there might not be enough of him to tell his mom and dad that they were grandparents.

Jess raised from the bench. "You're not the first man who's resorted to prayer when they heard Lou coming."

Though Louisa was the baby, his sister was a force. Blessed with brainy wit and unmatched effrontery, Lou could make the toughest man cringe and run for cover, and McCrea had done his share of hiding.

When she flipped the ties of her bathrobe into a knot and gave him a gloating smile, he regretted not taking the back door.

"That eye looks painful." If there had been an ounce of sleep in those mischievous brown eyes of hers, it had been stomped out by cynicism the moment her bare feet touched the floor.

Jess yawned. "You should have seen it yesterday."

Lou wrinkled her nose as she walked past McCrea to the fridge for her morning OJ. "Is that maple syrup and," she sniffed, "chimney soot, I smell?"

McCrea lifted the front of his shirt to his nose. "You can smell that?"

"No," she admitted. "I just got off the phone with El. We had a long talk about chimney soot and pancakes."

"And to think I wanted details." Jess playfully shoved Lou out of his way as he reached for a coffee cup from the top cabinet. "When are you moving out?"

"When are you?" she returned, bumping him with her hip.

"I moved out three years ago."

"And yet, you're here for breakfast, lunch, and dinner," she reminded him. "And I bet your tighty-whities are in the laundry."

"I draw the line at carting my Superman underwear in for Mommy to wash," Jess said, filling his cup with coffee.

The conversation between his two younger siblings would deteriorate into idle threats and mild cursing, Lou being first, to do both. So McCrea was thankful Jess changed the subject. "I thought you found a house."

"Not a house, a small apartment," she said, taking sips of her juice. "I have an appointment with Mrs. Putney this afternoon about renting Dawn Shelly's old apartment above the flower shop. Dawn told me her boyfriend asked her to move in with him. But I know for a fact that she was evicted because customers were complaining about the lewd noises coming from up there on her days off."

"That apartment does have thin walls," Jess commented.

Lou faked a gag and opened a bag of whole wheat bread. "I don't want to know how you know that."

Jess sipped his coffee. "No, you don't."

Having snagged his travel mug from the truck this morning, McCrea flipped open the lid and poured in coffee. "You haven't been home for more than a couple of days, and you're already up to speed on all the gossip. Is there anything you don't know?"

She popped the bread into the toaster, and surprisingly, her response wasn't sarcastic. "I didn't know about Sophie. I would have never played matchmaker if I had."

Staring down at the cup, McCrea smiled. "If you

hadn't, I might have never known her." Lou came closer, looped her arm through his, and laid her head on his shoulder. "Does this mean you forgive me for what happened four years ago?" he asked.

She made a small measurement with her finger and thumb. "I'm this close," she said, staring up at him with those big brown eyes of hers the way she had when they were kids—full of love, and like he was the best big brother in the world. "But if you let her walk away again, I'll never forgive you." Her toast popped up, and she reached for it.

"I may not be able to stop her from leaving town again, Lou."

She bit into the toast. "I know that." Then she paused to chew. "All I'm saying is don't be such a prick."

"I'm never a prick," he argued.

Lou snorted. "Right."

"Hardin, stop that!" His mothers' low-key giggle echoed out of the dining room.

"I can't resist you, Belle," his father's deep baritone voice brought forth another giggle, but this time it was higher.

"Have you told them yet?" Lou questioned.

"No." McCrea stepped to the dining room door and eased it open.

He saw their embrace, the way he had witnessed it a hundred times over the course of his life in this house. They were standing near the window. His dad's arms were locked around his mother's waist, holding her tight against him, securing her in his love and life. He whispered something intimate in her ear, and she blushed and giggled as though she were a teenager again.

Youth overtook them, and their age fell away. The

magic of love kept them young. It healed whatever hurt they had, mended wounds, and refreshed them in a way nothing else could. Their love had that kind of power to it.

He didn't want to interrupt the private moment, just enjoy it. He missed living in a house with love, not seeing it or witnessing it. More than that, he missed not having it in his life. He wanted it. He craved it. He wanted someone he could love openly, without motive or fear, and he wanted that love returned.

"Do you think we'll ever be that lucky?" Jess asked from behind him.

"I hope so." That answer rooted itself deep inside him.

Lou shoved passed him and Jess, knocking them both through the door and into the dining room. "They were eavesdropping again."

"Again?" Belle laughed as Hardin kissed her cheek.

McCrea tossed his hat on the table, pulled a chair out, and sat down. "Do you know how traumatic it is for me to see you two making out in the dining room?"

Jess shook his head disapprovingly. "Yeah, I won't be able to sleep tonight." He took a ham biscuit from the serving plate in the middle of the table and sat down across from McCrea. He bit off half and ask, "Don't you two have a room?"

Lou stole a piece of his ham. "I think it's romantic."

"You would," Jess mumbled, smacking her hand.

Belle gave Hardin an impish smile. "I guess we shouldn't tell them what happened on the table before they came in."

McCrea couldn't help but grin. At first glance, his mother seemed out of place in the rough and dirty world of cattle ranching. But those who knew her knew her perfectly styled hair and flawless makeup were merely window dressing.

Belle Coldiron could be a sweaty-brow, work-'till-sundown, dirt-under-her-nails rancher. She was one hell of a good cook and the best mother anyone could have. Her spontaneity and dry humor made her fun and easy to be around.

"That's gross." Lou's tone was flat.

Jess stopped in mid-chew and held his biscuit protectively. "No, that's disgusting," he mumbled with a mouth full of food. He pointed to the two of them. "The dining room is off limits for your kinky sexual interludes."

"Oh, I'm joking. Lighten up." She laughed and did a double take at McCrea's black eye. "I thought you'd grown out of fighting."

"Did you win?" Hardin asked.

Jess laughed out, "No."

"He got punched in the face by a big guy named Hank, and they spent the night in jail," Lou rushed out.

Belles' face fell with the idea of her sons being incarcerated. "Jail?"

McCrea sat back in his chair. "Lou didn't mention that it was all a misunderstanding."

Lou smiled sweetly. "They were fist fighting in the parking lot, Mom." All that was missing were her braids and braces.

Jess poked her in the ribs with a finger. "Traitor."

Lou resorted to sticking her tongue out.

"We ran into Eleanor last night at a bar in Austin," McCrea explained.

Belle smiled. "She gave you the black eye?"

McCrea cleared his throat. "No, Hank did, then a cop showed up and our asses went to jail."

Hardin rubbed his jaw. "Is Hank her boyfriend?"

"Hank is her business partner. Her boyfriend is the cop," Lou filled in while wearing an obnoxious smile.

Belle covered her mouth to hide her amusement. "How is Eleanor?"

"All grown up," Jess said, before popping the last of the biscuit into his mouth.

"That was bound to happen," Hardin said.

Belle's phone beeped. "I have three missed calls from Mildred. Oh, she's calling again."

"Don't answer it!" McCrea shouted.

"Why not?" Belle questioned, then frowned. "Dear Lord, McCrea. What did you do?"

"It's complicated," he answered.

"It always is with you," Lou snickered.

"Hi, Mildred." Belle flinched and held the phone away from her ear. "He did what?"

Hardin leaned in to hear. "What is she saying?"

"Something about McCrea cooking bacon naked," she said.

Lou raised her top lip. "Eww..."

"Mildred, please calm down. Mildred, I can't hear you — She hung up on me!" Belle gave McCrea a mean eye and repeated her question. "What did you do?"

He told them about the break-in at Sunset Terrace Estates, the disappearance of his coin collection, and about Chaves's new position with the historical society.

"How did he manage that?" Hardin asked Belle.

"We didn't vote on hiring a dig liaison," she was quick to say. "And if we had, it sure wouldn't have been Tony Chaves."

"We also think Tony is the reason we've had so many rescues out near the Twisted J," Jess said.

"Hope looked a little better yesterday, don't you think?" Lou had taken a special interest in the mare, stopping by Promise Point every day to spend time with her. His sister could chew a man up and spit him out several times over. But there wasn't an animal she didn't love. She would be a dedicated veterinarian.

"It'll be touch and go for a while."

"Does Finn know about your suspicions?" Hardin asked.

McCrea took another sip of his coffee. "We talked about it, but he doesn't have the manpower to patrol a ranch the size of the Twisted J."

"I'll make some calls," Hardin told him. His dad belonged to several cattle, equine, and stock sale associations, and he had connections with ranchers from all over the Southwestern U.S. If Chaves were involved in the buying and selling of horses in any capacity, Hardin would find out.

"This is going to piss a lot of people off. It might even get you kicked out of the historical society," McCrea said.

"I doubt it. Mildred is the only bear in the group. Most of the ladies are sweet," Belle assured him.

"Sweet?" Jess nursed his backside. "Some of those gals are predators. I have a bruise from the last meeting you made me attend."

"Oh, hush. I'll have a talk with Mildred and have a luncheon for the ladies. McCrea, you can play hostess and served them cocktails. Are you free tomorrow night?" she teased, gathering the plates from the table.

"There's more," McCrea said, scrubbing the back of his neck. What was he going to tell his mother? That he had tried seducing Eleanor into becoming his wife to appease Wade, and now he was a daddy?

Hardin raised both brows. "More?"

Lou took the plates from Belle. "You need to sit down for this one, Mom."

He took a deep breath. "I'm a daddy."

Chapter Fourteen

leanor had dreamed of moments like this since she saw those two pink lines on the pregnancy test. Moments when Sophie would finally meet her family. But she had been a wreck since Mc-Crea told her they were having dinner with his parents.

Her frayed-bottom blue jeans and faded yard-sale t-shirts might have made her look like a rodeo drifter. But they were the practical choice for what she thought would be a working vacation at the ranch. She hadn't packed anything suitable for tonight's dinner.

She fidgeted with the pearlescent snaps of the dark blue and white checked western shirt she had dug out of the back of her closet. She could practically hear their screams as they strained to cover her breasts. "Are you sure the shirt isn't too tight?"

Had she just invited McCrea to look at her breasts? She had, and he was doing so. Thoroughly.

Desire darkened his eyes while humor tugged at his

lips. "You'll be fine as long as you don't take a deep breath."

"Thanks a lot," she said, letting out a long sigh that snapped the first two buttons. He chuckled, and she muttered a curse under her breath before snapping them back together. "They've gotten bigger since I had Sophie."

"I noticed," he said, tightening a hand around the steering wheel. "But you look beautiful. Now stop worrying. I don't understand why you're so nervous. It's just dinner."

After Eleanor came to live with her Grandma Rose, Rex tightened his hold on her mother and stepsister and forbade them from speaking to her again. It was hard at first, but Belle and Hardin had quickly welcomed her into their family by including her in every dinner, holiday, and birthday party. It wasn't like this was the first time she'd be sitting down to eat with the Coldirons. "How am I going to explain…? I mean, it's obvious we were more than friends."

He glanced into the back seat at Sophie and lowered his voice. "Are you worried because my parents know we've had sex?"

She twisted her fingers together. "No. Maybe. Yes." His laughter filled the cab. "It's not funny. What if they want to know why I haven't been back or why they haven't seen their granddaughter?"

"Mom and Dad don't care about any of that," he reassured her by giving her knee a gentle squeeze. "They were thrilled when I told them about Sophie. She'll be spoiled rotten in no time. They've always wanted grandkids."

Belle and Hardin were amazing people, and Eleanor knew Sophie would love them. With the

Coldirons she would always have a family and a home.

"You're right. I'm being silly." She relaxed against the plush leather seat. "It's been so long since Louisa and I really talked. Is she dating anyone?"

He maneuvered the truck around a pothole. "If she is, I don't know about him."

"How about Jess?"

"I doubt it, but I keep hoping there's something to his Salted Carmel Mocha Latte addiction."

"Since when does Jess drink lattes?"

"Since Violet Gates opened her coffee shop," he answered, cutting her a matter-of-fact glance.

"Oh, I see." She frowned, thinking about her friend's shy personality. "Violet doesn't seem like Jess's type."

Distaste twisted his lips. "She's nothing like Hallie, that's for sure."

No one had been overly fond of Hallie Collett, an ambitious and spirited barrel racer Jess had met while competing. Everyone expected them to marry. But the relationship was over shortly after a fall at the National Finals Rodeo ended his rodeo career.

A chill ran over her as she remembered watching Jess being tossed into the air, then stomped by his horse.

"But between serving as the executive director for Promise Point and rodeo stuff, Jess doesn't have much time for dating."

"Rodeo? I didn't think he'd be able to compete again."

"He won't," he said tersely. "He's working with Logan and Tyler Gates to bring the rodeo to Santa Camino."

Before the accident, Jess had been wild like the wind and ready for any challenge, no matter how dangerous. He loved cowboying, bustin' broncs, and riding fast. "Shuffling papers and rounding up sponsors can't compare to saddle bronc riding."

"I know." McCrea's eyes were on the road, but it was clear that his thoughts were elsewhere. "When I started the foundation, we both put in some long hours and lost a lot of sleep. He can't sit or drive for long periods of time, and desk work is difficult for him. But you know Jess. He never complains."

She did know Jess. He was a private man who didn't like talking about the fall, losing his career, his injuries, or his pain. "Is he riding again?"

"No," he sighed. "Lonnie Childers has been our trainer since we started the rescue, but he's retiring soon. I'm hoping Jess will want to take his place."

Six years without being on a horse didn't make the odds of Jess stepping into that position probable. But Eleanor wasn't going to take away McCrea's hope for his brother.

"I would love to see the rescue. Maybe you could show me around before I leave town."

He rested his palm on the top of the wheel, guided the truck down the drive, and stopped at the end. "We have a few minutes. How about I give you the grand tour?"

Eleanor turned to the backseat. "Ooooh, did you hear that, Sophie? Daddy wants to take us to see the horses."

"Horses!" Sophie yelled.

Laughing, he turned left at the end of the drive and drove west. After they passed the Coldiron Ranch, he flipped on his signal and turned up the road to Promise Point.

"Look, Mommy," Sophie shouted. "Horses!"

Eleanor turned her attention to the dozen or so horses grazing in the fields. "I see them, baby."

"We took in seventy-five horses the first year," McCrea said.

"Seventy-five?" she questioned. "I didn't realize there was a need."

"Thousands of horses are abused and neglected every year, and despite the efforts of rescue facilities like Promise Point, the numbers are growing."

Eleanor was overwhelmed by what she was seeing and the staggering facts. Horses were such magnificent creatures. They were intelligent, caring, compassionate, and devoted animals.

"And then there are the slaughterhouses," he said, with a grimness in his voice.

"Is that what's happening at the Twisted J?"

"The remoteness of its location makes it the ideal setup, but we haven't found proof of slaughter yet."

"Meaning if Chaves isn't stopped, it could escalate?"

"Yes."

"How do you know he's behind it?"

"He used to work for the rescue. He was new in town and needed a job. So when he cleared a background check, I hired him. But he would disappear for hours at a time. I began watching him."

"He was sneaking off to Vera la Luz," she deduced.

"Yeah, the bastard was looting. I fired him and a week later, two of our horses were stolen. We never found them. My guess is, they were loaded up and taken to Mexico to be auctioned off to kill buyers."

"God, that's horrible."

"We now use chip implants to keep track of all the horses at Promise Point." He laid a hand over the wheel and slowly guided the truck through the gate. "The mare we rescued the other night was pregnant. But Doc isn't sure either of them will make it."

"That has to be hard."

"It is. Some are so malnourished that they can't walk, and some have suffered such abuse that we never regain their trust."

"How can people be so cruel?"

"I ask myself that daily. But not all of our rescues are like that. Sometimes owners can no longer afford to care for them or have suffered health problems themselves." He pointed out her window to the pasture. "Remember Boaz?"

Her eyes darted from horse to horse until she found one she recognized. The sorrel gelding with the blonde mane was Colton Ritter's. He and McCrea had been best friends since the second grade and were thicker than thieves, until Sue and Reid divorced when Colton was sixteen. After that, Colton had moved to Montana with Reid to help run the family ranch and married Lauren after high school. McCrea stayed in touch, taking hunting excursions to the Lucky Jack Ranch every fall, and had been the best man at Colton and Lauren's wedding before Colton was deployed overseas.

"I thought Colton and Lauren were living in Montana."

"They were. But Colton had some problems after he was discharged from the Marines."

Colton came from a long line of servicemen. His father, grandfather, and great-grandfather had been in the military. So his choice to enlist or attend college hadn't been hard. A year into his tour, his platoon had been ambushed by a sniper. Colton lost a lot of his friends and the use of his left hand. But he had pulled through.

"Lauren and Little Jack are living at Sue's old place," he said as he continued driving up the road without explaining why Colton's favorite horse was at Promise Point or why Colton wasn't living with his wife and little boy.

"Friends come and go, but the ones you make as a kid are special," she said, hoping he would divulge more about Colton. But he didn't. Instead, he answered her with a simple nod.

He parked near a building that, according to the sign out front, was the office. Sophie was quick to say she wanted to see the horses and Daddy quickly obliged her. "Let's take a walk."

Her face beamed with anticipation as she skipped alongside McCrea. Eleanor walked behind them, taking in all the changes he had made.

Buildings, barns, paddocks, and stables sprawled out over the lower bottoms. Promise Point was a flourishing ranch; more than that, it was a refuge. A place dedicated to saving lives and giving second chances.

Four years ago, McCrea had been so passionate about building a ranch of his own, so determined he could make it work, that Eleanor had been envious of it. But the zeal he had had towards starting the game ranch was nothing compared to the zeal he had for the rescue.

He stopped, looking over his shoulder at her. "Is something wrong?"

The rescue ranch was a very important part of the man McCrea was now. The father, the caregiver, the rescuer, and she wanted to know more about all of them. "Nope. Lead the way. I'm right behind you."

He held his hand out. "I'd rather have you beside me."

She had waited a lifetime to hear him say those words. Beside him. With him. Together forever. Too bad they weren't in the right context. She lay her hand in his, feeling the warmth of his words and the gentleness of his hand escalate her curiosity to dangerous new heights.

He led them across the lawn and over to the fence. Sophie climbed up to the top as he pointed to a buckskin horse. "See that one? The light colored one with dark hair."

"I see it!"

"That's Milkshake. He's a sucker for a good chest scratch." He moved his finger up the field. "And that gray one over there is named Bisbee."

"Can I ride one, Daddy?" Sophie clapped her little hands. "Please."

He wrapped an arm around her waist and put her on the ground. "I promise to take you riding soon."

They visited the stables where some of the newer horses were being housed and moved on to tour the clinic. When they entered the double doors, Louisa was standing next to an older man with bushy salt and pepper eyebrows and glasses.

Louisa grinned when she saw Sophie. "God, McCrea, she looks just like you." She gave him a wink. "The poor girl."

"Sophie, this is your Aunt Louisa," he returned dryly.

Louisa crouched down next to her. "Hello, Sophie. I'm so happy to finally meet you."

Sophie gave her a shy smile. "Hello."

McCrea turned his attention to the man. "Doc, this is — "

"Charlie's granddaughter. You have your mother's smile."

Her Granddad Charlie had made friends and contacts from all over the country. Several of them had visited her grandma when she was a child. But she didn't remember Doc. "I'm sorry, have we met before?"

"It was a long time ago, and you were just a little girl when I last visited the ranch. All braids and braces as I remember," he said.

"How's Hope?" McCrea asked.

"About the same," he said and smiled down at Sophie. "But some company might help improve her spirits." He picked up his stethoscope and headed around the desk. "I'm leaving after I finish my rounds."

"Thanks, Doc." McCrea led them down the hall and to one of the back stalls. He lifted Sophie up so she could see where the mare was lying.

Sophie's face showed her sadness. "What's wrong with her, Daddy?'

"She's sick," he explained without details. "But we're doing our best to make her better."

Eleanor's heart broke for the poor mare. It would be a miracle if the foal survived. "She's so malnourished, so pitiful and poor."

Louisa propped her arms along the stall wall. "What I would give to get my hands on the person who did this to her."

"I think everyone feels that way," he said, letting Sophie down.

"I was just about to feed Skeeter," Louisa said,

holding out her hand for Sophie to take. "Would you like to help me?"

"Who's Skeeter?" Eleanor asked.

"Skeeter is more of a what than a who," he explained. "But Sophie will love him.

"Can I go, Mommy?"

"It'll be great." Louisa made a silly face that made Sophie giggle. "But he does slobber and occasionally, he spits."

"Yes," Eleanor said, laughing. "You can go, but try to stay clear of the slobber and spit."

Sophie took Louisa's hand, and they disappeared down the hallway.

"I'm not sure I trust a who named Skeeter around my daughter," she told him.

He held the door open for her and took her hand as they walked outside. "Skeeter is harmless unless you try to put a bridle on him."

"I see, so Skeeter is a lot like you," she said, biting her lip when he gave her a blank stare.

"Skeeter is a jackass," he explained.

She snickered. "You're making this too easy."

Grinning, he shook his head. "Yeah, I guess I am."

She listened as he explained the operations of the ranch. "We have twenty-five full-time employees and as many volunteers who undergo an extensive orientation before they are permitted to work with the horses."

"This place is," she paused, searching for the word. "Amazing, wonderful, impressive... I can't believe you did all of this."

"I didn't. Like I said before, Jess has been on board since the beginning. Lou volunteer s long hours in the summer and has plans on coming to work for us once she finishes veterinarian school. Ed volunteers and so does Sage when she's not volunteering at the dog shelter. Mom and Dad help find homes for the horses that are up for adoption or don't go into the equine therapy program."

"I've heard of those programs." But never in a million years would she have thought McCrea would have been involved with one.

"Our program caters mostly to returning veterans." He led her a short distance to a different barn, slid the door back, and proceeded inside. She followed him through the long hallway to the other side. "There's a substantial amount of evidence which shows animal-assisted therapy helps to improve the stress levels of people suffering from PTSD, depression, anxiety, and other chronic mental illnesses."

He walked outside and over to one of the round pens. With the click of his tongue, he called the horse inside it over. "This is Penelope. She's one of the horses that was accepted into the program. Her owners were no longer able to care for her, so we took her in. She's gentle and easy to communicate with."

"So how does the program work?" she asked, reaching over to pet the horse.

"Each client is different. Sometimes it's their first time being around a horse, so the horses aren't ridden or even saddled. We start out by letting the client get to know the horse and feel comfortable enough to move up to haltering and leading it.

"You know how horses are. They have heightened senses. They know when you're feeling happy or sad. They often perceive danger before we do. They can offer us immense comfort, and they can even help calm people in times of duress."

She rested her chin on the rail, looking into Penelope's eyes. Within those dark brown orbs was an intelligent soul capable of love, compassion, and even healing.

"Romeo did all of those things for me," she confessed.

"See," he winked. "You know exactly what I mean."

"It's just them and the horse, alone in the pen without judgement, pressure, or threat. I get it."

"At Promise Point, clients are given a chance to not only interact with the horses but also others who are going through or have been through the same situations." He took her hand. They walked back through the barn and out the other side. "We have a clinical psychologist who leads and monitors clients through the entire process."

"I'm very proud of you."

His walk slowed to a stop. "That means a lot to me."

She tightened her hand around his. "I mean it. Others may have helped, but Promise Point is your baby, your passion, your ingenuity, your dream."

His eyes searched hers. "It used to be, but like you, I have new dreams."

What were his new dreams? She was sure they included Sophie. But beyond that, she hadn't a clue.

Still holding hands, he resumed the tour. They walked down by the lake where they swam as kids. Live oaks and pinyon pine thicketed the banks and helped give cover for the plentiful white-tailed deer and quail that flourished around the area.

Promise Point was so much like the man who had longed to claim it. Defined by ruggedness, but strikingly attractive in a provocative way.

She looked westwards towards where the Mission was. Soon the sun would drop lower in the sky, creating a spectacular backdrop for the soaring limestone bluffs and rocky hills. A land filled with dangerously steep canyons and deep caverns of unexplored territory.

They made a circle, walking back to the office. They passed the truck and followed the incline up the hill. Eleanor knew where the road led. She had traveled it over and over in her mind a million times since she had left Santa Camino, replaying what had happened the night McCrea proposed.

As the sun disappeared behind the hills, the automatic timers on the landscape lights switched on, illuminating the cabin that sat just up the road.

The weathered and time-beaten tongue-and-groove logs were lighter than she remembered. The stacked-rock pillars had been replaced with a solid foundation. A new porch had been added along with new doors, windows, and shrubbery. From the wood shakes to the rock foundation, the old cabin had gone through a transformation. It looked nothing like the cabin she remembered. "You restored it."

"I needed a place to live, and it needed saving. It's been home sweet home for the past four years."

This was McCrea's home, the cabin where he had found her all those years ago. The place they'd had their first date. The place where Sophie was conceived, where love was made and lost.

A swarm of butterflies birthed in her chest. "It's beautiful."

He pulled her towards the steps. "I want you to see the inside."

The butterflies scattered and fluttered up to her

throat, causing her to pull her hand from his. "I don't want to be late for dinner."

Louisa's whistle cut through the air.

He spun around. "Something's wrong."

She waved a hand in the air. "Get down here!"

Alarm triggered her feet to a run, and he followed. "With Sophie?"

"No. It's the mare."

Seconds later, they met Louisa at the door. "I went back to check on her before we left, and she was having trouble breathing. I called Doc. He's on his way back."

The three of them raced down the hall to the stall where Susan and Patty worked to help Hope.

O n Wednesday nights, Doc Tolbert played poker at the Weller ranch, which meant he was only about five minutes away. When Doc rushed through the door, Jess wasn't far behind him. "I was on my way home and saw Doc barreling down the road. What happened?"

"She's crashing." McCrea fell to his knees beside the mare and worked at placing the harness under her so they could move her onto the gurney.

Jess did the same on the opposite side. "Can you save the foal?"

"We'll do our best," Doc said as they lifted the mare up and positioned the gurney under her. When she was secure, they rolled her out of the stall and down the hall to surgery.

Eleanor lifted Sophie into her arms to comfort her as only a mother could. "Will she be okay, Daddy?'

McCrea didn't want to lie to her. Death was an unfortunate part of ranching and rescuing. Sophie would learn that in time. But for now, he would do all he could to protect her from that heart-wrenching reality. "Don't you worry about Hope. She's a fighter."

He laid his Stetson on the receptionist counter and raked a hand through his hair. He pointed Eleanor to the waiting area on the left. She and Sophie took a seat on the sofa. "Someone should call Mom and tell her we won't be there for dinner."

"I'll do it," Lou volunteered. "I need something to do."

"I'll make some coffee," Jess said, rubbing his hands together.

Lou hung up and walked over to where McCrea was. "Mom's bringing dinner to us."

Jess walked by them with his coffee in hand. "Good, I'm starving."

"You're always starving," Lou mumbled and went back to biting her nails.

A half an hour later, Belle and Hardin arrived at the clinic. They packed in bags of containers filled with the food his mom had prepared for dinner. Roast beef, mashed potatoes, mixed vegetables, rolls, and a home-made cobbler. He and Jess pulled coffee tables together to make room for the food, and Lou found chairs for everyone.

Belle and Hardin became acquainted with their granddaughter, and McCrea knew by the smile on Eleanor's face that her anxiety about tonight's dinner was gone. She was with family: his family. Maybe she would see that it was where she and Sophie belonged.

"Thank god, Dimples got your good looks, El," Jess said, giving Sophie's belly a tickle that caused her to curl into a ball.

"Hey, now," McCrea cut in. "She looks more like her daddy than her mommy."

Sophie pointed to her face. "I have your eyes and your hair."

Everyone laughed, and she became the center of attention again. The laughter and conversation helped to keep everyone's mind off Hope and what was going on in surgery. But Lou continued to bite her nails, and Jess was checking the clock every five minutes.

With her belly full, Sophie curled up in McCrea's lap and fell asleep. And the room became quiet, too quiet. Belle began picking up paper plates and Eleanor helped her.

Jess tossed his hat onto a table and sighed. "Remember that time we put a dress on Mr. Jackson's milk cow?"

"Oh, God." Belle's eyes were wide with disbelief. "You didn't."

"We did," Lou said.

"Where on earth did you find a dress that size?" Hardin asked.

"From Mrs. Jackson's clothesline," McCrea answered.

"Remember when we all went riding, and we thought Jess got lost?" Lou looked over at McCrea. "We were afraid to go home without him because we knew Mom and Dad would ground us for months for going out so far."

"The four of us searched for hours trying to find him," McCrea said, shaking his head.

"I remember that." Jess grinned sheepishly. "But I wasn't lost."

Eleanor stopped beside him and ruffled his messy

hair. "We found you in the hayloft with Sandy Hubbard."

Jess wiggled his eyebrows as he looked up at her. "Ah yes, Sandy. Blonde hair, long legs, and big—"

"Jess," Belle scolded him with a distasteful look.

"What?" he asked, lifting his hands innocently. "I was going to say big blue eyes."

"Sure, you were," Lou said.

Eleanor walked to where McCrea was sitting and picked up the container of yeast rolls. "These two almost drowned me when—"

McCrea snagged the last roll and bit in. "You're exaggerating. You were nine, and it was a rain barrel."

"That was the first time. The second time, I was twelve, and it was the water tower."

"Oh yeah," he said, purposefully chewing slowly as if he had just remembered when, in fact, he remembered it like it was yesterday. "You wanted us to teach you how to swim, but you were afraid there were snakes in the lake."

"So, you thought climbing the water tower was safer?" Hardin chuckled.

"It was Lou's idea." Jess batted the blame to his sister.

"Shut up. Everyone knows I wasn't the wild and crazy one." She smiled sweetly. "That was you."

Jess grinned, taking silent credit for being both.

Hardin shook his head. "I don't know how the four of you ever made it to adulthood."

"We were kids. We could tuck, roll, and bounce a lot easier back then," McCrea laughed.

Jess stretched his leg and winced. "Amen to that."

When McCrea heard the doors to the surgery open,

he jumped to his feet and met Doc at the receptionist's desk. "How is she?"

"Alive."

The word brought a sigh of relief over everyone.

"And the foal?" Jess asked.

"Also alive," Doc smiled. "And doing good."

"Thank God," Lou whispered.

"But," Doc held up a hand. "Hope's not out of the woods. She has a long way to go."

"Thanks, Doc," McCrea said, giving his hand a shake.

"Now, go home, all of you," Doc ordered, grinning.

A THUMPING SOUND jerked Eleanor's eyes open to a tiny beam of light cutting through the crack in the bedroom window blinds. It came again and again until it registered that the thumping was someone knocking on the front door.

She found her phone and winced when she could finally make out the time. "Seven freakin' o'clock in the morning," she grumbled and kicked the covers back. With only one eye open, she made it to the landing as the knock came again. "I'm coming!"

She gripped the railing as she descended the stairs, and at the bottom, peeled back the curtain to see who it was.

McCrea had dropped them off at Redemption last night with a promise to Sophie that he would be back bright and early this morning.

He had kept that promise.

She slid the chain off, twisted the deadbolt, and slung the door open. His cheerful, full-blown, toothy smile made her want to throat punch him. "Do you know what time it is?"

"Aren't you just a ball of sunshine?" He laughed and stepped inside. "I told you I'd be here bright and early."

She groaned, swung around, and headed to the kitchen in a staggering zombie stomp.

"You used to be up before daylight, cleaning stalls and feeding," he reminded her. "What happened to you? Did the city make you lazy?"

She yawned, scratched her bedhead, and headed towards the coffee pot. "The bar doesn't close until two, and I usually don't get home until three or four. I'm so wired that I don't fall asleep until five or six. I couldn't go to sleep last night, so I stayed up packing." Another ear-popping yawn came, and she shivered. "I've only been asleep for an hour or so."

"Poor baby." His taunting tone jerked her middle finger into the air and rousted a deep laugh from him. "Now, is that any way to treat the man who brought you breakfast and coffee?"

Her hand dropped and for the first time, she noticed the coffee carrier and plastic bag in his hands. "Coffee? You brought coffee?"

"Fresh, hot, black, kick-your-ass coffee," he said, reaching her a cup.

She wrapped both hands around the Styrofoam cup and drew in the rich aroma before taking a sip. The bitter taste of the strong caffeinated brew closed her eyes with satisfaction and made her feel almost human. "I could kiss you," she said, opening her eyes to find Mc-Crea had moved closer and was only a few inches away.

"I'm easily trained, darlin'. And with that kind of positive reinforcement, I'll be here bright and early every morning with coffee."

His eyes found her lips seconds before he kissed her. He wasn't rough, but expectant and hungry. He tasted her with a tongue that roused an anticipating tingle deep in her belly and provoked her ovaries to cheer and twist with suspense.

In her hurry to get to the door, she hadn't thought about the short Rebel Road t-shirt she wore for a nightgown or that it barely covered her panty-clad butt. But she was thinking about it now.

And so was McCrea.

His fingers inched up the hem, skimming her bare thigh. His touch triggered the warning bells in her head, causing her to grip his hand. "We should really talk about those boundaries you keep breaking."

He nibbled on her bottom lip. "Sorry."

"I guess I am partly to blame. I did say I could kiss you."

He cupped her face, touching his nose to hers. "You did."

"And for coffee this good, I just might meet you at the door, Cowboy," she said, smiling when his grin widened.

"You've got yourself a deal, darlin'."

"But I'll be wearing my granny panties and a flannel nightgown."

He pulled out the takeout containers from the plastic bag. "Shame on you. What would officer Rebel think about that?"

"My granny panties and flannel gown?" she joked.

"No, you rewarding me with kisses."

She pulled her lips to one side. "Why would he care?"

"Because you two are lovers?"

"That's news to me," she said, taking a seat at the table. She opened one of the containers and inhaled the smell of bacon and eggs. "Though Tracey would love it if we were."

They weren't lovers? He sat down next to her. "Did Tracey introduce the two of you?"

"No," was the only answer she gave him. Because she wasn't going to volunteer any details about how she had met Nix.

"I thought we'd tackle the tack room today. Are you game?" she asked, loading her fork with scrambled eggs as he picked through his.

"Did he catch you speeding?" he persisted.

She scrunched her lips, thinking about how she could get out of explaining. "Not quite."

"Old Blue broke down and he came to your rescue?"

"Nix did come to my rescue, but—" she paused. "Are you sure you want to hear this?"

"I'm going to feel like a dick, aren't I?"

"Probably."

He sighed. "Go for it."

"It was the day I drove out to the ranch. The day Vanessa told me you didn't want anything to do with Sophie." His jaw tightened. "Anyway, I was on my way back to my apartment when the contractions started. They started out as lower back pain early that morning. But they grew intense when I hit the high-way. So I pulled over to the side of the road. Then my water broke, and I really started to panic."

He tossed his fork into the container and shoved it to the middle of the table.

"Blue lights flashed in my rearview window and there was Nix, holding my hand, and telling me everything would be okay."

He moved from the chair to the sink and braced his hands against the counter. "Was he there for the birth?"

"No." She collected their empty carry-out containers and tossed them into the garbage. Then she joined him at the sink. "But he did come to the hospital to check on us a few days later. I guess he felt sorry for me. He introduced me to Tracey and Hank, and the four of us have been friends ever since."

His chest expanded with a deep and pensive sigh as he stared out the window.

She couldn't count the times she wanted McCrea to hurt, to feel remorse for turning his back on her when she needed him the most, and for missing the birth. But the anguish on his face didn't satisfy her. It pained her. "I'll go up and wake Sophie."

"No," he said. "Let me do it."

Chapter Sixteen

McCrea had grown up and worked with some of the roughest cowboys around, so he had an extensive vocabulary of derogatory names and curse words. But none of them were foul enough to describe the man he was for not being there for the birth of their daughter. He should have been the one holding Eleanor's hand. He should have been the one comforting her.

But he hadn't. And he couldn't get those times back.

He climbed the stairs, pushed open the door to the bedroom where Sophie was sleeping, and walked over to the bed. Her little lips were parted, and dark eyelashes lay against her cheeks. She had his hair and eyes and Eleanor's smile and intelligence.

McCrea had witnessed the birth of hundreds of ranch animals and knew the dangers associated with breech births. Newborns and their mothers, no matter the species, were so weak and fragile.

Lying there in a tangled mess of pink blankets and pillows, Sophie didn't look much bigger than a newborn. But inside this tiny body was a vivacious and energetic life. Hope and her foal had reminded him of just how volatile life was, and of how it could change in the blink of an eye.

He combed back her hair and bent to kiss her cheek. "Hey, sleepyhead."

Sophie stirred, opened her eyes, and smiled. "Daddy."

His new title on the lips of his daughter made him want to cry. "Are you going to sleep all day?"

She shook her head no and stretched before crawling into his arms.

Within the hour, the three of them were headed to the barn to explore Charlie's tack room.

With a grand adventure awaiting them, Sophie skipped ahead to the hitching post near the entry of the barn. She latched onto it and swung back and forth. "Look, Mommy. I'm swinging."

"Careful, sweetheart. You'll get a splinter," he cautioned as they followed behind.

With knees drawn to her chest, Sophie giggled with the motion. "Wheeee!"

He stopped to shade his eyes with his hand as he gazed up at the trees lining the back fence. "Didn't there used to be a swing in the backyard?"

Eleanor pointed to the big maple where the tattered rope hung from the lower limb. "It was over there. Jimmy Ross put it up for me the summer I came to stay with Grandma. But it's been gone for years."

"Daddy will buy you a new one. One of those big ones with a tree house," he said as they walked into the barn.

Sophie's feet dropped to the ground. "Yay!"

"I think replacing the tree swing would be more practical," Eleanor said. "Unless you're planning on putting the new one at your house."

After a moment of thought, McCrea winked at Sophie. "Mommy's right. We'll fix the tree swing tomorrow. It will do for now."

Sophie launched into a complaining cry. "But I want to swing now."

"Tomorrow," Eleanor said flatly, halting Sophie's whiney rebuttal.

Knowing she would never budge her mother, she directed her theatrics at her daddy by lifting her chin and pooching out her bottom lip. McCrea could have sworn he saw it tremble. "But Daddy..."

"Sophia Rose." Her mother's stern tone, along with the use of her first and middle name, deflated the lip. She dropped her head. "Okay." With crossed arms, she stomped back to the hitching post.

"That dimple makes her adorable when she pouts," he chuckled. "She looks just like you when you don't get your way."

Eleanor threw him a scowl. "They're a sign of beauty that we inherited from my mother."

He pushed the front of his hat up and sighed. "That little girl was testing me, wasn't she?"

"Yup," Eleanor agreed, smiling.

"Did I pass?"

"You didn't give in. So, yes. You passed with flying colors."

He loved her praise, but more than anything, he loved what she had given him. Her love. Their daughter. "You know," he said, clearing his throat. "This is a place I never thought I'd be."

"Granddad's tack room?" she teased.

He watched Sophie swing. "Here with you and our little girl." The joy in his heart faded when he thought about how close he had come to losing them. "It scares the hell out of me to think I could have lost you both."

"But you didn't. Sophie came out all pink, puckered, healthy, and mad at the world. Oh, just so you know—" She laughed. "Harley's about to be a big brother, so you might want to prepare for questions about where babies come from."

"I'm prepared for that."

"Does it involve a long-legged bird with a huge beak?" she joked.

He moved behind her and put her hands on her hips. He reminded himself that there was no going back, only forwards. There was an indescribable beauty in birth that he hadn't had the privilege of witnessing with Sophie. But there would be more babies, more births, and more memories to make. Eleanor was a wonderful mother, and McCrea couldn't wait to feel her pregnant belly full of their unborn child.

He slid his hands lower to where her womb lay and was blanketed with an overwhelming sense of love. He heard a sharp intake of her breath and knew she felt it too.

He longed for another baby from the deepest part of his soul. He wanted to hear their baby cry for the first time, hold it, see its face, and know that they had made that love together. He had lain awake last night thinking about that future. Those babies. "Sophie's too smart for that."

"Yes, she is," she whispered, looking up at him.

"When we get pregnant, I'll tell her that Daddy loved Mommy so much their love made a baby."

IF THERE WAS a plane of higher existence where time stood still and the earth ceased to turn, Eleanor had just been sucked into it. She could hear her heart beating and knew she was alive. But she wasn't breathing.

"When we get pregnant?"

McCrea's desire-laced eyes were intense and focused on her as he ran a thumb down her jawbone. "Sophie needs a brother or sister to play with, don't you think?"

She didn't know what to think or what to say. Did Daddy love Mommy?

Sophie let out a cry. Eleanor knew from the sound that it wasn't anything serious.

But McCrea went running. "Oh, it's just a tiny splinter," his soothing voice quieted her tears. "You're tougher than that, aren't you?"

"Yeah," Sophie sniffed. "I guess."

One could hardly be blasé about a declaration of love, yet McCrea was. He tended to Sophie as if nothing had happened. Time hadn't stood still for him. So maybe it hadn't been a declaration at all. But babies?

"Are you ready to get some work done?"

His question jolted Eleanor out of the trance. "Ah —yeah."

He flipped the latch and swung the door open. Scratching the back of his head, he winced. "We might need a bulldozer."

She stared into the dark room, stagnant with the smell of dust and leather, and felt the urge to bite her nails. The small room was loaded to the threshold and cluttered from years of disregard. There were probably all kinds of critters making their homes in the moth-eaten bedrolls and buckets.

He stepped inside and removed a bridle from the hook. "This looks like mold."

"After Granddad died, Grandma shut the door and never ventured back in. The hands weren't allowed to use any of this stuff." She made her way around a bucket of rusty nails and over to one of her granddad's saddles that was draped over a wooden stand near the door. She ran a finger over the seat, wiping away a layer of dust. "I hope they're not all ruined. I'd hate to throw them away."

"I'm sure most of it can be cleaned," he said, looping the bridle over his arm. "Some of these things are pretty old. Are you sure you want to donate them?"

Over dinner, Belle had told Eleanor about the historical society's display focusing on local rodeo performers and the history of the sport in Santa Camino. Jess had donated some of his buckles he had won early on in his career. Her Granddad Charlie's trophies and memorabilia would be safe and well preserved for generations to come.

She shoved her hands into her back pockets and let her shoulders slump. Her granddad had passed away before she was born, but her Grandma Rose had brought him to life in the stories and memories she shared. "I never really knew him, but I know he loved the rodeo, so I think he would approve."

They continued to dig their way through piles of mothy blankets, dusty saddles, harnesses, lead ropes, and spurs. Some of the leather tack was ruined beyond repair, but there were still some good pieces.

"Oh man," he said, blowing away the dust from

something he had found on the back shelf. "Look at this buckle."

She waved the dust away. "Nice. Are there more?"

"Yeah. They're from all over the state," he answered after he'd found another one and frowned. "But these are for barrel racing."

She moved closer to examine the buckle.

He used his thumb to clean off the year. "Nineteen eighty-eight?"

"These aren't Granddad's."

"They're hers." He handed her a framed photo of a young woman accepting the buckle in his hand. "Do you recognize her?"

She stared at the picture, trying to place the woman. Something about her was so familiar. The eyes, the hair, the smile. It wasn't until she saw the dimple on the woman's cheek that she recognized her. "It's Mom."

"I didn't know she competed."

She sat down next to the saddle and held the photo to her chest as a deep sadness overtook her. "Neither did I," she said, near tears. "I've never seen her smile like this. She looks so happy and alive."

Here was the real Frances Mackenna. The daddy's girl and rodeo princess. The vibrant child her grandma spoke of. A zealous competitor with a promising life and career ahead of her. The young woman staring up at her had the light of a million stars in her blue eyes and dreams that knew no bounds. What had her mother dreamt about? How long had she held on to those dreams before the depression had snuffed them out?

A slight tremble moved her fingers lovingly over her mother's youthful face, wishing she could remember the woman in this picture, more of the good times, more of her mother's smiling face and laughter.

But she couldn't. Because she had been so young when her mother drifted over the edge of reality that the only good memories she had were of Mallory.

Her baby sister had been her own little ray of sunshine. But after she came to live with her Grandma Rose, her stepfather Rex severed her ties with her mother and sister. The Christmas and birthday cards she had sent them went without a response.

Eleanor knew coming home to a place full of memories and ghosts was going to be hard. But she had no idea it would hurt so much. Her heart ached so badly for her mother and for all that she had lost.

McCrea squatted beside her. "Are you okay?"

She nodded, unable to speak.

"We can take a break," he suggested, tucking a strand of hair behind her ear. "Or put it off until tomorrow."

"No. I need to get this over with." She tipped the photo back so she could see her mother's face. "I want to keep the photo and her buckles."

Rising, he looked around the room until he found an old crate. "We'll put them in here for now."

One by one, Eleanor laid the buckles inside and wondered what else she would learn in the days she had left at Redemption.

Chapter Seventeen

Eleanor moved around the large living room, studying the people in the photos. Some she had met, others she knew only by her grandma's recollections. Fathers, mothers, grandparents, aunts, uncles, cousins, and friends. Most were gone now. Some buried in the cemetery with Rose and others nearby. It reminded her of how alone she was.

Reaching out to take the picture of her grandparents' wedding day, she smiled at the memories Rose had shared about her husband. A handsome cowboy who lived and loved with all his heart. Her grandma had such faith in him and their love for one another. A Charlie and Aggie Rose kind of love.

Gently, she wrapped the picture in a layer of newspaper and placed it in a box. By ten o'clock, Eleanor had the photos and her grandma's knickknacks safely packed away in moving boxes. But stacking a lifetime of memories and love into the back of the storage building she had rented seemed wrong.

She raised, stretched her aching back, and checked the time. The grandfather clock in the hall was nearing ten o'clock. McCrea would be here soon to take Sophie riding, and she would have the house to herself.

Sophie had begged her to go, but Eleanor wasn't up for company. She was moody, and her soul was restless. Last night, she had dreamed of Rose. Her grandma had been standing in a field of flowers, waving goodbye.

She snagged her jacket from the coat hook, opened the screen door, and stepped out onto the front porch. She slipped her jacket on and sat on the wooden rocker. It would have been a peaceful Friday afternoon if not for the circumstances of her return to the ranch. A cool breeze mingled with a hint of warmth, warning that summer was on its way.

She rested her head against the back, watching a regal display of colors stain the western sky and bathe the sleeping fields of autumn with a golden light. She moved back and forth, syncing the creak of the old chair with the tick of the clock. It was something she had done as a child and something she still found enjoyable.

The country was abundant with simple things, good and wholesome things. Things people from the city often overlooked, took for granted or knew nothing about. The whinny of a horse, a sunrise filtered through an early morning fog, the soft flutter of birds in the brush…

The air was as it used to be in the fall, cool against her face and fragrant to her nose. But not everyone considered manure and dying leaves fragrant.

She drew in a deep breath, wishing she could catch the hint of apples from the orchard down the road. She and her grandma had baked pies for the fall festival, and the house would harbor those sweet smells for days after. Maybe she'd bake a pie before she packed up the kitchen. Or maybe she'd wait until they were back home in Austin. She and Sophie could start a new tradition of fall baking.

She opened her eyes to the overgrown flowerbeds beside the cracked sidewalk. Guilt tore through her. One could hardly tell the flowers from the weeds. Her grandma would be so upset.

"Sophie," she yelled, rising from the rocker. "Grab your jacket and come help me."

With one arm through her jacket, Sophie pushed the screen door open. Eleanor helped her other arm into the sleeve and buttoned her up. Down the steps and around the side of the house to the garden shed, they went. The old metal building leaned to the right and made her leery about going in. She opened the door to a curtain of dusty cobwebs.

Sophie snubbed her nose. "It smells funny, Mommy."

"It just needs airing out." Inside, Eleanor found a small shovel and dug deeper into the pile of discarded tools until she found Rose's garden gloves. She turned them inside out, and after she was sure they were free from insects, slid them on. They were a perfect fit.

"Can I have a bucket?"

Eleanor found a pink Easter basket. "How about this?"

Sophie snatched it from her hands and ran towards for the flower beds around front. Tools in hand, Eleanor followed. When she rounded the corner, she found Sophie perched on a rock near the porch. "It's a perfect day for gardening, Sophie."

She knelt beside the flower bed and dug the spade into the dirt, removing a chunk of weeds. Her grandma would be pleased to know she was finally taking an interest in gardening.

There was a special feeling about the ranch. The peace of being home, of safety and family, that cocooned her in calmness. It was something she hadn't felt in a long time. One that reconnected her soul to the soil beneath her nails.

The sudden death of her grandma had left a hole in Eleanor that she would never be able to fill. She missed the woman who had taken her in, sheltered her and loved her when no one else had.

"Can I have gloves too?"

"Here," Eleanor shed the gloves and held them out so Sophie could shove her tiny hands inside. "You can wear these. They were Grandma Rose's."

Sophie wiggled her fingers beneath the blue material and pointed to her chest. "Rose, like me?"

"Yes, just like you. She was so excited when you were born." Eleanor brought Sophie to Redemption a couple of times before Rose passed. Her grandma had been lonely and begged her to come home more. But Eleanor's visits were few and far between and never lasted more than a couple of hours. If only she had those days back.

Suddenly, the familiarity of Redemption brought with it an ache of loneliness and the heaviness of culpability because she hadn't taken an interest in gardening. She was weeding because she felt guilty about selling Redemption and about not being here during her grandma's last days.

"She loved you so much, Sophie Rose. I wish she were here now to dig in the dirt with us."

"I like digging in the dirt, Mommy."

"Me too," she agreed.

Before long, Sophie wandered off to the lower corner of the yard. She gathered acorns from the oak near the fence line, kicking the vibrant orange and gold leaves as she went.

The roar of McCrea's truck turning into the drive pulled her attention to the fancy black and chrome horse trailer it was pulling. He parked in the turn-around, opened his door, and stretched when his feet hit the ground.

He was dressed in a blue-checked western style button-up shirt, Wranglers, and a pair of comfortably worn riding boots. The blue drew out the darkness of his hair and cast his skin a deeper brown. Damn, he was a beautiful man.

"Daddy!" Sophie's little body sprung into a dead run across the lawn straight to him and wrapped her arms around his leg.

"Hey, sweetheart." He swung her up and into his arms. "Did you miss me?"

She nodded. "Uh-hu. Did you bring my horse?"

He laughed. "I did, and I brought an extra horse just in case you talked Mommy into going with us."

"She didn't," Eleanor answered, going back to her weeding task. "I have work to do, and I don't think gallivantin' all over Hill Country with the two of you will help me get any of it done."

"Could it be that Mommy has forgotten how to ride?" he asked Sophie before he put her down. "Or maybe the living in the city has taken the country out of the girl."

"That's it," she agreed sarcastically, and held up her dirt-covered hands for his inspection. "That's why I have dirt caked under my nails and calluses on my hands."

He squatted down, so he was eye level with her, and with his thumb, gently rubbed the dirt from her cheek. "You look good in dirt."

She smiled and batted her lashes. "You're so sweet."

He grinned. "Are you sure you haven't forgotten how to ride?"

Everything she knew about a horse she'd learned from McCrea the summer they met. He started her out on Winnie, an old broodmare who hadn't gone beyond a slow walk in years. Step by step, he showed her how to saddle, buckle, and mount the horse, and she'd taken in every detail of the lesson.

That was the first of many lessons she had learned from this cowboy. "You were a good teacher, McCrea. I haven't forgotten anything you taught me."

Why was she taking her grief and guilt out on him? It wasn't his fault she hadn't been there when her grandma needed her. Not coming back to the ranch had been her decision.

He dropped to his knees beside her and reached over to take the spade from her hand. "Mom says gardening is therapeutic."

"Grandma said that too," she said, sighing. "She had lost my granddad and my mom, and gardening must have helped her through it."

"We all have our way of dealing with death." He sat down, drew a leg up, and rested his arm on his knee. "Every meaningful conversation I had with my Grandma Sophie was in the kitchen. I didn't realize that until after she was gone." He glanced up at her. "Remember when we were kids and all of us would gather in the kitchen to help her bake?"

"God gave that woman a double portion of patience." She laughed.

"He must have," he agreed. "Everyone would disappear after the treats were gone, but I always stuck around to talk."

"She was something."

"Grandma Sophie had a type of radar. The kind that could see right through lies and bullshit. She was real and honest." His smile disappeared. "She didn't care about money, power, or land. She cared about people and loved with her whole heart. I don't know what she ever saw in my granddad."

"Love sees past flaws and failures."

"Yeah, I guess it does," he said, tapping the toe of his boot with the spade. "It may seem silly, but sometimes I go into the kitchen and talk to her."

"It's not silly. I've talked to Grandma a lot lately." Eleanor picked up her grandma's gloves that Sophie had laid to the side when she ran off. Time and countless hours in the garden had faded the cotton material to a dull blue. She slipped her hand inside and laid it over her heart. "It couldn't have been easy taking care of a child at her age. But she didn't think twice about it."

She had missed precious time cowith her grandma. A woman who was more of a mother to her than her own flesh and blood mother had ever been. A woman who had taken her in when she didn't have a home, sat up with her night after night when she had the flu. A woman who had held her while she cried from a broken heart. A woman Sophie would never know. "I should have come home sooner. I should have been here for her. I knew she was frail."

He scooted closer and drew her head to his shoulder. "Rose knew you loved her."

The tears she had been holding back rolled down her face. "I miss her so much."

His hand made gentle circles over her back. "I know, darlin'. I know."

Again, McCrea held her, comforted her, and let her cry her heart out. When her tears subsided, she raised her head and dried her eyes. "Thanks for letting me cry on your shoulder.

"It's always here for you." He moved to his knees and shoved the spade into the roots of a Blackfoot Daisy plant.

"What are you doing?"

He pried into the base of the plant, moving the spade back and forth. The hearty roots snapped and popped until they broke. He yanked the plant out of the ground and tossed it over his shoulder. "Weeding."

"Is that what you call it?" she asked, half laughing, half wincing when he targeted another plant.

"I like gardening," he declared.

"About as much as I like castrating calves."

An upward glance brought a mischievous grin to his lips. "You do like cutting a guy's balls out from under him, don't you darlin'?"

She snatched the spade from his hand, halting his assault on the defenseless daisies. "I dare say I could identify my target better. Are you sure you're not trying to blackmail me?"

"Go riding with us or the flower gets it?" he questioned, rubbing his chin thoughtfully as a villain would.

"Yeah, something like that."

"I don't think that would help our friendship any."

"And you think pulling weeds together will?"

"All the old women in Santa Camino gardened. And most of them have been friends for years. There's got to be something to it," he said, uprooting a handful of pink Asters.

"Stop." She pointed a finger at the perennials in his hand. "These are flowers." Her finger moved to the weeds. "These are weeds. Leave the flowers. Pull the weeds."

He nodded. "Got it."

"Good."

"Mommy." Sophie skipped up the sidewalk. "Can we have a picnic?"

"That's a great idea, baby. We'll have one tomorrow."

"Why wait until tomorrow?" he asked. "Come riding with us, and we'll have one today."

This is where she was supposed to say no and not let either set of those matching brown eyes sway her into saying yes. But she held her ground. "Those puppy dog eyes aren't getting you two anywhere."

Sophie pooched out her bottom lip. "Please, Mommy."

"Not today."

McCrea held out his hand. Eleanor eyed it, knowing he had ways of persuading a woman without speaking a word. When she accepted it, he tugged her to his chest. The brush of his lips against hers blanketed her with a heated wave of familiarity and desire.

Sophie giggled, causing him to lift his head.

Eleanor opened her eyes. "How's peanut butter and jelly sandwiches sound?"

"Perfect." He took her hand and pulled her towards the trailer. "But first, I have a surprise for you."

"I don't like surprises."

"You will this one. Now, close your eyes," he said, stopping near the back. "Come on, do it."

She closed them and waited. She heard the door open and a horse whinny. "I don't want to spoil your surprise, but you did say you brought a horse for me to ride."

"Keep them shut," he said, lifting her hand.

The horse's warm breath and whiskers tickled her palm, and she couldn't resist a laugh.

"Okay, open them."

She did and gasped. It was her silver roan quarter horse. The one she thought had been auctioned off after Rose died. "Romeo?"

The horse whinnied once more and then snorted.

"He recognizes you."

"I thought you were gone, boy." She ran her hand along the horse's neck and laid her head against his mane, fighting tears. "Please tell me he wasn't a rescue."

"He wasn't. I couldn't stand the thought of your baby being sold to a stranger, so I bought him and waited for you to come home."

Home. The thought made her want to fall to her knees and burst into a fit of tears.

Chapter Eighteen

Sitting in the saddle made a man feel tall. The power of the horse under him and the reins gripped firmly in his hands gave him the illusion that he was in control. But the reality was, a man was never in control. And the horse, no matter how tame, was as unpredictable as the beautiful woman riding next to him.

"Want me to lead?" Eleanor asked, the twist of her lips daring him to say no.

McCrea removed his Stetson in a graceful, swooping manner and bowed in his saddle. "Ladies first."

She nudged Romeo forward and cut him a sassy wink over her shoulder. "Try to keep up."

Oh, he could keep up and then some. But the view from the back was a hell of a lot better than the view from the front. The erotic thrust of her hips moving with the horse would make him take a back seat anytime.

As McCrea knew every inch of Coldiron land, Eleanor knew Redemption's. She led them around back to the barn and through the rusty open gate that once fortified the horse fields. It had been over twenty years since Charlie's death, and that was a long time for a ranch to go unkept. The fences, corrals, barns, and out-buildings were in disrepair and would need rebuilding before animals returned to Redemption.

He was careful as he guided his horse along the path. The precious cargo sitting in the saddle in front of him gasped with excitement at every turn.

Today would be something Sophie would remember for years to come. Her first horse ride through the ranch that would one day be hers. McCrea prayed it was the first of many memories the three of them would make together.

When the land became flat pasture, he moved Milk-shake up and joined Eleanor. Side by side, they rode. She lifted her face towards heaven and closed her eyes. Her hair fell back, exposing the smoothness of her ele-gant neckline. She held that pose for several seconds as if she were trying to drink in a healthy dose of sunshine and home. A slow smile eased the corner of her lips up. "Have you thought about what kind of grandparents we'll be?"

"No, I haven't."

"It's going to happen sooner or later," she said, reading his mind with just a glance.

"I know," he sighed. "But I've known I was a daddy for about five seconds. Let me enjoy it."

"I'll have blue hair and you'll start collecting bolo ties."

He winced. "I got one of those for Christmas last year."

"It's already happening." She snickered.

For him to be a granddad, Sophie would have to grow up, get married, and have children of her own. He wasn't ready for that and probably never would be. He tightened his hold as he looked down at Sophie. He held her safe and secure just like he had Eleanor years ago.

They kept to the flat land and followed the trail up to a hill just below one of the limestone overhangs. The rainfall had gorged the small creek that usually wasn't more than a ditch running through the ranch. The water rushed over the rocks, creating a robust waterfall and unspoiled backdrop for a family picnic.

McCrea led Milkshake down the hill to a shaded spot where the creek dwindled to little more than a swollen ditch. "How about this spot?"

Eleanor raised her hand to shade her eyes from the sun as she gazed up at the view. "It's perfect."

He dismounted and set Sophie on the ground.

Eleanor dismounted Romeo with the grace and fluidity of a beginner. Moving stiffly while holding her lower back, she winced and tossed him the blanket she had packed for their picnic. "Not a word," she warned.

He unpacked the food from the saddle bag. "I won't say a word about your dismount resembling a beached whale rolling over a sandbar," he teased.

"Oh, ha, ha," she scoffed while holding back a smile. "Unfold the blanket. I'm going to sit my wounded pride and numb backside down and let you do all the work."

Laughing, McCrea gave the blanket a flip and spread it out under one of the juniper trees before unpacking their PB& J sandwiches. After giving Sophie hers, he removed the cellophane wrapper from her straw and poked it into the juice box.

Eleanor crossed her legs, leaned against the tree, and accepted her sandwich. "Thank you."

"You're welcome," he said, biting into his. He stretched out on his side and propped his head on his hand. The sweetness of the grape jelly and the saltiness of the peanut butter coated his tongue, taking him back in time to the day they met. "Do you remember the first time we shared a PB& J sandwich?"

Licking her pinky finger, she shook her head. "Yes, I do. You wrapped me in your coat, shared your sandwich with me, and explained that problems couldn't be solved by running away."

He wanted to have that talk again, but he knew she didn't see selling Redemption as running away. And keeping her here was going to be a lot harder than sharing his coveted peanut butter and jelly sandwich with her.

Sophie sipped the last of her juice and grabbed the apple slices. "Can I feed the horses?"

"In a minute," Eleanor pulled out a small packet of wet wipes and began cleaning peanut butter from Sophie's face."

"Does your sister know about her?" he asked as Sophie lay down beside of him, yawning.

"No," she answered, looking towards the hills. "I tried contacting her when Grandma passed away, but I didn't have any luck. I haven't seen Mallory for so long that I'm not sure I would recognize the woman she is now."

The sadness in her eyes made McCrea want to pull

her into his arms and shelter her just like he had the day she ran away from Rex Montgomery.

McCrea could see her now. A little girl not much older than Sophie crouched up into a ball at the far corner of the cabin porch with a bloody lip. Back then, he had brushed it off as a cut or scrape, a result of her trek through the underbrush and thickets.

He lowered his lips to Sophie's brow, kissing her softly. It hadn't taken long for her to fall asleep.

Eleanor smiled briefly before she looked away. "Losing my dad really hurt my mom. By the time I was in the first grade, she had slipped into a state of deep depression. Some days were good, but most were bad, leaving me and Mallory with Rex."

The pain of losing her mother all those years ago was still fresh to Eleanor. With each room she cleaned, each box she packed, came more tears and unanswered questions. He wanted to take it all away, but he couldn't. And that frustrated the hell out of him.

He was beginning to understand that Eleanor's childhood demons were complex, hidden, and waiting to lash out.

Dragging them into the light where they could be dealt with would take time and a subtlety, he wasn't sure he had. She had never once talked to him about what happened the day she ran away. She had never confided in him or talked to him about her life before coming to live with Rose.

But why would she? He had brushed her to the side every chance he got. He flirted with her and teased her, using her crush to keep her at bay. Staying as far away from the marrow of caring as he possibly could.

He felt the weight of that pressing down on him. "Why didn't you tell me you were running from him?"

"To a little girl, Rex was a giant. A monster who couldn't be slain. Besides, what could you have done? You were just a boy."

"Something. Anything. I could have protected you."

"When you brought me back here, Grandma saw what he had done. If Rex had found me, he would have thrown me in the car and headed back to New Mexico. She would have never known. You protected me without knowing it. You were my way to Redemption."

McCrea wanted to tell her that he would be her way to Redemption again. He would be any damn thing she needed him to be if she would give him the chance.

Her smile was almost shy. "I know growing up I was a bit of a nuisance, but—"

"No, you weren't," he corrected with a raspy, guilt-laden voice. But to a teenage boy, she had been. And he had done everything short of tying her to a fence post to get rid of her.

She stuffed the uneaten portion of her sandwich back into the Ziploc bag. "You always had a way of making me feel safe and protected. I guess it was because you were the one who found me that day."

He hadn't been a protector or even a good friend to her. Eleanor had trusted him and opened her heart to him. In return, he had hurt her. And like Rex, he had caused her to run away.

There were a lot of things McCrea didn't know about Eleanor. Deep things. Meaningful things like the case in point.

He knew the top layer. The way she smiled when he flirted with her. The breathless way she laughed after a ride. The way she belted out a response to his teasing.

And he knew her body. From the rose-colored peaks of her nipples to the soft curves of her calves. He knew the intimate cry of her husky surrender when he had claimed her body. But he didn't know one damn thing about her. The real her and the derision of that sliced through him.

They both fell silent and let the songbirds take over the conversation. Their harmonies floated along the breeze and joined in with the sound of the cascading water.

Eleanor leaned back and rested her weight on her hands, smiling the way she had when they rode out. "Winding streams, tree-shaded groves, limestone bluffs, and woodland wildlife." She gazed out over the land. "That's part of the description Sage wrote for the advertisement on her website."

"It doesn't do it justice."

"No, it doesn't."

"Are you sure you want to give all this up for the Rebel Road?" he questioned.

She sat up, her smile melting as she dusted her hands. "I don't have a choice."

"Yes, you do."

"This partnership is a way for me to have financial stability. I want to do more than scrape by."

"Eleanor, you're not a single parent anymore. You don't have to worry about providing for Sophie."

"And you don't know how relieved I am about that. Really, you don't. But…"

"But what? I don't see the problem."

"Of course, you don't." She let out a short, snipped sigh. "Because you've never had to sacrifice anything you love."

How could he tell her that four years ago he had

made a sacrifice? One that helped her keep her beloved Redemption, but had cost him Promise Point?

She stood and dusted her backside. "We should be getting back."

HOPE HAD BECOME A CELEBRITY, and the clinic had been bombarded with calls from all over the state about her and her foal. Offers for adoption were pouring in, but McCrea decided that the unnamed filly and Hope would have a permanent home at Promise Point. The mare was still recovering and growing stronger every day. She was gaining weight and had bonded well with the foal.

Sophie sneaked her fingers apart and opened an eye. "Can I look now?"

"No, not yet." McCrea had missed out on birthdays and Christmases, and the foal would be Sophie's first gift from her daddy. With his hands on her shoulders, he turned her down the sidewalk and guided her towards the round pen where he had asked Lonnie to take the foal.

"But Daddy..." she whined.

"Oh, just a few more steps and you can open your eyes." Eleanor laughed, walking alongside them.

The chestnut filly was full of energy. Her eyes were bright, her whinny was strong, and her tail lively. With long legs and knobby knees, she leaped and trotted around the pen, ready for play. But she stopped to twitch a curious ear at her visitors.

McCrea moved Sophie up to the pen and crouched on one knee beside her. "Are you ready?"

Her little body vibrated with excitement. "Yes."

He glanced up at Eleanor—who had the same eager smile as Sophie—and winked. "Okay, open them."

She jerked her hands away from her face and opened her eyes. A squeal of delight rushed from her throat. "It's a baby horse!"

The filly reared on her hind legs, kicked the air, and leaped around the pen.

"She's a filly," he said.

"That means she's a girl," Eleanor added.

"Can we call her that?" Sophie asked.

"She's yours," he whispered in her ear. "You can call her anything you want."

With wide eyes, she clapped. "She's mine?"

Seeing the joy on his daughter's face and knowing he was responsible was better than anything he could imagine.

"Can I take her home with me, Daddy? Please. Please."

"She'll stay here at the ranch, Sophie," Eleanor was using her motherly voice.

Sophie climbed up the metal railing and poked her head through the middle of the pen. "But I want to ride her."

"She has a lot of growing to do before she can be ridden," he explained.

"Then can I take her home?"

Eleanor crouched beside him and pulled Sophie back through the railing. "I don't think Mrs. Bruce would approve of us having a horse in the backyard."

Sophie's brow crumpled. "I don't want to go back to that house. I want to stay at Grandma Rose's house."

Eleanor took her hands, glancing briefly at McCrea before she spoke. "We have to go back to our house in Austin, baby. Mommy's job is there, and what about Harley?"

Her shoulders sagged.

"Don't be sad," McCrea told her, reaching up to wipe away her tears. "You have a new horse to play with and to help care for. Did you know that horses have special powers?"

"They do?"

"Yes, they do. They can tell when you're happy or sad." He turned her around. "Filly knows that you're sad right now. You don't want her to be sad too, do you?"

Filly came closer, wiggling her nose to pick up Sophie's scent.

Sophie shook her head no and held her hand out for the horse to smell. Filly sniffed and whinnied, making her giggle.

This wasn't like the tantrum she'd had at the barn. Sophie wasn't throwing a fit to get her way. She didn't want to go back to Austin, and it wasn't just because of the filly. She had grown attached to her new family, to the horses at Promise Point, and to Redemption.

Chapter Nineteen

E leanor wasn't sure they would have everything packed and ready when the movers arrived on Sunday. But when Louisa suggested the four of them get together for coffee, she hadn't argued. She needed a break from the packing, from the unanswered questions about her parents, and especially from McCrea.

She hadn't come home to rekindle an old flame, but that's what was happening. The flame she thought she could smother out was burning hotter than ever. Being with him every day was taking its toll on her sanity and her willpower.

They worked side by side, day after day, but chaste kisses were all she allowed. And she felt traitorous for that. How could she even think about letting their relationship go any further? It had been easy for McCrea to let her walk away the, first time. What made her think this time would be any different? She couldn't sacrifice her heart for the sake of sex.

As she drove into town, she pushed her worries to the back of her mind and focused on the positive things that had happened since she had come back to the ranch. Sophie and McCrea were close, and she was bonding with her new grandparents.

It hadn't taken much persuasion on Sophie's part to hoodwink her Granddad Hardin into joining the club. Eleanor had watched Hardin squat and fold his tall frame into a pink Nantucket style child's chair that came with the set Belle purchased online, especially for Sophie. With a finger and thumb, Hardin had guided the miniature teacup to his lips and sipped the imaginary drink. Belle had eagerly offered to watch Sophie while Eleanor went for coffee. Later, she would drop Sophie off and pick up Charlie's rodeo memorabilia for the display.

With the morning sun in her rearview window, she passed the Baptist Church and the old Jericho Mill before making a left onto West Main. She stopped at the red light and drummed her fingers in beat with the radio.

McCrea had surprised her with a trip to the car dealership and told her to pick out a new vehicle. She argued with him about cost when he suggested one of the high-priced crossover models. But he had won the battle when the salesman showed her the safety features.

She hadn't gotten used to the luxury of a working radio or the convenience of a wireless charging station for her smartphone. It would take her days to figure out all the digital gadgets. But it felt good to know she and Sophie wouldn't be left stranded again.

When the light changed, she made a right turn. After parking, she grabbed her purse and walked across the street to where Louisa and Sage said they would be waiting.

Pixies was a little building sandwiched between a vacant rental space and the Bluebonnet Flower Shop, another business that had opened after she had left town.

Louisa looped her arm through Eleanor's and pulled her towards the door. "Hurry up or all the good tables will be taken."

Sage held the door open. "Looks like we're in time for the morning rush."

The shop's brick and mortar walls were sturdy, and a bit weathered, while the feminine pastel colors of the furniture and accessories added softness and welcomed customers in. The coffee shop was the mirror image of its owner. Hard and soft, strong and sweet. It was everything Violet Gates was, minus the smell of strong coffee and pastries.

Violet worked behind the counter, filling orders to the line of caffeine addicts rushing to jumpstart their morning. Her auburn hair was in its usual loose knot fashion at the base of her neck, and Eleanor knew that any second, she would be shoving those dark-rimmed glasses back up her slightly freckled nose.

Louisa stuck two fingers into her mouth and rolled out a loud whistle that nearly stopped traffic.

Violet swung around, and with eyes as big as saucers, ran around the counter to hug her.

"Hi, Violet."

Violet jerked back and giggled. "How's Austin? Big, right? And noisy. Tyler said the city is noisy."

"It is big and noisy," she agreed, laughing.

"What can I get you?" Violet asked, hurrying back around the counter.

Louisa took a seat at a table near the front. "Café Mocha with extra whipped cream."

Sage followed her. "Cappuccino."

Violet added chocolate syrup to a cup and poured espresso over it. "What about you, El?"

"I hear your Salted Carmel Mocha Lattes are excellent," Eleanor hinted, hoping Violet would say something about her potentially budding romance with Jess.

"Jess loves them," Violet said.

"I've heard that," Eleanor said and joined Louisa and Sage at the table. When the coffees were ready, Violet carried them and a plate of chocolate chip cookies out on a tray.

"It's busy this morning." Sage looked around the crowded shop. "Are you sure you can take a break?"

"Yeah, I just need to let Joel know." She sprinted to the kitchen door and poked her head in.

Louisa licked whipped cream from her upper lip. "Who's Joel?"

"I'm guessing he's the stunningly handsome dude who just walked out of the kitchen," Sage answered, and their eyes followed her finger to the counter.

Joel was built stocky, with jet black hair and biceps that strained the seams of his pink Pixies t-shirt.

Louisa's jaw dropped. "Holy shi—"

"Shh...here she comes," Eleanor whispered.

Violet bounced back to the table and sat down.

"How did you talk Logan and Tyler into letting David Gandy work for you?" Louisa asked.

Violet squinted and pushed her glasses higher on her nose. "Who?"

"That's a very good comparison," Eleanor threw in.

Sage snapped her fingers. "I thought he looked familiar."

"You mean Joel?"

Louisa gave Violet a what-the-hell look. "Yeah, I mean Joel."

"I told them he was gay," she said, sipping her coffee.

"Is he?" Sage asked.

"I don't think so."

"You're working shoulder to shoulder with a possible sex god, and you don't know if he's gay or straight?" Louisa asked.

Violet laid her forearms on the table, cocked her head sideways and assumed a very professional expression. "Joel's sexual orientation isn't any of my business."

"Violet, honey, we really need to talk," Louisa said.

"Oh, leave her alone," Sage chided.

Eleanor slipped an arm around Violet's shoulders. "I have missed your sweet disposition."

The four of them had become friends in summer camp, Eleanor's first year in Santa Camino. Though they varied in age — Sage being the oldest and Violet being the youngest — the four of them had instantly bonded. They had shared good times, celebrated achievements, and helped one another through all the bad things life had thrown at them. She had missed the sisterhood, love, and familiarity of her tribe.

Louisa shoved a bite of cookie into her mouth. "These things are phenomenal."

"Mmm..." Sage's moan was one of praise.

Violet broke one in half and took a nibble. "They're Joel's special recipe."

"The man bakes?" Louisa whined and licked the tips of her fingers. "Please, God, let him be straight."

"Do you really need a man who bakes?" Sage questioned.

"No," she said, dusting the crumbs from her fingers. "But I wouldn't mind eating cookies in his bed."

Giggles followed as they tried targeting the ingredients of Joel's phenomenal cookie recipe.

It was Violet who changed the subject. "Who's the mystery man buying Redemption?"

Eleanor shrugged. "I have no idea."

Sage gave the cookie in her hand a long examination. "The guy's lawyer is handling everything."

"Intriguing," Louisa said, as if there could be a conspiracy behind the purchase.

"Maybe he's a movie star," Violet offered with dreamy eyes.

"Here in Santa Camino? I doubt it." Sage chuckled.

"Maybe he's a cowboy movie star." Violet's fantasy developed further. "I wonder if he looks like Scott Eastwood?"

"God, I hope not." Louisa snatched another cookie from the tray. "We have enough of those running around Santa Camino."

"Cowboy movie stars who look like Scott Eastwood?" Violet crinkled her nose. "I don't think so; I would have noticed if there was."

"Me too," Sage threw in.

"And what's wrong with cowboys?" Violet pressed Louisa. "Your brothers are cowboys and so are mine."

Louisa stopped in mid-chew, considering her argument. "It's just that most cowboys are roamers and only want one thing."

Violet's brows arched. "What?"

Eleanor and Sage busted into laughter.

"For god sakes, Violet," Louisa groaned. "Sex. They just want sex."

The pink on Violet's cheeks darkened. "Why didn't you just say that?"

"I was afraid you might spontaneously combust in your chair," Louisa said with wide, googly eyes. "I swear, Violet. We have got to find you a man."

"Pay her no mind, Violet," Sage threw in while trying to keep a straight face. "Louisa was bitten by a cowboy as a child."

"That must have hurt." Violet tittered.

Louisa broke another cookie in half. "Laugh if you want, but I've been around cowboys my whole life. And their love 'em and leave 'em philosophy is not for the faint of heart. Once a cowboy, always a cowboy."

"My, my, my," Sage crooned, suspiciously. "You were bitten by a cowboy."

Louisa gave Sage an aloft roll of her eyes that landed on Finn, who had just walked in.

"Uh-oh, girls. There's a new sheriff in town," Sage announced, smiling behind her cup.

Louisa tossed Finn a polite smile. "Finny boy is one of the bachelors being auctioned off Saturday night."

The dreaminess in Violet's eyes morphed into contempt. "Clayton gave Tyler full access to any of the equipment Durant Resources has to help with the cleanup. But the damn fool turned him down."

The friction between the families hadn't lessened with time, and Eleanor wondered if they ever would. The affair between Thea Gates and Clayton Durant had left a shadow of perfidy looming over their children and had given Tyler a heavy burden to carry as the product of their adulterous union.

Violet narrowed her eyes into a vengeful glare and looked over her shoulder at Finn. "I think I'll bid on him just to make them mad."

"Careful," Sage warned, without taking her eyes off the subject matter. "I hear that particular roughneck is hard on a woman's heart."

Louisa snatched another cookie from the tray and bit into it like she hadn't eaten in days. "Yes, dear Violet. Under that pretty uniform is a very bad boy."

"Keep in mind that he will be wearing a tux at the auction," Eleanor added dryly.

"In my mind, he's not wearing anything," Louisa grinned, nudging Eleanor's arm with her elbow as she wiggled her eyebrows. "But speaking of the auction. You're bidding on McCrea, right?"

"Sure, she is," Violet joined in with a not-so-innocent twinkle in her eyes. "The word around town is the two of them are already cooking bacon naked."

Louisa laughed. "Oh, you're busted!"

Eleanor knew her face was red. "It didn't take Mouthy Mildred long to get the gossip going."

"Give us the details," Violet said, using the knuckle of her index finger to push her glasses back up her nose.

"They," Louisa pointed to Violet and Sage, "want details. I do not."

"Forgo the details," Sage said. "How are things between the two of you?"

Eleanor etched a pattern into her cup with her fingernail. "There aren't any details. McCrea is the perfect loving and attentive father every mother dreams her child will have."

"But," Sage prompted.

"I lie awake in the mornings waiting for the sound of his truck rolling up the drive. We work side by side, day after day, and I count the hours until it's time for him to say goodnight with a kiss that breaks the boundaries I've set. He's at the house every morning with coffee and breakfast and every night to tuck Sophie into bed. Tossing and turning has become a part of my nightly routine." She knew tonight wouldn't be any different. Her body was strung tighter than a banjo string. "It's taking its toll on my willpower not to give in."

"So give in." Violet's voice was bashful.

"Yeah," Sage encouraged. "I say let nature take its course."

"Knowing he chose Promise Point over me is a hurdle I can't get over," she confessed.

"What are you talking about?" Sage asked.

"McCrea proposed to me a week before I left town," she said, feeling the need to lay everything out on the table despite Louisa's presence. "I'm sorry, Louisa. I know he's your brother, but McCrea is one of those love 'em and leave 'em cowboys you warned Violet about. Wade told him that if he found a wife and kept her for at least a year, the land was his. He asked me after we had sex. I turned him down and he married Vanessa."

"I know about Granddad's ultimatum, and I also know that Granddad didn't want McCrea to find just any wife." Louisa pointed a finger at her. "Granddad wanted McCrea to marry you and only you."

Eleanor frowned. "What? Why?"

Louisa laced her arm through her purse strap and patted Eleanor's arm as she stood. "That's something you should ask McCrea. I'm going to check on Hope. I'll see y'all later."

Chapter Twenty

"What's this?" Jess pecked the top of the old trunk.

"Letters from Grandma Callie. Eleanor found them at Redemption. I thought I'd let Mom read through them."

"You two are just alike. Both of you would wade ass deep through a pile of hot manure to find a spittoon used by Washington's wig maker," Jess said.

Ordinarily, the analogy would have made McCrea laugh or at least smile, but he was too frustrated to do either. In the days since Eleanor and Sophie had returned to Redemption, the three of them had developed a routine.

He arrived early with breakfast and coffee. They worked until lunch, ate, and then worked until dinner. After dinner, they went for long walks, dipped their toes in the cold creek down by the barn, and got in some serious swing time. They made memories and caught up on four years. There were so many things he had missed out on because he had been afraid of her "I love you".

That regret stuck in his gut like a piece of rusty barbed wire. God, what he would give to hear her say those words again.

They talked, laughed, and indulged in safe kisses. But the evening always ended with him saying good night, never with them making love. And damn if that wasn't killing him.

He loved watching her move, loved hearing her hum as she worked around the house, the smell of her hair, the beauty of her smile, and the love in her touch.

He wanted to peel back the layers of Eleanor's heart that no one knew about. Learn her secrets. Her hurts. He wanted to see her scars. Learn every part of her body until he had it memorized like a road he traveled every day.

He ached to hold her, wake up with her in his arms, and hear her voice as it bid him good morning. He wanted to eat breakfast with her, take her to dinner, go for long walks, fall asleep on a blanket under the stars, and laugh with her. The way they had when they were kids. He wanted to grow old with her, laugh with her, and die with her face being the last thing he saw.

McCrea had never cared about lavishing any woman with gifts, but it was different with Eleanor. Everything was. The new car and ranch were just the start of what he wanted to give her.

"This one has potential." Jess brought McCrea back to business by handing him the resume he had just printed.

McCrea hitched a hip onto the desk as he skimmed over the candidate's work experience. "Brody Vance.

Three years in Wyoming, two in New Mexico. This guy moves around a lot."

"So did Lonnie," Jess said, with an overly dry tone.

The job duties for a horse trainer were simple on paper. They ranged from adapting the animal to wear saddles and bridles to training them for equestrian events. But in practice, the job was so much more. A good horse trainer had patience and a real love for the animal. Promise Point's trainer would have to work to correct behavioral issues sometimes related to abuse and trauma.

The last two interviews for the horse trainer position had been a bust. The first applicant was Carl Leary. He had worked at a horse-riding school in California. The second was a younger man who had just graduated from college with a degree in equine management.

Given the timid nature of Promise Point horses, each applicant was given a time in the round pen to show their horse skills with Skeeter, the spirited jackass Eleanor had compared him to. Neither had impressed McCrea.

"But Vance has a military background and a degree in psychology," Jess added.

McCrea tossed the application onto the desk and massaged his temples. He wouldn't have to spend hours going through job applicants if Jess would just take the damn job.

Jess closed the laptop. "I'll list the position on one of those job service sites. That will give us a better pool of candidates."

He stood and held to the desk for a moment before taking a step. The long night he had pulled helping Logan and Tyler had him visibly sore.

"How's the leg?"

"Still useless as hell," Jess answered grimly.

McCrea knew better than most about the pain Jess had gone through. The trauma his body had endured and that the road to recovery had been a long and excruciating one. He had helped with Jess's physical therapy, taking all the cursing and anger his brother wanted to throw at him because he could do that much. He couldn't take away the pain or erase the accident. But he could be the one Jess lashed out at when his body reached its painful limit and when he fell to the floor or couldn't walk another step.

"Jess." He didn't want to challenge him, but this conversation was long overdue. "You're my brother and I'd do anything for you, including tell you the truth."

Jess stared back at him. "And that is?"

"You belong on the back of a horse, not sitting behind a desk. Take the horse trainer job."

"I don't want the job," Jess said flatly. "I'm perfectly content being on the business side of things."

"But you're not content, whether you know it or not."

"So now you know me better than I know myself?" Jess scoffed.

"Even with the pins, you're still a better rider than any man in Santa Camino, including me. Get back in the saddle and back to doing what you love. It's evident that parts of you are still broken in a way that surgery or physical therapy can't fix."

Jess scoffed. "If the doctors can't fix my leg, what makes you think a goddamn job will?"

"We both know the problem isn't with your leg. Jesus, man," McCrea swore. "How long has it been since you've been out on a date?"

With a tightly clenched jaw, Jess grabbed his hat from the rack beside the door. "Last week."

"A real date with a woman who wants more than sex?"

"I don't have time for this," Jess said and headed to the door. He paused with his hand on the knob. "I'm driving over to the Gates Ranch to see how the clean-up is coming. I'll be back later."

McCrea thought about all the broken things in his life and how they were miraculously starting to mend now that Eleanor was back. Love was a powerful healer, and his brother needed a woman who could love the pain away. A woman who could make him feel like he was more than a man broken from a fall. And maybe Violet Gates could do that. "Can I offer you some advice?"

Jess raised his head towards heaven with a sigh. "Can I stop you?"

"Logan and Tyler are both good guys. But doing anything other than buying coffee from their little sister is suicide."

Jess turned away from the door with a slight smirk on his lips. "Don't' tell me they scare you."

"If I were interested in Violet, hell, yes, they would scare me. Mainly, because I favor my balls being just where they are. South of my belt buckle and not sadistically tied around my neck."

"Well, I can assure you that my balls are perfectly safe. I have no interest whatsoever in Violet." Jess crunched his face. "She's so...."

"Nerdy?"

"Yeah, kind of, but that's not it."

"Innocent?" McCrea offered.

Jess raised his finger when he thought of the word. "Naïve. That's the word I'm looking for."

McCrea picked up the resume to symbolically wave the white flag of a truce. "I've said what I needed to say. If you're not interested in the job, call this guy and set up an interview."

"Will do," Jess said, before walking out the door.

AFTER DRIVING BACK FROM PIXIES, Eleanor gathered her mother's rodeo buckles and pictures from the tack room and her Granddad Charlie's silver spurs and a promotional poster with him as the main attraction and put them to the side. Belle and McCrea arrived shortly after noon, and he loaded her Suburban. With the memorabilia gone, there would be more room for whatever was in the attic. A task she would eventually have to start and complete.

They worked in the dining room, packing her grandma's carnival glass collection first. Table clothes, placemats, napkins, and unused holiday candy dishes came next. When the last snowman was safely wrapped in newspaper, McCrea drove into town to pick up dinner from the diner.

After it was eaten, Eleanor left McCrea and Sophie on the loveseat to watch a Disney movie without her. She hadn't tasted a bite of her drumstick, not that what she had eaten could constitute as a bite. The fried chicken with all the fixin's would have hit the empty spot in her stomach if she hadn't been so preoccupied with why Wade wanted McCrea to marry her specifically.

She wasn't sure she needed to know the answer. Wade was gone, and Redemption was soon to follow. In a couple of days, neither would matter. What would remain was McCrea, Eleanor's feelings for him, and the mounting tension.

She bathed, dried her hair, dressed in her usual yoga pants and the Rebel Road t-shirt, and made her way back downstairs. The volume on McCrea's laptop was turned down and the living room was quiet. The lamp was off, and the only light was from the rolling credits.

McCrea lay across the short loveseat. The thing couldn't be comfortable for a man his size. His head was bent, pushing his chin into his chest. Sophie lay sprawled out face down on top of him with her arms hanging off the side. His right leg bent precariously over the armrest while his left stretched out and his chest rose and fell with the weight of Sophie's thirty-five pounds.

His long black lashes lay closed in sleep and a slight part was at his lips. Disheveled hair and relaxed frown lines gave him youth and drew her closer.

There had always been a tender side to McCrea, a side he didn't often let people see, but she had been fortunate enough to witness it firsthand when they were kids. But as he grew older, it slowly faded into the background. And a new McCrea had evolved. A man distant from the boy she knew and loved. But here he was, amid a bedraggled appearance, crumpled shirt, and a slight snore.

She suppressed a giggle, took her phone from the end table. She held it up, maneuvered them into the center of the camera, and snapped their first picture together. It wasn't frame worthy.

She grinned. Maybe refrigerator worthy with alphabet letters holding it in place. Sophie would love it and years from now ,would look back on it with fond memories of her time at Redemption.

They were leaving on Sunday, and Sophie would have to adjust to not seeing her daddy every day. And so would she.

"Enjoy your bath?" McCrea asked, opening his eyes to slits.

"Immensely," she answered, closing his laptop. "Did you enjoy the movie?"

He hooked an arm over the back of the couch and eased himself up with a tortured contortion to his lips. He massaged his neck and rolled his head around until it popped. "Immensely."

Sophie stiffened, stretched, and rolled to the crevice beside him. Dead to the world.

He eased her onto the loveseat and stood, stretching his back until it mimicked the sound his neck made. When it did, he sighed. He bent and gathered Sophie into his arms. "Come on, Rosy Posey. It's bedtime."

She stretched, wiggled, and settled back into his arms as if she'd been there since the day she was born.

Eleanor waited in the living room while McCrea carried her up to her room and tucked her in. She heard the bedroom door close and the soft tread of his bare feet down the stairs. He stopped on the last step, waiting for her to meet him. This was their usual routine, a long goodnight kiss at the bottom of the stairs.

She moved closer, staring up into his eyes. He wrapped his hands around her forearms, drawing her closer. "You've been awfully quiet today."

"I guess I have been a little preoccupied."

His slightly callused thumbs rubbing her wrists brought chill bumps to her skin. "With what?"

She moved closer, laying her head on his chest. "Questions."

"About your mom?"

Eleanor knew that if there was ever going to be more than kissing between them, McCrea would have to give her a damn good reason for letting her walk away. A reason other than Promise Point.

She raised her head, connecting her eyes to his. "No, my questions are about why you didn't come after me four years ago?"

McCrea flinched as though she had slapped him. Dropping his hands, he turned away from her and laced his fingers behind his head to stare at the ceiling. For a moment, she thought he might walk out the door without answering. But he took a deep breath, exhaling slowly before he spoke. "I'd trade every acre of land I own to have a life with you and Sophie."

"Would you?"

"Yes, I would, but things happened. Things you don't know about."

"Enlighten me, McCrea. Help me to understand why you traded us for Promise Point."

His arms dropped as he swung around to face her with a glower of disbelief etched into his face. "I didn't trade us for Promise Point."

She lifted the doubtful brow he hated and crossed her arms, daring him to prove her wrong. "Didn't you?"

The muscles in his jaw flexed tight as if he were debating. "How many times did Wade offer Rose money to help pay her bills? How many times did he offer to pay the taxes, fix the barns? Lend her money to meet payroll?"

Wade Coldiron and her Granddad Charlie had been best friends. Over the years, Wade looked in on her grandma and even offered Eleanor a job after she graduated college.

But Wade was a shrewd businessman who had expanded the Coldiron land by purchasing area ranches at rock-bottom prices. He could be polite and courteous, but also ruthless and demanding when he wanted something. "What are you saying?"

"Wade tried for years to buy the ranch from Rose after Charlie died. But she wouldn't sell."

She remembered Wade's frequent visits and the closed-door talks. But she hadn't thought much about it. Was that why her grandma had been so afraid she would marry McCrea? "Okay, so Wade wanted Redemption. What does that have to do with you and me?"

"Granddad had a way of getting what he wanted." His voice was gritty with animosity. "Once we were married, he would have railroaded his way in and taken over. There wouldn't have been a breeding program or new stables."

With a day of stubble on his face and the hint of blue under his eye, McCrea looked irresistibly handsome. In an outlaw sort of way. And for most of his life, he had been just that. An outlaw.

His I-don't-give-a-damn attitude and temper had always been his Achilles' heel. His eye was proof of that. And he always got what he wanted. Eleanor shivered, knowing that she was proof of that. "You've always gone your own way, McCrea, even when it got you into trouble. If you cared for me, you would have come after me. You wouldn't have waited until Wade died to inherit the land. Instead, you married Vanessa two months after I left town!"

He ran a hand through his hair and stared down at the floor. "I knew I'd lost Promise Point the moment I watched you disappear into the rain. But I thought maybe Wade would give in if I found a wife. I talked Vanessa into eloping because I didn't want my family and friends there when I said I do to the biggest gold digger in town. When Wade found out, he was livid. He revised his will and divided Promise Point between Jess and Lou. I got nothing from that man."

Eleanor had fortified herself against the truth she knew was coming, McCrea finally admitting that he chose his own selfish wants and desires over her love. She was ready to hear that. She needed to hear that. But she was in no way prepared for what he had just said.

"So I didn't trade us for Promise Point." He pointed to the floor and spoke with tight lips. "I traded us for Redemption."

Wade had wanted Redemption and when he couldn't cajole her Grandma Rose into selling it, he had blackmailed the one person who had idolized him. McCrea had done everything he could to please his granddad, everything except give him Redemption. "Why would you do that?"

"Because no matter how much you try to deny it, Redemption is a part of you. It's in your heart, in your blood, and it's where you belong." His throat muscles constricted with a hard swallow. "I couldn't be a part of taking it from you."

McCrea had sacrificed Promise Point, his pride, and his relationship with his granddad so she could keep Redemption. But again, his motives were about land, not love. She moved to the stairs, pausing with the first step. "Knowing you wouldn't be a part of Wade's plan helps to lessen the sting. But it doesn't get you off the hook. Wade died the winter I left. You could have told me then what his plans were, and this whole mess would have been avoided."

His chest heaved under the weight of her words, but he said nothing.

"Jesus, McCrea, say something! Anything! Don't just stand there looking guilty!"

"I don't want to argue," he answered calmly.

"Well, tough shit!" she yelled. "Do you know how long I hoped and prayed that you cared enough to come after me?"

"I did care."

"You had one hell of a way of showing it," she seethed. She started up the steps, only to have his hand latched onto her arm.

"I didn't come after you because I was afraid."

This man, who had gone nose to nose with guys twice his size and broken wild horses, was afraid of something? "Of what?"

He moved up the steps to where she was standing. "Of you, of how you made me feel. I knew that when I caught you, I'd take back my offer of a business arrangement and make sweet love to you until I was the man you wanted me to be."

"The man I wanted you to be?"

With his eyes trained on her lips, he smiled. "A man willing to submit to your romantic dreams of love, white picket fences, growing old together, and babies."

Chapter Twenty-One

Romantic dreams of love? White picket fences? Growing old together? Babies? All the things she told him she wanted the night they made love. He remembered it word for word.

"You're not a man who can be reined in by love, remember?" she challenged, taking the next step up.

"But here I am, grinning from ear to ear because I'm a daddy, drinking tea, fixing swings, and tucking my little girl into bed every night."

She poked him in the chest. "Don't bring Sophie into this. You made your choice. Why should I believe you suddenly changed?"

"Because I have changed," he said, easing a finger along the open neckline of her t-shirt. "And you know it. You feel it. That's why you're so scared of taking this relationship any further."

Was she that easy to read?

The soft glide of his fingers over her collarbone ignited a fire in her, but she kept her eyes fixed on the dark stubble of his chin. Like before, his fingers found the chain and urged her closer. "The night we made love, you said you loved me. Were you lying?"

It would have been so easy to stab him in the heart with a "hell yes", but she wouldn't lie about her feelings for him the night Sophie was conceived. She wouldn't taint the conception of their daughter or the memory of her love for him by copping out.

But how could she tell him how much she loved him then? How much she still loved him without making herself more vulnerable? She couldn't. She wouldn't.

"Just a yes or no," he urged.

"It's not that simple," she snapped.

"Isn't it?"

"No, it's not a simple question," she said, removing the chain from his grasp. "And this isn't a leash. Stop trying to lead me around."

Oh, he thinks that sexy little smile is going to get him somewhere.

And maybe it would.

She drew in a deep breath and tried to focus on the argument, not on his hands. She let herself go back to that cold, rainy day she fell in love with the boy from next door. Back before raging hormones and inheritance came between them. Being there was better than being where they were right now, standing inches apart, with an expanse of hurt wedged between them. "I was very much in love with the boy who found me the day I ran away. You were my knight in shining armor."

He trailed a finger down her cheek. This time, his touch wasn't lustful or guiding. It was affectionate, and she welcomed it. It reminded her of a time before either of them was old enough to care about land, love, or attraction.

She opened the bedroom door but paused before closing it. "But I know now that the boy I fell in love with grew into a man I didn't know."

His hand caught the door before she could ease it shut. "Do you want to know the man I am now? The man who values love and family above everything else?"

His question was loaded with possibilities that sent her heart racing again. God, yes. She wanted to know him. But she was torn between protecting her heart and relinquishing her body to the consuming passion of the night they made love.

She needed a place where her heart could be safe and sheltered. But she wanted his heart, an unexplored territory of dangerous love. Wild and reckless, heart-shattering love.

"Maybe, but I'll never love him like I did the boy," she said, moving a step back because the feel of McCrea's nearly naked body so close to hers ravaged her willpower. "Recklessly and without caution."

"Always guarded?"

She held her fingertips to his chest to set a boundary. "Our past causes me to keep you at arm's length."

But when he lifted her hand to his lips and gave her finger a gentle suck, she knew that was going to be impossible. The slow glide of his cowet lips and velvet tongue sent an electrifying jolt of pleasure through her body. His tongue marked a trail of fire to her wrist and circled her palm.

Tell him to stop.

He planted a kiss along her forearm and skipped over her shirt to her neck.

Pull away.

He kissed the line of her collarbone and moved lower to the hollow of her neck. He outlined the shallow dip with his tongue. "Never closer?" he whispered as his teeth nipped her earlobe.

"No," she answered, fighting the urge to reach out and touch him. His body had always been a captivating landscape of tanned skin and muscles that she hadn't explored in four long years. She wanted to slide her hand over the dark hair dusting his chest and to feel the hard, defined muscles of his stomach. She craved to taste the cleft between his pecs. To relish the flavor of his skin, the clean but sensual taste of him on her lips.

Her body tightened with the memory of the exciting foreplay, the consuming climax, and of how damn good it felt to soar with him.

"What about our future?" His breath was hot against her ear.

Did he think they needed to pretend they had a future? Maybe he thought her too frail to accept that they didn't. Or maybe, he thought, once they were lovers, everything would change. Fat chance. "Polite hellos and goodbyes during holidays and visitation," she managed.

McCrea slid his leg into the space between her thighs and slid his palm to her butt, pressing her hips against him.

"And our present?" he asked, watching her with those dark, sexy eyes.

The very real, very hard, very male present was pressing against her stomach.

"I — I'm here until everything is packed."

He guided her into the bedroom. "What about here? Now? Tonight?" he asked, shutting the door behind him.

She had mastered loving McCrea from a distance years ago but hadn't mastered letting him go. Her heart would never be free of him, but her body could be satisfied.

Blood pumped through her veins with the force of a raging river. And a white-water torrent beat against her senses, drowning out all sensibility. "McCrea, are we going to...?"

"Make love?" he finished with a rough voice. "Yeah, baby. We are."

Why was he using a four-letter word he knew nothing about? They were going to have sex, not make love. Because if this was just sex, her heart would be safe. So it was most definitely just sex.

She reached for him, lightly skimming her nails along the taut muscles of his stomach as she arched into him.

The sensual slither drew a growl from his lips, and in one quick motion, he dragged her t-shirt over her head. Her breasts were hot and swollen, and she had an insatiable need to feel his soft but abrasive chest hair rubbing against the tips of her aching nipples. He unclasped the bra and slid the straps down her shoulders.

Impulsively, she rubbed against him. The delicious friction bathed her in heat. He held the weight of her breast in his palm and delicately plucked the nipple. He teased the bud by gently pinching it, breaking her breath, and rousing a cry of both pain and pleasure.

"Damn," he said, taking pleasure in her response. "You make the sweetest sounds."

His hands skimmed to her back, to the curve of her hips, and lower. The soft scrape of his slightly callused palms over her sensitized skin heightened her ache and made her shudder.

Hooking his thumbs in the elastic band of her yoga pants and panties, he relieved her of both while his tongue offered her mouth a foretaste of what was to come. An erotic appetizer before the main course.

With his hands palming her butt, he pushed her against the wall. The thrust drew her legs around his hips and opened her crux to the rock-hard rise of his arousal. The course abrade of denim against her hot center summoned a low, throaty moan from her lips. She closed her eyes and arched into him, needing more.

He rolled his hips upwards, teasing her hot, wet center. "I could take you right here against the wall." He moved his hips again and abruptly stilled with a harsh curse.

She fought her way through the fogginess and opened her eyes. "What's wrong?"

He rested his head against her shoulder, his body clenched tight. "I didn't think we'd be having sex tonight. I bought condoms, but didn't bring one with me."

Eleanor hadn't thought about protection four years ago. She'd left that up to him. Having learned her lesson, she'd gone on the pill six months after Sophie was born. "I'm on birth control, and I haven't had sex since we — I mean," she stopped. "In — a while."

"How long is a while?"

When she didn't answer, he raised his head. The tempest of desire had cleared from his eyes, leaving clarity and focus. "How many lovers have you had, Eleanor?"

"You want me to talk about my lovers now?" she asked, glancing down at their bodies.

"No," he said, dipping his head to give her exposed

nipple a gentle tug. "Just how many you've had since you left my bed."

Since she left his bed? Why did that spark a fire through her? He sounded so...possessive.

"Answer me," he urged, circling the nipple with his tongue.

Damn, the man was a master interrogator!

She buried her hands in his hair to pull him closer. Admitting he was her last lover — her only lover— would strip away more than her pride. It would send the wall around her heart crashing down and allow him to see right through her. She bit her lip, trying to stay focused. "Wh — what about the women you've slept with?"

"I was a married man who practiced safe sex," he said, shooting down her attempt at diversion. With an arousing bite to the nipple, he asked again. "How many?"

"I — I — Can we have sex without talking?" she growled in frustration.

"No." His fingers bit into the soft flesh of her butt, pulling her into the rough thrust of his hips again. "And if you don't answer me, me and my dick are leaving."

McCrea was bluffing. She was sure of it. He wanted this just as much as she did. But unlike her, he had options. And probably a list of women more than happy to take her place 'tonight. But she wasn't giving in to his threat.

Her body screamed and fought against her decision, knowing it wouldn't be satisfied. She pushed against his shoulders. "I've changed my mind. Take your dick and go home."

His eyes held hers steadfast. "If that's what you

want, I'll go, but not until you've answered my question. How many?"

Odds were, this was about his over inflated ego. And it with it in charge, McCrea was less likely to attribute her celibacy to love.

She crossed her arms to hide her breasts and raised her chin. "There have been zero men."

And there it was. The prideful and arrogant glint of triumphant gold firing through his eyes. Glittering specs of satisfaction that told her he was damn pleased with himself. God, men were such vanity pigs.

"I'm the only man to have you?" he added in a way that made her wonder if he was going to jump on the bed and pound his chest with a feral roar.

"Now go home," she said, trying to ignore the way his eyes darkened and the way his chest expanded as he drew in a deep, controlled breath.

"Why haven't there been other men?"

Because you broke me. Oh, the insensitive prick would love that. But he had her pinned against the wall, literally, with no way out.

"What do you want me to say, McCrea? That one night with you ruined me?" She managed a deflated laugh that helped keep her from crying. "Or that you hurt me so badly I vowed I'd never let another man close?"

Over the top, Eleanor.

The darkness in his eyes shifted, making room for guilt. Well, she hadn't expected that, nor had she expected the words that followed.

"I don't want you ruined, baby," he said, grazing her cheek with his knuckles. "Or guarded."

He wrapped his arms around her waist and lifted her from the wall. She held onto his shoulders as he took her to the bed. He planted his knees on the bed, keeping her astride him. They were face-to-face, body-to-body, with only his jeans between them. He cupped her face tenderly, as if one wrong move would break her.

And God help her, it might. She felt so frail right now. So vulnerable and exposed and not just because she was sitting astride him, naked. He was unwrapping her layer by layer and peeling away her protective shell. "What do you want, McCrea?"

"You, baby. I want all of you." He was killing her, ripping her apart with his touch, and slicing into her soul with his words.

He bent his head and kissed her. His lips moved over hers slow and easy as if he were drinking her in. As if she were water and he was dying of thirst. As if he wanted to savor every drop of her.

Her plan was to keep her mind centered on the sex and not let love intervene at any time. But the more he kissed her, the more his hands touched her, the more love fought to surface. And the more she remembered about the first time they made love. The night she became his forever.

Eleanor felt the slow, sensual power of his kiss blanket her with love. The power of that overtook her and tears she couldn't hold back trickled to her cheeks.

He drew back a fraction. "Baby, don't."

She knew right now she must look like a wounded animal with its leg in a trap. A mangled mess of something once alive and vibrant, but now hurt and shattered, vulnerable and exposed. "This was supposed to be sex, but you're—" Her voice cracked. "Crossing the line."

He searched her eyes. "Is that what you want? A line we don't cross? Sex without anything else?"

Her lips trembled beneath the strain. "Yes."

He traced her cheekbone with his thumb. "That will never happen."

"Why won't it?"

"Because you love me."

Those words peeled away the final layer covering her heart, and Eleanor felt everything on the inside of her crumble.

Chapter Twenty-Two

McCrea didn't consider himself a brutal man. But as he sat there looking at a woman who was suffering under his scrutiny, he felt like a malicious bastard for disarming Eleanor with demands for truth when he hadn't done the same. The slow, silent tears spilling from her eyes were ripping fissures through him.

Damn his insensitive and prideful horns. Here they were again, destroying all the beautiful things in his life. They had their own selfish agenda, and he couldn't stop them. Why couldn't he have just kept his mouth shut? Why couldn't he have pinned her against the wall and taken what she was so willing to give?

The answer was simple. His ego needed to know why she hadn't taken other lovers, and his heart needed to know that she was still in love with him. There had been no other men.

He should have felt bad about that, but he didn't.

Not one damn bit. He was the sole benefactor of her sexual explorations. The embodiment of everything she knew about a man.

"I don't want to love you, McCrea," she said, looking at him with blue tear-filled eyes that made him unworthy of her love.

To a woman like Eleanor—a woman who was led by her heart and not her body—making love was just that. Giving herself to a man wasn't superficial. Which made seducing her four years ago feel more like sacrilege than a mere sin. Making love was the intimate joining of body and heart. The act of loving someone completely—totally. Of giving yourself to the selflessness it required.

McCrea hadn't known that the night he'd taken her virginity, but he knew it now. And he wanted to feel that love again. He wanted to lose himself in the arms of the woman he loved. He wanted to love Eleanor so fully that he became nothing, and she became everything.

But as he felt her tremble, he knew this wasn't going to be as easy as seducing her. This was a whole other ballgame and way out of his area of expertise. This wasn't sex or a quick fuck. This was love, their love and their future hanging in the balance of whatever came out of his mouth.

He wanted to tell her that he loved her, but knew he was on uneven ground, a fragmented surface full of pits and holes. One false move could ruin everything and send her running. So he let his heart lead the way. "I know, and that's my fault. Everything is my fault." She raised her hand to once again push him away. "Please, baby. Don't," he choked, catching her wrist. "Make love to me."

An avalanche of darkness blanketed her eyes. Her hand lowered to press against his heart as if she were searching for proof of its existence. "It's there," he reassured her, laying his hand over hers. "And fuller than it's ever been."

For years, it had beaten with a faint pulse. But the night they made love, Eleanor had brought a new cadence to his heart and transformed him into a man who believed in love.

McCrea cupped the back of Eleanor's head, bringing it closer to brush his lips against hers. "Love me here, now, and in this moment. Love me without fear. Love me recklessly and without caution."

The low sound that broke her parted lips could have been a cry of pleasure. But he knew it was something deep, something painful in a way he was only now beginning to understand. The sound was surrender. She lowered her lips to his, and he felt her body yielding to him.

He let her explore and taste him the way she had the night they made love. Shyly, lovingly, passionately, her tongue floated along the line of his lower lip. More experienced women had kissed—tempted him, but none had brought his body to a fever pitch so fast. None of them had loved him with such sweet and innocent abandon.

He broke the kiss to suck in a deep breath and let it out slowly to salvage his restraint. But the sensual dusting of her fingertips skimming his chest kept him from fully grasping control.

Her soft, wet kisses against his neck burned a trail of fire straight to his dick. Her hands drifted lower to his belt line and paused with indecision, bringing him back her innocent exploration four years ago. And there was no way in hell he could do that tonight.

He moved from the bed to strip out of his jeans and underwear and returned to the bed. He laid her back and moved over her.

Eleanor's heart, like her body, was naked and open for him and ready to be loved. He was ready to claim both. She turned her head, grasping his hand to pull it to her lips for a kiss. The touch of her soft, supple lips moving over his palm was sheer heaven and the sensuous nip of her teeth — hellfire.

A low groan left his mouth. Her innocent gestures were killing him. He shifted, lowering himself over her with most of his weight on the bed.

He kissed her gently, softly, as his hand grazed a path down her shoulder, arm, and over her hip. A thin layer of goose bumps spread across her flushed skin, deliciously enticing his hand lower. With a finger, he skimmed the curve of her small waist and the line of her pelvis until he came to the soft hair nestled between her thighs.

Sinuously, she arched. "McCrea."

"Patience," he growled, flicking her nipple with his tongue before his thumb found her soft, sensitive nub. The soft, mewing sound that escaped her throat vibrated through his body. Her reactions were so honest and real. With Eleanor, there was nothing forced or embellished.

With closed eyes and parted lips, she moved her hips rhythmically against his hand. And every move, every moan, brought him closer to the edge.

A hard shudder racked her body and drew her hungry mouth to his chest. Her breath burned him like a blue flame as her inner muscles tightened around his fingers and bathed them in her warmth. Breathless and panting, she began drifting down from the pinnacle.

But before she could reach the bottom, McCrea moved away from her, rose to his knees and lifted her foot to his mouth. With his tongue, he traced the arch of her foot, the feminine definition of her calf, to the slope of her knee. He paused, kneading the sensitive bend, and kissed his way lower to her inner thigh.

Her knees drew inward with an instinctual reflex to hide. But he wouldn't let her. He wanted to see her. To unfold her body and taste her.

He drew her knees apart. "Love me recklessly," he said, looking up at her as his lips traveled lower. "And without caution."

"N-no," she stumbled, on the verge of panic. The faint smell of her warmth enticed him closer and roused his appetite for the sweetness he knew lay within. "Yes," he breathed and nuzzled his cheek against her wet mound.

Her fingers laced through his hair with a soft mew of pleasure.

McCrea planted a kiss on her swollen nub. "Let me love you. All of you," he said, punctuating his words with sensual licks.

She gave into his coaxing.

When her legs relaxed, McCrea slid his fingers past her soft, wet folds and into her velvet channel. The "yes" that broke her lips rallied his need and left him trembling.

The silky glide of his fingers plunging in and out of her brought her closer to the edge. Her head rolled back with a low, throaty moan. With his slow, sensual thrusts and withdrawals, her body tightened, and her moans became short whines. Her body clenched, and McCrea felt her release. "Come for me, baby."

He rose above her in hopes he could catch the fleeting cascade of her climax. But when he positioned the head of his dick against her, her nails bit into his hips to hold him at bay.

Her body wasn't accustomed to lovemaking, nor had it gone through the natural process of childbirth. Although she wasn't a virgin, her body was still very much chaste.

He forced himself to take a deep breath and entered her slowly, testing her body's resistance. He watched her eyes widen, and her mouth open in a silent gasp. Inch by delicious inch, she took him in. And as her taunt body become pliant, McCrea pushed deeper, completely sheathing himself.

Knowing he was naked inside her was exquisite and summoned a visceral growl from his chest. An uncontrollable need to thrust overtook him. He flexed his hips slowly, at first, lifting them higher and higher. But as the pleasure built, the thrust became faster, harder, and quicker.

She rode the wave of pleasure, meeting each one until her body contracted and arched up.

Her cry and satisfaction propelled him to the brink of an earth-shattering orgasm, but he held it back. His jaw tightened. His fingers dug into the sheet, and his body vibrated with restraint. He didn't want this to end. He didn't want this to be over. He wanted to stay inside of her forever.

But with one twist of her hips, he was spiraling in a deadfall over the edge. An exploding spasm of gratification and release thrust his hips forward. A course cry broke his lips as the orgasm rocked him to the core.

ELEANOR STARED up at the ceiling with the weight of McCrea's body pressed against hers. Memories of the sensual way he had pleased her flooded her mind. They had made love.

He had been a tender lover, kissing her breathless and rousing her body to a painful ache. Then he had satisfied her, repeatedly.

The euphoria of lovemaking made every fiber of her being tingle. There was no fear, no worry, only love.

Love me recklessly and without caution. His plea had unraveled her and brought to light her darkest secret. He knew there hadn't been other men, and he knew why. She loved him. She wanted to bury her face in his shoulder and live the rest of her life in this bed.

Closing her eyes, she smiled. Life was funny. A flat tire had introduced McCrea to his daughter and brought about a truce to their relationship. But this was more than a truce. They were lovers again, and Saturday night, she'd be bidding on him. Her eyes popped open. "Damn Brook Tidwell."

He braced his hands against the mattress and raised his head. "What was that?"

"I said, Damn Brook Tidwell. You're mine."

"All the way down to the soles of my boots," he said with a roughish smile.

He rolled onto his back and took her with him. She laid her head on his chest, listening to the sound of his heartbeat. She had felt it earlier, beating fast beneath her hand as he pleaded for her to make love. He had always been a kind and gentle man, but the heart of the man he was now was selfless and without pride or guile. What had brought about these changes? Was it because he had broken away from Wade's hold and gone his own way? Or was it something deeper? Something tied to Colton and Boaz?

She raised her head and slid her hand under her chin while he twirled a strand of her hair around his finger. "What happened to Colton?" His fingers stilled, and Eleanor knew her question had hit a raw spot. "Why isn't he living with Lauren and Little Jack?"

His eyes grew hooded and dark as he laced his fingers behind his head and stared out into the room. "After you left town, things got bad. Real bad."

She raised onto an elbow. "What do you mean?"

"You were gone. Granddad had disowned me, and I was married to a woman I hated. I was one miserable son of a bitch. I started drinking and feeling sorry for myself. I thought, to hell with Texas. I'm going to Montana."

"To the Lucky Jack?"

He nodded. "I packed a bag and left in the middle of the night without telling anyone where I was headed. I called Colton to tell him that I was driving up, but I heard there was a snowstorm coming to the Big Belt Mountains. I knew if I wanted to beat it, I'd have to fly up. So I caught the first flight out and rented a four-wheel drive at the airport in Billings."

"Go on," she urged, seeing anxiety build in his eyes.

"I beat the storm and was looking forward to a warm fire and a strong drink from the bottle of whiskey I knew Colton had hidden in the barn. I parked, grabbed my bag, and knocked on the door. No one answered. Colton wasn't expecting me until the next day. So, I let myself in with the key I knew he kept over the door.

The house was empty. There was no furniture, no beds, no crib. There was nothing. The place was like a ghost town."

"Where was Colton?"

"I found him in the barn, saddling Boaz up for a ride. We had a few shots of whiskey, and he said he was going to help his foreman get the heard, ready for weaning. I offered to ride with him, but…" his words trailed off.

"And the storm?" she asked, hoping Colton had made it back before the snow fell.

"I ended up passing out. When I woke up the next morning, the storm was over, and Colton hadn't made it back."

She saw him wipe his eyes. "McCrea."

"I knew Lauren had left him and taken Little Jack. I knew he was hurting, and I knew he was struggling with PTSD. But I ignored it all because I wanted a drink. I hadn't seen him in over two years, and all I could think about was a drink."

Chapter Twenty-Three

Eleanor dozed off somewhere around three o'clock and woke to the tickle of McCrea's chest hairs against her back. The hard contours of his thighs cradled her backside. His arm circled her waist while his lips brushed her ear with the soft breath of sleep.

She slid her hand up his bicep, savoring the softness of his skin, the warmth of his body, and the arousing scent that was McCrea. So,, this was what the morning after was like. Peace and contentment wrapped around her in a warm blanket of McCrea's love. They had both fallen asleep without any more said about Colton, and she was glad. She didn't want to start the day off with something as horrible as Colton's death looming over them. She lay perfectly still, taking in this moment of heaven.

"Good morning." The gritty growl of his morning

voice rippled through as his arm tightened around her waist.

She turned over, so she lay facing him. "It is, isn't it?"

That lopsided smile of his drove her crazy. He slid his hand over her hip. "The best one I've had in years."

"I've been thinking."

His hand migrated down to her butt as he trailed kissed across her shoulder. "It's too early in the morning for that."

She pushed him over and crawled on top of him. "I'm serious."

His hips flexed up, pressing his hard temptation against her. "So am I."

She slid her hand down and encircled him. "Do I have your attention?"

He made a hissing sound.

"I thought so." She winked, enjoying the sensual play. "I have nothing to wear to the auction."

His jaw rolled from side to side. "I'm sure Sue can fix you up with something nice."

"I don't want to look nice." She slid both hands under her hair, lifting it from her shoulders. "I want to look fantastic."

Lustful admiration darkened his eyes as he palmed her breasts. "Something black and strapless."

"Mmmm," she moaned. "I like the way you think."

The loud ring of her cell phone caused her to jerk. McCrea's hands circled her waist, keeping her in place. "Don't answer it."

"It might be important."

"Then they'll call back." With a shift of his hips, he entered her.

She arched her back and rode the rhythm of his

thrusts. His fingers bit into the soft flesh of her hip, pulling her into each upward thrust of his hips. Desire spiraled through her, coiling tight in her belly. The urgency in which he took her was unlike anything she had ever experienced. McCrea had been so careful and restrained last night. But this was neither. It was the down and dirty of sex, of physical need and satisfaction.

And it was so good.

A moan left her lips as she felt the orgasm take hold. The pain split into pleasure, and McCrea's hold on her tightened. His gratification came with a hard thrust and a growl. After the fleeting remnants of her orgasm sparked, Eleanor drifted back to earth. McCrea made no attempt to withdraw from her.

She twisted her hips and felt him grow inside her. "How...?"

"Can I get rock hard after I've just had you?" he asked, kissing her shoulder before pulling from her. "You aren't the only one who hasn't had sex in four years."

She rolled onto the bed. "But you said you practiced safe sex."

"Abstinence is as safe as it gets," he said with a touch of humor to his voice.

She stared at him. "Abstinence? You and Vanessa didn't —"

"No, we didn't," he said, before sitting up to check the time on his phone.

"Married couples usually have sex," she said bluntly.

He stood, ran a hand through his tousled hair, and set out to find his jeans. "We weren't a couple. The marriage wasn't consummated. We never had sex, slept in the same bed, ate at the same table, or lived in the same house."

McCrea and Vanessa hadn't been lovers. The marriage had been a crudely arranged agreement with the intent of gaining his inheritance.

He had spent the last four years very much alone. So had she, but at least she'd had Sophie. "It sounds so cold, so unemotional and detached."

"Business agreements usually are."

"Then I'm glad I didn't accept the one you offered me."

His head snapped up. "Our marriage wouldn't have been like that."

It was on the tip of her tongue to ask why, but she wasn't that brave. "But if it were only an agreement, why didn't you sleep with other women?"

His brows pinched. "I may have married Vanessa for the wrong reason, but I still married her. I made a vow, and I kept it."

She'd had doubts about his faithfulness when he proposed to her, but keeping his vow to a woman like Vanessa took conviction. The vows—to have and to hold from this day forward, for better, for worse, for richer, for poorer, in sickness and in health, to love and to cherish, till death do us part—were sacred to McCrea.

"I'll be busy at Promise Point for most of the morning. But we can start in the attic when I get back."

She raised on an elbow to admire his naked form. Tanned, tall, and lean with muscles, she loved to run her hands over. "It's fine."

He found his jeans and jerked them on before heading down the hall to the bathroom. In a few seconds, she heard the shower turn on.

Eleanor's heart was telling her that McCrea's proposal four years ago had been more than a business arrangement. It was also telling her that last night and this morning hadn't been about coaxing her into anything. It hadn't been about land or marriage.

McCrea had made love to her because he loved her. The revelation of that possibility sank in, and her stomach did a mammoth-size flip flop. Oh, God. What if he was in love with her? What then? Would he want her to stay in Santa Camino? And why did that scare her? Wasn't that what she'd always wanted? For McCrea to love her? Yes, but she was sure he would want marriage because he wanted Sophie to have a stable home as he had said before.

Her cell rang again. She picked it up. "Hello."

"I was beginning to worry," Sage's motherly voice answered back.

"Sorry. What's up?"

McCrea walked back into the bedroom, whistling what sounded like a Jason Aldean tune.

"I have everything ready for you to sign." The shuffling of papers drowned out the whistling. "Can you meet me at Pixies at nine? My office is still a mess."

It was almost eight-thirty. It would take at least a half an hour for her and Sophie to dress and another fifteen minutes to drive to town. "Can we do it this afternoon?"

"I'm sorry, El. I have a full schedule this morning and Chloe has a doctor's appointment this afternoon. I won't be in the office tomorrow because of the bachelor auction, and Sunday I'm helping with the animal shelter bake sale. But we can wait always wait until Monday."

The movers would be here on Sunday to haul the furniture and boxes to the storage building. The house would be empty, and her reasons for being at Redemption would be gone. "Sophie and I are heading back to Austin on Sunday." She glanced up to gauge McCrea's reaction to the news, but there was nothing there. No thought or concern was on his face. A twinge of hurt rippled through her. "And I'm working Monday night. So I won't have time to drive back. I guess I'll see you at nine."

"Okay, I'll see you then," Sage said, and the phone went dead.

She tossed her phone on the bed. "That was Sage. I'm meeting her at nine to sign the papers."

"Have you seen my shirt?"

She untangled his shirt from the quilt at the bottom of the bed and held it out to him. "Did you hear what I said?"

"I heard," he said, slipping it on. "I can take Sophie with me and drop her off on my way to work if that helps."

Maybe she was wrong about last night. Maybe this was it. Maybe he was fine with her leaving. "Sure. If you have time, that would be great."

He stopped in mid-button. "What's wrong?"

She pulled the sheet over her breasts. "Nothing."

He sat down next to her and gave her a considering look. "Are you having second thoughts?"

About us? About you? "No—uh. It's just hard. You know, to let go." Hard wasn't the word. What if this was just sex? What if this was nothing more than physical for McCrea...

"Don't overthink things. You're one step closer to that partnership."

She had forgotten about the bar. It was, after all, the reason she told herself she was selling the ranch.

He cupped her chin and raised her head. "It'll all work out, darlin'. Trust me."

She did trust him, but at what cost?

He leaned closer to brush his lips against hers. "I'll wake Sophie and get her ready while you get dressed. Mom will make her breakfast."

When he was gone, she fell back onto the bed. He was right. She was overthinking again. He wasn't upset about her selling the ranch because he knew it was what she wanted. He was happy for her.

Sophie assured McCrea, with the determination of her mother, that she could dress herself. So after getting her clothes out of her Hello Kitty bag, McCrea left her to it. Then he hurried down the stairs to start the coffee.

He felt good, damn good, and he knew the reason wasn't that he had just had the best sex of his life with the woman he loved. Although waking up with Eleanor in his arms did put a spring in his step and a whistle on his lips. No, the euphoric harmony that coursed through his veins was because tomorrow was the day. He had everything arranged, the ring, the horse, and the proposal.

He filled his travel mug, jogged back up the stairs, and eased the bedroom door open to check on Sophie's progress. She tugged at the hem of her Dora the Explorer t-shirt and used both hands to push her unruly hair from her eyes. "I did it, Daddy!"

"You did a great job, Rosy Posey," he agreed,

moving to a knee in front of her. "Now, let's get your shoes on so Daddy isn't late for work."

"And brush my hair," she reminded him.

"Right. I knew that." His interview with Brody Vance was at nine and it was eight forty-six. It would take at least twenty minutes to swing by his parents' house to drop Sophie off and drive back to Promise Point. But this was part of being a dad, of managing work and family, and part of being a responsible husband and loving father. It was what he had missed out on.

He was sure he would eventually get the hang of braids and matching socks. But for now, running a brush through Sophie's hair and finding two different shades of purple socks was all he had time for. He gave her hair a few careful strokes with the hairbrush and tied her shoes. Then he fished his cell phone out of his pocket to text Jess. *Running late. Dropping Sophie off at Mom and Dad's. Be there soon.*

He picked her up and started to the stairs. "Let's find your jacket."

Sophie snuggled her head against his shoulder and wrapped both arms around his neck. "I love you, Daddy."

McCrea's heart melted. How could such a tiny person bring him to the brink of tears? "I love you too, sweetheart. More than anything on earth."

Eleanor met them at the bottom of the stairs, fully dressed in the dark jeans and a black sweater with her hair hanging loosely around her shoulders. He couldn't wait to see her in that strapless black dress. Sophie was spending the weekend at his parents' house. That meant he'd have Eleanor all to himself.

With the expertise of a seasoned mother, Eleanor

had the jacket on Sophie and was buttoning it up in a matter of seconds. "Remember, if you want to come home, have Grandma Belle call and Mommy will be right over to get you. Okay?"

"Okay."

"She won't need to call. Grandma Belle has all sorts of fun things planned for the sleepover, and Granddad Hardin is taking her riding tomorrow."

Sophie patted her little hands together, and her eyes brightened with excitement. "I get to go riding!"

"Tell Mommy bye," McCrea instructed.

"Bye, Mommy."

Eleanor gave Sophie a kiss and handed McCrea her art bag. "Goodbye, baby. I'll see you tomorrow."

"She'll be fine, darlin'."

He opened the front door and stepped out onto the porch.

Eleanor followed. "I know, but it's a mother's job to worry."

McCrea hurried down the steps to his truck and buckled Sophie into her car seat. After he shut the truck door, he ran back to the porch and up the steps. He snagged an arm around her waist and yanked her to him. "And it's a father's job to remind the mother that she worries too much."

A smile nudged her lips up. "It's a hard habit to shake."

He pulled out his wallet and handed her a credit card. "Here."

She frowned. "What's this?"

"For the dress, shoes," he wiggled his eyebrows. "Lingerie, but don't make undressing you too complicated."

She slipped the card into his front pocket. "I don't need your money."

"I like buying you things and it's as much for me as it is for you. I want you to look stunning when you win the bid." He gave the card back to her and brushed his lips across hers. "I'll see you in a little while."

"Okay," she agreed.

As he drove down the drive, he adjusted his rearview mirror so he could see Eleanor. She waved and watched until they were out of sight. The vulnerability in her eyes as they made love last night would always be with him and remind him of how fragile her heart really was. It had been hard for her to give in, hard to admit that he was her only lover, and even harder for her to trust him. But she had.

She hadn't held back. She hadn't shied away. She had loved him. She hadn't let those unanswered questions about their future hinder a second of the time they had together. She had done what he asked. She had loved him recklessly and without caution.

Eleanor was the missing piece of him. She was the unmeasurable portion of love in his heart. And he wanted to spend the rest of his life loving her.

Chapter Twenty-Four

When McCrea arrived at his parents' house, Jess's truck was parked in the drive. He unbuckled Sophie and hurried inside. In the foyer, he removed her jacket and set her art bag by the door. "Go find Grandma."

Sophie set out for the family room. "Grandma, I'm here!"

"There's my girl," his mother answered back from the living room, and the two quickly busied themselves with chatter. Sophie had both of his parents wrapped around her little finger.

The noise prompted Jess and another man, who Mc-Crea assumed was his nine o'clock interview, from the kitchen.

"I'm running late."

"Don't sweat it. Brody was early, so I put him in the round pen, and then we drove over here for coffee." Jess held up his cup. "We're out at the office. Brody, this is McCrea, my brother, the guy who will be signing your paychecks if you get the job."

The guy had a good inch on Jess's six feet. He was physically fit, with dark hair that grazed the edge of his pressed white collar. He wore a dark brown corduroy jacket, but no tie.

Brody stepped forward and offered McCrea a firm and quick handshake. "I'm Brody Vance."

Callused but clean hands, fresh jeans, scuffed boots, and a Stetson that had seen a lot of road and weather. "I didn't mean to keep you waiting. I'm still adjusting to fatherhood," he explained, holding up Sophie's purple jacket.

Brody's mouth lifted at a corner. "Not a problem. Family comes first."

"That's good to know," he said, hanging her jacket in the hall closet. "Do you have kids?"

"Damnation." Lou's curse vaulted out of an upstairs bedroom, stopping Brody's answer. "I'm going to be late."

Jess winced, and Brody cleared his throat with an entertained expression on his lips.

"Not that kids are a requirement for the job," Mc-Crea joked, wanting to draw the attention away from his cursing sister.

Brody made a dismissive gesture with his hand. "No, I get it. You want to know if I'm planning on putting down roots here."

"Are you?" Jess asked.

"I'd like to." He sighed. "God knows I've done enough roaming, but first I'll have to −"

"Damn it." Another curse came from upstairs. "I hate being late. It ruins my entire day."

"Find the right woman," Brody finished, watching Lou hurry down the stairs.

She ignored Brody completely as she approached Jess. "Have you seen my car keys?"

"No," Jess answered and pointed to Brody. "Louisa, this is Brody Vance. He's applied for the horse trainer position at Promise Point."

Lou spun around on her heel and raised an eyebrow as she gave Brody a long, leisurely once over. "Hello, Brody Vance."

Brody dragged his hat from his head. "You and your husband have a fine-looking home, Ma'am."

Lou raised her brows, then threw her head back and laughed. "This yahoo isn't my husband." She pointed to McCrea. "And neither is this one. They're my brothers."

"Oh." Brody's reply was short as his lips twisted with the urge to grin. "Sorry, my mistake."

She tilted her head to one side and crossed her arms over her chest. "But you already knew that, didn't you?"

"No, Ma'am."

She crossed her arms and cocked her head to the side. "Why don't you stop beating around the bush and ask me if I'm available?"

Brody ducked his head and tried corralling his grin again. "Okay, Louisa," he said, stepping into her personal space to gaze down at her with a level stare. "Are you available? Or did you pour your ass into those tight jeans just to be a tease?"

"Oh, shit." Jess laughed and covered his mouth.

Damn, this guy was ballsy.

Lou considered her prey through narrow eyes, but instead of pouncing, she dropped her arms, spun around, and walked to the door. "I would love to stay and argue, but I have somewhere to be."

Brody dangled a set of keys in the air. "You might need these."

Her mouth dropped open. "How did you—?"

"They were lying on the ground beside that sleek little sports car out front."

So much for intelligence. Brody should have known that when a bear charged towards a man, his only chance at survival was to drop to the ground in the fetal position and play dead. But instead of playing dead, he was shaking those keys to bait her closer.

"I like him," Jess said from the corner of his mouth.

A man who could wrangle Lou into a corner without a fight was worth hiring. "He has finesse, that's for sure. How did he do in the round pen?"

"He got a halter on Skeeter."

"Damn, really?"

Jess nodded.

Brody shook the keys again. "Are you sure you don't want to stay and argue?"

Hell, yes, she wanted to argue. Lou loved to argue, especially with guys who thought they had a chance. But Brody had rattled her cage and couldn't be cut down by her sharp tongue. If anything, he seemed to enjoy the sting of it.

"Maybe some other time," Lou said before she snatched the keys from his hand. "But thanks for finding my keys."

He gave her a wink. "Anytime."

"You'll have to forgive our sister, Brody," McCrea said after Lou was out the door. "She lacks social grace and refinement."

Brody set his hat back on his head. "I like her. She's got grit."

Jess snorted. "Is that what you call it?"

"Jess can show you around and get you acquainted with everything," McCrea said.

Brody's brows rose in surprise. "I got the job?"

McCrea held out his hand. "I think you're a good fit for Promise Point."

"SIGN HERE." Sage pointed to a blank line at the bottom of the page and flipped it over. "And here."

Against the background noise of Pixies' morning rush, Eleanor signed her name on both lines and laid the pen down.

Her grandma was gone, Romeo was gone, and now Redemption was gone.

Sage stacked the papers in a neat pile and deposited them into a manila folder. "The money will be deposited into your account within two business days."

Louisa snatched the folder from Sage's hand. "Are you sure about this?"

"Yeah, El. Are you sure?" Violet asked, slurping the last of her iced coffee. "I mean. you and McCrea are cooking bacon naked, and we've all gotten used to having you and Sophie around…"

"Ladies," Sage interjected and snatched the folder back from Louisa. "You're here to make things easier for her, not harder."

Eleanor felt hollow, empty, and lost. But she put on

a smile to reassure them. "I appreciate your concern, but I'm fine."

"But we just got you back," Louisa said with a small, sad smile.

"Austin isn't the far side of the moon." She was going to miss having them. She stood, gathering her purse and her coffee. "Now, I have a ton of things to do before the auction tomorrow night."

If she'd had an ounce of common sense, she would have loaded Sophie up and driven back to Austin as soon as she left Pixies. But nothing she had done in the past two weeks made sense. So why stop now?

She had one more thing to do before she left town and that was win the bid on McCrea in tomorrow's auction. She didn't need a black strapless dress, earrings, or high heels to do that. But when she walked into the Tall Oaks ballroom, she wanted to look like a million bucks.

The high of finding the right dress for the auction ended when she walked through Redemption's door.

She closed the door and felt the echo of an almost empty house rattle through her. The pale blue walls were bare, as were the windows and hardwood floors. Boxes were taped, labeled, and stacked in the corner. She had donated clothes and dishes to the church and hauled away a truckload of junk to the landfill. What remained would go with the movers to the storage building.

All that was left was the attic. A task she dreaded almost as much as selling Redemption, but she couldn't put off any longer.

She set her purse on the table by the door and tossed her keys inside. She shrugged out of her jacket and hurried up the stairs to the second floor to hide her dress. She didn't want him peeking. Then she climbed the narrow steps to the attic and hesitantly turned the knob.

The door screeched open and a curtain of cobwebs clouded her path. She wiped them away and coughed. She switched on the pull string light and let out an exasperated breath. There were stacks of old newspapers —some of them dating back to the early 1900s—and National Geographic magazines from the 1950s.

A large headboard and dresser sat along the right wall and an antique wash basin, which she knew was her great- Grandma Maggie's, occupied a corner near the door. Eleanor ran a finger over the old upright piano that used to sit in the dining room as she walked deeper into the dark abyss of her family history.

As a child, she had been terrified of the house-settling noises that originated from the room her grandma labeled off limits. As a teenager, she hadn't been curious about what secrets were hiding in her family's attic. As an adult, she wanted to say that had changed. But this mission into the dark garret wasn't exclusively for packing. A part of her yearned for answers about her father and why her mother had left Redemption. But another part of her feared what she might find.

With a heavy sigh, she sat on the floor and chose a vintage boot box as her next rummaging victim, knowing there would be anything but boots inside.

She opened the lid and shook her head. It was full of black and white pictures with unfamiliar names scribbled on the back. Some had years, others had nothing. Towards the bottom, she found one of her Granddad Charlie. A much younger version than she was used to seeing, but it was him. The Mackenna men all had the same long, straight, and dignified nose.

She tossed the photos into the box and slid it to the

side, knowing one day she would have to go through them. She came to her knees and reached for a larger box. It held ribbons and photos of Charlie's '59 win. More memorabilia for the historical society. She found six more boxes with similar ribbons and photos.

She stood, dusting her backside, and placed the boxes in a section of the room she designated as "storage". Then she arched backward, stretching her back, and caught sight of a small steamer trunk on the opposite wall. She pulled it to the middle of the floor and lifted the lid.

It was full of yearbooks and photos of her mother. "Jackpot." Her mother hadn't talked about her granddad, which made Eleanor believe that father and daughter hadn't been close. But the photos told a very different story. There were hundreds of them, of her mother and Granddad Charlie. Some were of them riding and roping, others were simply quiet moments her grandma had caught on camera. Eleanor dug deeper into the chest, searching for answers. She leaned the photos against the wall, sorting through years of her mother's life.

The fair-haired, blue-eyed, chubby-cheeked little girl wearing a pink fringed cowgirl dress and matching hat was her mother. And so was the toddler sitting on Santa's lap.

Birthdays, graduations, and holidays were all celebrated and gave proof to the happiness Rose told of. "So what happened?" And why were the photos up here, hidden and out of sight?

In the next photo, her mother was older and probably in her late teens or early twenties.

The front door opened downstairs, drawing her attention from the photo.

"Eleanor?" she heard McCrea call out from the second floor.

"I'm in the attic," she yelled.

He sprinted up the stairs.

"I thought you'd be busy for most of the day. So I started without you."

"I finished early." He let out a whistle as he looked around. "You weren't kidding."

"It's like a montage of all the Indiana Jones movies. All that's missing is Harrison Ford and a whip," she joked and waved him closer. "Look at this."

McCrea crossed over the boxes she'd moved and stepped in behind her, wrapping his arms around her to look over her shoulder. "Is this your mother?"

"Yeah, but the photo looks weird. It's off center, like half of its missing."

"Or folded back," he said, taking the photo from her. He flipped it over and slid the cardboard backing down, disclosing the hidden part of the photo. When he slipped it out, a folded piece of paper fell to the floor. He handed her the photo and bent to pick up the paper.

She carefully unfolded it and stared at the man holding her mother's hand. He was built like a tank, muscular and stocky with gray eyes, dark hair, and a beard. "I wonder if this is my dad?"

When McCrea didn't answer, she glanced up at him. He'd unfolded the paper and was reading it. "What is it?"

His eyes didn't give anything away as he handed it to her.

She read it silently. *Franny, I pray one day you can forgive me and yourself for what happened. But know that my heart will always be with you and our little girl.*

Love always, J.E.

Chill bumps covered her arms. Tears rimmed her eyes. Was the letter from the faceless man who had haunted her dreams? The man who had abandoned her and her mother?

"That's it?" she questioned, feeling more pain and disappointment settle into her chest. "'I'm sorry, Franny?' The bastard left us and 'I'm sorry' is all he could manage?"

"Come here." McCrea pulled her into his arms, and the tears in her eyes were unleashed.

It wasn't just the unanswered questions about her dad that made her want to drop to the floor and have a temporary meltdown. It was also this, McCrae holding her, comforting her like he had on the side of the road. It was her not knowing what was going to happen between them when she left Santa Camino. Because no matter how hard she tried, she couldn't shake the uncertainty of his motives and his true feelings for her.

"We can hire a private investigator —"

"No," she said, withdrawing to collect herself. "If the man didn't care enough about me to stick around, then he's not worth the time or money it would take to find him."

She brushed away her tears, tossed the photo and letter in a nearby box, and closed the lid on her unanswered questions, her emotions, and her fears.

SOMETHING HAPPENED when Eleanor closed that lid. It was like a switch inside her head flipped. She began rearranging boxes, furniture, clothes, and magazines into piles of what would go and what would stay.

She was cleaning out everything, years of memories, heartbreak, and loss. And there was no stopping her. She was composed, distant, and quiet. The questions from her childhood were eating away at her.

By late afternoon, he was sprinting down the stairs with the last box from the attic. He held it above his head and maneuvered his way across the living room to the stack of boxes with her granddad's rodeo stuff. "This is the last of it."

The wooden floor of the old house creaked beneath the weight of his body.

"That sounded like a weak spot," she said, blowing a strand of hair away from her eyes.

He took a seat on the arm of the couch. "This old house has a lot of life left in it. It just needs a little TLC."

"Maybe the new owner can afford to give it the upkeep it deserves," she said, walking towards the kitchen. "Violet thinks he's a movie star."

He grinned. "Here in Santa Camino?"

She returned with two bottles of water and handed him one. "A cowboy movie star, no less."

He twisted his open and chugged down a couple of gulps. "I know an excellent carpenter."

"You can refer him to the new owner." She bit her bottom lip and shoved a hand into her back pocket. "I'm sure they'll be a lot of things he wants to change to make it more modern."

McCrea didn't want to change anything. He loved the old house just the way it was. There was a homey feel, strength and durability modern homes didn't have. Generations of Mackenna's had built a life here. A life of love and longevity, of children and love. It was a life he wanted. It was a life he craved and a life he wanted to make with her.

There wasn't a doubt in his mind that he loved her. He knew he could tell her a hundred times a day how much he loved her. But Eleanor needed to see, hear, touch, and feel that love. He prayed to God he'd done that.

But he wondered if he was making a mistake by proposing. Eleanor had seen firsthand what a loveless marriage was like and couldn't let go of the uncertainty of what was ahead for them.

McCrea wanted to make those vows in front of his family and friends. He wanted to slide that ring on her finger, kiss her, and hear the minister say, "I now pronounce you husband and wife." He wanted that commitment and trust from Eleanor.

He closed his eyes and listened to the silence, the peace and tranquility of the place that felt like home. But still, there was something missing. "The house is so quiet without Sophie."

"Yeah, it is," she sighed. "I know you don't want to talk about us leaving, but —"

"You're right. I don't." He had avoided talking and thinking about it. Eleanor would accept his proposal, and they would never discuss visitation.

"I don't want Sophie to wonder if and when her daddy will show up." Her arms crossed, and her shoulders drew inward. McCrea watched the woman shrink back and the little girl emerge. "I need to be able to tell her when she'll see you again. She needs reassurance that you haven't left her."

"Darlin'," he said, knowing these were her childhood fears, not Sophie's. "We'll see each other every day."

"How? Are you going to drive to Austin every day?"

He should just do it. Get down on one knee and ask her to marry him. He had been carrying the ring around in his pocket for days.

But he wanted this proposal to be special. He wanted it to be right, to be memorable and perfect. He wanted this one to wipe away the memory of the first one.

"If that's what it takes, then, yes, I'll drive to Austin every day."

"Be serious."

He tucked a loose strand of hair behind her ear. "I promise we'll talk about it soon. But this is the first time we've had the house to ourselves."

The worry in her eyes gave way to interest. "It is, isn't it?"

"So you can hardly blame me for not wanting to waste it on talking," he teased.

She moved between his thighs and wrapped her arms around his neck. "I see your point."

"I knew you would."

"What will we do in this big ol' house all by our-selves?" she asked, looking at him with those soft, sexy eyes that made his dick twitch.

He rose from the couch, laced his fingers through hers, and playfully tugged her up the stairs to the bed-room they had shared last night.

Chapter Twenty-Five

If someone had told Eleanor two weeks ago that she would be riding in a limo to a bachelor auction charity event for the Promise Point Foundation to bid on McCrea, she would have snorted in the most unladylike way and told them when hell organized a bobsleigh team.

But here she was, doing both. The limo had arrived promptly at six o'clock, just as McCrea said it would. By six-fifteen, the door opened, and Eleanor placed her black high heel on the cobblestone sidewalk outside the Tall Oaks ballroom.

Several guests had already arrived and were in the tasting room adjacent to the ballroom. From the schedule handed to her at the door by a rather pompous looking fellow, Eleanor knew that there would be wine and icebreaker games to follow. Oh, goodie.

Eleanor was a cheese spread and cold beer kind of

woman, but when she walked into the tasting room, she felt like Cinderella.

All eyes were on her. She had checked her makeup and low chignon bun before getting out of the limo. So it had to be the dress. Sue said the black mermaid style dress was perfect for her, and Eleanor had liked that it made her look sexy and sophisticated. It fit snug to the shape of her hips and flared out at her calves. But the dipping neckline made her a little self-conscious.

She adjusted the matching wrap and headed to where Sage was standing next to one of the tables.

"Oh, El," Sage gasped. "You are stunning."

"It's not too revealing?" she asked, giving Sage a peek under the wrap.

"Absolutely not. I wish I could wear something that daring."

The teal wraparound party dress Sage was wearing was flattering and accentuated her brown eyes. "I think you look beautiful."

"Thank you."

Eleanor took a glass of wine from a passing server and stepped over to the door leading into the two-story ballroom. There were dozens of elegantly decorated banquet tables set up, as well as two large screens on either side of the stage. "This place is something."

Sage joined her. "Nestled in the hills of central Texas, Tall Oaks Winery is a rare gem which offers a unique and elegant venue for every occasion. Its three thousand square foot, Tuscany-style winery sits majestically among fifty acres of opulent grapevines. The Grand Ballroom is large enough for weddings and corporate events yet provides an intimate space for cocktail parties and family gatherings." Sage paused to explain.

"I use the information from their website as one of my selling points to potential buyers."

More guests had arrived, and the tasting room began to fill. "It must work. There are a lot of people I don't recognize."

"These people are from all over the country," Sage said, pointing to the two gentlemen who had just walked in. "That's Jasper and Bill Baxter. Jasper's daughter went through the Equine Therapy Program and Bill's son was on his third deployment overseas. They're great guys and die-hard supporters of the Promise Point Foundation."

Eleanor scanned the crowd for McCrea. Some of the other bachelors had arrived and were mingling with the ladies. Brook had the arms of bachelor's number six and nine. But Eleanor knew she would still be bidding on McCrea. Soon after, Ed and Sue arrived.

Sage leaned closer. "Aren't those two the sweetest couple?"

"They are," she agreed, watching the man behind them. He was tall with dark brown hair and a face that was so familiar. He shook hands with Jasper and Bill, and when he smiled, Eleanor felt as though she'd seen a ghost. "Is that Colton Ritter?"

"That's him. Colton is a living, breathing testament as to why the foundation is so important."

"I thought — I mean —" Words failed Eleanor, but relief poured over her. She suddenly understood just how important the foundation and the ranch were to McCrea. Promise Point wasn't solely about rescuing horses. It was about saving men and women like Colton. It was about helping families regain their loved ones. Little Jack hadn't lost his daddy.

Sage raised her glass when Colton looked their way.

"Colton is a spokesman for the foundation. He does speaking engagements and conducts educational seminars to inform the public about the importance of the work they do with veterans."

"Is he one of the bachelors being auctioned off?"

"Oh, no, Colton is still a married man." Sage motioned discreetly to where Lauren was sitting alone at the bar.

As Colton walked closer, Lauren dipped her head. His hand opened and closed as if he were tempted to reach out and touch her. They spoke quietly to each other without eye contact. Then Colton shoved his hands into his pockets, and Lauren covered her mouth before rushing towards the bathroom.

"It always ends like that," Sage said with a sad undertone to her voice. "Lauren hasn't been back to the Lucky Jack since McCrea found him."

"Why do they stay together?"

Sage sighed. "Who knows? Maybe for Little Jack or maybe because they love each other. We all keep hoping they'll work it out."

"Hey, girls." Louisa bounced in between them, making them jump. "Did you bring your checkbooks?"

"We did," Eleanor answered, feeling the effects of her second glass of wine kick in.

Louisa adjusted the short hem of her red Bodycon dress and snapped her fingers. "Good. Now, let's get this party started."

"Where's Violet?" Sage asked.

"She's here somewhere." Louisa lifted her head to look for their friend. "I saw her walk in with Joel. Oh, there she is."

Dressed in a white, sleeveless party dress that did

nothing but compliment her figure, Violet accepted the glass of wine Joel offered her.

"Do you think Logan and Tyler believe Joel is really gay?" Eleanor asked.

Louisa shrugged. "He's still breathing, isn't he?"

When the icebreakers started, McCrea was still nowhere to be found. Eleanor left the tasting room and walked into the ballroom, hoping to find him. She made her way down the hall and into the kitchen where the staff worked at preparing dinner for the guests. But McCrea wasn't there.

She walked back to the ballroom and was about to take a seat when she saw him. He was standing outside on the terrace. Quietly, she made her way to the door and opened it. He was near the edge with one hand tucked inside his pocket as he leaned an elbow against the railing.

The position gave her a side view of his rigid jaw and hard expression as his eyes searched for something on the horizon. His shoulders were fixed as if they bore the weight of the world. What was he doing out here alone? What was he looking for? What was he thinking about? Why did he look so worried? Was it saying goodbye to Sophie? They hadn't talked about custody. Or was it her?

A nagging fear worked its way up her chest and into her throat. When McCrea made the deal with her, they had been at the early stages of trying to mend fences for Sophie's sake. Maybe he expected it to be all fun and games with their relationship never going past sex. Maybe buying the dress and playing the part of an attentive lover was his way of lessening the sting of what he thought would be a hard goodbye.

Hadn't she always known it would end this way? With

them parting as friends when she went back to Austin? Tears threatened her eyes, but she wouldn't cry. If this was his plan, she wouldn't cry and ruin her makeup, throw a hissy fit or cause a scene. She wouldn't make this awkward or difficult for either of them. She would enjoy their last night together. This time, she would leave Santa Camino with her dignity. "The icebreaker games have started."

Her voice pulled McCrea's eyes away from the view and onto her.

"And since I'm only interested in you, I didn't want to play."

With a slack jaw and wide eyes, he looked her over.

She tried smiling, but his lack of words made her uneasy. "Do you like it?"

He shook his head as if trying to regain his senses and blinked a couple of times. "Like isn't the word, darlin'. I— I'm flabbergasted."

"No." She waved a finger at him. "You're not getting off that easy. I want words and sentences. How do I look?"

McCrea pulled her to the middle of the terrace and locked his hands behind his back in a studious fashion. He walked around her slowly, studying every detail of her body. The adoration and desire in his eyes were as enthralling as chocolate and sex. "You are lovely and exquisite. A regal goddess with an unsurpassed beauty. You are a sweet rose whose sensual fragrance entrances me." Having made a full circle around her, he stopped, awaiting her response.

"Much better," she said, wrapping both arms around his neck. "I was so eager for you to see me as a woman the night we had our first date, not your sister's annoying friend. So I dressed to tempt, fancied up my face and hair, and strolled into the Roadhouse determined to make you mine."

McCrea eased closer for a kiss. "You did."

She withdrew a fraction. If he was trying to let her down easy, this wasn't the way to do it. "Did I? Are you really mine?"

A slight frown darted across his brow. "You have to ask?"

"I do."

His eyes took in the details of her face as though each one was a new star he had just discovered. "You have all of me, Eleanor Mackenna. You own me. Heart, body, and soul," he said, sealing his avowal with a soft kiss.

"Heart, soul, and body," she whispered. "By my calculations, that equals love."

His lips lifted into a sexy, melt-your-panties smile, and he winked. "You always were good at math."

Her body began to tingle.

"Okay, ladies and gentlemen, let's get started with tonight's auction," the auctioneer's voice sounded over the PA system.

McCrea held out his arm and Eleanor accepted it, letting him lead her back inside. "Are you nervous about being on stage in front of all these women?"

His smile wavered. "Not nearly as nervous as I am about what happens afterward." Inside, he kissed Eleanor's cheek and headed backstage. What was going to happen afterward?

"Shall we?" Jess asked, taking the arm McCrea had just let go of.

"Hey, stranger." She laughed. "Why aren't you in the line-up?"

"My only job tonight is to make sure you're seated in the right place."

"The right place for what?" she asked.

Jess led her over to the table where Louisa, Sage, and Violet sat. He pulled out her chair and she sat down.

"Finn is up first," Louisa said, grinning.

"I wonder what his routine will be?" Sage asked.

"I heard handcuffs may be involved." Violet snickered.

The auctioneer stepped up to the mic and the large screen behind her lit up with the Promise Point logo. "Welcome to the Promise Point Third Annual Bachelor Auction!"

Cheers and clapping followed, as well as a few whistles.

"Mr. Colton Ritter would like to say a few words before we get started."

A spotlight centered on Colton as he stepped up onto the stage and took the mic. "We are so pleased you could join us for tonight's event. As you know, the Promise Point Foundation helps hundreds of veterans and their families throughout the U.S. each year. We could not do this without faithful volunteers and donors like yourselves." He laid a hand over his heart. "I thank you from the bottom of my heart."

A standing ovation followed, and Colton returned to his seat.

After the crowd quieted, the spotlight cut and the screen went black. Excitement built, giggles and chatter followed. Then Finn's face appeared on the screen and "Pony" by Ginuwine began playing.

"Oh, God." Eleanor laughed.

"Ladies, are you ready?" the auctioneer prompted.

The crowd roared to life with cheers.

"The first bachelor up for auction will make you walk the line… Finn Durant!"

Louisa stood and rolled out her signature whistle. The spotlight centered on the black curtain as it parted, and Finn walked out. Ladies jumped to their feet, ready to bid.

"We'll start the bidding out at one hundred dollars," the auctioneer said.

Louisa waved her number in the air. "One hundred!"

Finn reached into his pocket, pulled out his mirrored shades and slid them on. Then he walked to the end of the stage, twirling a pair of red-feathered handcuffs around his finger.

A lady across the room challenged her. "Two hundred dollars!"

"Three hundred," Sage yelled, shooting Louisa a sly shrug.

Louisa laughed, taking the challenge in good fun.

Finn worked the crowd with his mojo until the final bid was at twenty-five hundred dollars. But Louisa and Sage lost the date with a three-thousand-dollar challenge.

Louisa settled back in her chair and fanned her face with the schedule. "Damn, that was fun."

"Tyler's up next." Eleanor bobbed her head back and forth while grinning at Violet.

Violet winced. "Awkward."

"A date with bachelor number two may leave you covered in oil…. Ladies, meet Mr. Tyler Durant!"

Michael Jackson's "Give In To Me" began, and the curtain parted for Tyler. With a pipe wrench resting on a shoulder, he made his way down the stage. The bidding started, and Tyler used the tool in a suggestive, but tasteful way to raise bids.

Violet grimaced and covered her eyes with both hands. "Tell me when it's over."

The crowd was alive, on their feet, waving numbers, shouting bids, and having the time of their lives. Tyler left the stage with a final bid of two thousand.

McCrea was up next. Like before, the lights dimmed, and the crowd grew hushed in anticipation of the next bachelor. Then the music started.

Eleanor had heard the piano introduction before but couldn't place the song until John Legend began singing the tender ballad of "All of Me." The lights were still low, and McCrea's introduction hadn't started. Halfway through the song, the spotlight centered on the center of the curtain. It parted, and McCrea walked out.

Chapter Twenty-Six

McCrea was a man who hated soirees and could never be labeled as having savoir-faire. To him, parties and social get-togethers were more about beer and barbecue than about rubbing elbows with the town's well-to-doers.

Most people mistook his lack of élan as a characteristic of the strong, silent type. With the dressings of a suit jacket and tie, a dash of expensive cologne, and a drink in his hand, he could make it through without a single hiccup.

And by now, McCrea should have been at a corner table, slouching in his seat with a bored expression plastered across his face. Instead, the tough, leather-worn horse wrangler was about to take a walk down the catwalk for a charity he founded.

Absolutely amazing.

As he walked down the stage, Eleanor noticed a single red rose in his hand. Classy, but she had yet to figure out how he was going to use it to drive up bids. It didn't matter. She was ready. Damn that Brook Tidwell.

The spotlight followed him to the end of the stage and down the steps. Okay, so he was going to mingle with the crowd. Good idea, because the air was dead without a single whistle or yell. As he neared their table, their eyes locked, and Eleanor suddenly knew exactly what McCrea was doing.

He wasn't telling her goodbye. He was proposing. This was bad. This was so bad. God, please don't let him propose, she prayed silently.

"What's he doing?" Violet asked Sage.

"Shhh…" Sage scolded.

"Tell me this isn't happening," Eleanor whispered.

"It's happening," Louisa answered.

McCrea stopped in front of Eleanor and handed her the rose.

John continued to sing, pouring out his heart to the woman. Those damn butterflies were back, fluttering around in her stomach, making her nauseous. She clutched her midriff as the sound of her beating heart drowned out the music. This was it, the life-altering, catastrophic event that changed lives.

Again, all eyes were on Eleanor, but this time, instead of staying for the ball, Cinderella wanted to run. She didn't want to embarrass McCrea in front of his friends and family by turning down his proposal in public.

But she didn't have a choice. So, she turned, dropping the rose as she hurried across the ballroom and out the door. Pausing just outside the tasting room, she removed her heels and headed towards where the limos were parked. She didn't know where she was going, but she had to get as far away from McCrea as she could.

"Eleanor," she heard his voice call out from behind her.

She ran faster and faster until she reached the limo, but the door was locked, and the driver was nowhere in sight.

McCrea had finally caught up with her. "What are you doing?"

She burst into tears. "I had to get out of there. The song, the rose…I got spooked."

He wrapped his hands around her arms, pulling her to him. "This was supposed to be a happy night. Don't cry. I hate it when you cry."

"I'm leaving in the morning, McCrea," she sobbed.

"You don't have to leave. Redemption is yours."

She cleared her eyes and sniffed. "Redemption is gone, McCrea. I signed the papers this morning. You know that."

Reaching into his jacket pocket, McCrea pulled out an envelope. "Redemption is yours."

Hesitantly, she took it and flipped it over and lifted the flap to pull out the paper inside. She unfolded it. It was the deed to Redemption. "You're the anonymous buyer?"

"There was no anonymous buyer."

"But the money —"

"Is for your partnership. I know how important it is to have something of your own," he explained. "But rebuilding the ranch was always your dream. This way, you can have both."

Her brain scrambled to make sense of what was happening. "I don't understand."

What happened next was book two in the slow-moving train wreck saga that had started in the ballroom. From the same jacket pocket, McCrea produced a small white box. "Redemption is my wedding present to you. Marry me," he said, dropping to one knee as he opened the box.

A wave of prickly needles blanketed her body, evoking memories of his first proposal.

"I love you, Eleanor."

The butterflies fluttered to life again in a kaleidoscope of color. They flew higher and higher, lifting her above her doubts and fears. McCrea had said the words she had always wanted to hear.

I love you.

The man she had loved since she was eight years old was finally hers. Sophie had a father who loved and adored her. Romeo was hers and so was Redemption. How many times did a woman get everything her heart desired? One in a million, maybe.

"I've waited so long to hear you say that."

There was something open and yielding, something translucent and vulnerable in McCrea's eyes. "Make babies with me. Love me recklessly and without caution."

Eleanor wanted to savor having his love and of saying yes. She wanted to savor his words and the moment of having it all. She wanted to believe they could make marriage work. But her untrusting heart wouldn't let her.

"I'll stay and make babies with you," she agreed through tears. "And I'll love you recklessly and without caution. But I won't marry you."

He blinked once, twice, three times, then rose to his feet. "Why not?"

"Once we make those vows, neither of us will break them, no matter how horrible the marriage becomes. Think about Colton and Lauren and about how miserable you were with Vanessa."

"I told you our marriage wouldn't be like that."

"Why won't it? Because of Sophie?"

His frown was deep. "What? No! I love you!"

"You love Sophie. Marriage is binding, McCrea, and I need to be able to walk away after the new wears off."

A muscle in his jaw flexed as he snapped the box shut and returned it to his pocket. "You don't believe I love you?"

"No," she whispered. "There's too much at stake. I will listen to my head instead of my heart this time. I will never put Sophie through the hell I went through. She won't see a broken mother weeping for a man who doesn't love her."

"Eleanor, you are not your mother, and I'm not Rex. I love you."

No, they weren't, but love couldn't be trusted. It was volatile, so unstable and dangerous. It could snuff out vibrancy, beauty, and life. In the wrong hands, it had the power to kill, or worse, beat away at a person until they were nothing more than an empty vessel.

Frantically, she wiped her face and stuffed the deed back into the envelope. "Sophie was just an infant when I used to cry myself to sleep. She won't be this time, and I will never put her through the hell I went through. I should have faced the facts and walked away days ago."

"What are the facts?" he asked grimly.

"That my mother and I are cursed when it comes to love." With those words, fresh tears came. Because this was the heart of her problem. Not McCrea. Not what had happened between them years ago. It wasn't him. It was her. Her past, her childhood, and her fears.

It was all about her.

He stared at her for what seemed like hours. "Eleanor." His voice rattled with emotion as he stepped forwards to hold her chin. "I am sorry that you had such a shitty childhood. I'm sorry Rex was a son of a bitch to you. I'm sorry you had to watch your mother weep for a man you think didn't love her. I'm sorry your dad walked out on you." He let his hand drop. "But most of all, I'm sorry you don't know love when it's holding you."

Pain tore through her. She did know love. He had dark cognac eyes that sparkled when he laughed, hair the color of rich coffee, and a voice that soothed her like nothing else did. Love was standing in front of her, with a ring in his pocket and a shattered look on his face.

He took a step back, then walked around her. "I'll get the driver."

The ride back to Redemption was more than quiet. It was heavy and exhausting and by the time the limo stopped, Eleanor could hardly move.

She shifted the wrap higher on her shoulders and gripped it tightly with one hand while the other still held the envelope with the deed to Redemption. She held it out to him. "You bought it. It's yours."

He pushed it back to her. "Give it to Sophie."

"The money—?"

"Is for your partnership," he said, not looking at her.

"I can't take—"

"It's done." His tone was low but curt. "The money is already in your account."

Eleanor opened the door and stepped out of the limo. She watched until the lights faded to black. Dear God, how was she ever going to recover from this? She wouldn't. It was that simple. When she left tomorrow, her heart would stay where it had been since she was eight, with McCrea.

McCREA SLAMMED the office door and gave his hat a hard sling across the room. With the swipe of his hand, everything on the desk followed. "Goddamn it!"

The laptop cracked as it hit the floor and skidded under a chair. The trunk with the letters Eleanor had given him hit the wall and splintered in half. Papers quietly floated to the floor, and McCrea was left with a dismal reality. Tomorrow Eleanor and Sophie would be gone, and there wasn't a damn thing he could do about it.

He stepped around the corner of the desk and yanked open the bottom drawer. Then flung files and papers to the mess on the floor and dug until he found what he was looking for.

A bottle of whiskey.

He fell to the chair, and after twisting the lid off, lifted the bottle to his lips. He chugged a couple of long gulps to dull the pain that had settled deep into his bones. He was back to square one. Up came the bottle, and he began chugging.

He wiped his mouth and balanced the bottle on his thigh. He had done everything Ed told him to. He had manned up, confessed everything, and tried his damnedest to make amends. But it wasn't enough. Because he couldn't erase Eleanor's past. He couldn't make her trust love.

He leaned forward, braced his elbows against his

thighs, and let his head drop as his eyes came to rest on the name Callie Coldiron written on the envelope beneath his boot. The letters from the trunk were mixed in with business receipts, bills, and reports from the desk.

He didn't care about the letters or the goddamn gold. He took another swig and winced as the burn set in. Then he moved his foot, and the letter shifted, exposing the letter underneath. A letter addressed to Franny Mackenna.

He picked it up, his eyes dropping to the return address. Private First Class J.E. Carmichael. Marine Corps Base, Camp Pendleton, California.

He yanked the letter out and began reading.

Dear Franny,

How are you? I called yesterday, but Rose said you weren't feeling well...

His eyes skimmed to the bottom.

Love always, J.E.

"Who the hell are you, J. E. Carmichael?" He sat the whiskey on the desk and moved to his hands and knees, searching for more letters. There were over a dozen with the Camp Pendleton address.

One by one, he read the letters and soon knew the missing pieces of Eleanor's painful childhood. Rose had hidden the letters in the trunk to keep Eleanor from finding him, from making the connection to her biological father. The man in the picture with her mother. The stocky Marine with piercing gray eyes. The man who had abandoned Eleanor.

Private First Class J.E. Carmichael.

"That deceitful bastard," he hissed under his breath. Then scrambled to his feet, out the door, and to his truck.

By the time he turned into Tall Oaks, he was hell-bent for leather. He slammed the brake to the floor and pushed the truck into park. He ran through the empty tasting room and into the ballroom as the last bachelor was coming down the catwalk. He pushed through the crowd to the table where Ed and Sue were sitting.

"When were you going to tell her?" he shouted over the music and slung the stack of letters across the table.

Sue jumped, and Ed's back stiffened. "I wasn't."

"You've known all this time that she was your daughter."

"Daughter?" Sue asked, her eyes bouncing back and forth between them. "Ed, what's going on?"

Ed steeled his eyes. "It's better this way."

"For who?" McCrea blasted. "She thinks you left her."

Ed's head jerked up. "I did."

"She needs to know the truth. She needs to know what Charlie did."

"No."

"She's leaving, Ed," McCrea said, flatly.

Ed shook his head. "That's on you. Not me."

"She has some twisted notion that she's cursed in love because her father ran out on her, and her mother married an abusive son of a bitch." McCrea pointed a finger at Ed. "That's on you."

"I didn't know Rex was abusive. It killed me to know she'd been hurt."

"She's hurting now, and you have the power to stop it."

Ed dropped his head to stare at the faded letters. "No."

"I love her, and I want to make her my wife. I want the three of us to be a family. You remember what that's like, don't you, Ed? The feeling of loving someone more than you do yourself? Of knowing your life will never be complete unless they're in it?"

Ed's eyes closed. "Nothing I say will change her mind."

McCrea held the letters up with a shake. "These will."

"No, they won't," he said. "All they'll do is tarnish Charlie's memory."

"Fuck Charlie's memory!" he yelled, drawing everyone's attention to the table. "He was a son of a bitch for what he did—"

Ed came to his feet. "You don't know a damn thing about Charlie."

"Maybe I don't, but I know that down the road there's a woman we both love who, at this very moment, is packing her bags because she's hurt and scared. And tomorrow, she's leaving." He pushed the letters into Ed's chest. "She's taking my daughter and your granddaughter with her."

"Your granddaughter?" Sue repeated.

"Man up," McCrea gritted out. "Isn't that what you told me when I came back from Montana? Take some of your own advice."

"Go to hell," Ed ordered through tight lips.

Chapter Twenty-Seven

C offee was coffee, Eleanor reminded herself, and drummed her fingers impatiently against the kitchen counter as she waited for her morning joe to brew. Though she had spent most of her adult life drinking whatever brand was on sale at the grocery store, she had recently become spoiled by having hers hand delivered by a tall, dark-haired cowboy. But after being back in Austin for nearly three weeks, she knew that wasn't possible.

As they often did, her eyes moved to the picture on the refrigerator held in place by brightly colored alphabet letters. It was the photo she had snapped of Sophie and McCrea asleep on the loveseat.

For Sophie, the goodbye hadn't been as hard as Eleanor feared. She had been sad about leaving McCrea but had quickly bounced back to her happy self when he promised to see her soon. He called her every morning and every night. And he was never too busy to talk when she wanted to. Sophie trusted her daddy and never doubted that he would be there.

They handled visitation one day at a time, talked cordially over the phone, and exchanged friendly smiles when he picked Sophie up and dropped her off. But since they had left Redemption three weeks ago, Eleanor's life had been hell. She couldn't eat, sleep, or concentrate.

She filled her coffee to the brim, hoping the caffeine rush would kick in quickly.

"Is Daddy here?" Sophie's burst into the kitchen, caused Eleanor to jump. Hot coffee sloshed over the side onto her hand.

She bit her lip to keep from cursing and sat the cup on the counter. "No, baby. Daddy's not here yet. Mommy was talking to herself. Are you ready to go?"

"Huh-uh."

"Did you pack your toothbrush?"

Sophie grinned slyly. "I forgot."

"I thought as much. Hurry and put it in your bag. Daddy will be here any minute."

Sophie disappeared down the hall, and Eleanor knelt to clean up the mess. She unrolled a handful of paper towels and stopped, her mind going back to the night she and McCrea had had tea.

She burst into tears. Damn it! Why did everything remind her of him? Yesterday, she had burst into tears when a customer ordered a beer. It was beer, for god sakes. And this was coffee. She was crying over spilled coffee.

She was usually able to hold them back. But this morning, she felt like her whole world was falling apart. She couldn't do this, not now, not yet. She had to wait until McCrea and Sophie were gone.

"I got it." Sophie returned. "What's wrong, Mommy?"

"Nothing, baby," Eleanor assured her with a wide smile. "Mommy burned her hand. That's all." Gathering the soppy mess, she stood and threw it into the garbage can, then turned to see McCrea standing in the kitchen.

"Daddy!" Sophie exclaimed.

He pulled her into his arms. "You ready, Rosy Posey?"

"Yes!"

"Good. Get your bags."

Sophie sprinted up the stairs, and the silence between them became deafening.

His face was impassive as he removed his hat and raked a hand through his hair. "I knocked, but I guess you didn't hear me."

"No, I was trying to clean up the mess I made." God, if that were possible. But it would take more than paper towels to clean up the mess she had made. She unrolled another hand full and busied herself with the cleanup.

"How've you been?"

His polite question caused a sharp stab of pain to cut through her body. She had done it, pushed him to polite hellos and goodbyes during holidays and visitation. "Fine. You?"

"Good. Busy."

"Yeah." She forced herself to laugh. "Me too. How are Hope and Filly doing?"

"Good." He fumbled with the brim of his hat. "Eleanor, I…"

She held her breath, hoping he would say something, anything, that would make her feel like she wasn't being ripped apart. But this mess wasn't his to clean up. It was hers and she needn't look to him for help.

"I'm ready!" Sophie zoomed into the kitchen, grabbed McCrea's hand, and started tugging him towards the door. "Bye, Mommy."

"Bye, baby."

"Hold up, Rosy Posey." He laughed. "I'm coming."

Eleanor kept her smile in place. "You'd better go before she jerks your arm off."

"Yeah, I guess so," he said, following Sophie to the door.

"Mommy burned herself, Daddy," she heard Sophie explain. "That's why she was crying."

When the door closed, Eleanor fell to the floor and cried. She had burned herself. Badly.

CASE JACKSON, a returning performer at the Rebel Road, churned out one tune after another. His deep, soulful voice and good looks always drew a crowd on Saturday nights, and Eleanor had been behind the bar since her shift started at six.

Two waiters had called in sick, and the bartender's little boy had fallen at the playground and broken his arm. So, with three employees missing, she and Hank were filling in where they were needed.

But she liked it busy. It helped to keep her mind off the second deed she had found yesterday after Sophie and McCrea left.

Promise Point was hers. He had given her the land, the business, and his dream.

Nix planted himself on a bar stool shortly after nine and started ordering longnecks. There was nothing unusual about that. He came into the bar on a regular basis, usually with a woman. But tonight, he was alone. And looking more tortured than ever.

She could count on three fingers the number of times she had seen him drunk. He didn't blow off steam by getting wasted or kill his cares with a bottle. So why was he sitting here drinking like a fish?

When Case finished his rendition of Blake Shelton's "Boys 'Round Here," Nix narrowed one bloodshot eye at her. "So, what are you going to do with the ranch?"

Knowing Tracey had filled him in on all the details, she lifted a shoulder as she snagged the empty bottles next to him. "I don't know. I haven't had time to think about it." She chucked the bottles into the garbage can and came back to wipe the rings away.

Nix's face contorted into a drunken scowl. "That's bullshit. You've had plenty of time." The finger he had hooked around the top of his beer pointed to her. "You don't want to deal with it. You're trying to ignore it like it's a bad case of the crabs."

She'd had almost a month to think about what she was going to do with Redemption, and she hadn't indulged in a single second of thought. Because thinking of Redemption made her think of McCrea. And when she thought of him, she cried. "If by it, you mean him, then yes, I am."

He tilted the bottle to his lips and swallowed. "He won't go away, El."

"I pray he never does. Sophie needs her daddy."

Nix gave her a drowsy wink. "And so do you."

"But I'm a big girl. I'll get over it."

"No, you won't," he said and emptied the bottle.

She hadn't had a chance to apologize for the argument they'd had before she left, and though he didn't seem to be waiting on one, she felt she was partly to blame for his surly mood. Nix was always in control, in and out of uniform. He kept his words few, his advice short, and his ghosts under lock and key. This was the closest he had come to ever letting her see them.

She picked up the bottle and gave the bar a swipe. "I'm sorry for what I said the other day about you running from Sabrina."

"Don't be. You were right. But unlike you, I won't get a second chance."

Dread settled in the pit of her stomach. "Why won't you, Nix? What happened to Sabrina?"

His glazed eyes met hers. "She died."

A sharp stab of pain hit her in the chest. "Oh, God, I — I'm sorry."

"Yeah, me too," he said, his voice raw with emotion.

His darkness was death. How could anything she had been through compare? No wonder the poor man looked tortured.

In McCrea's arms, she felt whole, and if her heart had beaten before he'd made love to her, it was a melancholy rhythm at best. She fought the fear of never loving again, of never having the intimate joining of body, heart, and soul.

"Forget the petty shit. Life's too short."

In terms of what had been lost, she knew she came in second. Death couldn't be measured by a broken heart and betrayal. But she wasn't being petty. She was being smart by protecting both their hearts.

"Forget the past and forget the hurt. If you love this guy, don't let him go."

She did love McCrea with all her heart. "You're supposed to be on my side."

"I am. That's why I'm telling you that life has a way of working itself out. And just when you think you have it figured out, it turns a different direction. This may be its way of correcting itself, setting right what went wrong four years ago. What you have to decide is how you're going to handle it. Do you give this guy a second chance or run like hell in the opposite direction?"

She hadn't considered her time with McCrea as a second chance. To her, it had been about second risks. But Nix would gladly give his soul in exchange for one more minute with the woman he loved. Yet she was forfeiting hers out of fear.

She suddenly felt awful for not taking it, and his honesty dug in deep to draw out her worst fears. "And what if you're wrong?"

"If I'm wrong, you can bury yourself in this place and buy a goddamn cat."

"I hate cats."

He stood and slid a palm over his chest. "Then you can pet me instead."

"Oh, you'd love that."

"Damn right I would." He dug into his pocket for his keys. "And so would Tracey."

"You're not in any shape to drive," she said, reaching over to snatch the keys from his hand. "I'll call you a cab."

"Don't bother. I have a designated driver."

"Who?"

"I'll let you know as soon as I find her," he said with a wicked grin as he staggered out onto the dance floor. A couple of minutes later, she saw him leave with a brunette.

Eleanor didn't get her name, and she knew Nix wouldn't either. Tomorrow, he would wake up to a stranger with his ghosts safely locked away once again.

After escorting the last customer out, Eleanor locked the doors and took her time cleaning up. Then she flipped off the lights and walked down the hall to the office where Hank was. "I'm done up front. Do you need help with anything?"

He glanced up from the computer screen and rubbed his eyes. "It's after three. Go home."

She groaned and plopped down on the couch. "I don't want to go home."

A trace of amusement twisted his lips. "Tracey and I would love to have the house all to ourselves every once in a while."

"Yeah, well, I'm flying solo. So going home to a lonely house isn't something I look forward to."

Get used to it. This is the way it's going to be. You and that damn cat.

Hank pinched the bridge of his nose and leaned back. "It's not too late to back out of this partnership."

She sat up from her slouching position. "You know I want it."

"I know you used to, but since you came back from Santa Camino, it's like you're just going through the motions. Your passion is gone. Or is somewhere else?"

Her passion was at Redemption among dusty barns, overgrown hayfields, and horses. But she couldn't live that dream. Because eventually, McCrea would marry again and have those babies he talked about. And that would be a living hell for her. So, she needed to be as far away from him as possible, not living a few miles down the road. "Going home was hard—"

"And leaving was even harder," he said, tapping the

end of his pen against the desk as he spoke. "Don't feel like you owe us an explanation. Just follow your heart, El."

"My heart doesn't make my decisions for me."

"Maybe that's your problem," he said, before turning his attention back to the computer.

First, Nix had accused her of being petty. Now, Hank was telling her to trust her heart and forget about the partnership. Was there some higher power at work here? Who was next? What was next? Maybe Morgan Freeman was waiting outside in a time machine, waiting to give her a glimpse at her future.

Cats. That's your future, Eleanor.

"Here," she said, tossing him Nix's keys. "He'll be looking for these tomorrow."

Hank caught them with one hand. "Think about what I said."

She unhooked her jacket and purse from the coat rack. "I will. All the way to the door. 'Night, Hank."

She slid the jacket on and stepped out onto the sidewalk. Bars on the Dirty Sixth closed at two, but the streets stayed crowded. She had learned how to maneuver her way through the crowd of patrons and sometimes rowdy partyers quickly and without much thought.

But tonight, her walk was a little slower as she thought of Santa Camino. She missed sunsets on the porch and coffee at Pixies. She missed taking walks by the creek and pancakes. But more than anything, she missed McCrea.

She missed the sound of his boots scraping across the hardwood floor, the feel of his callused palm when he cupped her jaw. The smell of his cologne, his laughter, and his passionate whispers as they made love.

It would be dawn in a couple of hours. Maybe she would drive to Lou Neff Point and watch the sunrise. Or maybe she would binge watch something on Netflix and eat a pint of ice cream.

She picked up the pace and headed for the Brazos Street Parking Garage where her car was when she saw a familiar face step into her path. "Ed?"

Ed's mouth hinted at a smile. "It's me, honey."

Chapter Twenty-Eight

Her old boss had driven to Austin and inserted himself into the vein of party central to see her? Okay, this was just weird. "What in the world are you doing here?"

"I came to see you," Ed said, dodging a group of college students. "Can we talk?"

Ed had always shown her a fatherly affection. He had taken her under his wing and given her a job when she was sixteen. He had looked out for her and made sure everyone treated her with respect. "Uh—well, I was on my way home…"

"I'll walk you to your car," he volunteered.

"Oh, okay, sure." She pointed up the street. "It's this way."

The crowd thinned, and the noise lessened as they neared Brazos Street, but Ed didn't offer to speak until they were inside the garage. "I'm glad you've decided to keep the ranch." She started to say that she hadn't decided on anything, but he didn't give her a chance. "Charlie always said he wanted it to stay in the family."

She took the lead, walking to the row where her car was parked. "You knew Granddad?"

"I worked for him as a ranch hand."

Santa Camino was a small town, and it wasn't strange that Ed knew her grandparents, but it was strange that he hadn't mentioned it before. "You worked at Redemption?"

"I'd enlisted in the Marines and needed a job to see me through until I was to report for basic training."

There was a part of her that knew where this was going. The part that chose not to see the similarities between the man in the photograph with her mother and the man she had worked for as a teenager. "When did you work there?"

"Charlie hired me in the spring of ninety-three."

She began counting back nine months from her birthday. Her mother had gotten pregnant in April of ninety-three. "You knew my mother."

"Yes, I knew Franny."

"Franny." She expelled the name with the breath she had been holding and leaned against the car for support. "You're J. E. Carmichael, aren't you?"

"James Edward," he confessed. "The boys in my platoon gave me the nickname Tubs. And Rose thought it was best that I go by something other than Carmichael, when I came back to town after leaving the Marines."

Ed was the secret her grandma had been hiding. "You're my dad."

"I am, honey."

She spent her childhood living for this exact moment. The day she would finally meet the man who had abandoned her. Bitterness worked its way up her throat, filling her mouth with a vile taste. "You left us."

"I didn't," he countered. "Franny left me."

"You're lying. She loved you! Do you know how many nights she spent crying for you?"

"Eleanor," his voice was soft and patient. "I wanted to marry Franny before I left for basic training. But when Charlie found out she was pregnant, he went off. He kicked me out on my ass and told Franny that if she married me, he'd disown her. He said his little girl deserved better than a ranch hand. And he was right."

Despite her bitterness, the humbleness on Ed's face made her want to defend him. He had always been good to her, and now she knew why. He was a kind and generous man who deserved a chance at love. But instead, her granddad had shunned him for being a ranch hand? If so, then Charlie Mackenna wasn't the man her Grandma Rose said he was.

"They argued, and Franny told Charlie she hated him and that she never wanted to see him again. The next morning, Charlie was dead. He'd had a heart attack in his sleep."

She closed her eyes, empathizing with the pain and guilt her mother must have felt when she found out Charlie had died. The pictures of father and daughter she found while at Redemption flooded her mind. Happy and joyful occasions, torn to shreds by a single moment of anger.

"Franny fell apart. The funeral was horrible. She just sat there, looking lost and alone. I tried to comfort her, to tell her that it wasn't her fault, and that Charlie knew she loved him. But she couldn't forgive herself."

He reached into his back pocket for a stack of letters tied together with a single blue ribbon. Her mother's favorite color. "I reported for basic training the week after. I wrote Franny, regularly and sent her money. But she never wrote back. I called, but she wouldn't talk to me."

"By the time I tracked her down in Santa Fe, she was married to Rex and expecting his baby. And she'd changed…" A deep sigh left him. "The Franny I fell in love with died with Charlie."

All those times her mother had cried herself to sleep weren't because the man she loved had left her or even because she had made the wrong choices. Her mother's tears were because she couldn't forgive herself for Charlie's death and from walking away from a man who truly loved her. "All this time, I thought…"

She let him take her hands because she needed to experience the loving touch of a father just once in her life.

"I know I've never been a father to you. But you need to know that your mother and I loved each other." He gave her hands a gentle squeeze before letting go.

She watched Ed turn and walk toward the exit. He wasn't Morgan Freeman. But he had given her a glimpse of her future by showing her the mistakes of the past. She held the letters tight against her chest, seeing the overwhelming similarities between herself and her mother. She had tried so hard not to make those same mistakes, but she was. McCrea loved her and Sophie and she was throwing away her chance at happiness.

God, Nix was right. She was running and if she didn't take this second chance, with McCrea and with Ed, she would regret it for the rest of her life.

She was a grown ass woman with a daughter of her own. She should be over needing her daddy. But she did. Inside, she was still that little girl, crying out for him. She needed to share birthdays and holidays with him. She needed to feel his hugs and hear his praise.

And life was too short for petty shit.

"Ed! Wait," she yelled, running to wrap her arms around his neck. "Thank you."

He held her tight. "Don't let what happened all those years ago between me and your mother keep you from making the right choices. McCrea is a good man, and he loves you, honey."

"I know, Ed," she whispered. "And I'm ready to go home."

THE SMELL of coffee opened McCrea's eyes to the smooth pine finish of the cabin ceiling. He blinked a couple of times and gave his reoccurring dreams of Eleanor and Redemption credit for the heavenly smell that had dragged him from sleep.

Groaning from another restless night, he sat up and swung his feet to the floor. With a long sigh, he snagged his duffle bag from the floor and hunted through it until he found his last pair of clean jeans.

Sophie had spent last night with his parents, so she could attend Sunday school this morning. She was happy here, and he hated that he had to take her back to Austin on Monday. He hated saying goodbye, and he hated that he had to call Eleanor to schedule a visit with his daughter. He didn't want shared holidays, and he didn't want to spend the rest of his life living on doorstep glances of Eleanor. He wanted them both living with him. But he couldn't compete with her fears. This was the way life was going to be, and he would make the best of it.

He had the morning alone to be grumpy, drink coffee, and think about how he was going to tell Eleanor about the letters. She deserved to know who J. E. Carmichael was and the real reason she had grown up without a father, even if it didn't make a difference in her decision to walk out of his life.

He slipped the jeans up his hips without bothering with the zipper and opened the bedroom door to a percolating coffee pot and the woman from his dreams.

Eleanor smiled up at him from the kitchen table. "Good morning."

He blinked. He was dreaming. Yeah, that was it. This was a dream because there was no way in hell Eleanor was sitting at his table, drinking his coffee.

But her she was raising an eyebrow in the direction of his open zipper. "Rough night?"

His mind had accepted that it was over between them. It had been the easiest to convince. Because logically they were both better off this way. At a distance. She didn't trust him or love him. And he wouldn't live with a line they never crossed. But his heart would never be over her. It would never heal, and every time he saw her, it would ache. Just like it was doing now.

And he would always want her, in his arms, in his bed and in every part of his life. She knew all of that. "No rougher than usual. How did you get in here? The door was locked."

She held up the spare key he had in the office. "Your new horse trainer told me where the spare was at. Nice guy."

"Who obviously doesn't know a damn thing about privacy."

"Oh, don't be too hard on him. He put up a fight until I showed him the deed with my name on it. Coffee?" she asked, getting up to pour him a cup without waiting for his answer. "I picked up this morning's paper. They arrested Chaves and Vanessa and a stolen antiquities dealer at the travel lodge. The article says they found several artifacts in the trunk of her car."

He scrubbed a hand over his face and focused on the headline: Stolen Antiquities Found. Police Arrest Three. He tossed the paper onto the table. "Yeah, Finn called me yesterday. The coins were among the stolen artifacts. We weren't able to prove Chaves was the one selling the horses, but he'll be going away for a while."

She smiled. "That's good."

He pulled out a chair and planted himself in it. "I thought we agreed I'd have Sophie until Monday."

She handed him a cup and sat down. "I'm not here for Sophie."

"Then why are you here?"

"I came to give you this." She unclasped the chain from around her neck and laid the necklace on the table. "Add it to your collection. I don't need it anymore."

She was returning his gift from the night they had first made love. The night Sophie was conceived. She couldn't have been any clearer that what they had was over. But something in his gut told him she was here to do more than return the necklace. "Is that all?"

"No, I want to know why you gave me Promise Point."

"Why does it matter?" he asked, lifting the cup to his lips.

"Well, technically, all of this is mine. The land, the

rescue, and even the chair you're sitting in belong to me now."

"So, are you here to tell me to hit the road?"

"No, of course not," she said, shaking her head. "I need someone to run the day-to-day operations."

"Someone to run..." His words ended with a satirical laugh. "Thanks, but no thanks. Jess is the executive director. You don't need me."

Her eyes softened. "But I do need you, McCrea."

Her words were like a slap to the face. "You could have given me the necklace when I dropped Sophie off. So, again, why are you here? Why aren't you in Austin living your dream of a partnership in the Rebel Road?"

"I turned the partnership down."

"Why?" he asked in an even tone, unwilling to let her see his surprise. Was it possible she had given up the Rebel Road for him and a life at Redemption?

She rested her elbows on the table and leaned closer. "You first. Why did you give me Promise Point?"

He raked both hands through his hair, feeling caught in a game of cat and mouse. "Because I wanted to prove to you that my dreams have changed. That I wasn't a man who valued land over love."

He saw her throat flex with an arduous swallow. "'I'd trade every acre of land I own to have a life with you and Sophie,'" she said, softly repeating his words.

"Yes," he admitted.

"How hard was that to say?" she asked.

"The first time, it was the easiest thing in the world, but now..." His voice faltered. "What do you want, Eleanor? Why are you here?"

She moved from her seat to behind him, slid her arms around his neck. The soft suppleness of her breasts pressed against his back, the brush of her lips against his ear, and the warmth of her arms were like a soothing ointment to his aching heart. God, she was killing him.

She lowered her chin to his shoulder. "To ask for forgiveness and a second chance?"

McCrea thought he knew heartbreak. Watching her and Sophie drive away damn near killed him, but this was a hundred times worse.

Her touched enticed his body while her words gripped his heart so tight, he thought it might stop beating. He wanted to say that there was nothing to forgive. He wanted to grab her and kiss her and make love to her. And he wanted to give her that second chance. But doing those things would only prolong the inevitable. Her leaving. "A second chance at what? Ripping my heart out when you walk away again? Because that's what's going to happen."

"I've been so selfish," she whispered. "I'm sorry I hurt you."

He loosened her arms and shifted around in his seat so that he was looking at her. "What good is a second chance if you can't believe I love you?"

"I do believe you love me," she confessed.

Did she? Would she ever be able to see that she wasn't her mother, and he wasn't her father? "I can't spend the rest of my life fighting your demons, darlin'."

"You don't have to. I read the letters." She lovingly touched his jaw. "I know my mother felt so guilty over Charlie's death that she ran away from the pain, from Redemption, and from the man who loved her. I know the tears she cried were because of the mistakes she made. Not because my father left her."

"About your father..."

She smiled through her tears. "Is J. E. Carmichael. I know. Ed came to see me last night."

Relief washed over him. He might kiss that cranky old bartender the next time he saw him. "I wanted to tell you, but I didn't know how."

"You knew?" she questioned.

"I went back to the office after I dropped you off, intent on drowning myself in a bottle of whiskey, and found the letters hidden in the trunk you gave me."

Disappointment hooded her eyes. "My Granddad Charlie—"

"Did what he thought was best for his little girl," he cut in to help comfort her. "How are you with knowing Ed's your father?"

"A dear friend made me see that life is precious and short, and that I was a fool if I let whatever happened in the past stand in the way of the happiness I had ahead of me. Ed and I have a lot of catching up to do, but I want him in my life. I want him in Sophie's life."

"I'm happy to hear that." Ed deserved to be a granddad.

"But honestly." She smiled. "Even if Ed hadn't come to see me, I don't think I could have gone much longer without you. I knew I'd made a mistake by leaving, but I was too afraid to admit it."

"Then why did you give me the necklace back?"

"It seems so silly now, but the necklace became sort of a talisman that kept me safe from love. And it reminded me of the promise I made the night I left four years ago. To guard my heart at all costs."

He stood and wrapped her in his arms. "Your heart will always be safe with me, Eleanor. But I want all of it, not just a piece. And not with lines we don't cross."

Though her cheeks were wet with tears, her smile was joyful. "You have it all. You always have."

He didn't have to question her sincerity. He could see it in her eyes and feel it in her touch. The fear that had been holding her back was gone. "Then you'll marry me?"

Her smile widened. "Yes. I will marry you. I want a big wedding with all our friends and family there, and I want Ed to walk me down the aisle."

"It will be the biggest wedding this town has ever seen," he promised.

"I'm tired of running," she said, lifting her lips to briefly brush them over his. "I'm tired of being afraid and tired of not being happy. You make me happy, McCrea."

His heart swelled with love. "Darlin', I'll do everything in my power to keep you that way."

"Just love me."

"I do. I will. Forever and always," he swore before he kissed her.

McCrea didn't have an acre to his name or the business he had worked so hard to build. The woman in his arms held everything. His life, his dreams, and his heart.

THE END

The Fallen Cowboy

CHAPTER ONE

The dull, almost constant throb in Jess Coldiron's right thigh had become such a part of him, he could hardly remember what his life had been like before bad luck and love had tossed him into the air and tried stomping the life out of him.

But he'd had a life before the fall, a life of bucking broncs and trophy buckles, of cheering crowds and adrenaline rushes, and of flinging his hat high into the air when he made eight seconds.

Most days, he didn't think about that life. But some days it crept in, and all he did was think.

He snatched his faded brown Stetson — a hat that was older than any of his relationships — from the dash of his truck and let out a weighted sigh as he scrubbed a thumb over the hoof print near the back of the brim.

He and the old hat had plenty in common. They'd both seen a lot of airtime, been knocked around, stomped on, and reshaped.

Nowadays, the hat kept the sun from his eyes, his hair in place, and reminded him of everything he had lost.

Jess's position as the executive director for the Promise Point Horse Rescue Ranch was nowhere near as demanding or rewarding as competing in the Pro-Rodeo circuit, but it was a lot safer.

On a good day, sitting behind a desk didn't bother him, but on a bad one — when his thigh felt as though it were in a vice and under the merciless twist of a vengeful woman — it was hell. A hell he hated because nothing, including the pain pills the doctors liked to throw at him, helped.

After his fall at the National Finals Rodeo eight years ago, he had undergone countless surgeries and months of grueling therapy just so he could walk again.

He'd learned to live with, and to an extent alleviate, the physical pain of his injury. He stayed in shape, worked out regularly, ate well, and was doing daily stretches. But this morning, he'd been in a hurry to get the workday over with.

He was paying for that now.

Jess put in long hours because he enjoyed his job, his locally hand-crafted desk, his well-worn leather office chair, and the embossed stationary set his sister Louisa, had given him last year for Christmas.

Most of all, he liked his title. He liked seeing his name on the office door. Not because he needed to be some high falutin administrator. That wasn't Jess's style. He hated wearing a suit and tie and having to shave daily. His office attire was his scuffed-up Justin boots, a t-shirt, and faded jeans.

He liked his title because it kept him away from the

shit and shovel part of the Rescue. The hands-on, horse, hoof, and halter part.

Holding to the pinch, he set the hat on his head, opened the door, and eased from his truck. He shifted his weight to his left foot and massaged his right thigh until he was sure he could walk before taking a step.

"You're doing it wrong."

"Oh, for God sakes, Logan," Violet moaned and threw up a hand in her brothers' direction. "Will you please shut up and let Ty fix the damn thing?"

"Stay out of this, Vi," Logan warned.

On top of the pain in his thigh, Jess would probably have to play referee between two of his best friends and the woman responsible for his daily dose of caffeine.

Logan and Ty would forgive him for breaking up their family row. But Jess wasn't so sure Violet wouldn't punch him in the gut if he got in her way.

The baby of the Gates family could be a hard cup to measure. But Violet wasn't a pistol with a sensitive trigger like his sister Louisa. She was usually a sweet and somewhat callow woman who was often all smiles.

But lately, Violet had a rebellious side that often reared its ugly head when her brothers were too protective or dismissive. The woman could be as mean as a pissed-off grizzly when she was angry, and she was, all the way down to her petite pink sneakers dotted with brown and white drops of caffeinated beverages and high- calorie pastry frosting.

"Why?" she demanded, curling her fingers into fists. "Why do I have to stay out of this? I'm a part of this family, and a third of that rusty heap is mine."

"Hey!" Ty shouted from under the belly of the ranch truck. "Don't disrespect the Green Machine."

"Fine, you stubborn asses!" she threw up her hands. "Do whatever!"

"How many times has this damn thing died?" Ty asked, not waiting for an answer. "And how many times have I been the one to resurrect it?"

"Can't help it," Logan said. "Obviously, practice doesn't make perfect, little brother."

Holding back a groan, Jess slammed his truck door and slowly started down the incline towards the brothers.

Violet mumbled a heated curse as she stomped past him on her way to her baby 4x4 parked in front of his truck. "Those dunderheads have been messin' around with that damn thing for almost three hours." She pointed to a stain on her pink Pixies Coffee Shop t-shirt." I have grounds and caramel sauce all over me. I'm tired, hungry, and need a shower. They're all yours."

"Thanks a lot," he grumbled.

"Oh." She stopped in mid-stomp and swung around on a heel, the hard scowl on her face relaxing. "How's Eleanor? I haven't had a chance to call her. Have there been any changes?"

Five years ago, his niece Sophie had arrived without much warning and almost made her appearance on I-35, so his brother and sister-in-law, and every other member of the Coldiron family, were on high alert in anticipation of the couple's second child.

"No," he said, looking at his watch again. "I was on my way to Redemption to check on her when Logan called me for a tow."

His brother, McCrea, had handed over the long-distance rescues to Brody Vance, the horse trainer they'd hired last year, so he could be there when the baby was born. This afternoon McCrea was on his way back from a rescue on the other side of the county, but would be home in time for supper.

His parents usually took turns checking in on the expectant mother. But his mom and Louisa were shopping in Houston, and his dad was out of town at a cattleman's meeting in Fort Worth.

If Eleanor went into labor, Jess was flying solo.

"Well, good luck at getting Ty to give up," she said with a blistering glare in their direction before she climbed into her truck. "Maybe you can bait him out with beer and beanie weenies."

Jess shuddered — remembering the atomic cloud that lingered in the air after Ty consumed the two — and started towards the twenty-year-old heavy-duty diesel that should have been hauled to the junkyard years ago. "What's the problem?"

"The problem is," Logan said, raising from his bent position under the hood of the truck, "Ty doesn't know his ass from a hole in the ground."

Predictably, the brothers exchanged derogatory insults about holes and hoses before Jess intervened.

"What's wrong with it this time?" He leaned over the grill to take a look at the motor.

"Hell, if I know," Logan said, fidgeting with the fuel line. "It started choking and sputtering a few yards back. Then it just died."

"Sounds like it's out of fuel." Jess threw in his two cents.

"It's got half a tank," Ty answered from below.

Logan closed his eyes as if he were asking the Almighty for patients. "Is the gauge working?"

Ty rolled out, stood, and dusted his backside. "It's not the gauge."

"Then what is it, genius?" Logan asked.

"I thought it had a fuel leak last week, so I crawled under to see if a line had busted."

"And?" Logan prompted.

"It's not a line," Ty said, walking to the bed of the truck for his toolbox, a thought-filled pull pleating his brow. "I think it's losing oil pressure from a clogged valve."

And just like that, Ty had the problem figured out. Heading back to the front of the truck, he opened the beaten and battered hand-me-down box and started digging through it for sockets.

"You *think* it's losing oil pressure?" Logan asked, sparring another argument.

A clogged valve was going to take longer than ten minutes, and Jess wasn't going to add to Ty's troubles by telling him to hurry.

Logan had that covered.

Ty was an excellent mechanic. Working in the oil-fields and on the ranch had taught him how to improvise. And Jess had no doubt the truck would be up and running soon if Logan left him the hell alone.

"Just get in the damn truck and let me tow you back to the ranch," Jess said.

"I've almost got it," Ty said, unwilling to throw in the towel just yet.

"I'm leaving in ten minutes," Jess told them, catching sight of a long grease streak across the middle of his t-shirt. "With or without you."

"I only need five," Ty assured him.

"And a good mechanic," Logan threw in.

Jess snagged the hem of his t-shirt and yanked it over his head. He wasn't going to stand by in the July heat while the brothers verbally duked it out.

He let the tailgate of his truck bed down and hoisted

himself onto it. Then he eased around and leaned his back against the inside of the bed, drew his good leg up, and stretched his bad leg out, feeling the tendons and scar tissue in his thigh tighten as he did.

He plucked his hat from his head and dropped it on his knee, then scrubbed a hand over his head, noting he should have made time for a haircut before his date with Brandi tonight.

The beautiful blonde executive of Winsor Rodeo Productions wouldn't mind the length of his hair, only his performance and stamina after dinner. With that in mind, Jess tried to drown out the sound of the bickering brothers.

But the distant hum of a vehicle brought his head up.

The gravel road, which was off the beaten path, ran through the heart of the Gates Ranch and rarely saw traffic, so whoever was behind the wheel of the dust cloud was either lost or looking for one of them.

More than likely, when the dust cleared, a face similar to Ty's would be staring back at them. But Jess would never let his friend know that he favored Clayton Durant, Ty's biological father, more than he did Emmett Gates, the man who had raised him.

"Yo, Ty." Logan swatted his brother's leg, thinking the same as Jess. "You've got company."

"What?" Ty called out without looking up.

Logan's voice went cold. "Clayton is here."

That got Ty's attention. "What the hell does he want?"

"He's probably a man short for some shit job," Logan said, staring flatly at the road, ready and waiting to face a man he despised, but tolerated for Ty's sake.

But as the vehicle sped closer, the outline of a motorcycle and its rider emerged from the dust.

Jess scooted from the tailgate. "Since when are bikes the vehicle of choice for Durant Drilling?"

"You couldn't tie Clayton to one," Logan answered, cleaning his hands on a grease rag from the floorboard of the truck.

Ty joined them as the bike slowed and then stopped about twenty feet from them. When the dust cleared, the curvy feminine form of the rider appeared.

The woman removed her helmet, freeing a crop of dark, mahogany hair and a face that looked nothing like the always-frowning roughneck, Clayton Durant: high cheekbones set against an oval face, a straight, elegant nose and lips that begged to be kissed.

A pair of stylish aviator sunglasses added to the mystery and stirred Jess's male curiosity.

The ends of her long locks were tousled and wind-blown from miles of road and sun. She gave her hair a shake and offered them a friendly smile. "Hi, guys."

The coarseness of her voice blew across Jess like a sultry breeze, arousing more than Jess's curiosity.

"Holy shit," Logan murmured.

"Fuck me," Ty whispered under his breath.

"She looks too smart for that," Logan returned without taking his eyes off the woman.

What she looked like was a hot, sexy fantasy plucked straight from the cover of a motorcycle magazine. The sight of her firm thighs straddling chrome and leather were enough to entice the most sainted man. And Jess had always been one step closer to hell than to heaven. Judging from the lustful expression on Logan's and Ty's faces, he wouldn't be alone in the descent.

"Boys," Jess cleared his throat. "Remember your raisin'. Let's not act like primates."

"Says the man who has drool drippin' from his chin," Logan murmured.

Ty extended his hand to Jess. "I bet you fifty bucks I can get her number in under five minutes."

Usually, before Jess would have taken a bet like that, he would have upped the ante with, "I can get it in two." Because this woman — sitting astride a bike that alone gave him a hard-on, with slender legs clad in a pair of dark denim jeans and leather chaps, a trim waist and full breasts that pressed tight against her riding jacket — was exactly his type.

But something about *this* woman made Jess err on the side of caution and kept him from accepting that bet.

"She could be a reporter," Logan suggested.

She was relaxed and at home on the back of the fully blacked-out motorcycle. Reporters looking for a story about gold or rescued horses were usually more discreet, more plainly dressed, and never, ever sexy.

Jess swallowed, trying to dislodge the dry knot that had suddenly formed in his throat. "I haven't seen hide nor hair of a reporter in months, and I've never seen one on a murdered out Indian Chieftain Dark Horse."

"Yeah, you're right," Logan said, handing Ty the grease rag. "I don't think she's here for a story. But she could be part of the archeology team."

"No way," Ty disagreed. "She's too pretty to be diggin' in the dirt with those academic needle heads up at Vera la Luz."

Ty was probably right. Over the last two years, Jess had met several of the archeologists and grad students involved in the excavation of the old Spanish Mission atop Promise Point. Not one of them resembled this woman. Her complexion was too evenly colored and smooth for an outdoor occupation.

She tucked her helmet under an arm and glanced over her shoulder at the road as if she were waiting for someone to catch up with her.

Satisfied there wasn't, her eyes went back to them. She shifted her ass to the other side of the seat as her full lips pulled to one side in consideration. "Excuse me."

The cord tightened, stirring lust low in Jess's stomach. It pivoted downward when she lodged the tip of her leather-clad finger between her teeth and slid her hand free. It was an innocent but sensual gesture that made him hard.

"Maybe she's lost and looking for the interstate," Logan suggested.

"Reporter… archeologist." Ty adjusted the waist of his dirty jeans and grinned. "I'm readily available for whatever Beautiful needs."

She lifted her face towards the sun, then closed her eyes, momentarily soaking up the rays. The smooth lines of her face were almost angelic. The woman was a tempting mixture of seductive innocence and alluring beauty. It was a combustible combination that caused caution to stir inside Jess's chest.

With a huff of frustration, her eyes opened, and again, she focused on the three of them. "Yo, fellas!" She impatiently slapped the side of her helmet to get their attention and pulled her sunglasses to the end of her nose, giving Jess a view of her dark eyes. "You guys speak English or something similar? I'm not fluent in grunts and scratches, but I'll figure it out."

Jess grinned and held up a hand to signal he was on his way. "A hundred bucks says I can send Beautiful packing in two minutes."

Ty's face contorted with confusion. "Why the hell would you do that?"

"Yeah, man," Logan agreed, speaking from the side of his mouth. "She's a knockout."

Jess had experienced lust at first sight more times than he cared to admit. The rodeo had been oozing with gorgeous women willing to share his bed as he climbed the ranks.

Some had been clingy and demanding. Some had acted innocent and accommodating. All of them had intentions of claiming a piece of him after they left his bed. Only one had come close. But that one had taught him trouble and heartache could come wrapped in a pretty package.

And as sure as there was Texas dirt and sun-fried grass beneath his boots, Beautiful was a biblical proportion of both. "Something's not right about her. She's trouble."

"If she's trouble, give me a double dose," Ty said and started towards her.

"Hold up," Jess said, halting him with a hand to the mid-section. "I'll handle this."

"Oh, he'll handle it," Logan mocked.

"Yeah." Ty laughed. "I know what he wants to handle."

Ignoring the brothers, Jess made his way up the incline to the road. His steps were slow, his gait jerky and stiff. It was hard for a man to feel confident when he could hardly walk, but Jess held his grin.

"Can I help you?" he asked, noticing that her eyes weren't brown but hazel.

"Ah…yeah," she said, glancing at his leg. "I hope so."

Jess was used to drawing pity stares and brief looks of interest. His way of dealing with it was by ignoring it. But Beautiful's empathetic glance was a double punch to his manhood.

"I'm trying to find Redemption. Charlie and Rose Mackenna's ranch."

The Mackenna Ranch was next to his parents' ranch. McCrea and Eleanor had begun remodeling the old house soon after they were married last year. But all that had been put on hold until after the baby was born.

The last few weeks had been stressful for the newlyweds, and Jess wasn't about to add to their problems by giving Beautiful directions to Redemption until he knew what she wanted.

He gave her a flirty wink. "Now what would a pretty thing like you want with that dilapidated old horse ranch?"

"I — ah." Her eyes squinted and her lips did a cute little twist of annoyance. "It's urgent that I speak with Eleanor Mackenna. Do you know her?"

Jess pretended to think. "The name seems familiar."

She motioned towards the bike's instrument panel. "I followed the GPS —"

"Those things aren't reliable out here," Logan interjected, walking up to where Jess was standing.

"A lot of these back roads are nothing but horse trails," Ty added, stuffing the end of the grease rag into his back pocket as he joined them.

She took a deep breath and let it out. "Great."

"Don't worry." Jess widened his grin. "I'll give you directions."

Relief relaxed her shoulders. "You will?"

"Sure," he said, walking closer. "What kind of gentleman would I be if I didn't help a lady in need?"

Other Books by Mina Beckett

BOOKS BY MINA BECKETT

Coldiron Cowboys series

The Fallen Cowboy

Breaking the Cowboy

Coldiron Cowboys Collection - includes all three books plus, the novella.

Crossfire Canyon series

A Cold Montana Christmas: A Crossfire Canyon Novel

Rough Creek series

A Cowboy Charming Christmas

Hollywood Cowboy

Coming soon in the Texas Heat Series

Roughneck Cowboy

For more book news, visit minabeckett.com